W9-DIB-327

## Praise for *New York Times* bestselling author Kristy Woodson Harvey

"A major new voice in Southern fiction."
—Elin Hilderbrand, *New York Times* bestselling author

"Sweet as sweet tea on the outside and strong as steel on the inside . . . Kristy Woodson Harvey is a natural."
—Ann Garvin, *USA Today* bestselling author
*I Thought You Said This Would Work*

"Southern fiction at its best . . . Beautifully written."
—Eileen Goudge, *New York Times* bestselling author

"An author whose carefully crafted paragraphs stir my imagination and touch my heart."
—Leslie C. Moore, editor, *Sasee*

"There's something about Woodson Harvey's writing that just feels as calming as sipping sweet tea on a warm summer night."
—E! Online

## Praise for *Under the Southern Sky*

"A heart-wrenching tale of love and loss . . . Fans of women's fiction will devour this."
—*Publishers Weekly* (starred review)

"Pack your beach bag, Harvey's back with another delightful story of the magic of southern coastal towns . . . As with Mary Kay Andrews or Patti Callahan Henry, Harvey spins romance around well-drawn characters, complete with strengths and weaknesses, and always mindful of the beauty that comes from living in the modern South."
—*Booklist*

"A warm-hearted mix of hometown charm and the sort of thoroughly modern problems that bring us back to the people who know us best and the places that remind us of who we really are."
—Lisa Wingate, #1 *New York Times* bestselling author of
*Before We Were Yours*

"Perfect for: fans of beach reads, *P.S. I Love You*, and anything by authors Jennifer Weiner and Elin Hilderbrand."
—*Country Living*

"[Kristy Woodson Harvey's] best novel yet . . . You'll need plenty of tissues—and maybe some of Cape Carolina's beloved bourbon-spiked sweet tea—to make it to the end. Deliciously plotted, intricately constructed, gorgeously written, and brimming with hope, *Under the Southern Sky* will steal your heart."

—Kristin Harmel, *New York Times* bestselling author of
*The Book of Lost Names*

## Praise for *Feels Like Falling*

"Only Kristy Woodson Harvey can make sense of the sometimes devastating, oftentimes delicious dilemmas faced by the protagonists of her newest perfect beach read. Readers will fall in love . . . Buckle up, buttercups, because *Feels Like Falling* feels like your next summer sizzler!"

—Mary Kay Andrews, *New York Times* bestselling author of
*On Ocean Boulevard*

"Pitch-perfect tones . . . Harvey's optimistic tale just might convince readers that bouncing back can actually land a person in a better place than where they started."

—*Publishers Weekly*

"Kristy Woodson Harvey has the voice of a best friend; [she is] a story-teller of the finest sort. This is more than a novel about friendship; it is also a story for friendship: you will find yourself sharing it with everyone you love. Dive in; the storytelling is delicious!"

—Patti Callahan Henry, *New York Times* bestselling author of
*Becoming Mrs. Lewis*

"Harvey creates genuine, capable, flawed protagonists and fun secondary characters, and readers will appreciate the thoughtful depiction of women supporting one another in an easy, breezy story. Fans of Mary Kay Andrews and Mary Alice Monroe should add this to their beach read lists."

—*Booklist*

## Praise for the Peachtree Bluff Series
### *The Southern Side of Paradise*

"Kristy Woodson Harvey has done it again! Perfectly tying together the stories of Ansley, Caroline, Sloane, and Emerson (and their men!), *The Southern Side of Paradise* is full of humor, charm, and family. Fans of the Peachtree Bluff series will not be disappointed!"

—Lauren K. Denton, *USA Today* bestselling author of *Hurricane Season*

"As the eldest of three sisters, I know you're not supposed to pick favorites—but *The Southern Side of Paradise* is Kristy Woodson Harvey's very best. . . . This novel had me laughing, crying, and wanting to hop on a plane and head south. I loved every page."

—Camille Pagán, bestselling author of *I'm Fine and Neither Are You*

"Woodson Harvey has been called a major voice in Southern fiction, and her latest novel—the third in the Peachtree Bluff series—delivers a healthy dose of her signature wit, charm, and heart."

—*Woman's World*

## The Secret to Southern Charm

"The characters will leap off the page and into your heart, and you'll find yourself rooting for them so fervently, you'll forget they're not actually real. Kristy Woodson Harvey has delivered another masterpiece . . . Let's just say that this one had better have a sequel too, because I'm not ready to leave these charming ladies behind."

—Kristin Harmel, internationally bestselling author of
*The Room on Rue Amélie*

"Harvey's growing fan base will find another great beach read in this second novel in her Peachtree Bluff trilogy . . . Harvey is an up-and-coming Southern writer with staying power."

—*Booklist*

## Slightly South of Simple

"Kristy Woodson Harvey cuts to the heart of what it means to be a born-and-bred Southerner . . . It's easy to see why everyone is buzzing about *Slightly South of Simple*."

—Cassandra King Conroy, bestselling author

"My prediction is that writers come and writers go, but Kristy Woodson Harvey is here to stay. The warmth, wit, and wisdom of this novel pave her way into the exclusive sisterhood of Southern writers."

—*HuffPost*

"With a charming, coastal Southern setting, *Slightly South of Simple* is a heartfelt story about the universal themes of love, loss, forgiveness, and family. I'm thrilled to hear that this book is part of a series and look forward to getting to know this cast of strong Southern women even better."

—*Deep South Magazine*

## ALSO FROM KRISTY WOODSON HARVEY
## AND GALLERY BOOKS

*Under the Southern Sky*
*Feels Like Falling*

## THE PEACHTREE BLUFF SERIES

*The Southern Side of Paradise*
*The Secret to Southern Charm*
*Slightly South of Simple*

# *Christmas in Peachtree Bluff*

*A Novel*

# Kristy Woodson Harvey

## G

## Gallery Books

New York    London    Toronto    Sydney    New Delhi

# G

Gallery Books
An Imprint of Simon & Schuster, Inc.
1230 Avenue of the Americas
New York, NY 10020

Copyright © 2021 by Kristy Woodson Harvey

First Gallery Books trade paperback edition October 2021

GALLERY BOOKS and colophon are registered trademarks of Simon & Schuster, Inc.

For information about special discounts for bulk purchases, please contact Simon & Schuster Special Sales at 1-866-506-1949 or business@simonandschuster.com.

The Simon & Schuster Speakers Bureau can bring authors to your live event. For more information or to book an event, contact the Simon & Schuster Speakers Bureau at 1-866-248-3049 or visit our website at www.simonspeakers.com.

*Interior design by Erika R. Genova*

Manufactured in the United States of America

10  9  8  7  6  5  4  3  2  1

Library of Congress Cataloging-in-Publication Data
Names: Harvey, Kristy Woodson, author.
Title: Christmas in Peachtree Bluff : a novel / Kristy Woodson Harvey.
Description: First Gallery Books trade paperback edition. | New York : Gallery
   Books, 2021. | Series: The Peachtree Bluff series ; volume 4 |
Summary: "In the newest installment of USA TODAY bestselling author Kristy
   Woodson Harvey's Peachtree Bluff series, three generations of the Murphy
   women must come together when a hurricane threatens to destroy their
   hometown—and the holiday season in the process"—Provided by publisher.
Identifiers: LCCN 2021019916 (print) | LCCN 2021019917 (ebook) | ISBN
   9781982185206 (trade paperback) | ISBN 9781982189402 (library binding) |
   ISBN 9781982185213 | ISBN 9781982185220 (ebook)
Subjects: GSAFD: Love stories. | LCGFT: Christmas stories.
Classification: LCC PS3623.O6785 C49 2021 (print) | LCC PS3623.O6785 (ebook) |
   DDC 813/.6—dc23
LC record available at https://lccn.loc.gov/2021019916
LC ebook record available at https://lccn.loc.gov/2021019917

ISBN 978-1-9821-8940-2
ISBN 978-1-9821-8520-6 (pbk)
ISBN 978-1-9821-8522-0 (ebook)

*To my brilliant fellow Friends & Fiction authors—*
*Mary Kay Andrews, Kristin Harmel, Patti Callahan Henry, and*
*Mary Alice Monroe—our spectacular managing director Meg*
*Walker, and the extraordinary members of our*
*Friends & Fiction Facebook Group.*

*This holiday season, all of you are truly my greatest gift.*

# Ansley: A Southern Lady

*The Day before Thanksgiving*

FOR MAGAZINES AND TRAVEL GUIDES, globe-trotting Insta-grammers and hotel reviewers, Peachtree Bluff, Georgia, was a beach destination best enjoyed during the heat of summer. But as I leaned on the counter at my waterfront design shop, looking out over the Intracoastal, I realized that fall in Peachtree might be our best-kept secret. Yes, summer was great—the sun glinted on the water, the wild horses roamed the islands, and the wind blew more softly through the trees than anywhere else in the world. But fall and winter, when the weather was slightly cooler and the streets less crowded, were glorious. And, if you asked a local, nothing beat Christmas in Peachtree Bluff.

I perched on the gray-and-white Parisian bistro stool behind the counter, stack of receipts in hand, to review the sales from the day before. It was the day before Thanksgiving, but already, the trees flanking the picture window were trimmed, the Christmas music was playing, and my store, Sloane Emerson, was overflowing with the goodies that I hoped would be mostly gone after this weekend. Between online sales and foot traffic from locals, the store made one-quarter of its profits in the weeks between Black Friday and Christmas, so it was paramount that everything be just right. That included my middle daughter, Sloane's, collection of miniature paintings for sale, arranged on a round antique mahogany table in the center of the shop: reindeer, the Star of Bethlehem, a shining menorah, and, my personal favorite, the Grinch.

The quiet and calm, with everything in its place, made this the best way to start the day. It was a time when a woman could do some thinking. Of course, coffee helped. Coffee was key. And, as of yet, no coffee.

It gave me a pang for Kyle, the previous owner of Peachtree Perk, not only because I missed his piping-hot and always-on-time lattes—which I did—but also because I missed my daughter Emerson and my granddaughter Carter, who went with him to California three years earlier.

The idea that they were somewhere in the air over Montana right now, on their way from LA to Peachtree Bluff, made my stomach turn. I liked it better when my children were on the ground. But the idea that they were on their way *here* to see me was almost too thrilling to bear. I went through my mental checklist. I had ingredients for Emerson's green juice, baby Carter's organic milk, Kyle's favorite double-dipped chocolate-covered peanuts from the candy shop on the corner, and IPAs from our local Blackbeard Brewing. I couldn't wait for them to get here.

As the door to the store opened, the familiar tinkle of the bell rang out happily. "Every time a bell rings, an angel gets her wings!" I exclaimed.

This morning, like so many mornings, it was my friend Hippie Hal who walked through the door. I could see his grin across the store even underneath his beard, which he let grow in more fully for winter. It was a chilly morning, so he had layered two of his signature white oxford shirts he always wore with jeans—and a piece of rope as a belt.

"I got your latte," he said somewhat grimly as he held it out to me.

"Oh no," I said, standing up and walking around to the front of the counter. "Again?"

He nodded. Kyle's cousin Keith had taken over Peachtree Perk when Kyle moved with Emerson to LA for her to take a once-in-a-lifetime acting role. When Keith had discontinued Kyle's famous coffee delivery service, we had been aghast. But, finally, after years of complaining, he had decided to resume delivery.

"What did Keith bring you?" Hippie Hal asked.

"Nothing," I said gleefully, as I took the cup from his hand and smiled. He rolled his eyes, so blue amidst the darkly tanned, deeply lined skin of his face.

The bell tinkled again and Leah, my design assistant—well, really more like my right-hand woman—walked through the door, her wavy red hair flowing over her shoulders.

"This is convenient," she said. "I got a flat white today. Now I don't have to run all over town looking for you."

Leah handed Hal his usual coffee order and crossed her arms. "Y'all, I get it. We like Keith. Keith is nice, and we're happy he's here. But this is ridiculous. We have to tell him that he gets our orders wrong."

I knew she was right. This was lunacy, and we couldn't let it continue.

"I'll tell him," Hal said. "It should come from a man."

I snapped my fingers. "Or we let Kyle tell him when he gets here! Things are better when they come from family."

Leah shook her head. "Things are so much worse when they come from family."

I considered that. Maybe she was right. I couldn't be sure. I hadn't had any caffeine yet, after all.

The bell tinkled a third time and in walked Jack, the love of my life, and now, after decades of being apart, my husband. I still got a thrill just seeing him walk through the door, so polished and handsome but also the right amount of rugged. His salt-and-pepper hair was thick and full, and he had the kindest smile I'd ever seen. Our tiny dog, Biscuit, ran to me, and I leaned down to rub her white, furry head. Jack kissed me quickly.

Then he turned and said, "Miss Leah, you are the proud winner of a cinnamon spice latte."

"Yes!" she said. "The day can begin!"

"We're three for four now!" I said happily.

Leah rolled her eyes. "Ansley, your tolerance is too high."

"It has only been a couple weeks. I think we need to be more patient and—"

"Oh!" Jack interjected. "Keith told me to let y'all know that he baked loaves of fresh pumpkin bread for all his regulars. They're waiting and you can grab one at your convenience."

Hal, Leah, and I groaned in unison.

"What?" Jack asked. "Do y'all have something against pumpkin bread?"

"No," Hal said. "It's just that every time we decide to do something about the messed-up coffee orders, he does something so nice that we can't."

"He did just donate that money for the new bleachers at the high school too," Leah said.

"Traitor!" I said, pointing at her. "You're the maddest of all, and you cave the fastest."

A tinkle of the bell and Kimmy, our resident produce woman, walked in, basket of squash, sweet potatoes, and lettuces in hand. She had been growing out her short, spiky hair, and it was almost to her chin now. And pink. She'd gone back to her natural black for a while last year, and it just felt wrong.

"Oh, good, you're here," she said, handing the basket and a cup to Jack. "These are all your Thanksgiving veggies—and your plain black coffee. Ick."

Jack raised his cup to us like he had just won the lottery. "Good things come to those who wait."

"Or complain!" Kimmy countered. "Why can't one of you tell him that he's screwing up the whole town's orders?"

Kimmy was by far the snarkiest of the group and cared very little about anyone's feelings. "Why don't *you* tell him," I countered, "if you're so bothered?"

"Because he's my second-biggest client! Do you know how many strawberries that man buys? I can't be on his bad side."

She looked around the circle expectantly. Jack put his arm around her shoulder. "No takers here, Kim. Let's go down to Page and Stage. Claudia certainly has a mean streak." He paused and perked back up. "And, hey! Maybe she has your coffee too."

"From your mouth to God's ears," she said.

He turned back to me. "Five days days, Ans. Five days."

"I know, love," I said back. Five days from today, Jack and I would leave for three weeks for a trip we had wanted to take since we were teenagers. I never would have imagined that, decades later, after I had been a widow for sixteen years, he would come back into my life, and we would fall in love, get married, and finally be able to cruise the Australian coast like we had dreamed—and explore Indonesia as a bonus.

I had some qualms about coming home only a few days before Christmas, but my daughter Sloane, who was living next door to Jack and me with her sons and husband, would be the one hosting this year anyway. She was in the big house, the one my grandmother had left to me, so she inherited the family gatherings. Thanksgiving was relatively small for a Murphy celebration, so we would do that at Jack's. Sloane had promised me that she would decorate the tree to my exacting specifications and make plenty of cookies and I would come home to a fridge full of everything I needed to make Christmas Eve dinner. She was nothing if not dependable, my Sloane.

I knew she could handle it. I just wanted to be there to handle it with her. The thought of missing Taylor and AJ's Christmas program at school filled me with dread.

As if they knew I was thinking about them, the door flew open and five-year-old Taylor ran through, with seven-year-old AJ on his heels. They were both tall for their age, little clones of their father, with dark hair and a penchant for trucks and toy soldiers. But Taylor had Sloane's bow mouth, and AJ got her eyes. Every now and then it struck me in moments like these, took my breath away how quickly they were growing. But they weren't too big to run into my arms, nearly knocking me down, so that was good. They had just seen me last night, but their enthusiasm made it seem like it had been months.

I kissed both their chilly cheeks and smiled at their little backpacks. My grandsons could walk to our neighborhood elementary school and stop by to see me on their way there. It was a sweet and special magic.

I looked up to see Sloane coming in behind them, messy bun atop her head, fresh paint already smattered on her white, long-sleeved T-shirt, smiling down at me, sipping her coffee. Even with no makeup and little attention to her appearance, she had such a fresh glow about her. She was a natural, effortless beauty. Always had been. "Who had your coffee this morning?" Hal asked.

She shrugged. "I couldn't deal with it. I'm just drinking someone's coffee with cream and sugar or something."

Leah, Hal, and I gasped simultaneously. Drinking someone else's coffee order was strictly forbidden.

She put her free hand up in defense. "I know, okay? I drink someone else's coffee and this entire idiotic system of traipsing around town returning coffee falls apart. I get it. I hear you. But I'm a mother of two young sons, my husband is still overcoming PTSD, I am a full-time artist, and I run three stores with my sisters and my mother. I need my caffeine, people! And today, I needed it now!"

A hush fell over the crowd. Sloane was the quietest, mildest-mannered of my daughters, so when she raised her voice, she was mad. Really mad.

"You should just tell Keith, you know," Leah said, faux concern lacing her voice.

Sloane waved her finger at her. "No, ma'am. I see what you're doing. Of everyone in town, I think we all know I'm the least likely to tell him. I hate confrontation." She blew me a kiss and said, "Come on, boys! Time to get to school."

I hugged the three of them goodbye. "We'll see you later! Leah and I need to get to work!" The comment was aimed at Hal, who was now lounging in one of the club chairs in the corner, holding the NO SITTING, PLEASE sign in his lap. He was a good friend, but sometimes he lacked the wherewithal to realize when people needed to cut the visit short. Whether it was just his personality or a side effect of the copious amounts of pot he smoked, I couldn't really be sure.

"All right," I said, hinting again. "Mrs. Milton wants a full remodel now that Mr. Milton is dead."

Hal laughed. Mr. Milton was absolutely loaded but never spent a single dime. Mrs. Milton cried at his funeral, spent three days accepting casseroles, and then, like a caged animal set free, went on a spending spree that probably made the fiscal years of most of the businesses in town. You wouldn't hear me complaining. "Unlimited budget" was the most beautiful phrase in the English language.

"Yeah, I hear you," Hal said. "I just wanted to be sure that you'd heard about Hurricane Pearl making her way through the Gulf."

My heart raced at the prospect, but I waved my hand casually, like that was the farthest thing from my mind. "It's almost Thanksgiving, Hal. We never have hurricanes this late." I smiled. "Plus, a

Southern lady like Pearl would never ruin the holidays in Peachtree Bluff." If I had learned one thing from a lifetime here, it was that roughly three-fourths of our potential hurricanes were all talk and no show.

He laughed. "I just want you to keep an eye on it with you leaving for your trip and all that. Just because we don't usually have hurricanes this late doesn't mean it isn't still hurricane season."

I nodded. "Okay. Well, thanks."

My phone beeped. A little shiver of excitement ran up my spine. Caroline.

Vivi, Preston, and I are at JFK. Thank God. Be warned: my daughter has made the complete transition into the spawn of Satan.

I laughed out loud. Caroline hadn't exactly been easy when she was a teenager either. But I did empathize with her problems. A moody daughter was rough under the best of circumstances, but when you had a toddler and were going through a divorce it was even worse. Vivi, who was usually such a sweet-natured child, had been giving Caroline a run for her money: arguing with her over everything, talking back, even sneaking out and threatening to live with her father full-time. It was breaking Caroline's heart. I felt like a few days in Peachtree Bluff, away from the hustle and bustle, the pressures and stresses of the city, would do them all a world of good.

Plus, I was totally convinced: there was nothing that Gransley's homemade pecan pie—made from my own grandmother's recipe—couldn't fix.

# Caroline: Non-Legal Family

WHEN WE WERE LITTLE, MY sisters and I put on Christmas "shows" almost every day of the holiday season. Sometimes we did a spin-off on Santa and his reindeer or the nativity, but mostly, we were Christmas princesses or fairies or unicorns. Born bossy, I was a natural organizer and director, while Sloane, the artist, could create sets that were stunning. Emerson, the actress, had a flair for the dramatic even as a toddler and was always cast as the lead. Sloane would sometimes get mad about this, but that was showbiz. I never felt jealous that Emerson shone so brightly onstage or that Sloane could turn a blank piece of cardboard into a fairyland. We all had our strengths, and that was that.

Now, leaning back in my surprisingly comfortable airplane seat on our flight from New York to Georgia, my sweet three-year-old, Preston, who always fell asleep on planes, breathed deeply in the seat beside me. And for the first time in maybe my entire life, I actually envied Emerson. I was jealous of my sister who was on a six-hour, cross-country flight with a wiggly two-year-old who did *not* fall asleep on planes. I wouldn't have realized it when I was living through it, and I certainly wouldn't have believed anyone who had told me, but the terrible twos were a piece of cake compared to the fearsome fifteens. Actually, I could think of a better f-word to describe this year of my daughter's life . . .

As if I didn't feel guilty enough already about putting her through a divorce, she had to act like everything on the planet was my fault.

I looked across the aisle at Vivi, highlighted hair across her face, headphones on, glued to her iPad. Her therapist had suggested that perhaps too much screen time was making her moodier—and more downright awful. So I tried taking the thing away from her after her appointment a few weeks ago, but that made it even worse. Instead of being occupied on her iPad, she turned her fury toward me for a larger percentage of the day. So I made excuses to myself as to why I was ignoring the therapist's suggestion in order to make my life easier. Today's excuse? *Of course she can have her iPad now. We're on a plane, for heaven's sake.*

Seeing her face soft and relaxed, away from all our problems on the ground, assuaged my mom guilt. Sometimes, now, after a huge fight, I'd go in her room to watch her sleep, to remind myself that the daughter I once knew was still in there somewhere, that I could get her back.

When I had asked last week what she was packing for the trip, she had screamed, "How could you make me be away from my father for Thanksgiving? Just because you don't love him or care about him doesn't mean I don't!"

It is amazing how deeply a skinny teenager's words can hurt. I was trying so hard to be kind about James. And, in truth, that deep, visceral anger I'd had at him more than three years ago, when I found out about his affair, had all but passed. No, living together and trying to become a family of four again after Preston was born hadn't worked out. I couldn't trust him, and I decided I had to choose myself, my happiness, and sanity. Maybe it had been the wrong choice. But he had been the one to appear on *Ladies Who Lunch*, the most popular reality show on TV, with the model he was cheating with. So I was confounded at how all this anger was now, suddenly, turning on me.

Preston stirred as the captain came across the speaker. "Flight attendants, prepare for landing."

I looked at Vivi as she put her seat back to its original, upright position. As if feeling my glance, she turned to glare at me, that cold, devilish stare she'd recently mastered. At least she hadn't tried to sneak out last night. But still. She had done it several times before—once at my house, twice at James's, not that I was keeping score—and it was the most terrifying thing that had ever happened to me. A fifteen-year-old girl in New York City alone is a recipe for disaster. She could have been kidnapped, raped, murdered, anything at all.

So even though she'd screamed at me when I had told her last night that, yes, once and for all, she was going to Peachtree, her anger was still better than if she snuck out. At least she was in her room. At least she was safe.

I looked down at Preston, into the big blue eyes of my precious little bundle of love. It wasn't fair how sweet and dear he was in comparison to my daughter. Not that I loved him more. But I would admit that I liked him more, at least right now. He stared up at me. "What are you looking at, sweetie?" I asked.

"You're so pretty, Mommy," he said, sighing.

Preston was the most magical gift on earth. He didn't scream at me and tell me he wanted to go live with his father. At least, not yet.

As we landed a few minutes later and I retrieved our bags from the overhead compartment, Vivi took Preston's hand. Curiously, she was sweet as pie to her brother, which was something to be grateful for. She shot me another icy glare as we started to move off the plane. Yup, it seemed like her fury really only extended to me.

My children walked off the jetway before me, and I heard squeals of excitement and peals of laughter before I looked up and saw my blonde, blue-eyed, beautiful sister Emerson, her ungodly handsome boyfriend, Kyle, and their two-year-old daughter, Carter, with hair so blonde and eyes so blue she looked as though she was one of the Christmas fairies we used to play come to life, plucked out of the enchanted forest. I snapped a quick pic of Carter and Preston hugging—literally the world's cutest sight. It was only right to share it on Instagram. Happy tears would be shed the world over. Then I squeezed my modelesque little sister so tight I thought her guts might come out.

I pulled back to look at her, tears coming to my eyes out of the pure relief of being with someone who loved me, of being away from my problems at home. Away from James and divorce lawyers. Away from Sloane Emerson New York and the ordering and paperwork. I didn't realize until then just how much I needed a palate cleanser. Plus, Vivi had always listened to Emerson. Maybe because she was only twenty-nine and still pretty cool, but mostly because she was famous, I think. Hopefully she could talk some sense into her.

I hugged Kyle and kissed him on both cheeks. "You know it isn't safe for you to be here. They will try to lock you in that coffee shop and keep you there forever."

He laughed. "Good thing I have my security detail with me." He put his arm around my shoulder. I reached down for Preston's hand.

"Aunt Emmy, do I still get to come see you at the Golden Globes in February?" Vivi asked, coming up to join us.

We shared a look. Emmy was none too thrilled about what her niece had been putting me through lately. But even still, as soon as we had found out Emmy was going to present a Golden Globe, we had all planned to be in LA to celebrate with her afterward. It was something my daughter should see. I nodded and Emmy said, "Of course you do. You're my date." Then she leaned over and whispered, "But only if you can be nice to your mother."

"You don't understand," she whispered back, the two of them walking arm in arm toward the exit, pulling their rolling suitcases with their free hands.

To which Emerson replied immediately, "No, Vivi. *You* don't understand."

Vivi looked back at me with slightly less venom than usual, and I wondered if being back with our family was working already, if it was making her remember I wasn't the enemy.

"Did you hear there's a hurricane coming?" Kyle said, adjusting the duffel bag on his shoulder as he walked, holding Carter's hand.

A shudder ran through me. Peachtree Bluff hurricanes terrified me. I nodded, fighting the urge to turn around and get back on the plane. "Yeah, but it's way too soon to really know what its path will be. Most of them peter out this late in the season before they make landfall."

Kyle nodded. "I hope Pearl gives up the ghost."

"Who's Pearl?" Vivi asked.

"The hurricane," said Emmy.

Vivi laughed. "Hurricane Pearl. That sounds like a little old lady with a purse on her forearm. How bad can a hurricane named Pearl be?"

We all laughed.

"I just hope it doesn't mess up Jack and Ansley's trip," Kyle said. "Wonder if Sloane and Adam and the kids will want to come back with us if they have to evacuate."

I nodded. Kyle and Emerson were already planning to make a pit stop in New York for a few days to do the whole Christmas-in-New-York thing with Carter. I couldn't wait. "Oh yes!" I said. "They should come even if there isn't a hurricane. It would be so fun for us to get together for a few days."

"That would be so fun!" Vivi said. It was the first time she had agreed with me in months.

"I need more art from her than I even want to tell her, and I could really use her at Sloane Emerson for a minute." I smiled up at him. "Win-win. Kyle, this is why you're my favorite non-legal family member."

He squeezed my shoulder. "Someone won't marry me," he said loudly.

"Not having this conversation today," Emerson called back

breezily. Her blonde, sun-kissed hair was long and loose down her back, in beachy waves, while Vivi's was shorter and darker. But their build and walk were so similar as they made their way to our rental Suburban that it made me laugh.

Kyle scooped Preston up into his arms, making him giggle, and I picked up Carter and covered her little face with kisses.

This was going to be a great holiday. I just knew it. And, seeing how happy Vivi was, surrounded by her family, gave me the best idea. Maybe an extended vacation in Peachtree could do Vivi some good. Now all I had to do was figure out how to get my mother on board.

# Vivi: That One Percent

THERE ARE NO HOT GUYS in Peachtree Bluff. Some of my friends would think that's a problem, but I think it's kind of great. There's no one to look good for or impress, so I can just put on a pair of jeans and a T-shirt and not worry about it. After a long day of flying and a long night of catching up, I definitely slept later than anyone else, but they couldn't ever get motivated for breakfast until like ten anyway. Which, I mean, is kind of early for me, but I guess I was sort of excited to see everybody—and Gransley makes really, really great pancakes. Plus, Emerson and I were going to go paddleboarding later, before everyone started running around getting ready for Thanksgiving dinner.

"Good morning, sunshine," Mom called as I walked into Gransley and Jack's dining room. Everyone was lounging around in pj's, and Mom's were these pale pink silk ones that made her look super glamorous. Her dark hair was wavy and loose, and she already had her makeup on. I rolled my eyes. Who put makeup on for Thanksgiving breakfast with their family?

It smelled like turkey. It was kind of weird to stay at Jack's house when Gransley's old house was right next door. Sloane and Adam were living there now, and Kyle, Emerson, and Carter were staying in their guesthouse. Dad had bought Mom a house down the street, which she super selfishly was stealing away from him in the divorce. I mean, it was just as much his house and his town as it was hers. But everything was about Mom these days. There was no way I was staying with her, so I stayed with Gransley and Grandjack instead.

Grandjack went to bed kind of early—I think on purpose—and I helped Gransley make pie and stuffing and the breakfast casserole some of my family was already eating. It was cool to have Gransley all to myself. I never knew my grandfather Carter—who Emerson named my cousin after—so it wasn't like I was mad at Gransley for marrying Grandjack. But it was still weird to have to share her.

She didn't say anything to me about being mean to Mom, but I knew she wanted to. And, yeah, I felt pretty embarrassed that she knew about all that. But she didn't understand me. She didn't get how it felt when your parents got divorced because your mom couldn't get over some dumb mistake your dad made. Didn't she know that we were supposed to be family? I had a right to be mad. That's why, when we got back to New York, I was going to go live with Dad.

When I walked into the room, AJ, Taylor, and Preston all came running toward me at full force. I was lucky I made it to the couch in time because they knocked me down and made a big pile on top of me. Carter, who was trying so hard to keep up with them, crawled up beside me on the couch and smiled like she was one of the big kids.

"Vivi!" she squealed.

"You made it!" I squealed back, hugging her.

They got tired of me pretty quickly, though, and ran over to the insane amount of toys Gransley kept in her living room.

I sort of half waved at everyone, got my plate, and scooped myself a small piece of breakfast casserole from the sideboard. I wanted to save room for the main event: Thanksgiving dinner.

"Viv! You want pancakes?" Gransley asked.

"No," I said, even though I did. She looked so comfy in her robe with her coffee I didn't want to bother her.

"So what are you wearing to Thanksgiving?"

I looked down. "Um, this?"

Gransley laughed, and Mom said, "No, ma'am, you are not."

I rolled my eyes at her. "Mom, who cares what I wear to Thanksgiving? It's just our family."

Aunt Sloane chimed in, "But those are the most important people! Don't you want to look good for us?"

I knew she was trying to be funny, but she really wasn't. Every day in New York I had to worry about what I wore and what my hair looked like and how my eyeliner was done and how designer my purse was. "It's not like anyone in this hick town even knows if I look good or not," I said under my breath.

I knew that was going to piss my mom off. I can't even really explain why I do it. I mean, my mom is one of the fiercest people I have ever known. She's pretty good at controlling herself with me, but I guess maybe I test her, see how far I can push her before she snaps, which she does every now and then—and it is terrifying. So when I said this, I knew she was going to react, and it made these bubbles in my stomach. Not the good ones like when Lake—who I have a *huge* crush on—hugs me in the hall at school. Like bubbles out of a horror movie.

But Mom didn't have a chance to say anything because *Grand-jack* chimed in, "Vivi, you're not going to disrespect your mother, aunt, and grandmother at my breakfast table."

He was super calm and didn't raise his voice or anything, but he was *Grandjack*, for God's sake. He wasn't my family; he didn't have any right to scold me. Who did this guy think he was?

So I got up super dramatically, almost knocking my chair over, grabbed my plate, and marched up to my room. I was trying to be really nonchalant about the whole thing, but tears were stinging my eyes. Grandjack didn't even *know* me; he didn't get to tell me what to do. But as I got to my room, I realized I was maybe more upset that I had embarrassed myself in front of my whole family. I was trying to embarrass my mom. But she wasn't the one who looked bad. I did.

Maybe this was why people sent little kids to their rooms. Because it gave them time to think about stuff like this.

I set the plate of breakfast casserole I didn't want on the end table next to my unmade bed and plopped down, the white duvet fluffy and cozy underneath me. Then I called my dad. "Hey, kiddo!" he said, kind of loud, into the phone.

"What are you doing?" I asked.

"I'm on the chairlift. We weren't sure if there would be snow, but there is."

Picturing him with his gorgeous blonde new girlfriend, on a ski trip in Telluride, made me jealous. Was she going to replace me in his life? It did sort of make wonder if Aunt Emmy was right—as hard as this was for me, it was probably a million times harder for my mom. My dad hadn't left me. He'd left her. And not for just this girlfriend, but for, like, a few.

Even still, my mom was a nightmare, and she probably deserved it.

"Daddy," I said. I only called him Daddy when I really wanted something. He had probably caught on by now, but still, it worked like ninety-nine percent of the time. "Can I come live with you after we get back from Thanksgiving?"

He sighed. "Oh, honey. You know I would love that. You know I'd love nothing more—"

I cut him off. "So it's settled, then. I'll bring my stuff on Monday."

"Viv, look, you know I love you more than anything, and I would love to have you with me all the time. But I'm not doing this to Mom, and neither are you. We have a custody agreement, and that's how it is."

"But, Dad! I'm fifteen. I can choose who I want to live with."

"Viv, you're fifteen. Mom and I are going to choose who you live with. And, for now, you live with me every other weekend and half the summer and some holidays. If you want to spend a week here and there and your mom and I agree, then fine. But you don't get to run to me every time you don't want to follow Mom's rules."

"This is because of your new girlfriend!" I spat into the phone and immediately hung up.

That was a bad move. I never yelled at my dad. I needed him to be my safe place when I had to get away from my horrible mother.

Ninety-nine percent of the time calling him Daddy worked. But then there was that one percent . . . I felt tears coming to my eyes again. My door opened slowly. "You can't come in!" I called. But then I saw it was Biscuit. The little fur ball ran and jumped onto my lap, licking my tears away. I snuggled into her soft fur.

"At least *you* wanted to come check on me," I said.

My stomach sank again, thinking back to the phone call. I hated when my dad was mad at me. He was the one who always rescued me, no matter what, who spoiled me and took care of me even when my mom was mad.

Speaking of men who would rescue me, I was pretty sure now that I shouldn't have blown it with the closest thing I had to a grandfather. The only man who loves a girl possibly more than her dad is her grandad. I was going to have to work harder on being nice to Grandjack. Every girl knows you need a backup in your corner—especially when it feels like your whole world is falling apart.

# Sloane: High Water

*Thanksgiving Day*

MY BRILLIANT, FIERY, BEAUTIFUL SISTER was broken. You could see it in her shoulders, in her jawline, around her mouth. She was tired. She was defeated. And I could tell in my infinite sisterly wisdom that it wasn't only because of her divorce from James. It was also because of her daughter.

We all sat in silence around the antique pub table in Jack's dining room for a few moments after Vivi stomped off. The smaller kids were playing happily in a little cluster in the corner, not even noticing anything weird was going on, thank goodness. As I looked at my amazing husband sitting beside me, I wondered how Caroline did it. I wondered how she faced the hurricane that Vivi had become each day alone, without a good man to weather the storm with her.

"Jack, you shouldn't have stepped in," Mom scolded.

Caroline shook her head, tears springing to her eyes. "No, he should have. Thank you, Jack. It felt really good to have someone come to my rescue."

"Well, if I had known that . . ." Adam started. I looked up into his kind eyes. Sometimes it still startled me to see how long his hair had grown. I was so used to his cropped military cut. I squeezed his knee, bare beneath his khaki shorts, as everyone laughed, my heart fluttering at the very thought that this man was so good. No doubt about it, my military hero of a husband would have come to the rescue if Jack hadn't gotten there first. Man, woman, child, dog, bat, field mouse—if you were in trouble, Adam was your guy.

Caroline smiled at him. "Trust me, Adam, we all know you are always available for a rescue."

"I feel like I should step in here, but as the least manly, least dominant male at the table, I imagine it would be useless at this point," Kyle interjected.

Caroline shook her head, wrapping her hands around an oversized coffee mug. "No, Jack is her grandfather. He can scold her."

"Caroline!" Mom glared at her.

"Okay, she doesn't *know* he's her *actual* grandfather . . . but he is. Whatever. I don't know. Guys, I'm just tired. I'm so tired. I don't know how much longer I can deal with this."

"We can stay in New York a little longer to help," Emerson said. But, really, how much could she help? She had a two-year-old and a grueling full-time job. She loved it, but it was all-consuming.

"How can we help?" I said. "We have more time than Em." That probably wasn't strictly true. But, well, Em was the little sister.

"Oh!" Kyle interjected. "That reminds me. With that hurricane coming and Ansley and Jack leaving, you guys should come to New York with us."

"That hurricane is not coming here," Mom said. "Y'all need to calm down. These things almost always veer off course or get downgraded. It's fine."

"Even still," Caroline added. "You haven't been in forever, and it would be fun." She paused and grinned at me. "Plus, I could really use your help at the store."

That was fair. We were all part owners, and, while creating the art for Sloane Emerson, Sloane Emerson New York, and Sloane Emerson LA was a big job, it was the fun part. Mom and Caroline were left with most of the drudgery: the bills, the ordering, the inventory, the paperwork. Emerson, as the baby, was required to do very little. Because that's how it was. Even still, even now, we always stepped up to do what needed to be done for her. It was the unspoken system.

I looked over at Adam, who looked at Jack. Jack and Adam owned Peachtree Provisions, the corner grocery and deli, and it was packed at all times. Tourists coming in—of which there were many—counted on the store for their provisioning. And, with its laid-back atmosphere and amazing sandwiches, it had quickly become a local favorite too.

"Sloane, I love the idea," Adam said slowly, "but with Jack taking this trip, I need to be at the store. I don't think a visit to New York is in the cards for us."

"But there's a hurricane coming," Caroline interjected. "You might have to board the store up, at least for a few days."

"There isn't going to be a hurricane!" Mom protested.

"Mom," Caroline said dully. "Just because you say it over and over again doesn't make it true."

Jack shrugged. "You know, Adam, maybe this is the time to put Alisha to the test. We've been talking about making her manager. Let's see how she does for a few days with us both gone. Obviously, if we evacuate, she isn't going to stay here either. But if the store opens before you get back from New York, it will be a good time to see if she's up for the challenge. I had great managers that I trusted at every one of my hot dog shops before I sold out. I couldn't have grown without them."

Adam nodded. "Agreed." He turned to me. "I'm in." Then he got up, took his plate, and walked to the sideboard for more break-fast casserole.

"Yay!" Emerson, Caroline, and I said at the same time.

As Adam and I walked out Mom's front door, AJ and Taylor in tow, I couldn't help but smile. The antique-looking streetlamps were already adorned with huge wreaths with red bows and twinkle lights. The sun glinted off the water. I took a deep breath, feeling the breeze in my hair. Neighbors waved as they walked by.

Adam took my hand. "So, I know we decided no store-bought gifts for each other this year."

I nodded. "Yes." We were trying to build our nest egg. Plus, I had Adam and my kids and Peachtree Bluff. What else could I possibly need?

"This is admittedly harder for me than for you—"

"Babe," I interrupted. "Seriously, don't even worry about it. I don't want a thing."

He grinned widely, his dimple showing. "No, what I was going to say was that even though I *thought* this would be harder for me, I think I finally figured out something that you might like."

As I reached our gate—well, Mom's gate—Adam dug into his pocket and pulled out an envelope and handed it to me. It just said *Sloane* in his distinctive penmanship on the front.

I gasped. "Is this what I think it is?" I asked.

Adam shrugged. "Might be."

I smiled. "Can I open it now?"

"Well, I'm writing you one every day between now and Christmas, so if you want to keep up, I think you should."

I squealed and kissed him. "This is the best gift ever."

Wow, how different a letter from Adam felt now than when he was in the military—it was less of a lifeline and more of a wonderful addition to an already rich, full existence. Honestly, when Adam went MIA three years ago, I never imagined that we would be in this place, where we would all be together again, happy and healthy. And we wouldn't have gotten through any of that without Mom and Jack. I wasn't sure Adam would have made it through life without the military—he had too many lasting injuries to ever be back in the field—if Jack hadn't stepped up to help him start a business. We were so richly blessed to have them.

As if he were reading my mind, Adam said, "Babe, I wanted to talk to you about something: We can wait until after the holidays, but do you think it's time to start looking for our own house?"

My stomach gripped at the mere thought. I looked up at the white clapboard house with the black shutters and wide double front porches where I had spent my summers as a child, where I had healed after the death of my father, where my husband and I had started our life over again. It was still Mom's house, even though she was kind enough to let us rent it. Well, she'd wanted to let us stay there for free, but Adam wouldn't hear of it.

Adam opened the gate on the white picket fence, and the boys ran inside the front door. He let me go first. "Well, I mean, we could move," I said, "but aren't things going well as they are now?" I was trying to hide my horror.

Adam nodded. "Yeah, of course. But we can't mooch off your mom forever."

"We're paying rent! Plus, you know she'll never sell it, and she and Jack are living at his house."

I was being a little spoiled. But we were living in a big, beautiful house on the water, next door to my mom. It had all my memories—and seven-piece hand-carved moldings. And while, yes, Adam and I had worked hard over the last few years and really saved some money, we couldn't afford anything like my mom's house.

"We need to start building equity in something we own," said Adam. "We're throwing away money every month."

I stopped and looked at him, at the scar over his eye he'd gotten while he was held captive in Iraq. He still limped just a little, but with the number of injuries he had sustained, the recovery he had made—especially mentally—was a miracle.

"Plus, don't you think your sisters resent it a little?" he asked.

I scoffed. "Um, no. Caroline already has a house here, and Emerson and Kyle seem to have hung their life on gathering as few possessions as possible. So no, I don't think they resent me."

Plus, if they did, Caroline would tell me.

"Maybe after the holidays we'll start getting an idea of what we could afford. And maybe we can save a little longer for a bigger down payment so we can get something closer to what we really want and not have to move again in a few years."

Adam leaned down and kissed me, smiling, amused. "So what you're saying is *I'm not moving come hell or high water?*"

It was just a saying, but it gave me a chill. I looked out over the peaceful inlet, finding something eerie in its stillness. *High water.* I took a deep breath, and suddenly I could smell it, an electric charge, a ferocity in the air. *The calm before the storm.* It was a smell, a feeling that I knew well. My mother was dead set against it, but I knew then that she was wrong. A storm *was* coming. All that was left to find out was how big it was going to be.

# Emerson: Her Very Soul

*Thanksgiving Day*

"TUR-KEY," I SAID AGAIN, LOOKING down at Carter, the giant bow I kept trying to make her wear sliding down her wispy baby hair for the umpteenth time.

"Tur-tey," she repeated, her face scrunched in concentration.

I grinned down at her, scrunching my nose back, not even worrying about the Botox I was going to have to get from constantly mimicking her sweet expressions.

I handed Carter another tiny piece of turkey off the stove and pinched a bit of cookie dough off one of the perfect rolls on the marble counter and popped it in my mouth.

"Emerson Murphy!" Mom scolded, walking into Jack's kitchen, her signature shirtwaist dress swishing at her ankles.

Ugh. Just like when we were children. That woman was *everywhere.*

"You're going to get salmonella poisoning," she said as I mouthed the words to Carter at the same time.

She crossed her arms. "Well, if you know what I'm going to

say, why don't you listen?" Then she leaned down and picked up Carter. "Your mommy doesn't listen."

"No!" Carter said.

"You don't have to gang up on me. It isn't nice." I grinned at them, taking in the smaller but still beautifully gleaming white kitchen Mom had created at Jack's. It was certainly different having Thanksgiving at his house—well, I guess Mom's and Jack's now—but I was getting used to it. I was getting used to the idea that Mom was married to someone who wasn't Dad. I was even getting used to the fact that he was the long-lost sperm donor my parents had used to get pregnant with my two sisters after fertility treatments failed, that they got a replacement dad and I didn't.

Jack entered the kitchen, rolling up the sleeves of his blue checked oxford tucked into his khakis. He ran his hand through his damp salt-and-pepper hair. "Hey there, Starlet. It smells awfully good in here!" Fresh from the shower, Jack added a clean Dove-body-wash scent to the turkey smell.

"Turtey!" Carter announced joyfully, throwing her fists into the air.

"That's right!" Jack said, squeezing her chubby leg. I would miss the stage where she could wear her cute little bubble outfits with her chunky thighs hanging out. It was still in the high sixties here, basically the same as LA, so she could get away with it. New York in the winter was going to be a rude awakening for all of us. Even though I loved seeing my family, I wasn't looking forward to the cold. But what I hadn't told my sister is that I wasn't just coming to see the windows decorated for Christmas and the Rockettes: I was auditioning for a starring role on Broadway. The mere idea gave me chills. I had worked my entire life for this.

And, pinching more cookie dough, I realized how delightful it was to be able to gain five pounds and not have it evident to everyone behind the camera. The stage was much more forgiving—especially when you were playing the role of a young Queen Victoria and wearing dresses that hid literally everything. I could be nine months pregnant if I wanted to . . . I grinned down at Carter, at how big she was getting. Something to consider, for sure. As if on cue, Kyle walked in, kissing us both quickly.

Jack picked up the silver carving knife and fork and rubbed them together. "Is it time for my big moment?"

"Are you ready?" I asked him. "This is do or die. Make or break. No pressure."

Kyle reached over and tore off a huge hunk of turkey. "Break a leg!"

That man loved a pun. I loved him anyway.

I walked out onto the front porch, where Sloane and Caroline were fussing over flowers and candles. Jack's house didn't have a dining room big enough to hold all his guests—again, I didn't know *why* we weren't just doing it at Mom's, but I had the feeling that she didn't trust Sloane to clean and organize to her exacting standards. But I loved eating outside and having all of our family and friends gathered around one big table, so I didn't mind the change.

"Em, can you be in charge of cocktails when everyone gets here, please?" asked Caroline, the party general. I saluted.

I agreed so willingly because Kyle was an ace with the drinks. I would just get him to do it. The first time we met, he actually invented a drink for me called the Starlite Starlet. He was the perfect man, the perfect partner, the most supportive human on the planet—and so laid-back. I was so grateful for his willingness to help me live out my dream always—but especially on Thanksgiving.

"Where's Viv?" I asked Caroline, who rolled her eyes and shook her head.

I laughed. "Yeah. Forget the terrible twos. The terrible teens seem pretty rough." Even so, she was my niece. My *favorite* niece. Okay, my only niece. But still. "I'll go find her."

I walked back inside and up the stairs. Below, I could hear Keith's voice and Kyle's whoops as he greeted his cousin. Hippie Hal's voice was unmistakable as well. I smiled, remembering these voices that had all played such an important role in the story of my life. It really was the most wonderful time of the year.

I knocked halfheartedly on the door before I opened it. The sun pouring through the windows was so bright, it made me squint. The walls were a pale warm gray with the tiniest hint of lavender, and the iridescent abalone-shell chandelier hanging above the bed was such a focal point. It was too gorgeous a room for anyone inside it to be so irritable. Vivi was lying in her bed, scrolling through her phone, still in her jeans. "Get up!" I said cheerily. "Everyone is here and waiting for you."

"Why do we have to have all these randos at our special day?" she asked sulkily.

"Because these 'randos' are friends so good and so close that they are family. And, as I recall, a few years ago all you wanted, more than anything, was to move to Peachtree Bluff. It was the birthday gift that you absolutely had to have."

"Hm," she said.

"Whatever. But I'm wearing this." I crossed my arms. Then I turned, opened her closet, and pulled out the first dress I saw. "Nope. You're wearing this."

"Why are you being like this?" she asked, giving me the eye that I knew Caroline got about thirty-seven times a day.

"Look," I said, sitting down on her bed. "I know it has been tough for your parents to get divorced. I get it. But their being together and unhappy couldn't have been a picnic either."

She cocked her head as if considering this.

"Your mom is my big sister, the protector of all. But after what I saw this morning—after what she has told me about what's been going down lately—I think she might need a little protecting herself. Her heart is breaking already because of your dad, and now it's breaking a million times more because of you. So quit sulking, put the damn dress on, and pretend for one dinner that you still have some manners."

I smiled brightly at her.

"But you and Mom don't understand," she said. "You've never dealt with this before."

I knew Caroline walked a really thin, tight line with Vivi, but I didn't have to. I was the aunt, and this aunt was incredulous. "I'm sorry. Is that a joke? Our father *died*. Yours moved downstairs. Our father was killed, probably slowly and painfully, in our country's worst tragedy. So forgive me if I don't bow down at your altar of pity here and spray my sympathies on you. A divorce is a big change. It's hard. I get that. But you get to have both your parents. They get to see you be this hateful fifteen-year-old. I never got that. So don't tell me that your mom and I don't understand what it's like to have your world rocked."

She didn't hug my neck and say, *Aunt Emmy! You're so right! You're a genius!* But she did get up and put the dress on, which I considered a giant win. Before we left the room, she said quietly, "I actually never thought of that."

"It's okay," I said. "Teenagers, as a species, are selfish assholes. But there's no excuse for treating your mom the way you do. She has sacrificed everything—including her happiness, her very *soul*—for you on more occasions than you will ever know. So maybe you could give her fewer reasons to call the police."

She gave me a half smile, and I put my arm around her. And, well, I couldn't help but think that what goes around, comes around. Because my sister Caroline had probably been the most difficult teenager to ever walk the face of the earth.

"What are you doing when you sneak out, anyway?" I asked, partially to get the scoop for Caroline and partially because I missed being young and on the verge of my whole future and was a little jealous. But doing something yourself when you're young and stupid is totally different from growing up and realizing how dangerous those young, foolish actions could be. I worried about Vivi.

"Well, my friends and I usually just hang out. Or we go to a party or something." She shrugged like it was nothing, but I could tell from her smile it was fun.

"You have to be careful, Vivi. You could get hurt." I stopped and looked at her seriously. "You aren't drinking or doing drugs or anything, are you?" My pulse started pounding at the thought.

She shook her head so vehemently I believed her. "I'm not smoking either," she said, pointing at her boobs, which, depressingly, were already bigger than mine.

We both collapsed against the hallway wall in laughter. Three years ago, I had caught Vivi and a friend trying to smoke a cigarette. I told them that if they smoked, they'd never get boobs. Now I clutched my chest, gasping for air. "You remembered! My aunt wisdom got in there somewhere!"

We composed ourselves and made our way down the stairs. She was still in there, my sweet little niece. And I felt like the laughter had been just as important as the talk.

We all sat down in chairs that ran the length of Jack's front porch. Mom had covered a row of plain plastic folding tables with antique linen tablecloths. Topped with her china, silver, crystal, and beautiful blooms from her backyard, it was absolutely exquisite. The view of the sound and Starlite Island across from it was the icing on the cake.

Caroline, assessing her happy, well-dressed daughter, shot me an impressed smile. Kyle held my hand—Carter on his lap—and, surrounded by all the people I loved most in the world, I couldn't help but remember how lucky I was. I had grown up with something so traditional, so by the book. I had spent years in Hollywood, a world of independence and convention bucking, and had convinced myself that I should buck convention too. But as I looked at the kindest, most handsome man I'd ever known—and the beautiful girl on his lap—it occurred to me that I wanted more of it: more traditions, more family, more children. So maybe it wouldn't be the worst time to finally get a husband too.

# Ansley: Best Man

The Day after Thanksgiving

PEACHTREE'S BIGGEST, MOST FAMOUS HURRICANE took place in 1916. Obviously, technology wasn't what it is now. There were no storm trackers that could pinpoint the hurricane's every movement, and part of the reason the storm was so deadly was that it came on quickly, with very little warning. All I knew is that I never wanted to be put in that position, especially not now. Even though I was unconvinced that the hurricane was actually coming, I was grateful that we were going on our trip and wouldn't be here if it did.

Jack, always the early and prepared packer, folded another pair of pants and put them into his suitcase, which was perched on the end of our bed. Then he jogged around to my side, where I was lounging with my laptop, reviewing next week's orders and periodically tracking the path of Pearl, and kissed me.

"It's happening, Ans! This trip is happening!"

I had never seen Jack this excited. Maybe on our wedding day. *Maybe.* But I was excited too. I had never considered myself a cruise person, but this small ship was so luxurious, so highly rated that I could imagine I was going to become one. And I couldn't think of a better way to explore all the places we were going to visit in such a short amount of time. I loved the idea of everything being planned out for me, of not having to juggle dinner reservations and hotels at every stop along the way. Literally, all I had to do was show up with my suitcase. And it appeared that if I forgot my suitcase, the boutique aboard was so lovely that that would be okay too. In fact, maybe that was a better plan . . .

I looked out the window at the flags on the end of the dock blowing in the gentle breeze, the sun setting over the water. How could a hurricane be coming here, when we were about to embark on the trip of a lifetime? As I flipped back to the hurricane tracker, I glanced up at the top right-hand corner of my Mac and gasped. "Jack! The tree lighting is in thirty minutes!" Peachtree's annual tree lighting was the official beginning to the Christmas season and one of my favorite events of the year.

He looked at me, puzzled, and pointed out the window. "It's a sixty-second walk. Maybe not even that."

I gave him a patronizing smile. Jack, who had only been a part of this family for three years, hadn't totally gotten used to our dynamic yet. The man simply couldn't comprehend the time it took to wrangle three daughters, five grandchildren, and various and sundry spouses/partners. Thirty minutes was going to be pushing it. But what he had learned already was that I absolutely could not, would not, be late for huge town events like this one.

"Viv!" I called to the only other person who was actually in my house.

"Grans!" she called back, appearing from her bedroom in a pair of jeans tucked into some very chic boots, her dark blonde hair half up, half down. She looked so much like Caroline in that moment it took my breath away. It made me feel nostalgic. Then I remembered Caroline as a teenager. Not *that* nostalgic.

"Are you ready?" I asked enthusiastically.

"Can't wait!" she said. "Do you think they'll have hot chocolate like last year?"

I nodded. "Oh yes. You can't have a tree lighting without hot chocolate. It's un-American."

"I can't believe that they're even doing this thing," Jack said. "They're just going to have to turn around and take the tree down. Mayor Bob told me at coffee this morning that if Pearl doesn't change course, we're going to have to evacuate by the middle of next week."

I rolled my eyes and turned toward him. "Jack, did Mayor Bob seem worried?"

He shrugged. "Not particularly."

"Right. And he didn't seem worried because this hurricane isn't coming. It's Thanksgiving weekend, for heaven's sake. It's the beginning of the Christmas season. Peachtree never has hurricanes this late. We can't. It ruins the spirit of things."

Vivi laughed at that. "You tell 'em, Gransley. If Pearl tries to come, we'll just say we have the flotilla lined up, and she can't stay."

The interesting thing about teenagers and toddlers was precisely the same: they were terribly unpredictable. This one, who had been so moody, sullen, and downright awful yesterday, was a peach today.

"Why don't you two go get Sloane, and I'll work on Emerson?" I said.

Jack elbowed Vivi. "You notice how she gave us AJ and Taylor, the impossible-to-tame duo, while she got Carter, the easiest two-year-old on the planet?"

Vivi laughed. Not politely. Actually.

Jack had been lamenting last night that, though he had made huge gains in his relationships with my girls—well, our girls, I guess—and the little ones, Vivi was a tougher nut to crack. I'd assumed scolding her at the breakfast table hadn't done much in that department, and I'd promised him that I would try to help however I could. We had discussed talking points and activities that teenage girls might like, fun things they could do for some quality time. I told him to ask her about her life, her friends, the music she listened to. In my experience, kids liked to talk about themselves. It was truly adorable how much of an effort he wanted to make with her. I really appreciated it.

"Hurry up!" I said, looking down at my watch. "Twenty-four minutes." They started down the steps, and I called, "I'll grab Caroline and Preston on my way past their house!"

I stepped out onto the front porch of Jack's house. No, our house. Three years later, and I still had trouble with that. I would never have told him, but I missed my family home. Jack's had a pretty view of Starlite Island, but mine also had a view out into the inlet. His front porch was quaint, but mine was wide and rambling. And, most of all, mine could hold my entire family, while his couldn't. That was the major drawback to Jack's. Our extended family couldn't stay under the same roof. When we were in the same house, we could stay up as late as we wanted to talking, could get up for coffee and congregate before we even changed out of our pajamas. But, most of all, it felt like old times. Jack was worth it, most certainly. But it was a change. And change was always hard.

I took a deep breath, admiring the dark pinks and burnt oranges of the vivid sunset. I was looking forward to Australia. But I couldn't imagine that anywhere in the world had sunsets as beautiful as Peachtree Bluff.

I turned to see Kyle walking up between our two houses. "Hey!" he called. "Ans! I was looking for you."

I looked down at my watch. "Where are Emerson and Carter? The tree lighting is in twenty-two minutes. The lighting waits for no one."

He laughed and lazily made his way through the fence. Didn't he know Peachtree Bluff events were sacred?

"I need to talk to you," he said quietly.

"Right. And I'm looking forward to it. After the tree lighting."

He laughed that casual, laid-back laugh again. Where was the disconnect coming from? This was not a laughing matter.

He walked up to the porch and sat down on the black swing.

Oh my gosh. There was no time for sitting! He patted for me to sit beside him.

"Kyle, if this is important, maybe we should wait until after—"

As if he hadn't even heard me, he said, "Ans, you know that I think the whole world revolves around Emerson."

"Uh-huh," I said with a hint of edge to my voice. I loved Kyle, but the man had a penchant for long soliloquies. *Yes, you worship*

*my daughter, even though neither of you have any regard for roots,*
*tradition, or stability. I get it. I love her too. You don't have to tell*
*me constantly.*

"I know she's pretty happy with the way things have been
between us, and so am I."

Great. State of the union. I glanced down at my watch. Nine-
teen minutes.

"But, Ans, I really want to move forward in our relationship. I
know we want more kids . . ."

He trailed off. I searched his face for what he wanted me to say
besides, *Hello, Southern grandmother here who is just barely*
*getting okay with the idea of this bohemian, no-rules, we-don't-*
*have-to-get-married-to-procreate thing.*

Before I could formulate a response, he said, "We haven't had a
real talk about it, but you know Emerson and I are soul mates. It's like
I can feel what she wants and needs even when she doesn't say it."

*Gag.* I squinted at him.

"And I think we both feel it's time for us to get married."

"What?" Now he had my attention.

He nodded. "I just feel it, you know?"

I leaned back on the swing and sighed. This actually *was* more
important than the tree lighting. I smiled at him. "Kyle, you know
nothing would make me happier, but haven't you asked her, like, a
few times?"

I didn't want to be insensitive, but I wasn't sure where Emerson was going to land on this one.

He shrugged. "I've asked her casually to test the waters, but
never with a ring and a plan. So that's why I'm here."

I raised my eyebrows. "What's why you're here?"

"Well, I want to ask your permission to marry your daughter. Ans, I love her like no one else could. I will always make her happy. I promise."

I laughed and patted his hand. "Kyle, you've been together for three years. You share a child. Yes, you definitely have my permission to marry my daughter."

I glanced at my wrist. Okay. Sixteen minutes. We were still going to make it. Although, where *were* Jack, Vivi, and Sloane's family? Not to mention Emerson and Carter?

"Right," he said. "But I don't want you to say yes just because of the optics of the thing. I want you to feel my heart."

I took his hand and looked him straight in the eye. "Kyle, you worship at the altar of Emerson. I read you loud and clear. People who have never met you read you loud and clear. You are literally the perfect human for her. I know. If you can talk her into marrying you, no one will be happier than I will."

He beamed. *Awesome. Right answer. We might just make it.*

"But that isn't the only thing I wanted to ask you."

It took all my patience not to groan. I loved Kyle before Emerson did. I had known him since he was just an unshaven kid delivering the most magical coffee concoctions on the planet. He was warm and funny and more handsome than any human had a right to be. But if he made me miss this tree lighting, so help me God.

"Yes, Kyle. What else do you need from me?" *A blood oath? A hair sample?*

"I want to make her proposal really, really special. And I was hoping maybe you could help me. I really want to do it over

Christmas when the whole family is together. I know the Murphies are a package deal, and I want everyone to be there to take part in this special moment. I thought maybe we could plan a post-engagement party?"

For just a second, I quit worrying about Christmas trees and hot chocolate and whether the Downtown Association, which partnered with Peachtree Perk to provide said hot chocolate, was getting low on the little marshmallows. They never got enough, and what good was hot chocolate without the marshmallows? I bit my lip.

I didn't want Kyle to be publicly humiliated in case things didn't go as planned.

"You don't want to plan something?" he asked.

I shook my head. "No, no. Of *course* I do. It's just that, don't you think . . . What if she says no?"

He shook his head now. "She'll say yes. I know it. I know it in my *bones*. Soul mates, remember?"

Kyle popped up off the swing, making it wobble uneasily. "We'd better go get the rest of the family! Can't be late for the tree lighting. And you know Keith never has enough marshmallows. I give him the numbers I used to use every year, and he still never has enough. Maybe third time's the charm."

I watched him walk away, stunned. I didn't know what to do. If I told Emerson about Kyle's plan, I'd be ruining the surprise. If I didn't tell her, she might just break Kyle's heart. Or worse, she might feel like she had to say yes because so many people were watching and break her own.

I didn't have time to worry because AJ and Taylor burst out

the front door, wrapped in scarves and gloves, which I assumed were for effect—it was seventy degrees outside—yelling, "Gransley! Let's goooooo!"

Finally! Someone on my page. "Yes!" I called back to them, running down the steps and out the gate, taking their little warm hands in mine. When we reached the corner, I said, "Go get Aunt Caroline and Preston. I need to make sure your mom knows I have you."

I looked back to see the rest of my family trailing behind me. Amazing. We were going to make it—and with time to spare! "I've got them, Mom!" Sloane called, as Caroline, still on her porch, called, "Mom! Can I talk to you for a minute?"

"You can talk to me for lots of minutes after the tree lighting," I called back.

She crossed her arms. "Mom, it will take like five minutes."

I glanced at my watch. "And we only have ten."

I could see her glaring at me even at a distance. "Fine," I said, trudging up the steps and closing the gate tightly behind me.

Ellie May, the goat Caroline had gotten a few years ago when Hal instituted his new goat plan to reduce lawn mower noise and pollution downtown, bleated at me loudly. I patted her head. She really was quite tame now. And it was more than convenient for Jack and me to bring our food scraps down here. Compost without the worms.

When I reached the porch, Caroline looked around.

"Vivi! Wait for me, please. Let's walk together!" Caroline called.

Vivi kept walking down the sidewalk, clearly pretending not to hear her mother.

Caroline and I sighed simultaneously.

"Do you see how she is to me?"

I did see. I would see more sympathetically *after* the tree lighting.

"Well, now that she's gone . . . Mom, I really need your advice."

I nodded, trying to focus on her.

"When I let it go, it doesn't help. When I punish her, it doesn't help. I feel like we need some time apart, but, Mom, this is so sad . . ."

"What?"

"She asked James if she could live with him."

I could tell she was trying not to cry. I could feel my nerves rising. No matter how hard my girls had been at one time or another, they were stuck with me. This was different. If James agreed, Vivi was old enough to choose to live with him. The thought made my stomach turn, but my job right now was to make Caroline feel better. I rolled my eyes. "Car, that's because he doesn't have any rules. He lets her do whatever she wants."

Caroline pointed at me. "Maybe. But it still makes me feel awful."

"Honey, I think this is a Sloane, Emerson, you, me, and a bottle of wine conversation." Caroline—much to my chagrin—sat down. "No, totally, Mom. There is so much to talk about."

Over the town loudspeaker, Mayor Bob called, "Five minutes until the tree lighting! Get your hot chocolate. We're running low on marshmallows . . . again."

I looked at Caroline, who appeared not to have heard him. She was very deep in thought. "I hate to even suggest this. It's a big ask. A huge one. But Mom, I'm not just worried about Vivi's emotions. I'm worried about her safety. And there's only so much trouble a kid can get into in Peachtree Bluff . . ."

She trailed off, and I sat down now too. She couldn't be saying what I thought she was saying. I had a husband to think of now. He had all these plans for the footloose and fancy-free life we were going to have, full of travel and fun. We weren't old by any stretch, but we were in our early sixties. The time for adventures was now, before a health crisis struck. I couldn't offer what she was clearly asking.

"Please don't make me say it, Mom. It's too much. But I was thinking, if you and Jack were okay with it, she could stay here for a few weeks and then I'd take her home after Christmas. Maybe if she's away from me for a bit, she'll hate me a little less when she comes back." She looked down at her hands. "If she goes to live with him, I'll lose her. I just know it."

I felt awful for her, but I shook my head. My hands were tied. "Caroline, Jack and I are going on our trip. I can't—won't— take that away from him. And what about school? And James?"

She just shrugged. "I'm not going to dig too deeply into it unless you think it might work. But lots of kids at Vivi's school go to Florida for the winter, so they are well equipped for her to do school from anywhere. That wouldn't be a big deal." She paused. "And, honestly, James and I have really been on the same parenting team. He sees what she's putting me through. I think he'd be okay with it."

I let out a long exhale. "Car, you guys are always my priority, but I honestly don't know how to broach the subject with Jack. I mean, suddenly having a child—and, no offense, but kind of a pill of a child at that—isn't exactly easy."

She crossed her arms. "What if James and I both died?"

"Well, she isn't *that* awful, Caroline."

We both burst out laughing, and I hit her on the arm lightly. "Don't even say that. You know I would take care of her—and all of my grandchildren, for that matter—at any time."

"Sloane gets my kids if we die anyway. But, you know. I just had to test you a little."

I rolled my eyes and put my arm around her. "Let me think about it. Okay?"

She nodded. "That's all I'm asking. And it might be crazy. If you say no, I totally get it. I'm just at my wits' end."

I grimaced. "It shows."

Her turn to hit me.

"Ninety seconds, Peachtree Bluff residents! Ninety seconds until we ring in another Christmas season."

Caroline and I both popped up and looked at each other briefly. "Run!"

I raced down the steps. "Oh my God! I forgot Preston!" Caroline exclaimed, turning back into the house to grab him.

But I didn't follow her. That girl could run at Olympic speed. She'd beat me even with her Preston detour. As I jogged down the street, I could see the bright lights of the square coming into view and the dull but large star at the top of the town's Christmas tree. By the time I had found the rest of my family and Caroline had caught up to us as well, I was out of breath. "Thirty seconds!" Bob bellowed.

The town square was packed with people—my people. I waved at Hippie Hal and Mrs. McClasky, one of the town's most enthusiastic volunteers, a few clients, Leah, and some friends from Azure, one of my favorite local restaurants. It seemed that everyone had gathered just in time to celebrate.

"There's my girl!" Jack said, cutting through the throngs of people standing shoulder to shoulder, handing me a cup of cocoa. With marshmallows! I leaned over and kissed him. "You are the world's very best man."

He smiled and kissed my nose. "I know about the marshmallows. This isn't my first day here."

We were way in the back of the crowd, which was okay with me—the back had the best view of the star. Bob was standing by the tree in shorts and a red scarf, holding a small box with a control button that, God willing, would enact the whole tree-lighting ceremony. In the other hand, he held a bullhorn and was counting down along with everyone else: "Three, two . . ."

Lights, camera, action. Bob punched the button, and that giant Christmas tree lit up like the Fourth of July. The crowd cheered as the star shone bright and thousands of twinkle lights glowed. Jack kissed me again, and I squeezed Vivi's arm.

"Was the stress of getting here worth it?" Jack asked.

Carter clapped and squealed, and the boys ran circles through the crowd and around the tree. And, for just a moment, the briefest of seconds, time stood still. There, in that Christmas-movie moment, we were all bound as one, united together in the spirit of a season that could still, even after all these years, leave me awestruck. Around that tree were people who had faced losses and struggles this year. They had fretted over next career steps, contemplated scary diagnoses, and worried about paying the bills. But in that brief moment, all of us were smiling, still and quiet, reminded of the simplicity of a holiday that was, perhaps, bigger than all of us.

# Caroline: A Sleepover

I HELD PRESTON UP A little higher on my hip so he could see the star. "Yay!" we yelled as it sprang to life, thousands of dazzling lights blinking on the thirty-foot-tall tree. I looked over at Vivi, who was standing next to Mom, a few yards in front of me.

"Did you know that I used to hold your sister just like this every year for the tree lighting?" I asked Preston.

His eyes went wide. I was sure he couldn't imagine his big sister ever being as small as he was.

As I cooed at Preston, a man that looked vaguely familiar caught my eye and smiled. I didn't know who he was, but he sure was cute. I smiled back, and he started walking toward me.

As Preston wriggled down to join his cousins, who were running around the square, I scanned my mental directory for how exactly I knew this man—this very, very handsome man, I might add. "Hi, Caroline. It's Wes Jenkins."

"Oh my God, Wes!" I put my hand up to my heart.

I laughed. Wes Jenkins was the boy who had finally convinced me, after we moved from New York, that maybe, just maybe, Peachtree Bluff wasn't so horrible. And now, twenty years later, here he was again.

"How have you been? Where are you living now?"

He nodded. "Pretty good. I'm in Atlanta." He paused. "Well, Atlanta and here. You?"

"New York."

"Still playing bingo?" he asked casually. I doubled over in laughter—and he did too.

In 2002, only a few months after my father died, my mom moved us all to Peachtree Bluff, into the waterfront home her grandmother had left her when she died. Today that house is a *Southern Living*–ready showplace. But back then? It was a dump. Not only had it not been renovated in decades, but it was also in the place that I considered the armpit of America. Yes, Peachtree was pretty, and yes, I liked Starlite Island, the beach across from our house, where my sisters and I spent hours and hours. But otherwise, I considered it a cultural wasteland with weird people.

Peachtree has seemingly millions of absurd traditions, which, as a grown-up, I find adorable. As I kid, I found them abhorrent. One of those traditions is Tuesday-night bingo. Practically everyone in town goes. You don't play with your family. You're assigned a random table when you walk in the door, which I now see as a part of its charm. Then, it horrified me.

But, one night, after months of living in Peachtree Bluff, Emerson finally convinced me to go. Emerson could—then and now—

convince me to do most things, which was funny because I generally considered myself the convincer, not the convincee.

I still remember walking into the church parish hall that night, with its faded green indoor-outdoor carpet and bad lighting. Tables were crammed every which way, covered with horrific plastic tablecloths in no semblance of a matching fashion.

People were wandering around filling up their plates with fried chicken and barbecue, brownies, lemonade, and other travesties of health-destroying Southern cuisine. I remember thinking, *Emerson can force me to come, but she can*not *make me eat this trash.*

I looked around for table eight, feeling torn between keeping my promise to Emerson and escaping out the side door. But when I approached the table, the most adorable blond-headed boy was sitting there. He was very Southern-looking in his khaki shorts and polo shirt—a huge negative—but he had these dimples and this gravelly voice when he said hello. One glance at him and I was hooked.

"Want to go get some barbecue?" he asked.

I don't remember everything about that night, of course. It was like twenty years ago. But I do know that Wes and I only made it through the first two of the eight games of bingo. And that I found myself eating and discovering that potato salad—that vile yellow, lumpy concoction—was actually kind of delicious. When Wes handed me half his brownie, I actually took a bite. When he told me about school and baseball, I listened, and, for the first time, I realized I might be excited about finishing high school here if it meant I got to be with Wes.

When it was time for all *N*s and *O*s, he took me out to the church softball field, and we sat on the bleachers, cuddled up— presumably because it was breezy but really because we wanted to be close—looking at the stars.

"I think you'll like it here if you give it a chance," he said. "The people are really laid-back. Not stuck-up at all. And I'll introduce you to everyone."

I smiled at him then, noting that I hadn't felt butterflies like this since I had broken up with John Richardson, my boyfriend back in the city, a few months earlier. "That's really nice of you," I said. "I am a little nervous about having to start over like this with no friends." Vulnerability was usually the enemy for me. Not now. Because after I'd bared my soul, Wes put his arm around me. "You've got me now. Nothing to be nervous about."

I don't know if it was the brownies or the lemonade or just him, but, when Wes's lips touched mine, he tasted so sweet. He *was* so sweet. Those six months I was in Peachtree Bluff before I went back to Manhattan to start NYU, we were inseparable. But our breakup wasn't dramatic. I was always going back to New York as soon as we graduated. Until then, Wes and I went to school dances and spent long days on the beach with friends, working on our tans and holding hands. We played bingo on Tuesday nights and went to all the Peachtree parades. He taught me to fish, and I taught him to sail.

But we had never, I was now realizing, had a Peachtree Bluff Christmas together. I smiled at him. When he grinned back, he looked so much like that boy he had been. He was handsomer now, with a few lines around his eyes, less cushion around his pronounced jaw. His eyes were still a piercing green, and there was still something in them that told me I was going to have a good time.

For just a second, I was a teenager again, on the beach in my bikini with a cute boy who made me realize that Peachtree Bluff—and the people in it—weren't so bad.

"So, are you home for the holidays?" he asked.

I nodded. "Just Thanksgiving. But we'll be back in Peachtree for Christmas. My daughter, Vivi, my son, Preston, and I." I realized I had amended that "we" to not include a husband very deliberately, and I was a little embarrassed I had. Had I become so desperate and obvious? And, if so, why now? I had turned down plenty of great offers from men in New York. "What about you?"

"Yeah. My son is with my ex back in Atlanta. She has him for Thanksgiving, so I'll be here with my parents for a week or so." He paused. "At least, that was the plan. With the hurricane coming, I guess I'll have to go back inland."

I shook my head. "If you want to ignore that it's coming, just chat with my mother for a while. She has deemed a late-November hurricane in Peachtree Bluff completely impossible."

"Well, there you have it," he said. "If Ansley says the hurricane is canceled, then the hurricane is canceled." We both laughed again, and it felt nice.

"Want to get some hot chocolate?" he asked.

I surprised myself by saying yes. I was generally a no-sugar kind of girl. But it was the tree lighting, and it was chilly-ish and everything was sparkling, and that kind of moment necessitated hot chocolate.

"Are you going to stay in Atlanta?" I asked as we walked over to the red hut decorated with wooden candy canes and gumdrops. As of tomorrow, it would house Santa until Christmas. But, for now, it was the official hot chocolate station.

He smiled. "I really don't know. I only have my son on weekends and holidays, and he prefers to spend his time with me in Peachtree fishing." He smiled. "Which, coincidentally, is all I want to be doing too." He shrugged. "I bought a little house here and have a condo in Atlanta."

I felt my eyes widen, even though I didn't mean for them to.

He paused and put his hand up. "Don't pity me. It's not the sad, cardboard-box-filled divorced dad apartment you're picturing. It's a really great condo."

I laughed. "I wasn't picturing that at all."

I was. I totally was envisioning poor Wes in a folding chair in one of those sad, lightless condos that always seemed to have sirens blaring outside.

"The condo was supposed to be temporary, but my son and I have spent so much time here with my parents that it seemed better to get a house in Peachtree and keep it simple in Atlanta."

I nodded as we finally reached the front of the line for hot chocolate.

"Hey, Keith," I said at the same time as Wes said, "Two, please." He handed me a steaming cup. Looking around at all the joyful people, for the first time in my life, I actually understood how living in Peachtree could be appealing. I couldn't imagine ever leaving the city. But there was something nice about this town welcoming you into its fold. And right now, it was just what I needed.

As we walked away from the stand, I scanned the crowd, spotting first Preston and then Vivi. Shew. I'd assumed my mom was watching them—sometimes I forgot that she had five little people to keep an eye on. Preston, who was running back and forth with his cousins between Sloane, Mom, and me, called, "Mommy! We're having a sweepover tonight!"

"A sweepover?" Wes questioned.

I laughed. "Well, a sleepover. Preston, AJ, and Taylor love to have sleepovers and then they stay up too late and are grumpy and untenable for days."

"Ah, yes. The good old days. Although, even at twelve, Brad can still be kind of a pill after a sleepover."

*Vivi's a pill even without the sleepover*, I thought. Although, at the moment, watching her laugh with my sisters by the now-lit tree, I sort of forgot about all that. The old, light-filled Vivi I knew was back for just a moment. I loved seeing her here, like this. I wondered briefly if I'd overstepped by asking my mom if Vivi could stay here until after the holidays. Maybe it was a cop-out on my mom job, but I really was worried about her safety. These ridiculous pop-up parties were all the rage in New York now. Some kid would post a "flash" Instagram post announcing the time and place. I'd think my daughter was at a friend's house and then realize that, instead, she was in some sketchy parking lot with a van and loud music and strobe lights and so many bodies all crammed together . . . It was terrible. When I was her age we were at least partying in cool old churches and spray-painted warehouses.

At any rate, I had a feeling that Peachtree was for Vivi—like it was for me—a reset button of sorts. I also mentally thanked my sisters. I knew what they were doing, occupying Vivi so she wouldn't notice I had been talking to a very handsome man.

I hadn't even considered dating since the whole James debacle. But, really, our marriage had been over for more than just the year we had been separated. It had been three years of total turmoil, of being in and then out, up and then down. I could truly say that I had given my marriage every possible chance. It was over. James knew it. I knew it. And he had moved on. Well, maybe not "moved on" necessarily. But he was dating. And that was more than I could say for myself. Not that Wes wanted to date me. But that smile he was giving me . . .

We stepped out onto the wooden boardwalk and walked down out of the crowd. I leaned onto the railing, taking a deep breath and admiring the beauty of the boats. "How long have you been divorced?"

"A year," Wes said automatically. "But, to be honest, it was never quite right. My ex got pregnant; we got married. And we made it work for twelve years. But at some point, you just want true love, you know? Life is too short to live without it."

My stomach clenched, and that feeling that had kept me hanging on to a bad marriage returned. James's very public affair with Edie Fitzgerald, the hottest new model in town, had nearly killed me. But I also had this bright, shining, seemingly inextinguishable flame that I carried for him, this man who had brought me so much love and so much joy. I wanted to recapture that. It took me years to realize that was impossible.

"I get that," I said. "I totally do. I think that's why I stuck with James for so long. We had that once."

Wes nodded. "Yeah, Caroline, everyone knows you're tough, but I can't imagine what you've been through."

The kindness in his face made me look away. I didn't want him to see the tears in my eyes. They weren't for James now. Not really. They were for Wes's understanding and sympathy. I smiled and turned back to him. "You'll find that woman, Wes. You deserve every happiness."

He looked down at his shoes and then back up at me. "Look, I haven't done this in a while, and you're the frankest person I know. You probably got the sense that I was about to ask you out, so was that your nice way of blowing me off?"

I laughed. "No! Not at all."

"Oh, good," he said, grinning so boyishly that I wanted to kiss him right then and there. "Because I was going to see if maybe I could take you to dinner when I come back to Peachtree for Christmas."

I felt something then that I realized I hadn't felt in a long time: joy. Real, true excitement. Not excitement for my children, but something that was all my own. "I thought you might ask me back to the softball field."

He laughed and put his hand up. "Whoa, Caroline. This is moving a little fast." We both laughed now, and it felt so good. I AirDropped my contact to him and said, "Well, I'd better get back to my family before my very suspicious fifteen-year-old gives me a lecture."

He nodded and held up his phone. "I'll be counting down the days until you come back."

I was surprised that I actually meant it when I said, "Me too."

It had been a long time since I'd had a crush on a boy. I really thought I liked it.

# Sloane: Christmas in New York

*The Day after the Tree Lighting*

Dear Sloane,

I remember moving into our first little duplex on Post and telling you how we wouldn't be there long, how we'd move up, make more of our lives. But do you know what's funny? I would give anything to be back there now. The simplicity of the two of us and knowing that our adventures together were just beginning. It was one of the best times of my life. Whenever I was away, I only had to think of you and, suddenly, I was home. It's still that way. No matter what decision we make, no matter where we go or what we do, you, Sloane, will always be my home.

All my love,
Adam

The best part of everyone being all in one place again was the noise. The cooking smells were wonderful, and seeing all the children—miniature versions of my sisters and me—playing in one place was great. But the sounds of happy laughter really took the cake this evening. I stretched, paintbrush in hand, and looked back at what I had been creating. I had already finished my limited-run holiday minis, but Caroline needed about a million abstracts for our three Sloane Emerson locations. And yet here I sat at my easel overlooking the water, in what had been my childhood room at my grandmother's house, finishing the painting I'd begun this morning of the lemon-yellow sun rising over the water, birds soaring in a perfect V overhead—despite the fact that the sun was actually setting right now. It wasn't what Caroline needed, but, alas, it was what I was creating. Caroline, the type A poster child for perfection, didn't quite understand why I couldn't always paint on demand. Well, no—I *could* paint on demand. No one feels inspired to create 172 miniature Grinches. But my large paintings, my real art, were where I let my feelings out.

You didn't have to be Freud to realize that capturing the very real view outside my window was a representation of all the beauty I didn't want to leave behind. Adam and I hadn't discussed moving again, but I knew he still wanted to. My heart sank at the idea of leaving this house, this room that had been mine for as long as we'd lived in Peachtree Bluff.

This was once my bedroom, but, now the bed was gone, the TV moved, and tables and canvases, brushes, and palettes stood in their place. And that was for the best because, for months after Adam came home, I couldn't walk into this room without thinking about how I'd spent weeks here, unable to get out of bed. When I found out he was MIA, I felt like I wanted to die. The thought of living without him, imagining him being tortured, was entirely too much to bear.

As I put the finishing touches on the last bird, the anticipation for the night's main event became too much. With only an hour until dark and the flotilla—the annual boat parade in Peachtree Bluff—I could see Jack and Kyle down on the dock lighting the fire pit. Judging by the increasing volume of voices coming from downstairs, the excitement had reached a fever pitch. The children's squealing, screaming, and loud footsteps were almost as distracting as the distinctive cookie smell rising up through the ceiling. I was glad Carter was in the guesthouse napping. This was not a restful environment, to say the least. But, man, was it happy.

I walked down the steps just in time to see three little boys whiz past me, Adam on their tail. "My beautiful bride!" he yelled as the door slammed.

I pointed to the kids.

"They're going down with Kyle and Jack to the dock." He wrapped me up, kissed me, and said, "How was the painting?"

"It was good," I said.

"You know how I was telling you the other night that Jack and I are thinking about building on top of the store and renting out office spaces?"

I nodded like I remembered exactly, when, really, that was all pretty vague. I was bathing the kids and, as much as I hated to admit it, sometimes my focus was a little divided.

"I was thinking that if we move, maybe we could save one of

the waterfront offices for you. You could have a studio space all your own, outside the house, with the best view in town."

I opened my mouth to protest, but, well, I had complained for years that I couldn't separate work from home because it was all in the same place.

Before I could respond, Adam said, "Well, think about it. And good luck with all those little monsters, babe. Daddy slash Uncle Adam is going to work out. Those three gave me a run for my money."

I laughed. "Well deserved. But don't be late for the flotilla."

I opened the door to find the rest of the family sitting on the front porch. Mom, Jack, Caroline, Vivi, Emerson, and Kyle all turned to look at me as Carter—who was evidently up from her nap—took off at full speed to try to keep up with the bigger boys.

"What are you doing?" Caroline scolded. "Get back up there!"

I crossed my arms. "I'm not missing the holidays with my family because you need paintings. People can wait."

She rolled her eyes. "Well, I guess being sold out isn't the worst business strategy. It does create demand."

"They sure are wound up," I said, pointing at the kids.

"Mommy!" Taylor said, flying at me. "Gransley made us cookies!"

"You don't say . . ." I smiled at him and kissed his chocolate-dotted cheek.

Vivi nodded. "Hey, want me to take them down to the dock to fish while we wait for the flotilla?"

"Oh my gosh, yes!" Caroline said. "But they all need life jackets."

She nodded.

"Isn't that kind of a lot on you, Viv?" Emerson asked.

Vivi smiled. "Maybe. Grandjack, want to come with me?"

He looked like he had just won the lottery. "Me?"

She nodded. "Yes. The only one of my grandfathers on the porch."

He stood up. "I would love to."

Kyle said, "In that case, Keith wanted me to help him go over a few things at the shop, so I'll go do that now and let y'all have your gossip time."

"Gossip time?" Mom asked.

"Uh-huh," Kyle said. "You pretend you don't want time for the four of you, and I'll pretend like I'm not leaving to get a beer."

I laughed. He wasn't wrong. Having everyone together was incredible, but when it was just the four of us it really felt like coming home. "So what's that all about?" I asked, nodding to Vivi and Jack when they were out of earshot.

"Oh, she's up to something, all right. I'm too relaxed to care what it is right now," Caroline said. "But that man should be very, very afraid."

"Speaking of men that should be afraid," Emerson said, "looks like Wes Jenkins threw himself in front of the firing squad again."

"I'm sorry," Caroline said coyly. "I don't know what you're talking about."

"So he didn't ask you out?" I questioned.

She looked out over the water. "I'd rather not say."

"Well, I think that's great," Mom said. "You need to get back out there, Caroline. You're young and beautiful."

The subtext that hung in the air was, *And you might not be for much longer.*

"Yeah," Emerson added. "James has his bimbo. You should definitely one-up him."

"She's head of investments at Morgan Stanley," Caroline said. "So maybe not a *bimbo* exactly."

"Well, you're head of a multimillion-dollar chain of luxury home décor stores," Mom said.

"Head?" Emerson interjected. "Since when is she the head?"

I scoffed. "Em, she's been the head since the day she was born."

We all laughed. And really, Em and I helped only a little. Although Mom had started it all, it was Caroline who, with her savvy and connections, had turned Mom's sweet gift shop in a sleepy town into a thriving empire. I felt guilty every single month when I got my check, because Caroline did most of the work while Emerson, Mom, and I received so much of the benefit. I reasoned that Caroline needed the creative outlet, the distraction to pour herself into. But she didn't need the money, no matter what she said. Half of what James had was more than enough. But Sloane Emerson took care of all of us. And Caroline, despite her snarkiness and devil-may-care attitude, wanted to do that. I could feel my heart swell with pride at the mere thought of it.

"Seriously, though," I said. "Are you going out with Wes?"

She nodded and grinned. "I am. When we come back for Christmas. I'm super excited about it, actually."

"What's his story?" Mom asked.

She shrugged. "I don't really know. I know he's divorced and has a twelve-year-old son and does something in private equity.

And I think he's going to move to Peachtree Bluff, at least part-time."

Emerson groaned.

"What?" Caroline snapped.

"Poor Wes. Here we are again. Caroline sweeps him off his feet and then dumps him for New York while he stays in Peachtree and pines for her."

"You are so dramatic," she shot back. "It's one date. And I'm in my late thirties. I don't sweep people off their feet anymore."

That was laughable. As a teenager, Caroline had been all the things a boy wanted: pretty, aloof, just out of reach. Now, as a woman, she was stunning, self-assured, and a force of nature. She was Teflon. Everything was attracted to her, but nothing quite stuck. Yes, Wes would probably be a heartbroken man once again. But I thought it was good for Caroline to get out there.

Mom stood up, shaded her eyes with her hand, and looked down toward the dock as she counted the kids. "All present and accounted for," she announced.

"I feel like Jack would go after the boys if they fell in," I said.

"Good," Caroline replied. "Because I can tell you Vivi wouldn't. Not after all the time she spent blow-drying her hair this morning."

Jack and Vivi were sitting on the top step of the dock, shoulder to shoulder. Carter was snuggling into Jack's lap as the boys stood in a straight line, casting their fishing rods. It was the only time I ever saw them still.

"That is really cute, isn't it?" Mom asked. "Jack has been all out of sorts about how to get in Vivi's good graces, so this is going to tickle him to death."

Emerson shrugged. "Maybe being stern with her made her respect him more?"

"Or she wants something, and she knows he's her best shot," Caroline countered.

I snapped my fingers. "Yup. That one." We'd all been there. "If Mom says no, ask Dad. Or, much better yet, Grandad."

Mom sat back down on the outdoor sofa beside Caroline and, clutching a black-and-white-striped pillow, said, "Car, are you going to tell her? About Jack?"

Caroline sighed. "Yeah. I mean, I will. I just don't really know when. I don't even think it will be that huge of a deal to her, but everything I say right now explodes into some tremendous drama. It's all more evidence of how terrifically I have failed her as a mother."

"Sounds familiar . . ." Mom said under her breath, and Caroline smiled apologetically at her. "I wasn't that bad, was I?"

"You were worse," Emerson said.

Took the words right out of my mouth.

"I guess I just don't get why it is that James is the one who has the affair—on TV, no less—but then, when I'm the one who finally decides to leave, I'm the villain. It's not really fair."

"Well, my love, motherhood never is," Mom said.

Caroline and Mom both looked so sad. "It's not your fault, Caroline," I said. "It never was, and it never will be."

"She just has all these feelings right now," Mom added. "And she knows that she can take them out on you, and you'll love her anyway. You're the only mother she's got. No one else is going to keep coming back every time she is awful to them because no one on the planet loves her like you do."

"So, really, this is good," Emerson said. "She's awful to you because she's so secure in how much you love her."

We all laughed as Caroline said, with no enthusiasm at all, "Yayyyyy . . ."

"Mom, are you packed?" I asked, changing the subject.

She nodded. "We've been planning this trip for so long I never thought it would get here."

"I'm proud of you, Mom," Caroline said. "You're being so adventurous."

The door opened, and a freshly showered Adam appeared with a tray of glasses and two bottles of Veuve, so cold you could see them already beginning to sweat a little. He had Biscuit's leash—which was actually attached to her for once—wrapped around his arm. "Flotilla sustenance!" he exclaimed. "Follow me for champagne."

"Don't have to tell me twice," I said. I would have followed that man anywhere, champagne or no. Well, anywhere that wasn't a new house.

I sighed. He had moved to Peachtree Bluff for me, started an entirely new career for me. Should I move for him? This was important to Adam, as his letter to me this morning made me realize. Us having something of our own meant a lot. And so I had to at least be open-minded. Although the idea of telling my mother we were moving made me feel broken inside.

We walked across the dark street and, when Jack and Vivi heard us, they got up and opened the gate to the dock. Soon, the decorated boats would begin to make their way down the waterway, one after another, like floats in a parade. "How many boats signed up this year, Jack?" I asked.

Jack knew all the town scoop from his morning coffee group, which met every Tuesday and Thursday at Peachtree Perk to "strategize about town affairs" slash gossip like old ladies at the beauty parlor. "I think seventy-five," he said. "Big year. Should take about ninety minutes or so."

I smiled and rubbed my arms. The darkness had made it the slightest bit chilly. We each took a glass from the tray, and Adam popped the cork with a practiced flick of his thumb. Kyle rushed down the dock to join us, and he, Adam, and Jack grabbed glasses too.

Just as AJ yelled, "They're coming, they're coming!" we all raised our glasses in the air.

"To family," Mom started.

"To second chances," Jack said.

"To happiness," I added.

"To children's laughter," Kyle said.

"To freedom," Adam said.

"To perfect nights," Emerson said.

And Caroline brought us home: "To Merry Christmases and the memories that last forever."

We all clinked our glasses as "I'll Be Home for Christmas" filled the air from the first boat in line, all lit up with Christmas lights and a pair of singing reindeer on the back. Biscuit took off like a shot to the end of the dock to unleash her most ferocious tiny bark at the reindeer. I sat down on the end of the dock and pulled AJ and Taylor to me, snuggling them in close for one of my most favorite Peachtree Bluff traditions.

Carter squealed, "Olaf!" from behind me where Kyle was holding her on his shoulders. The second boat was lined in blue-and-white *Frozen*-esque lights, a blow-up Olaf sitting proudly on the bow, with women dressed as Anna and Elsa waving on either side.

The happy sounds of family and Christmas music filled the air, almost making me forget, just for a moment, what was coming in a few days. The noticeable beeps and buzzes from all our phones at once made me remember. Goose bumps sprang up all over my body. I knew what that meant.

Adam and I locked eyes as Jack said: "The National Weather Service has officially issued a hurricane warning for Peachtree Bluff." Jack turned to look at Mom. "I think Pearl is coming, sweetheart."

"Let's go get the sandbags first thing in the morning, and then we'll board up the doors," Adam said.

"Thank goodness for working shutters," Jack interjected.

"I'm so glad I'm here to help," Kyle said. "And everyone not going to Australia has to come to New York. No excuses."

"Christmas in New York sounds better than hurricane in Peachtree," Adam said.

"Y'all are wearing yourselves out for nothing," Mom said, sticking to her party line. "They issue these all the time and nothing comes of them."

Mom was our rock, our guiding light, the knower of all truth. But I had to think that, this time, she was wrong.

# Vivi: Naughty or Nice

*The Day after the Tree Lighting*

I WAS A GENIUS. A bona fide, should-be-in-Mensa genius. I was already imagining how amazing all my Insta pics were going to be. I mean, three entire weeks on a yacht in Indonesia and Australia? Yes, please.

Once my dad said I couldn't live with him, I knew if I was going to figure out a way not to have to go back to New York with my mom, I was going to need a plan B. And Peachtree was super fun. But what was more fun than Peachtree? Australia. I honestly hadn't been sure I would have the nerve to go for it when Jack and I first walked down to the dock. But he seemed to have forgiven me mostly. And he was so nice that I found myself saying, "I wish I could just stay here for a while. I need a break from New York."

Jack had gotten my drift even quicker than I could have imagined. He pulled his phone out. "You know what? I got an email today from our booking agent that there were two staterooms left on our cruise and they were trying to fill them. You should come to Australia with Gransley and me!"

Poor Jack. That man had a lot to learn about grandparenting.

Even I knew that you couldn't just offer something like that to a kid without a massive amount of consulting with her parents and grandmother. But, well, what Jack didn't know was getting me exactly what I wanted. So I gasped. "Do you mean it?"

I could see his face cloud over, realizing that maybe he'd made a mistake. But I didn't falter. I hugged him sideways as best I could while still sitting on the dock steps. "I promise I will be on my very best behavior. I can do virtual school every day from the boat!"

He just smiled and said, "Well, you know we have to ask your parents."

That would be no problem. I could totally talk them into it. I would miss Preston. Sort of. I wouldn't miss him waking me up at six in the morning—or at least trying to. I would miss my friend Carson's birthday party. Her parties were pretty epic. But I'd be away from school and avoiding my parents' drama for three weeks. A little FOMO would be worth it.

The problem with New York was that all my friends' moms were friends with my mom—and they were all so gossipy. They thought *we* were rude? Please. Someone would see my dad out with some supermodel and all the moms would talk about it—and then all the kids would talk about it too. It was so annoying. I wanted to be like, *Get some friends your own age to talk about.* It was really embarrassing.

The flotilla was winding down, and everyone was clapping and cheering because the best boat was coming: The Peachtree Oars, the women's group that rowed almost every day in these old-timey, huge rowboats. And, instead of their coxswain on the bow, they had a very special guest: Santa!

As the boat passed by our dock, the kids started freaking out. AJ, the oldest, the ringleader, who knew this drill by now, shot down the dock toward the gate. Preston, Taylor, Carter, and Biscuit followed, the adults chasing after them. It was so cute with all the lights and music. I wasn't sure if my good mood was because of the boats or if it was because of my conversation with Grandjack, but, either way, I felt something I hadn't felt in a long time: happy. Like, actually happy. And then, just like that, the flotilla was over.

They all ran ahead down the street, trying to get to the Christmas Hut before Santa, but Jack and I hung back. "So what's the plan?" I asked.

He grinned at me. He was sort of handsome in that old-man, George Clooney kind of way. Maybe it was gross to think that about him. But it wasn't like he was my real grandfather or anything. I don't know. Anyway. He looked really excited. "You have to let me ask them by myself," he said.

"But I think it's better if we double-team," I protested.

He shook his head. "No way. That will make Gransley and your mom mad."

I wanted to argue, but he was my only chance.

"It's like when you're a little kid and you ask a friend to spend the night in front of them," he added.

"Ohhh . . . Yeah. You're right. That's totally true."

We were almost to the square, which was crammed with people and lots of little kids waiting in line to sit on Santa's lap after he'd gotten off the rowboat. They had no idea how good they had it. Life was so simple when you were a kid. You ran around, your mom made you snacks and poured your milk, and no one talked about you on social media. No one posted pictures to rub in that you weren't invited somewhere.

Not that that would happen with my best friend Carson. We would never do that to each other, and that was pretty cool. I started to feel guilty about leaving her all alone in New York without me for support. But, well, I'd only be gone for a few weeks.

"Are you sure you can do school online while we're gone?"

I laughed. "Grandjack, like half the kids in my school move to Palm Beach for the winter. Everything is online." He didn't look convinced. "The joys of private school!" I said.

Okay. So maybe it wasn't half the kids who did online school. It was more like five. But even still, that was one of the selling points, one of the things that made parents fork out giant tuitions. If you wanted to move for part of the year, it was a possibility. I wondered if that was what Kyle and Emerson would have to do with Carter. I couldn't see Emerson ever settling down in one place, especially since she was on location a bunch and Kyle always went with her. They were relationship goals for sure. And I didn't care what Gransley said, it made total sense not to get married. Just look at my mom.

"I don't know if they're going to go for it," Jack said cautiously. "So don't get your hopes up."

"Jack," I said, crossing my arms. "You can talk Gransley into anything. You talked her into marrying you, didn't you?"

He laughed. "That I did. That I did." He paused. "But, well, it's your mother I'm worried about." He leaned down and whispered, "She's a little scary."

Gransley walked over then and handed me a paper cup of hot chocolate. I was going to turn *into* hot chocolate at this rate, but whatever. It was Christmas. I stirred the candy cane that was hanging on the side and took a small sip. Yum. Mint and chocolate. Almost as good as chocolate and peanut butter.

"What are you two plotting over here?" Gransley asked.

"Us?" Jack asked innocently. "What would make you think we were plotting?"

Gransley rolled her eyes. "Viv, do you mind getting in a picture with Santa and the other kids?"

That was the problem with being seven years older than your next-closest cousin. I took out my phone, snapped a selfie with the cute red, lit-up hut in the background, and said, "Fine, Gransley. Fine."

I walked into the hut beside Santa, where the little kids were already gathered. Carter, who was on Santa's lap totally freaking out, held her arms out to me. I picked her up and said, "Don't cry, little girl. Trust me, you want to be on Santa's good side."

I wiped her tears and tickled her chin and she laughed and leaned her head onto my shoulder. She was so cute. We all smiled for the camera, while Gransley, Emerson, Mom, and Sloane took about a million pictures until we were all completely blind from the flash.

Then I snapped another selfie of Carter and me with Santa and put it on my Instagram story with a poll: "Naughty or Nice?" Before I was even out of the hut, the first response popped up. My heart fluttered when I saw who it was from. *Lake.* He had chosen naughty. He wished.

"Viv! Get your hair out of your eyes," Mom called.

I looked at my mom, and it was like my eyes just rolled themselves. Nothing was ever, ever good enough for her. I remembered being a kid and her reading me this book I loved over and over again. *Alexander and the Terrible, Horrible, No Good, Very Bad Day.* When everything goes wrong, Alexander decides he's going to move to Australia. That kid had the right idea. For three weeks, anyway, I was going to do the exact same thing.

# Emerson: Jim Cantore

## *The Day after the Flotilla*

THE DAY AFTER THE FLOTILLA was always Christmas-tree day. Well, "day" was sort of an overstatement. "Crack of dawn" was more like it. I looked down at my watch. It wasn't even eight a.m. yet. I thought Mom was joking when she said she had gotten the Rotary Club to open their tree lot an hour early so we could get a jump on picking out a tree. She had not been, in fact, joking.

"Remember when we thought I had aplastic anemia and y'all didn't make me do this stuff?" I asked, spitting pine needles out of my mouth. If I hadn't been so grossed out, I might have realized that they actually tasted kind of good. Christmasy. A little like rosemary. Or some sort of weird fringe drink that Kyle would create and people would go so nuts, it would suddenly start trending on Twitter.

Caroline laughed. Mom did not. "Don't ever talk about that, Emerson. I mean it."

Mom was not a fan of talking about when I was sick.

I set the bottom end of the tree down, balancing it on the edge of the stand inside Mom and Jack's living room, and then helped Caroline slowly lift it up. It almost touched the ceiling, meaning Mom would love it.

I brushed myself off and stood back to admire it once Jack had secured it in the stand. It really was pretty.

"I believe it's the prettiest tree we've ever had," Mom said. She said that every year, but the fact that nothing ever changed around here soothed me. Except, of course, this being Jack's house.

"Remind me," I asked, "why we didn't have the boys do this?"

"Because the boys are going to have to spend the day boarding up houses, and they don't need to have to get trees too."

Caroline groaned. "Mom, this is insanity. Why would we get Christmas trees when everyone is evacuating?"

She crossed her arms. "Caroline, we always get Christmas trees the day after the flotilla. Plus, this storm is going to be a non-event."

Well, that was progress. At least she was now admitting that the storm was, in fact, coming.

"Good morning, ladies of Murphy Row!" a familiar voice called.

I turned. "Keith! The man with the coffee!" It actually gave me the slightest pang of sweet remembrance for the days when Kyle was just a man I had a crush on, when he was the one concocting beautiful drinks to make me happy, when the mere thought of his delivering coffee could make my heart race. Although, I had to admit, having him around all the time was even better. I sighed, feeling content.

Keith handed me a cup. I was about to raise it to my mouth when I realized that, over his shoulder, Mom was frantically shaking her head. Caroline and I shared a glance as Keith handed her a cup and then Mom.

"Your tree looks great," Keith said.

"Oh, thanks so much, sweetie," Mom said as he made his way out.

"Stay safe during this storm!" Keith called as the door swung closed behind him.

"We will certainly stay safe, because it's going to be a small storm," Mom said under her breath.

I wanted to ask her why she was being so weird. We had hurricanes here nearly every year, and everyone usually evacuated, if not once a year, at least every other. But I guessed maybe she was a true local now. They didn't get worked up about hurricanes. Although "storm of the century" did sound scary.

"Please, sweet Jesus, why can't I drink my coffee?" I asked.

"Because it isn't yours," Mom said briskly.

The door opened and an annoyed Kimmy reached her hand out to Mom. "Your vanilla latte," she said.

"Girls, what do you have?"

"I have black coffee," Caroline said after taking a sip, sounding confused.

"Well, that's easy!" Mom said brightly, as Kyle came in the room from the back door. "That's Jack's, so we'll just run it out to him."

"I have a flat white," I said, looking at the writing on the cup, getting more confused by the minute.

Kimmy sighed. "I'll take it to Hippie Hal. He might have my Americano."

"Wait," Kyle said, looking at the scrawled pen on his. "I have an Americano." He paused and looked from one to the other of us. "What is going on here?"

Kimmy and Mom shared a glance as if they were deciding something. "Well . . ." Mom started.

"Your idiot cousin brings everyone in town the wrong drinks, but he's so nice no one has the heart to tell him," Kimmy said.

Kyle burst out laughing.

"Wait, I'm sorry," Caroline said. "So y'all just drink the wrong coffee every morning?"

"No!" Kimmy said, getting more exasperated by the minute. "That would be downright sensible. Instead, we spend the first hour of the morning playing this long-drawn-out game of finding the recipient of the wrong coffee we got and trying to find our usual order."

Now Caroline burst out laughing too, and I joined her.

"It's not really funny," Mom said.

I was laughing so hard tears were coming down my cheeks and, gasping for breath, I said, "Mom! You have to see how this is a little funny."

I don't know if it was the realization of how ridiculous the situation was or the sight of Caroline, Kyle, and me laughing so hard, but she finally joined us and then Kimmy did too.

"Oh my God," Kimmy said, catching her breath. "We all belong in the loony bin."

"Every last one of us!" Mom said as Jack walked in.

"What did I miss?" he asked.

Mom handed him his coffee, and that set us all off again. Mom filled Jack in, and he said, "Gosh, I guess I'm so used to it that it's just part of the routine. In fact, if he starts getting our orders right, I'm going to miss seeing everyone in town every morning."

More laughter.

Kyle kissed my cheek and followed Kimmy out the door. "Kim, let's go straighten this out."

"Be nice!" Mom called behind them.

"I don't have that setting!" Kimmy called back.

She was lying. Kimmy was one of the nicest people I knew. She just hid it really, really well.

"Ansley, Caroline," Jack said. "I need to talk to you."

Mom looked exasperated. "Jack, we have a tree to decorate."

He shook his head and wrapped his arm around her. "I want to remind you that we're evacuating tomorrow, but I have a feeling that that argument will have no bearing on whether this tree gets decorated today." He sighed. "I will even help you in a minute if you will sit down, please," he said, motioning to the couch and pair of chairs.

I cocked my head. "Um, do I have to leave? I will. I totally will. But I'm going to hide behind the wall and listen like usual." Growing up, everyone thought they were hiding all the good stuff from poor little Emerson. But they weren't. I was always sneaking around, gathering information. I guarantee that I knew more of the gossip in our house than anyone else did at all times.

Jack laughed. "You can stay. They're just going to ask your opinion, anyway."

I looked around. "Where's Sloane? Don't we need her?"

"She is painting!" Caroline snapped. "Disturb her and die."

I rolled my eyes.

Jack sat down on the edge of the ottoman in front of the fireplace, where he was facing all three of us. He looked like a defendant pleading his case to a jury. He twiddled his thumbs nervously. What had he *done*?

"So, I urge everyone to keep an open mind," he began.

We all shared a look. *The* look.

"Caroline, I know you have been having a lot of trouble with Vivi, and I hope you don't mind that Ansley has shared that you thought a short break from New York might be helpful."

"O-kay . . ." Caroline said. "True."

"And, as you all know, Ansley and I will be gone until right before Christmas."

"During which time someone is going to have to water that darn tree every other day," I said under my breath.

Mom popped me on the leg with the back of her hand and smiled.

"So I was thinking that maybe we could take Vivi with us. She will be on a boat, so there isn't anywhere she can get in trouble. She can do school online, and maybe a break from everything will do her some good. Then you can pick her up when you come for Christmas."

We all sat in stunned silence.

"I told you she was working him," Caroline said.

I laughed. That girl was good. And I was a little jealous, honestly. If any of the Murphies were going to get to go on the trip of a lifetime, shouldn't it be the daughters?

As if she were reading my mind, Mom said, "Jack, this is the least of my concerns, but the cost of that trip is astronomical. And we don't even know if they have room. Plus, it isn't fair to the other grandkids."

Forget the grandkids. What about me?

"Well," Jack said, "I did call, and we can get two adjoining rooms. And, Ansley, I'm retired. I sold my company. What's the use of having money if I can't spend it on my grandkids?"

I nodded. "So, like, just your real grandkids?"

I was sort of joking, but Mom pointed at me. "This is why we have to tell Vivi. Something like that is going to slip, and it's going to be bad."

"There will be a right time," Caroline said. "I don't know when it is. It can't be manufactured. But somehow, some way, there will be a right time to tell her, and that will be that."

"And, you know," Jack continued, "it made me think: What if we do this for all the grandkids? We take each of them on an amazing trip of their choosing during their teenage years?"

"What about Carter?" I asked sulkily. "Does she get a trip?" She was the only one who wasn't biologically Jack's grandchild, after all.

"Shut up, Emerson," Caroline said. "Quit acting like a child."

Jack was more empathetic. "Emerson, of course. Of course she does. And any other future children you might have."

Mom groaned. "Emerson, if you're going to have more children, could you please do your old, tired mother a favor and get married?"

Jack nudged her, and whispered behind his hand, "Don't

encourage her, Ansley. These grandkids are going to cost us a fortune."

We all laughed, that warmth I'd been feeling lately over the idea of marriage growing inside me. Whenever I looked at Sloane and Adam or Jack and Mom and thought about being connected to Kyle in that deeper way, I had to admit I kind of liked it. It wasn't a lightning-bolt moment; it was an evolution of my feelings.

Mom and Caroline looked at each other, having one of their eye conversations that none of the rest of us were privy to. I hated when they did that, but I guessed I shouldn't be complaining. I at least got to sit in here for the talk. Sloane was going to be so mad she missed it.

"Caroline and I had actually discussed Vivi staying here," Mom started. "But I thought the trip made that impossible."

"I actually think the trip is what makes it work," Jack said. "The worst thing would be that she's banished here for her bad behavior, stored away so no one has to deal with her."

"Worse than getting rewarded for her bad behavior with three weeks on a luxury yacht?" I wondered aloud.

No one responded yet again. Was I even here? But then, after a long pause, Caroline said, "You know, I hadn't really thought about it like that." Then she put her head in her hands. I almost thought she was crying until she looked up, her face crumpled, and said, "This last year with her has been hell. Being in Peachtree for these few days, it's like I can see who my daughter used to be. So maybe it isn't about rewards or punishments. Maybe it's just about making her happy so that she can get back to her old self again. That's honestly all I care about."

Mom got up, grabbed Jack's hand, and said, "We have some details about this trip to discuss in private, so let's put a pin in this." Then, to Caroline, she said, "But if we decide that it's okay, is it okay with you?"

Caroline shrugged. "I mean, yeah. I guess it's okay with me."

Mom and Jack started up the steps as Caroline got up and grabbed a small box of lights, threw me another one, and started unwinding the first string for the tree. "Say something to keep my mind off of everything," she said.

"Looking forward to your date with Wes?" I asked dramatically, and she laughed.

"That's a good start. What else you got?"

She was unwinding from her box, and I was unwinding from mine, and I said, "In light of what you've been through this year, what do you think about marriage? Worth it? Not?"

Caroline stopped her movement and peered at me. "Well, Emerson Murphy, I never thought I'd see the day."

"Me neither," I said, grinning.

"If you mean marriage in regard to you and Kyle . . ."

I had so much more to discuss, more to say, but, before I could, Kyle walked through the front door.

"Okay," he said, rubbing his temples. "As it turns out, not everyone is meant for coffee delivery."

Caroline chuckled.

"I kept a list of everyone in town's 'usuals' taped to the wall, but Keith had a small toaster fire that incinerated part of it. He could see the list of drinks but not the names, so he's just been running around town handing out drinks and hoping he was getting it right." Now Kyle squeezed the bridge of his nose.

Caroline and I burst out laughing. "This has been going on for weeks!"

"Weeks!" I reiterated.

Kyle shook his head. "I *think* I have helped him come up with a new system." Kyle, who was rarely irritated, was very, very annoyed. "I leave my flagship store for one minute and it all goes to hell."

"And yet no one even thinks to complain about it!" Caroline interjected.

For just a moment I was so wistful, so overcome with love for Peachtree Bluff, that I almost didn't want to leave tomorrow. I needed to get outside in the fresh air, enjoy the water, and be *in* this town for a few hours until we left first thing in the morning.

"Mom!" I called. "Come down here! Let's go on a walk!"

"Coming!" she called back. "Let me find Biscuit!" That was super important, especially considering Biscuit would walk about a block and Mom would have to carry her the rest of the way.

"You in?" I asked Caroline.

"Always."

"You come too, babe," I said to Kyle.

He shook his head. "I can't. Adam and I are going to get y'all's three houses boarded up, and then we're going to go help everybody else."

Caroline put her hand to her heart. "You're going to do mine?"

"Of course," Kyle said.

"Oh, great. Do you think you could get Ellie May trailered and down to the barn at the vet while you're at it? They're going to handle her evacuation, since what to do with a goat in a hurricane isn't exactly my specialty."

He looked horrified, and she laughed. "I'm kidding, Kyle. I'm kidding. Someone from the vet's coming to get her any minute."

Mom's footsteps thudded on the stairs. Kyle held his hands out to her.

"What?"

"I'll take Biscuit so the vet can pick her up with Ellie Mae."

She looked stricken. "Oh, that's okay . . ."

"Mom!" Caroline scolded. "You're taking her in like two hours. Let them save you a trip."

"I'm having second thoughts about boarding her. Maybe you guys could take her with you to New York?"

"Mom, you aren't serious," I said.

Caroline sighed. "I will take her to New York, but that kennel is a pet palace. She'll have all that room to play and get to socialize with other dogs."

"She does love the other dogs," Kyle said.

Mom looked hesitant, but then she kissed Biscuit's head. "Be a good girl while I'm gone. Sloane and Adam will get you after the storm and take good care of you."

I rolled my eyes as Caroline said, "Remember when Mom didn't like dogs?"

Mom crossed her arms. "Well, I'd never had one. Now I love her, and I won't apologize."

Kyle laughed, took Biscuit, and said, "She'll be fine, Ansley. It will only be a few days until Sloane and Adam come back to get her."

I opened the front door and called, "Sloane!" at the top of my lungs, as Mom dabbed at her eyes.

"I swear, Emerson," Caroline said. "I *just* said to leave Sloane alone!"

The window opened from next door, and Sloane popped her head out.

"Let's go walk!" I said, defying Caroline and grinning at her as I did.

"Yes! I need a break!"

"No, that's fine," Caroline said. "I hope you can quit acting and become an art forger, because you're going to have to chip in to get all these pieces finished for the store."

"Why don't you just stock more artists? Quit making poor Sloane work to death."

She crossed her arms. "The store is *Sloane* Emerson," she said, as if that were even an answer.

We made our way to the sidewalk with Mom as Sloane jogged out the front door.

We all linked arms, crossing the street to the boardwalk. I was feeling light and happy until, as I turned the corner, I ran directly into my past.

"Oh, hi, Mark!" Mom called. I was grateful. She was covering my gaffe. It was very clear that seeing him had stopped me in my tracks. I pasted on a smile.

"Hi, Murphies," Mark said. A familiar, deep dread entered my stomach as I unlinked arms with my sisters and gave my ex-fiancé an awkward hug. "How are you?" I asked, trying to seem normal.

He smiled like he was completely unaffected by seeing me. "Pretty good," he said. "I saw you on that new Peacock series. You were great."

Oh my God. Did he not even remember that we had once thought we were the loves of each other's lives, that we had called off our wedding? It was like it had never happened. "Oh, thanks. It was really fun."

"I'm so happy for you, Em. I'm happy you finally got what you wanted," he said, smiling, but there was a slight edge to his voice.

Ah. There it was. The sarcasm. The main reason we had broken up was because Mark's family business required him to be in Peachtree, and I couldn't imagine life without LA. I was willing to travel back and forth, but Mark, unfortunately, was not. Did it make me a bad person that his emotion finally showing through made me a little happy?

"Well, I need to get back to work. Y'all have a good day!" he called, slipping past us.

"Awk-ward!" Caroline sang under her breath once he was out of earshot.

It wasn't the first time I had seen Mark since we'd called off our wedding, but it wasn't like we bumped into each other often enough to get to a new, better place about things.

"But, see," Sloane said, "bumping into Mark is a good thing. Marriage seemed scary to you when you were with Mark because he wasn't your soul mate. Now, with Kyle . . ."

The knot in my stomach began to unclench at the mere sound of his name.

I took a deep breath and kept walking. "Yeah. No, you're right. That's actually kind of true. Weird."

"Loving the right man can change your mind about things," Mom said knowingly.

As the concrete under our feet turned to wood, I said, "These talks are my favorite. I'm going to miss y'all, but at least we got our Thanksgiving visit in before we had to evacuate."

Mom sighed deeply.

"Mom!" Caroline scolded. "What is your deal? It's a monstrous hurricane. It's coming. Why the attitude?"

"We just don't have late-November hurricanes here," she said.

"Well, we are now, Mom," Sloane said. "Like it or not. Don't you watch the news?"

"No," she said. "It's their job to make us panicky and dependent on them for the next moment's sliver of dread. I'd rather just not watch."

Sloane gasped and put her arms out straight to keep us from going any farther. "Do you know who that is?" she whispered, her gaze locked on a man in front of us on the boardwalk. He was leaning over the railing, looking out at the water.

I studied him for a moment and then gasped, as did Mom and Caroline, in unison.

All at once we said, "Jim Cantore," making the Grim Reaper of the Weather Channel turn to look at us. Jim Cantore was known for only coming to places where really big, bad, news-making storms were going to be. If Jim Cantore was here, we were doomed. I smiled and waved at him, trying to make things less awkward, even as my stomach gripped.

"Oh my God," Sloane said again. "It's Jim Cantore."

Mom looked at me, and I looked at her. And that was the moment it finally sank in. I could see it on her face. The storm of the century was, in fact, coming. And Peachtree Bluff as we knew it might never be the same.

# Ansley: Murphy Row

*Two Days after the Flotilla*

IN PEACHTREE BLUFF, HOMES ARE referred to by the name of the person who originally owned them. So, Jack's house was the Sloane house, Caroline's was the Turner house, and so on and so forth. It didn't matter that the house where Adam and Sloane were currently living had been owned by my family for four generations. It would, forever and always, be the Thomas house. I loved the sense of history here, so that was totally fine by me. But it did fill me with glee that, with our house, Jack's house, and Caroline's house on the same street, our block had been granted the nickname "Murphy Row."

Yesterday, after we finished decorating the tree and walking, we had done everything we could to batten the hatches on Murphy Row. We closed and wired the shutters shut, hammered plywood over the doors, and piled sandbags in front of them. We had taped the insides of the windows up so, if they shattered, the mess might be more minimal. Kyle and Adam had done most of the heavy lifting, but we had all chipped in, even the kids.

Now, I walked slowly—one last time before we left for our trip—down Peachtree's beautiful boardwalk. I had never, not in all my years here, seen this harbor completely devoid of boats. Many of them were fine to ride out a small hurricane, so they were often in their slips during storm warnings. So the fact that the dock was totally empty filled me with dread. Usually, the boardwalk and town dock were the epicenter of Peachtree, bustling with activity from both the townspeople and visitors. But now, there wasn't a single car downtown, and every window was boarded up and lined with sandbags. Many of the stores had spray-painted messages on their plywood. GO HOME, JIM! Or PASS OVER US, PEARL!

Dockmaster Dan approached, and I waved at him sadly. He was thin and weathered and looked as if he had been here as long as this boardwalk. And, as usual, his NO THINKIN', JUST DRINKIN' hat was firmly atop his head.

"You getting ready to leave?" he asked.

I nodded. "You?"

He gave me his sideways grin. "Nah." He patted the dock rail. "She's my ship. I gotta be here to protect her."

I looked out over my beloved Starlite Island one last time. Her dense layer of trees and foliage had protected this town for as long as she had been here. I was hoping it would be enough to protect Peachtree again as my phone beeped in my hand. Mandatory Evacuation for Peachtree Bluff, Georgia, 5 pm. Good Lord. Suddenly, it all felt too scary, too ominous. I needed to get out of here.

"Please be careful," I said.

He nodded. "Will do." Then he was off to continue his pacing, to keep his watch over the section of town that he alone was responsible for.

I turned to walk back to the house, reassuring myself. We were ready. Or as ready as we could be, anyway. It was impossible to know what to expect. If we moved everything from the first floor to the second, would we lose the roof? And if we moved everything from the second floor to the first, would it flood? My house—well, Adam and Sloane's house now—was built up, making it one of the highest points in Peachtree Bluff, at least a few feet above sea level. Technically, it wasn't in a flood plain. But who knew what the storm of the century would bring? I shuddered at the thought, and, despite my proclamations that this storm wouldn't, couldn't come, I was so grateful for the technology alerting us when to get off the island to safety. It was killing me to imagine being on a boat so far away from Peachtree, to not be here to assess the aftermath of the storm. But, as Jack reminded me, Sloane and Adam could handle it.

I forgot sometimes that they were grown-up adults. I forgot that they didn't need me to micromanage every moment of their lives. Letting go was hard. Although three houses and two businesses were a lot for anyone to handle in the aftermath of a hurricane.

I made my way back to the house. I knew all the kids would be leaving soon, and even though we were leaving too, it made me sad that our few days of fun were over. Even the promise of the beauty of Australia wasn't as wonderful as my children and grandchildren being all together.

As I walked up the driveway, Emerson was slamming the back hatch on one of a pair of hired Suburbans. "There you are," she said. "We have to leave in a few minutes."

I followed her onto the back porch of Sloane and Adam's house, my house, and saw everyone gathered in the kitchen. I put on my brave face.

Caroline had Vivi by the shoulders and was in the middle of a speech. "And don't forget that the school wants a three-page paper on your experience in addition to your keeping up with your work." Caroline wrapped Vivi in a hug, and it looked to me like Vivi actually hugged her back. It was a sweet moment. "Promise me that you'll behave. Do not give Gransley and Grandjack any reason to worry."

"I promise, Mom," Vivi said. "Our rooms are adjoining, and I'll never leave their sight unless I'm doing schoolwork and they are out exploring."

It hit me then that being responsible for someone else's child in a foreign country was huge, even when it was your own grandchild and they'd be staying next door to you. It wasn't that I didn't want to be on the boat with her, but there were so many things that could go wrong. She could run away or get sick or lost or hurt. I reminded myself that doctors were aboard and we could be flown home at a moment's notice. Security abounded. But Vivi was right about one thing: I wouldn't let her out of my sight.

Caroline gave me a big hug and kissed me on both cheeks. "I love you. Thank you so much for doing this for me. There is no way to repay you ever."

I smiled like I was delighted by the prospect of Caroline owing me. "There's no need to thank me. I'm happy to get to spend some quality time with my granddaughter. I'll bring her back tan and cultured and in one piece."

"See you Christmas Eve Eve," Caroline said, grinning.

"Gwansley!" Preston called, running up to me. He held out a conch shell, and I gasped like it was the first one I'd ever seen. Come to think of it, it felt like that. So many of the marvels of Peachtree Bluff did: dolphins jumping, a full sand dollar, the staurolite or fairy stones—as they were often called—that inhabited our favorite island. It was a brand-new thrill every time. I picked up my grandson and gave him a big kiss on the cheek. "Love you," I said.

"Wuv you," he said back.

To Sloane and Adam, I said, "Thank you for taking care of the house." I paused. "All the insurance information is in the safe at the store. Just in case."

"Ansley, promise me you won't worry," Adam said.

"I could, but we both know I'd be lying," I said, smiling. I looked at my family's now-empty hands. "Let me get you some drinks and snacks for the road."

"Remember the old days when Kyle brought us coffee whenever we left Peachtree?" Emerson asked, coming over to kiss me. She was as nostalgic as I was. "Love you," she said. "It's all going to be fine. We'll all be back for Christmas, and it will be like the hurricane never happened."

"We have plenty of snacks and drinks in the car," Sloane said, hugging me, AJ and Taylor each grasping one of my legs.

I finished kissing everyone goodbye and sent them on their

way. It gave me a moment's pause that my entire family—minus Jack and Vivi—was boarding the same plane. I wondered if other people had macabre thoughts like this or if I tended toward the dark side of tragedy because of the out-of-the-blue horror of losing my first husband. I rarely ever told a member of my family goodbye without wondering if this would be the last time I saw them.

I peeked my head in the back door. "Viv and Jack, I'm headed down to the store to tie up loose ends. I'll be ready to go in about an hour!"

"Okay!" they called back in unison.

"I'm almost finished packing!" Vivi added.

As I made my way to the sidewalk, I saw Kimmy. "Don't forget we've got to be out of here by five o'clock," I said.

She shook her head. "I'm not leaving."

I gasped. "Kimmy, you have to leave!"

"I can't leave my crops, Ansley. You know that. If something happens, I need to be here."

"If something happens, you need to be gone," I argued. "Even you are no match for the storm of the century." Simply uttering the phrase gave me cold chills. "Kimmy, they open the drawbridges, and you are stuck here. No way in, no way out."

She grinned. "Just like I like it."

I shook my head. I couldn't imagine. "Do you have enough provisions?" I asked.

She nodded.

"Plenty of water? People forget that during a hurricane the water often gets contaminated."

"Ans, I have plenty of water and food and booze and flashlights. I have blankets and firewood and everything I need. My brother and parents are staying at my house too."

I shook my head in disbelief. "Why would anyone in their right mind not evacuate?"

She laughed. "My baby brother isn't in his right mind. He's a total weather nerd. His life goal is to be a storm chaser."

"Like those idiots on TV who drive into tornadoes?"

She nodded. "When he heard Jim Cantore was here, there was no keeping him away."

"And your parents just let him stay? They don't want to evacuate?" I knew that Kimmy's brother was still in high school.

She shrugged. "They're crazy locals now too. They aren't that worried."

"Well, you're all nuts," I said. "I have lived through what were considered small Peachtree hurricanes, and I never want to do it again."

"We'll be fine," she said. "I promise."

No one could make promises when it came to Mother Nature or acts of God. That I knew for sure. "Will you text me?" I asked.

"I will. I'm not sure how good your reception is going to be in the middle of the ocean, but I will."

I nodded.

"Hal is going to bunk up with me, and so are Keith and Roger. Get themselves out of downtown." Kimmy's farm was a better choice since it was a few miles off the water. She usually fared pretty well. And probably would do especially well considering Roger, our mailman, was staying with her. I had long had my suspicions that he and Kimmy were a bit of an item, but, in true Kimmy fashion, she would never cop to it.

"That makes me feel a little better. At least you won't be alone. Take care of yourself—and the rest of your family too."

I turned and kept walking down the street, not even surprised that Hal, Keith, and Roger weren't evacuating either. It made me kind of furious that I had to worry about so many of my friends. I mean, what part of "mandatory evacuation" did these people not understand? Sure, they'd never evacuated before. But this was the "storm of the century," for heaven's sake.

Leah was standing right by the front door of the store when I opened it. "Let's go over these final few details for the redesign proposal of Dr. Wyatt's office, and then, Ansley, we need to get the heck out of Dodge."

We reviewed the plans for a few minutes, and then I looked around, going through what we'd done yesterday to prepare for the hurricane. My little store looked so sad. We had moved everything we could as far back as we could to protect it from floodwaters, which, since the building was at sea level, were nearly inevitable. It wasn't whether they would come through the door; it was how far they would make it.

The door opened again, and a man almost ran right smack into me. "Oh, hi," he said.

"Wes," I said, smiling.

A boy coming to my store in search of Caroline was far from an uncommon occurrence. It had been happening for decades. It had even happened with this same boy many years earlier.

"Oh," he said again, noticing Leah. "Sorry to interrupt. I was just looking for Caroline."

I smiled sympathetically. Again, not my first sympathetic smile to a boy in my store about Caroline. "She's already on her way to New York, sweetie," I said.

He nodded. "Oh, okay. I just wanted to make sure y'all were okay." He paused. "Can I help with anything, Ansley?"

A boy being helpful so I would get him on Caroline's good side was really my favorite kind. I shook my head. "I think we're all set. But you need to get out of town. We all do."

He shoved his hands in his pockets. "Yeah. Looks like it's going to be a big one." I almost thought he blushed as he said, "Hey, um, Ansley?"

Leah looked extraordinarily annoyed and walked off as she said, "I'll just be over here when you're finished."

Wes bit his lip, paused, and then said, "Not to put you in a weird spot, but . . ."

"Yup," I said. "I think she likes you."

He laughed. "Am I that transparent?"

"Yup!" Leah called from the back.

"Sorry," I said. "No one here is trying to embarrass you."

"I am!" Leah called again, and we all laughed.

I shook my head. "Seriously. She needs to move forward. It's time."

He smiled. "I hope I can help." He paused. "Hey, be safe out there."

As he left, Leah walked back to me and sighed. "Welcome to the Caroline Murphy dating center."

I laughed. "I've placed the order for the office's fourteen chairs," Leah said. "We need a huge piece of art for the hallway, and I was hoping Sloane would do it."

I shook my head. "She doesn't have time. Let's find someone else."

Leah nodded, and I patted her arm. I had a feeling she was using this project to procrastinate and avoid the very real fear welling up in all of us. "It's time," I said, my stomach fluttering. "We've done all we can, and we need to go." I smiled, probably looking braver than I felt. "Leah, please be safe."

"I'll come back the minute the bridges are open, and if I can't reach you on the boat, don't worry. I promise I'll still take care of everything."

I knew she would. "I'm not worried about the store. I'm worried about you. So please don't come back until it's safe."

In truth, I was a little worried about the store. I looked around at my dark, boarded-up shop, all its contents covered in tarps.

"Do you think it will all be gone when we come back?" Leah asked quietly. "Can it survive the storm of the century?"

I smiled, acting braver than I felt. "This town has made it through hundreds of hurricanes. One won't destroy it now," I said, trying to comfort her.

*Especially not a nice Southern girl like Pearl.*

# Vivi: Delicate Balance

*Two Days after the Flotilla*

THEY WERE GONE! THEY WERE all gone! I was free. I texted Carson.

Leaving tonight. Will snap tons of pics. Love you lots!

Can't believe you're leaving me, the reply came almost instantly. I don't know what I'm going to do without you! I'll keep you updated on all things Lake.

I sent her an eye-roll emoji, the only one she approved of. But, secretly, my insides were flip-flopping around. Now that she mentioned it . . .

I texted him. Life is better Down Under . . .

But I'm not there, he said.

I smiled. Hm. What to say back? Something flirty. Not too serious. Something that made me seem interested but also unattached. Something that would keep *him* interested but that wasn't a picture of my boobs. Mom had given me that lecture enough times. As I stared at the phone, all I could think of was one of Gransley's favorite sayings: *Absence makes the heart grow fonder.*

I was absolutely *not* texting the hot sixteen-year-old I was talking to *that*. I held up my phone and sent him a kissy-face selfie instead. Not clever, but it got the point across.

Wish you were here, he typed back. Then right after. No, wish I was there . . .

I clicked my phone screen off. Perfect. Well played. I left him with something to hang on to and stopped texting first. These things were a very delicate balance.

I bounded down the stairs at Gransley's, feeling the butterflies that people should feel when they were about to leave for the best trip ever. The house was super dark because all the windows and doors were boarded up. It was actually kind of creepy. And I had gotten major brownie points with my mom because not only had I been polite, but I had also helped get the house ready. I know. Maturity.

I had wired all the downstairs shutters shut, and I had ridden with Adam and Grandjack when they went a few miles out of town to store Grandjack's boat in the boatyard. That had actually been kind of fun. Grandjack's boat—the *Miss Ansley*—was absolutely huge. Grandjack and Adam let me help drive it from the dock at Grandjack's house to the dock at the boatyard. I had done a lot of pointing and gesturing and yelling, "Stop!" really loud during the docking process, which, if you thought about it, was pretty much the most important job. At the boatyard, they pulled it out with a forklift.

Then, all afternoon, while the grown-ups were packing and boarding up, I had kept four small and very rowdy children at Gransley's from drowning, playing with knives, or catching themselves on fire. So, basically, no one could say I hadn't done my part.

I hoisted my very full tote bag back on my shoulder. Lucky for me, I kept pretty much all my summer clothes at our house on the corner, so I had plenty of stuff to pack.

Grandjack was in the kitchen, slathering peanut butter on Oreos. He handed me one.

"This is so good," I said, popping it in my mouth and putting my hand over my lips so I didn't spray crumbs on him.

"I know," he said. "And I'm betting they don't have these on the ship. It's a little more five-star than Oreos and peanut butter."

"Then I don't want to go!" I said very seriously.

We both laughed.

"Hey, do you think we'll be able to leave from Atlanta? I mean, what about the hurricane?"

"It isn't coming that far inland," Grandjack said. "We'll be fine."

"Do you think the house will be okay?" I asked, biting into a second Oreo.

He nodded. "This house has been through more hurricanes than we can even imagine. Hundreds. Did you know there was a monster hurricane here in 1916?"

I did, sort of, but I said, "No," anyway.

He nodded. "It was during World War I, and legend has it that, with most of the men away, pirates had planned to use the chaos of the hurricane to pillage Peachtree Bluff."

There was so much history in this town. "Did they? Did it work?"

"Well, supposedly, a group of Peachtree Bluff residents banded together to save the town."

"Cool," I said.

"And legend also has it that the man who led the attack on the ship, who saved the town, lived in this very house."

I could feel my eyes widen. "Like right here?" It was kind of neat to think that more than one hundred years ago something that important had happened in this spot. Maybe right where I was sitting.

"Right here," Jack said. "And supposedly, somewhere in these walls, the pirate treasure is still hidden."

Now he *really* had my attention. "Seriously?"

He nodded. "Ansley and I kept hoping we'd find it when we did the renovations a few years ago, but no such luck."

Lost treasure. Now, that was pretty cool. It made me want to get one of those metal detectors we used to have at the beach when we were kids and search the walls. I mean, even if there wasn't that much money, how cool would it be to find pirate treasure in your house? "Do you think it's still here?" I asked.

He shrugged. "Honestly, the whole story is probably made-up. There weren't that many pirates in America by then." He paused. "Well, some, I guess. Famous ones like Roaring Dan Seavey."

"Do you think it was Roaring Dan Seavey they took down?" I asked, feeling my interest in this story rising by the moment. I mean, treasure! What if it really was here?

He shook his head. "I don't think so. But I guess for every famous pirate there are a lot of unfamous ones, right?"

I nodded seriously. That made sense. "Right. I mean, think about how many unfamous actresses there are for every one you've actually heard of."

We both laughed, and it struck me that this was a really nice, un-awkward moment. I had been mad when Jack scolded me in front of everyone at the beginning of the trip. But he'd really come around. It wasn't like I could be mad at him now. I suddenly felt so incredibly grateful.

"Thank you for taking me on this trip," I said because I really hadn't thanked him yet.

"Anytime," he said.

"No, I'm serious. I know it's a really big deal you're letting me come to Australia, and that it's super expensive. It's so cool that you would do this for me, especially since we aren't even technically related and stuff."

He didn't say anything, and it made me think that maybe I'd offended him. So I backtracked. "I mean, I guess we kind of are. I didn't mean it like that." I paused. What was the right thing to say? "I guess I just mean that I wish you were my real grandfather. That's all."

What he said next was something I never, ever would have expected. It was something that made me race out the door. It made me forget all about Lake and Carson and the Oreos. It even made me forget about the storm of the century. And, looking back now, I'd have to say that maybe that was my first really big mistake.

# Sloane: Northern Side of Paradise

*Two Days after the Flotilla*

Dear Sloane,

I might be cheating with this letter today. I'm not sure. Is stealing from your previous letters cheating? Let's just call it "reiterating." That sounds better. Because I know that there is one letter that you read more than any other. So, today, as you're facing your fear of flying, getting on that plane to New York, I wanted to remind you of what I wrote you all those years ago while I was deployed:

"There are moments to advance, to lunge forward with purpose, with power, but most importantly, with passion. Because any action taken without passion? Well, it's simply a waste of time."

I am so grateful that now, this time, I get to be with you as you face your fears, as you advance. I get to board that plane with you just like we boarded up those houses. You

*don't have to be afraid anymore, because I am always here to*
*keep you safe.*

*All my love,*
*Adam*

I touched the edge of that letter in my pocket as I sat with my family around the tiny pre-boarding area at the Peachtree Bluff airport. Even with Adam here beside me there was something about his words that emboldened me. "You aren't going to believe how fun Christmas in New York is, buddy!" I said to Taylor, who had been to New York before but had been too little to really participate in all the Christmas activities. Being upbeat and focusing on my children was distracting me from being terrified about two things: the hurricane that was probably getting ready to destroy my town and everything in it and getting on this stupid airplane.

I didn't admit my fears out loud, but Adam sensed my nerves. He wrapped his fingers around mine and squeezed. He smiled at me supportively. And that helped. It really did. After my dad was killed in 9/11, I refused to fly. My fear would have made more sense if my dad had been on one of the planes instead of in one of the buildings, I guess, but even still—there was something about tragedy, his being gone, and flying that were inextricably linked in my subconscious.

When Adam was MIA, Emerson had half tricked, half blackmailed me into flying to the Hamptons to see Caroline get a huge award—for her philanthropy, of all things. And it was one of Adam's last letters that convinced me to take that huge leap, to get on that plane and never look back. I smiled at him. He—and those letters—had helped me. My fear still existed, but it was much smaller now.

I leaned my head against Adam's shoulder, breathing in the smell of him. On that first trip years ago, I was facing the fact that life as a single mother might be my fate. Now, yes, there was a hurricane coming, and, yes, there were still things to worry about. But they were nothing compared to the idea of having to face life without Adam.

"Do we get to go ice-skating with Santa again?" AJ asked excitedly, standing in front of me. He had stopped, for the moment, wheeling his suitcase around in circles. The airport outside of Peachtree Bluff only had two gates and a few flights a day, so it wasn't super crowded. Still, I didn't want the kids to be too obnoxious.

"If we are going ice-skating with Santa at Rockefeller Center again, we better have some sort of fast pass," Emerson said. "I'm not waiting in line like last year."

Adam groaned. "That was awful."

Caroline, who was sitting in the chair behind us, facing the other direction, said, "We're doing the Santa brunch, and fast passes are included with that. No line."

"Hooray!" we all cheered. The kids joined in too, not even knowing what they were cheering about. Everyone in the airport turned to look at us. Yeah. We had officially crossed the line past a little annoying.

Kyle, who was sitting in a bench perpendicular to us, with a sleeping Carter on his chest, glared.

"There's not much I can do about the line for the Rockettes, though," Caroline said. "They were out of VIP tickets, so we're going to have to wait."

"Yeah, but that's a fun line," Emerson said. "Everyone is so excited and in the Christmas spirit."

"And they aren't in the ice-skating line?" Adam questioned.

Emerson shrugged. "I'm just trying to be positive, okay?"

"What else, Mommy?" Preston asked, jumping up and down. "What else are we doing with my cousins?"

I smiled. He was so cute. No, they were all so cute, the bunch of them together. I felt a little badly for Carter, the lone girl amidst all these boys. Maybe we'd give her another girl cousin closer to her age. We had talked about having another baby, now that Adam was feeling better and everything seemed to be settled. Although I sure didn't want to have another baby if we were getting ready to move. That sounded like a terrific nightmare. But three kids seemed right. Maybe even four.

"Well," Caroline started. "You know how much your cousin Carter loves *Frozen*." All the boys nodded. "We're going to go see it on Broadway!"

"Yes!" they were all saying, doing superhero moves and tumbling into each other. I was positive my two had no idea what Broadway meant, but I loved that they could get this excited about anything at all.

"I got our mortgage preapproval back this morning," Adam said.

My stomach rolled. "Already?"

I thought that was going to take weeks. *Damn small Southern town banking.*

Adam nodded. "Yeah. They are preapproving what we asked for—even with your credit." He nudged my ribs playfully.

I laughed, but it wasn't really funny. I had gotten us into a mound of credit card debt a few years earlier, but had been working to rebuild my credit ever since.

"You're sure you want to start house hunting now?" I asked. "I mean, we could wait a while, have one more summer on the water."

"I think it's time. I still say it isn't fair to your family."

"Hey, Car and Em," I said. "Do you think it's time for us to move out of Mom's house?"

"What?" Emerson said, gasping. "No. Absolutely not!"

Caroline turned around in her chair, her legs tucked up underneath her. "I need more. Why would you move out of Mom's house?"

"Well," Adam said, "tell the truth. Don't you sort of resent us living there?"

"No!" Caroline retorted as Emerson said, "Um. Definitely not. Why would we?"

I smiled triumphantly at him. So that excuse was over.

"Would you tell us if you did, though?" Adam asked.

Caroline peered at him, and before she could answer, Kyle interjected, "Man, I think you've forgotten who you're talking to."

We all laughed.

"I'm just thinking that the boys need a bigger yard to play in," Adam said.

"I have a big yard!" Caroline said. "You should buy my house!"

I scoffed. "Yeah. That's right in our budget." I paused, her statement registering. "But why would you sell your house?"

She shrugged. "It's just, you know, the house James bought when he was trying to win me back. I don't want it. I never wanted it. I come to Peachtree to see Mom. And y'all. Why do I want to stay down the street when I'm there to be with you guys? I was miserable this whole trip."

Adam pointed at her. "See. And she can't even stay at her own mother's house because we're in it."

She shook her head. "Between the guesthouse and Jack's house, there's plenty of room for all of us. You're not pinning this on me."

"I get it, man," Kyle said. "You need something that's your own, that isn't a part of Murphy world."

"Exactly," Adam said.

I didn't know how to feel. Offended? Understanding? I loved him madly, but my family was everything. I paused, mulling it over.

I didn't need anything outside of Murphy world, but maybe I could understand why Adam did. Even Jack, bless his heart, who had never wanted a family, knew that marrying Mom came with a hefty price tag: all of us. It meant no more worriless days, no more date nights, and no trips unencumbered by some hindrance, as Vivi had handily proven this week. Still, I couldn't apologize for sweeping Adam up into the very best part of my life.

"Is that how you feel?" Adam asked Kyle. "You want something of your own too?"

Kyle shook his head. "No. Murphy world is the only place I want to be. But I get how you need your own thing."

Emerson blew him a kiss, and Adam rolled his eyes.

"I just feel like we're throwing away money on rent," Adam said.

"Or," Caroline countered, "you're saving money by not having to pay insurance, taxes, and tremendous upkeep on a historic house."

"Or," Adam said back, "we could buy a newer house a few blocks down and a few blocks back and get equity, a bigger yard, and our own home."

Emerson gasped. "Are you saying what I think you're saying?"

"Are you considering moving to the Northern Side of Paradise?" Caroline asked, keeping up the shocked façade.

Paradise Pub was the oldest building in town and the dividing line between the town's old and new sections. Murphy Row was on the Southern Side of Paradise and was the part of town that people associated with Peachtree Bluff: beautiful, historic homes and charming, quaint shops. The new section was great, don't get me wrong. It was just hard to think about leaving the neighborhood I'd called home for so long.

"I still say I should try to sell you my house," Caroline said. "I'll give you a good deal, and we could work something out."

I didn't want to hurt Adam's pride more than it had already been wounded, so I said, as if it were on me, "Thanks, Car, but I can't conceive of a way in which that would be possible."

"Even if I throw in a goat?" We all laughed. Caroline nodded. "Well, you should still put their swing set and soccer goal in my yard. Then they can play over there while you look for another solution."

Caroline's eyes met mine, and we shared a look, a secret, like we had done so many times since we were children. Her look asked me if moving was even a consideration. My look back told her that my house and living beside Mom were important, but my husband was more so. She smiled at me. She understood. Because if I knew anything about my sister, it was that if she could rewind time and go back to the days where her family was intact and happy—before her world was irreparably shattered—she would do it in a heartbeat. She knew how important what I had right now was, and we had talked about how sometimes that meant compromising when we didn't really want to.

"What will happen to the house if you guys move out?" Kyle asked.

Caroline shrugged. "It will sit there, I guess."

"Ansley won't rent it?" Adam asked.

"She only let us pay rent because you insisted," I said. "She'd never rent it to anyone else."

"It will probably just be overflow for guests and family," Emerson said. "I'm totally positive she would never sell it."

The agent behind the check-in counter a few feet away from us interrupted our conversation with an announcement. "Ladies and gentlemen, we'd now like to begin pre-boarding for flight one-one-nine-seven to New York's LaGuardia."

Pre-boarding. "That's our call," I said.

I wrangled my sweet tots and braced myself for a couple hours in the air. Adam pulled me in close to him, and I marveled at how safe he made me feel, how protected. Loving him had let me step out of my shell and into the world again. And that, I reasoned, was more important than any house could ever be.

# Ansley: Insignificant Things

*Two Days after the Flotilla*

I GAVE MY TWO BOARDED-UP houses, the ones that had been a part of my life story, my family's life story, for generations, a final once-over. I remembered playing jacks with my grandfather and hopscotch with my grandmother on the very same walkway where I now did those same things with my grandchildren. My stomach clenched at the thought that, in a few weeks, I could come back here to something completely different. I wanted to cry, but instead, I steeled myself. My family was healthy and well, and, even if Peachtree changed after this storm, it would still be Peachtree. Plus, we'd had thousands of hurricanes here. This might be the storm of the century. But these houses had held tight through the storms of the last two centuries and been just fine.

I walked around the back of my house, expecting to see Vivi and my husband champing at the bit to get started on the nearly five-hour drive to Atlanta. Vivi had made us a dinner reservation somewhere along the way. We were packed and boarded up, and now I was getting nervous. I could feel the storm coming. The wind had picked up the tiniest bit, and the air felt sinister. Jack said people couldn't actually smell the ions in the air, but he was wrong. I could.

I opened the back door, the only entrance to the house that hadn't been boarded up yet. "Jack!" I called. "Vivi!" No answer. I grabbed my cell off the counter and realized I had two missed calls from Jack. Weird.

I called him right back. "Don't freak out," he said.

Immediately, my mind jumped to the plane that held my entire family minus two.

"What?" I practically cried.

"Well, um. I can't exactly find Vivi."

"Oh," I said, brushing it off. "I'm sure she just ran to get coffee before Keith finishes boarding up. But she'd better hurry up, because we need to get out of here."

"Well . . ." Jack said. There was something he wasn't telling me. "Hang on."

The back door opened, and Jack walked in, blinking. The darkness in this boarded-up house was hard to adjust to. "Something happened," he said.

My heart sped up again. "Jack," I said, "I'm really on edge today. Can you please just tell me what's going on?"

"You know how the other night we were all talking and Caroline said that when it was the right moment to tell Vivi I was her grandfather, we'd just know?"

*Oh God. Oh no.* "Uh-huh," I said warily.

"Well, we were talking and having such a good time and she said, 'I wish you were my real grandfather.'"

I gasped and put my hand to my mouth. "You didn't."

He bit his lip and shrugged guiltily.

I put my hand to my forehead. "Good Lord, Jack. That should have come from Caroline, not you. Vivi's such an emotional wreck right now anyway and . . ." I put my hands up, composing myself. "It doesn't matter. We have to find her, and we have to get out of here. That's what's important." I paused. "Where have you looked?"

"She can't be at Sloane's house, because nothing has been disturbed, not even the sandbags. There's no way in or out without it being obvious." He paused. "I should have followed her. But I just thought she was going down to her house when she ran out. I was trying to give her a minute. But she definitely isn't there either."

I called her phone, but as expected, she didn't pick up. Now that I knew what had happened I was worried, but not *that* worried. Men were notoriously terrible at searching for things.

"Okay," I said, composing a group text to Hal, Kimmy, and Keith. Vivi is missing. If you're out and about can you help us look for her? She isn't at Sloane's house or Caroline's or Jack's.

Immediately, they each responded that they were downtown and could help. Kimmy added, I'll get my brother on it too. Peachtree Bluff was a small island. It couldn't take long to find her. At least, it had better not, because we only had three hours until the bridges closed.

I picked up my phone again and hit BOB.

"What do I do?" Jack asked.

I put my finger up. "Bob," I said when the mayor answered. "Are you still here?"

"Riding it out, Ans. I feel like it's my responsibility as mayor to be here for those who are left on the island."

I nodded. He was entirely too old to be riding out a Category 4 hurricane, but he was a good man. "Bob, I can't find my granddaughter Vivi. I know everyone is occupied with hurricane prep, but if anyone can help, we've got to find her and get off this island."

"That you do," he said. "I'll get everyone on this right now. We'll find her, Ansley."

I hung up and looked at my phone. It was two o'clock already. Why had I wasted time going to the store? Why hadn't I stayed here? I should have known better.

"I'm so sorry, Ansley," Jack said.

I was angry with him. And I was angry with Vivi for running off when she knew what danger we were in. And I was angry with Caroline for leaving this volatile child in my care, knowing what could happen. But it didn't matter. Right now, we needed to find Vivi. We had to make sure she was safe.

I walked outside, and Jack followed me. It warmed my heart to see that my friends were already on the porch. They all worked within a two-minute walk, but still. "I'm heading down to the coffee shop to look for her there," Keith said, "and I'll check anywhere that looks even remotely open or hideable."

"Thank you," I said.

"I'm going to drive around town," Hal said. "Jack, why don't you come with me?"

Jack looked pleadingly at me. "Yes," I said. "That's a good idea."

"I think you should stay here, Ansley," Kimmy said. "Someone needs to be here in case she comes home."

I wanted to protest, but she was right. *When* she came home, I needed to be the one to smooth things over, to help soothe all the very complicated feelings she was having.

"Can you track her phone?" Kimmy asked as Hal and Jack got into his car. I snapped my fingers. "What a great idea! Although . . . Caroline is on a plane right now, and I don't have Vivi's phone connected to mine." I thought for a second. "James! I'll call James!"

She nodded. "I'm going to go start knocking on doors." She paused. "My brother is out on the hunt for Jim Cantore, so I sent him out after Vivi too." She smirked. "If you want to find a fifteen-year-old girl, there is no one that can sniff out her trail like a sixteen-year-old boy."

I was annoyed that she was joking at a time this serious. A gust of wind shot a dagger through my heart. The sky was beginning to darken. We had to find her. I didn't want to call James and admit that I had lost his daughter. He was going to panic. So would Caroline. I was here, at least. I could look. I could do something. They were so very far away.

I took a deep breath and hit James's contact. "Hey, Ans!" he yelled into the phone as if we were old friends, not almost-ex-in-laws. "I hear you're taking my girl on the best trip ever!" Between the wind here and the wind wherever he was, I was glad he was yelling so I could hear him.

"James," I said. "I don't want you to panic, but Vivi has run off and we can't find her."

He paused. I waited for him to freak out. "Damn," he said. "Yeah, she does that. She's done it to me a few times."

Okay. That wasn't exactly what I had expected, but I was glad of it. I couldn't possibly feel worse than I already did, so I doubted any anger would have had much impact even if he had been mad. "Look," I said, "we have to be out of here in a couple hours. Can you track her on your phone?"

"Oh! Good idea," he said. "Look, I'm on a ski lift right now, and I have horrible reception up here. I'll go into the lodge and see if I can track her down. I'm not her favorite person right now, so she might not pick up, but I'll call her too."

Yes! I hung up and called her again. No answer. I walked back into the house, pulled out a pad and a pen, and started writing. Sometimes it could jog my memory, and I was racking my brain for anywhere she might go. Her house was an obvious one, as was mine. But she wasn't there. Starlite Island was an option, but she obviously wasn't there. The weather was getting bad, and all the boats, kayaks, and paddleboards within a five-mile radius had been stowed. I stood up and walked down to my store with purpose. It was the only other place I could think of that she might possibly feel a connection to. But when I got there, the front was still completely boarded up. She definitely couldn't have gotten in that way. I walked around the back, where the only other door was solid steel and locked. I unlocked it anyway. She didn't have a key, but I wanted to check just in case. "Vivi!" I called, squinting in the dark. No answer. I flipped on the lights and did a thorough search of every nook and cranny. Nothing.

My phone rang. I willed it to be Jack or Bob or Kimmy with good news. But it was James.

"Hey," he said. "This is strange . . . It says her last location was Marine Supply Warehouse. Do y'all even have that?"

That *was* strange. "We do, way out on the highway, several

miles from here. But she would have had no way to get there." I texted Hal while still on the phone with James. She isn't at your house, is she? Maybe took a bike?

He texted back immediately. We've looked there. And I had to take all the bikes in, so they're locked up.

"Hm," I said to James. "I'm not sure how she would have gotten there, but I guess we could check. Hal said she definitely didn't take a bike or anything."

"I don't know," he said. "Could she have Ubered or something?"

I was annoyed now. "James, how many times have you taken an Uber in Peachtree Bluff?"

"Exactly zero," he said. "Do you guys even have Uber drivers?" We did, but only two or three. He chuckled, which struck me as odd. Her father was clearly not getting the gravity of this situation. "I know my child, Ansley. I can promise you she isn't at any marine supply store."

I shook my head. "James, I'm panicking," I confessed.

"I am too," he said. "But, look, she does this. I know Caroline has told you. She runs off, and we panic. But she always turns back up." He paused. "Want me to get on a plane?"

"You couldn't if you wanted to. Because of the hurricane."

"What?" he practically spat.

"Yes! You didn't know that? That's why I'm freaking out. The bridges are closing at five. Caroline and Vivi didn't tell you?"

"Vivi's mad that I won't let her live with me, so I haven't talked to her all weekend. And Caroline and I texted about the trip, but she didn't tell me about the storm!" He took a deep breath. "Oh

God, Ansley. You have to find her. I'm going to stay right here and keep tracking. If anything new pops up, I'll call you right away." Then he added, "Caroline is supposed to call me when she lands. Do you want me to tell her?"

Did I want him to? "I wish you could. But I think I need to be the one to do it."

Because that's how life worked. The right people have to tell you the right things at the right time. That was a lesson Jack would do well to learn.

I sent a group text to everyone on the search. James said his phone is tracking her at Marine Supply Warehouse? I doubt she's there—but if there's anywhere around there you can think of, please let me know.

I looked around the store one last time, thinking how stupid it was that I had been worried about these simple possessions, these silly, insignificant things, only a few hours earlier. Then I locked the back door up tight and booked it back home. On the way, I prayed harder than I ever had that, when I got there, my grand-daughter would be there to meet me.

# Caroline: The Storm of the Century

*Two Days after the Flotilla*

WHEN WE WERE LITTLE, THE number one role Emerson liked to play was the bride. The pictures are pretty comical. Tiny Emerson in the middle with Sloane and me, seven and five years older, respectively, towering over her on either side, the unhappy bridesmaids. She had an entire trunk of thrift-store gowns and veils, hideous rhinestone heels that clomp-clomp-clomped as she tried to walk around in them on her miniscule feet. It was the grandest of ironies that, out of all of us, Emerson—the consummate bride— was the most reluctant to get married.

I was telling her that very thing on our flight to New York. "Kyle is a god. You know that, right?" I asked Emerson as I sipped my rosé, sinking back into the wide, comfortable first-class seat.

She nodded. "Oh, I totally know. And I feel as though I worship him appropriately." She was so straight-faced when she said it that we both burst out laughing.

"Do you? Because your not-even-husband is back in coach

with your daughter and my son so that you can sit in first class with me. That's a good man right there." I smiled at her. "If my disastrous attempt at marriage taught me anything, it's that sometimes the little sacrifices, the tiny things that show someone how much you love them, really are the most important."

Emerson sighed. "I know. He's the greatest man in the whole world."

I was trying to feel Emerson out since we got interrupted by Kyle last time I'd tried. Mom had confided in me that Kyle had approached her about wanting to marry Emerson, but she wasn't sure whether it was a good idea. We all loved Kyle and Emerson together, and the last thing we wanted was a brokenhearted Kyle back in Peachtree Bluff while Emerson continued on with her fabulous LA life. Well, I mean, truthfully, having Kyle back in Peachtree Bluff wouldn't be that bad since his coffee—and delivery—skills beat the pants off of Keith's. But I *guessed* my little sister's eternal happiness was more important. Not to mention that there were tiny Peachtree Perks in our New York and LA stores, which would further complicate a disentanglement.

Before I could make any more offhanded comments that might help me dig further into the situation, Emerson leaned over and whispered, "I have a secret to tell you."

I gasped. "You're pregnant!"

She held up her wineglass and shook her head.

"Oh, right."

"I don't want you to get too excited because it's a huge long shot, and probably nothing will come of it."

It was too late—I was already excited. "What? What?"

She pursed her lips and said, "I've been asked to audition for a leading role on Broadway."

My mouth fell open, and I got chills all over my body. Yes, that would be great for Emerson and her career and blah, blah, blah. But, really, I'd get to have my little sister in New York! Maybe even for years on end!

"Does Kyle know?" I whispered.

"Of course Kyle knows. If I get the part we're going to have to move to New York."

"Have to?" I said skeptically. "If he moved to Toronto and Atlanta for you, I feel like New York isn't asking for too much. Seems like a step in the right direction."

She rolled her eyes. "New York is the only city in the world; nowhere else matters. I get it."

Now we had to figure out how to make this dream a reality. "I need the names of all the important people," I said, springing into action. "You know, producers, casting agents, any and everyone."

She nodded. "Thanks, Car. You've been my biggest supporter from day one."

I shrugged it off, but I knew it was true. Almost ten years ago, when she'd forgone college for LA, I'd paid Emerson's rent so she could focus more on auditions than waitressing. I'd asked favors from every friend James and I had that might know someone in the business. But she was my sister. I would do literally anything for her.

"So when's the audition?" I asked.

"In three days," she practically squealed.

I gasped. "Oh my God. What do we need to do? How's your singing? Should we practice your tap dancing?"

She laughed. "It isn't a musical, but that does sound kind of fun. Want to do it anyway?"

I nodded enthusiastically. "Got to keep up your skills because you never know what might happen."

Emerson looked down at her watch. "Okay. I'm going to go switch with Sloane."

It occurred to me as she got up that we had never even discussed my switching from first class to coach midway through the flight. At first, I felt sort of vindicated. All these years of big-sister rule had really sunk in. But then it hit me: Did they just feel sorry for me? They both had these amazing men in their lives to sit with and I didn't.

But when Sloane sat down, she looked so smiley and warm that I decided maybe I was being just a tad ridiculous. So I didn't bring it up. She sighed and said, "I've been wanting to ask you for days, but there's always someone around: Are you dating at all? Like, in New York?"

Well, now. That was fast. "Um, no. Why?" I said, not wanting to admit, even to myself, that Wes came to mind when she said it. Which was utterly preposterous. I lived in New York. He was moving to Peachtree. But it wasn't like I wanted to get married. And maybe it would be nice to have someone waiting for me underneath the mistletoe.

"I don't know," she said. "It's just kind of unlike you. You're not one to really be without a man."

"What does that mean?" I asked defensively. But I knew. Since seventh grade I had had a boyfriend pretty much every second until I married James.

Sloane just crossed her arms.

So I said wistfully, "I'm taking this time to get to know who I am without a man."

"Car, no offense," she said, "but you know who you are better than anyone I have ever met."

I smiled at her. "I do, don't I?" That didn't mean I always liked who I was. But I never felt the need to take a sabbatical or get lost in the woods to soul-search. Even after I finally decided, for good, to leave James, I was still me. I'd always been me. And I guessed it was comforting to know that, no matter what was going on around me, I always had myself to come back to.

I sighed. "No, I mean, you're right. I do want to find somebody. I do want to fall in love again. I'm not jaded and cynical—"

"You've always been jaded and cynical," Sloane interrupted.

I glared at her. "Well, not about *love.*"

She nodded. "True. You have always been sort of shockingly romantic."

"I have had some good offers on the table, but I just haven't been ready," I said. "And I don't know. If I do this again, I don't want to jump into a relationship with James 2.0." And that was going to be hard because James was my type: handsome and confident and successful. I knew I was a lot to handle and that I had a big personality. And, for some women like me, a man who was calm and compliant was the way to go. But I knew from experience that I would bulldoze right over a man like that. I needed someone who could stand up to me when I was off base. "I need an equal," I said.

Sloane patted my hand and took a sip of Emerson's wine. "The fact that you think you could even have an equal shows some real progress."

The flight attendant interrupted, refilling our glasses. She looked from Sloane to me a few times, but she didn't say anything, even though it was against the rules for us to switch seats. It wasn't like we could quietly replace Emerson anymore. Everyone knew who she was.

"Do you think Mom and Jack are going to have fun on their trip?" I asked, changing the subject.

"I think they would have before Vivi was tagging along."

Truth. We both laughed.

A few minutes later, we landed. I felt surprisingly calm and rested. When I turned my phone on, the incessant dinging of messages coming through didn't set any alarm bells off in my head. But when I started scrolling, I panicked.

"Oh my God," I said.

"What?" Sloane asked, her alarm now matching mine.

I dialed Mom as I said, "They can't find Vivi."

"We have everyone looking for her," Mom said without even saying hello. "Everyone in town, all the police and firefighters. I promise you we'll find her."

"What about the weather?" I asked, my panic rising further.

"Well, it's holding off for now," Mom said. She was lying. I could tell.

"Oh my God, Mom. Why did she run off like that?" I mean, not that there had to be a reason. She didn't like her hair. Her lip gloss was the wrong shade. Mom ran out of Topo Chico, and *no one* understood her.

"Look, Car, we can hash all that out later. For now, can you track her?"

I pushed the speaker button and tapped on the Find My Friends app. "Huh," I said. "It says she's at Marine Supply Warehouse."

"That's what James's said too," Mom said. "But she's definitely not at Marine Supply. We've done the legwork."

I managed a small snort. "I could have told you she wasn't there."

Then, remembering that my daughter was lost in a hurricane, I said, "What else can we do? Get an Amber Alert or something?"

"I've already tried," Mom said. "But you an only do that if you think the child has been abducted."

I knew Mom had to have been freaking out, but not as much as I was. She said, very calmly, "Peachtree is very small. We will find her, and we will bring her home, and it will be fine."

"I'm coming back!" I said frantically.

"Car." Mom was even calmer now. "You can't come back. They've closed the airport, and the bridges go up in an hour. There's no way for you to get back here before the storm."

My insides felt like they were being ripped apart. My daughter was missing. The storm of the century was coming.

I hung up and called James. "She's going to be fine, Car," he said first thing.

"You don't know that she's going to be fine!" I practically screamed. "She's lost in a hurricane."

"Not yet," he said. "There's no hurricane yet."

"Right," I said, willing myself to *calm down*. "Not yet. And they'll find her and get off the island before it gets there."

"Exactly," he said. "Look, I tried to get to Peachtree, but they've closed the airport."

*So I'm just going to stay in Telluride with my new piece of ass* was the implication. But what he said next made me do a 180.

"So I'm coming back to New York so we can figure out what to do next."

I nodded even though he couldn't see me. That was kind of nice. "It's going to be okay," he said. "Everything is going to be okay."

He couldn't know that. But it did make me feel the tiniest bit better. That was when I noticed that everyone was off the plane but my family, who was standing around looking at me. I knew I needed to get up, put one foot in front of the other.

"My bag," I said in a small voice as I got up out of my seat. "My baby," I added, feeling tears begin to run down my cheeks.

She was out there somewhere in the great big world, so far away from me.

A few hours ago, I would have sworn I'd never met a Pearl I didn't like. But life is like that. Sometimes it changes in an instant.

# Vivi: A Girl Worth Saving

*Two Days after the Flotilla*

SITTING IN THE SALON OF Jack's boat in the boatyard, where it was being stored during the storm, I realized something: this was actually the worst idea I'd ever had. But, in my defense, you couldn't even really call it an idea. It was more like an impulse. I mean, I felt like Jack and I were kind of having a moment when I told him I wished he was my grandfather. He even made up that cute treasure story for me like I was five.

So I don't know why I ran out of his house like that. I realized that I wasn't mad at him for telling me. I was mad at my mom for *not* telling me. It was just another lie, another secret.

But, oh my God, who *cared* right now. The wind was whipping, it was starting to rain, and it was cold. I'd made a big, big mistake. The storm of the century was coming, and now I was stuck on this boat. My heart started racing out of my chest. I had to get out of here. I had to do *something*.

I walked into one of the cabins, took the comforter off the bed and wrapped it around me like a cape. If only I could turn

into a superhero and fly back to Gransley's. All the way to Australia would be fine too. Then I started digging around the galley again for anything that potentially looked like a phone
charger.

When I had stomped out of Jack's house, I realized there
wasn't anywhere to go. All the houses were boarded up. I don't
know why I thought of Jack's boat. Maybe because I'd helped
Jack and Adam with it. I knew where the hidden key was, and I
knew I could get in. I wasn't planning on staying there or anything, just blowing off some steam and making them worry for
like an hour. Enough time that they knew I was gone but not
so long that we weren't able to evacuate. So I'd Ubered over
here.

"Why haven't you evacuated yet?" I'd asked the driver.

"I'm waiting until the last second in case someone needs a ride
off the island," he said. "But the other two drivers are staying. You
know how locals are. Think they're above a hurricane and that the
evacuation applies to everyone but them."

Once we'd gotten to the boatyard and the Uber left, I stood
around looking at all the boats, congratulating myself on this great
plan. The wind was just starting to rustle in the trees around the
very full boatyard. I was about to make my way toward Jack's boat
when I heard a tiny crying sound. I had to investigate.

I started looking around and under boats, walking toward the
noise. And then I realized that something I'd previously thought
about Peachtree Bluff was totally untrue: there were cute boys here
after all.

This super-hot guy around my age, maybe a little older, was

crouched up under one of the huge supports in the boatyard that was holding a gigantic yacht. He'd evidently heard the sound too. He put his finger to his lips, and I smiled and squatted down beside him.

Fortunately, I had done my hair and makeup in preparation for our night out in Atlanta. I was even wearing my cute new rain boots, so I looked hurricane chic. I gave myself a mental shake. What was wrong with me?

Tucked up behind one of the big pieces of wood holding up the boat was a tiny kitten. I put my hand to my heart. "I think she's scared," he said.

I nodded. "I can get her."

He was tall and broad, too big to crawl up to where the kitten was, but it was no problem for me. So I inched closer to her, talking in soothing tones the whole time. "It's okay, little kitty. We've got you. You're going to be okay. Let's get you out of here before the big, bad storm comes."

I was shocked that she didn't even try to run when I reached my hand out to scoop her up. I scooted out and stood, snuggling her tiny, soft body up to my face.

Handsome-in-jeans-and-a-flannel-shirt grinned and reached out to rub under her chin. "Where's your mama? Huh?" The kitten purred and snuggled deeper into me. I guessed I was her mama now.

"I'm Vivi," I said, forgetting for just a minute that a hurricane was coming and that I had run away from home.

"Tyler," he said. He had dark eyes and dark hair and his nose was slightly crooked. You could tell he had broken it. Judging from the size of him, my guess was he'd broken it playing football.

"Do you live here?" I asked, batting my eyelashes the tiniest bit.

"My sister has lived here for a while, but my parents just retired a few months ago and we decided to move here."

"Are you evacuating for the hurricane?" I asked.

He lit up. "No. My sister is one of those hard-core locals who thinks evacuating is for tourists." He paused. "Plus, I want to be a meteorologist when I grow up. Well, a storm chaser. So hurricanes are kind of my deal."

I laughed. What a cute thing to say. He was so cute. I thought of Lake. But it wasn't like we were dating. And, please. Like he wasn't flirting with everyone he saw right now?

"What are you doing here?" he asked.

"Oh, um," I stuttered. "Just checking on my grandad's boat." *My grandad.* Wow, that had really taken on a whole different meaning now. I pointed to the *Miss Ansley,* up on blocks. I was going to have to find one of those rolling staircases to even get up on the thing. I really should have thought this through better.

"So, what should we do with the kitten?" I asked.

"I can take her to my sister's," he replied. "Kimmy lives on a farm. One more cat won't be a big deal."

"Kimmy! You're Kimmy's brother?" I was wondering if maybe I'd miscalculated. Kimmy was super old. Like, probably at least twenty-six or twenty-seven. My heart sank. Her brother couldn't be my age, could he? "So, um, your parents just let you ride out a hurricane?"

"Yeah. Our parents are pretty laid-back, so we're all riding out the storm together. And, I mean, I'm responsible."

"Besides the whole chasing-hurricanes thing?" I asked.

He laughed. "Yeah. Besides that. I only have a year and a half left of high school, and I know I have to do well if I want to get into meteorology school. It's pretty competitive, believe it or not."

"The weather?" I asked coyly. "The weather is competitive?"

He just grinned. Okay. Whew. So he was only a grade above me. Perfect. Perfect for what, I couldn't say. I was leaving for three weeks, but, you know. A girl's gotta know her options. He held his hands out to me, and, for just a second—a mortifying second—I seriously almost held my hands out to him. Then I realized he wanted the kitten.

Tyler looked around. "Um. Do you need a ride or something?"

"Oh, um . . ." I thought about it. But I wasn't ready to go back to Gransley's just yet. Plus, this guy appeared to be a cute brother of Kimmy's, but I didn't actually know him. So it probably wasn't the best idea to get in the car with him. Not that I knew the Uber drivers . . . But didn't they have to be, like, registered or something at least? "I'm okay," I heard myself saying before I'd even really decided.

"I'm not a serial killer or anything," he said, grinning at me.

I eyed him flirtatiously. "Right. But isn't that what a serial killer would say?"

Looking back now, as the rain pounded on the salon roof, I knew I should have said yes. *Yes, handsome boy who's Kimmy's brother, I really need a ride so I can get off this island before I get blown to smithereens or starve to death in this boat because my phone is dead and no one knows where I am and I'm going to die.*

I slammed the last galley drawer. Who doesn't keep spare phone chargers on their boat? Although I wouldn't know how to turn on the generator even if I could find a charger. The only food was a tiny bag of pretzels and a bunch of dry rice and beans. Great. Could human stomachs even digest raw rice and beans? Could I survive if I was here for like a week? Oh my God. This was bad. This was so bad. I looked out, past the driving rain. There was no one around. No one at all.

Were they even looking for me? And what time was it? Ugh. I needed my phone really, really badly. I had left at like two or two thirty. It had to be at least four. *Oh my God. What have I done?* My stomach was in knots.

Okay. A plan. I had to make a plan. I went through every cabinet and drawer in the entire boat again. I found one more bag of pretzels and one Lärabar. There was a case of water, so that was good. I wouldn't die of dehydration. And I could soak some of the beans and eat them even if I couldn't cook them. Right? Isn't that what people did with dried beans?

I thought about my mom. She was an expert boat captain, and I really wished I'd listened more all those times we were out on the water and she'd tried to teach me about emergencies and boat safety. Not that this boat was going anywhere . . . At least, I hoped it wasn't. But hadn't there been that megayacht that blew completely over last summer in the Hamptons and its hull cracked? Surely, the hull was stronger than my skull. Okay. *Think. Think.* I could try to run for it, even in the storm, but I hadn't paid attention during the drive here and didn't know how to get home. I snapped my fingers. The VHF! I could radio out and hope that someone—another boat or person at the Coast Guard station—heard me.

I opened the door to the salon, the driving rain pouring in and the wind nearly blowing me back inside. These were not ideal ladder-climbing conditions, but I had to get to the bridge. That's where the radio was. Did the radio work without power? Was it on a separate battery switch? And where would the battery switches on this boat even be? Maybe there was a panel inside the salon. But I didn't remember seeing it.

I made it up the ladder slowly, holding on for dear life. My fingers slipped off the metal rails more than once, but my rubber boots held fast. I reached for the radio beside the helm, shivering in the cold. I held down the side button and prayed. "Please, God." Nothing. No glorious static. I was going to have to find the battery switches. There would be a control panel. I could do this. I could figure it out.

But before I could, I heard a voice calling, "Vivi!"

*Oh, thank God.* I started crying. I was saved.

"Vivi!"

"Up here!" I called, shivering.

A head popped up from the ladder.

"Tyler?"

"Hurry up!" he yelled. "It's coming in quick."

He wrapped one arm around my waist as I climbed down, which I was grateful for. It was gusting enough now that I would have blown right off. I grabbed my dead phone from inside, locked the salon door, and got down from the boat with Tyler's help. I'd say we made a run for it to the car, but there was no running in wind and rain like this. Simply walking was a full-on effort.

Once we finally got inside, drenched and panting, Tyler gave me a look. "Are you insane?"

"You're the one who wants to do this for a living!" I said.

"Vivi, I'm serious. The entire town is freaking out looking for you."

He typed quickly into his phone, and I heard a text go through.

"I'm sorry," I said. "I didn't mean for this to happen. I was only going to stay gone for like an hour, but then my phone died, and I couldn't figure out what to do."

"Why didn't you let me take you home earlier?" he asked.

"Because I didn't know earlier that my phone was dead."

He shook his head. Great. Just fantastic. Now the cute boy was mad at me too. And he didn't even know me. Not the first impression I wanted to make.

He pulled out of the parking lot so slowly it was like we were barely moving—and I could see why. No one should be driving in this weather. And especially not a sixteen-year-old who barely had his license. He leaned forward over the steering wheel for every extra ounce of visibility. A tree limb came flying at the windshield, and I screamed. Tyler, on the other hand, was totally in the zone, concentrating so hard that even a massive limb couldn't faze him. I was completely silent, holding my breath the entire way back home. I looked at the clock. 5:20. I felt nauseous as I realized that we were stuck here. Like it or not, we were riding out the storm of the century. Everyone had to be out by five, and this was why. This storm was whipping. Well, they were accurate, I'd give Jim Cantore's crew that.

My heart sank. I had ruined everything. I had ruined Gransley and Grandjack's trip of a lifetime. I had made it so that we had to stay in Peachtree Bluff during this storm. There was nothing I could do to ever make up for that. Even so, as we pulled into Jack's driveway, I felt like I could finally breathe again.

I looked at Tyler and said, as soberly and sincerely as I could, "Thank you. You saved me. You saved my life."

He smiled. "Anytime."

"Why?" I asked. "Why would you come back for me? Why risk your own safety?"

He grinned wider now. "You know, Vivi, from the second I met you, I felt like you were a girl worth saving."

I just hoped that, after all I'd put them through, my grandparents still felt the same way.

# Ansley: Boy Scout

*Two Days after the Flotilla*

DURING OUR CHILDHOOD SUMMERS IN Peachtree Bluff, Jack and his friends spent most mornings out fishing while my best friends Sandra and Emily and I sunned ourselves on Starlite Island or, upon occasion, by Emily's pool. The summer I turned seventeen, when the mere sight of Jack could make my pulse pound in my throat, Jack and his friends left early one morning before sunrise, as was their custom. They had been carrying on about the drum they were going to bring us and the hordes of bluefin—which were really only good when they were fresh and fried—they were going to sell to the local fish camp. They all had to spend their summers earning pocket money for the next school year, and, as it turned out, fishing was more lucrative than changing tires or bussing tables.

Their boat back then was barely seaworthy, just a little wooden hull with a small Mercury engine. But we were kids. We didn't think about safety. I was never afraid when Jack left on that boat in the mornings. But one afternoon, when the boys hadn't returned by one as usual, when the sky began to darken and the rain began to fall, I was panicked. Emily and Sandra were too, and they weren't even in love with any of the unreturned.

When Jack and his friends finally showed up a little before three, soaked to the bone, freezing and terrified, explaining that their engine had conked out and they'd had to figure out how to rig it up to get home, I had never been so relieved.

Not until this very moment, forty-five years later, that is.

When that text came in from Tyler on our group chain, I burst into tears. He had found Vivi. She was safe. I stood at the back door, waiting, and when his headlights came into view, I flew out the door and practically ripped Vivi out of the car. I had never hugged another human being so tightly. I was crying and yelling to be heard over the noise of the storm, not even caring about the driving rain pelting my face and soaking my clothes, saying the exact thing I had said to Jack all those years ago: "Don't you *ever* do that to me again!"

The strong wind was blowing tree limbs around the yard, and we probably weren't safe outside. But I was dizzy with relief.

"I'm so sorry, Gransley," Vivi said. "I swear I didn't mean to be gone this long!"

I looked up and finally noticed Kimmy's brother, Tyler. She was the one to come through, in her quiet way, like she did so often. She had been right. The sixteen-year-old boy had found my granddaughter. Now I could see that it *had* been a little funny. And totally true.

Tyler, squinting from the rain hitting his face, turned to get back in his car.

"Absolutely not!" I yelled over the noise of the rain, wind, and surf. "You can't drive in this. It's too dangerous. You'll have to wait it out with us." Kimmy's farm was probably only five miles from here, but at that moment, five miles might as well have been five hundred.

As I said it, anxiety rose in me. We were boarded up, but otherwise, we were completely unprepared. We had no supplies of any sort. Sure, there was some random food in the pantry, and we could scavenge up some blankets, flashlights, and maybe a case of water, but we were in no way ready for what was to come.

Jack ran out the door, arms full of sandbags, and said, "Tyler! Find a hammer and get the plywood off the house next door so we can camp out there!"

I texted Kimmy to tell her and her parents that Tyler was safe and riding out the storm with us. Vivi and I followed Jack, with much effort, to our family house. Tyler beat off the plywood on the back door with a hammer, and I, following suit, removed the sandbags.

"The water is rising already," Jack said. "This house is the highest point in town. This is where we need to be."

My stomach flip-flopped. He handed Vivi the supplies in his arms, and I pushed the door open. "Kids!" I said. "Go fill up every sink and bathtub with water. Then get all the cups, glasses, pitchers, any container you can find, and fill them up too."

"What?" Vivi asked.

"Now!" Jack said. "We'll explain later." Then he turned to me. "I'll do the same next door, and then I'm going to put the sandbags back after I finish boarding it up. Is there anything else you need?"

I was certain there was, but I was too frantic to even think. I shook my head. Jack grabbed the tops of my arms and kissed me hard. He looked me in the eye and said, "We're okay. It's going to be okay."

I nodded. Then I called Caroline. "She's okay! We have her!" I yelled into the phone, even though there was no real reason to yell.

"What?" she said back. "It's hard to hear you."

"We found Vivi," I said slowly, realizing that we must be starting to lose cell reception already.

"Oh, thank God," she said.

"I have to go, Caroline, but we're at Grandmother's house and we're safe. Okay?"

"Okay."

I could tell that she was crying. "You might not hear from me for a few days, and I'm sorry. I'll do everything I can to get in touch as soon as I can. But we're fine and we will keep Vivi safe. I promise."

"Oh my God, Mom!" she cried.

As thunder clapped loudly overhead, we all screamed. I knew that wasn't a promise I could make. But I knew I had to try.

"I have to go, Car. But I love you."

"I love you too," she said pitifully. There was really nothing else to say. Now we had to get as prepared as we possibly could.

A soaking-wet Jack, water streaming off his raincoat, entered the back door. Lining the interior with sandbags, he threw off his coat, leaving it in a wet heap on the floor.

"Tyler!" he yelled. The kids were running around the house filling sinks, and I wordlessly took over Tyler's job of filling up the downstairs bathtub as Jack said to Tyler, "Help me get this mattress off the bed."

My stomach gripped again. As the water ran into the sinks and bathtub, I took three deep breaths and walked into the bedroom. Jack was saying, "Take this end of the rope. We're going to tie it underneath the mattress, so we have something to hold on to."

With some effort, they removed the mattress from the bed and leaned it against the wall so there was just enough room for us to crawl behind it if a cyclone or tornado came and we needed an extra barrier.

"Jack, how will we even know if we need to get behind there?" I asked. "It's not like we'll be watching the Weather Channel for a tornado warning."

"Speaking of," Tyler said, running into the living room to, I presume, turn on the TV. I hadn't even owned a TV until a few years ago, when all the girls had come home at once and wanted to watch a movie Emerson was starring in. Now I was glad I had one. With the way the storm was raging, I couldn't imagine that the power would stay on for much longer, but I was grateful to have access to the outside world while I still could.

"Babe, not to scare you," said Jack, "but if a cyclone comes, we'll know. We won't need the Weather Channel for that." Chills ran through me. I closed my eyes, not really wanting to know what that meant.

I went back to the kitchen and grabbed flashlights in both arms, handing one to Tyler, one to Jack, and running upstairs to hand one to Vivi. "When the power goes out, it'll be too dark with all the boards to be able to see," I explained. "No light will be able to come through the windows or doors."

"Want me to start lighting candles?" Vivi asked.

"Not yet," I said, not wanting to waste them. Vivi had experienced power outages of a day, maybe thirty-six hours, during a snowstorm in New York. She didn't understand that, if this storm was as bad as they said it would be, we'd be lucky if our house was left standing, much less if we got power back in a few weeks. "But gather all the candles, matches, and lighters you can find and put them on the kitchen island," I said.

"Gransley," she said. "I can't tell you how sorry I am. I swear I didn't mean to do this. My phone died and I didn't know how to get home—"

I put my hand up. "There will be plenty of time for that later."

I ran back down to the kitchen. Tyler was glued to the Weather Channel. "Keep an eye on it," I yelled. "Let us know if we need to be high or low!"

That was the trouble with these storms. Between the flooding and the cyclones, the options weren't so great. It was a damned-if-you-do, damned-if-you-don't sort of situation.

Adam always kept a huge cooler in the back hallway. I opened the freezer and dumped all the ice into it. I had meticulously emptied everything in my fridge and freezer in the weeks leading up to our trip. Now I counted on the fact that Sloane had not. I cranked up the oven and put a frozen ham, some fish sticks, tater tots, and chicken nuggets in there to cook. That would get us through dinner and a few lunches.

I piled all the frozen fruit, fresh fruit, vegetables, yogurts, and everything else I could salvage from the fridge and freezer into the cooler, grateful that Sloane wasn't the type to remember to clean out her fridge before she left town. Jack, as if reading my mind, came into the kitchen. "We just have to make it until the flood-waters recede. Then I can get down to the store to reprovision. We're talking four, five days, tops." I groaned. "What's in the pantry?" I asked, still diligently sorting and finding what I could save.

"Look," he said. "Move the freezer stuff to the cooler, where it will start to thaw, and the fridge to the freezer. It will keep the food cold for a long time if we don't open it."

I smiled. "I knew I married you for a reason, you Boy Scout, you." Then I held up one of four packs of string cheese and said, "I hope you like this."

He stuck his head in the pantry. "And I hope you like Sesame Street cereal bars and Fruit Roll-Ups."

"I do, actually," I said.

"Oh!" he said, like he'd hit the jackpot. "Red Solo cups!"

"Fill 'em up," I said. I turned on the oven light. The tots were browning nicely. The wind howled. If we could just make it a few more minutes.

"I don't think we'll starve," Jack said.

I sighed heavily. "Note to self, always be prepared for a hurricane even when you think you're leaving."

He nodded. "Sloane sort of is. They don't have much water, but they have plenty of soup and beans. We can build a fire and heat all kinds of things." I stopped my hustling about to catch his eye. "We're going to fine," he said again.

At that exact moment, lighting bolted, thunder crashed, and

the power blinked out and came back on. I knew the oven would hold temperature for a while, even after the electricity was gone, so I figured the ham would be okay.

"Let's rustle around in these drawers and gather any extra batteries we can find."

"Hey, it's really starting to get going now," Tyler said, a touch too excitedly for my liking. "Where's your weather radio?"

Jack and I looked at each other as Vivi walked back into the kitchen.

"You live in coastal Georgia and don't have a weather radio?" Tyler said, incredulous. Jack shook his head. "Okay. Well, then, what about binoculars?"

"Oh! Adam has some really nice ones Sloane gave him for Christmas last year!" Vivi said excitedly. "Let's see if we can find them."

"Hey, Tyler!" I called after them. "The window on the third floor is too high to be boarded. You can use them up there—just don't get too close in case the wind surges. And don't forget your flashlights!"

With everything as generally organized and ready as it could be under the circumstances, I finally turned to look at Jack. I walked over to him, where he opened his arms. I leaned my head on his chest. "I'm so sorry about the trip, Jack. I am so, so sorry."

He shrugged. "There's nothing we can do about it now."

I pulled back to look at him. Maybe it was because my fear was so very much on the surface, but I felt like a raw, vulnerable wound had opened inside me. "Jack," I said hesitantly. "Is life with me more than you bargained for?"

He laughed so loudly it scared me. Then he kissed me. "Ansley, I can say with confidence that life with you is absolutely more than I bargained for." He kissed me again. "But in all the very best ways. I never knew how messy and chaotic and wonderful it was to have a family. And, yes, it is killing me that our trip got ruined. But what's done is done, and now we need to get through this. We can worry about our vacation later."

I nodded and kissed him again. He was a good, good man. The buzzer for the food went off. "I know we were planning on dining aboard one of the world's finest ships these next few weeks." I sighed. "But here, at Kitchen de Ansley, chicken nuggets, fish sticks, and tater tots await you, my love."

He nodded. "Sounds about right. I'm going to build a fire while I can still see to do it."

"Good idea."

I pulled out the trays of food that were cooked and closed the oven quickly so the ham would keep going. I looked around this beautiful kitchen I had redone not five years ago and wondered if my grandmother had ever lived through a hurricane of this magnitude. Had she felt this fear? Had she been terrified that she wouldn't be able to keep the ones she loved safe? Had she trusted this house to protect her from nature's rawest, realest power? I smiled then, thinking of her indomitable spirit—more powerful than any hurricane's—but as I did, the wind gusted, and, just like that, everything turned to black. And I couldn't help but think then, with a sense of dread: *That's the night that the lights went out in Georgia.*

# Emerson: Chart the Course

SWITCH TO PEACHTREE BLUFF. SWITCH to Peachtree Bluff, I silently willed the Weather Channel, which was playing softly on the large, flat-screen TV hanging over the lacquered console in Caroline's apartment living room. The good news was, since Jim Cantore was in Peachtree, my beloved town was getting a lot of screen time. The bad news was that it was getting so much screen time because it was getting hit so hard. I glanced down at my phone again, knowing that my mother couldn't text me, knowing that nothing had changed. It was nearly four a.m., which meant that Hurricane Pearl had been mercilessly pounding Peachtree Bluff for almost eight hours. I perked up when I saw Jim Cantore appear on-screen. As if she sensed it, Caroline walked in and sat beside me. Moments later, Sloane appeared at the other side. I knew neither of them would be sleeping. How could they? It was bad for Sloane and me, but it was worse for Caroline. Her daughter was in the midst of this chaos.

Jim Cantore was screaming into the wind. "Hurricane Pearl

was downgraded from a Category 4 to a Category 2 right before it made landfall here in Georgia, but this hurricane's true power for destruction lies in how slowly it's moving." We all scooted up in our seats as the camera panned behind Jim. The water was definitely covering the streets now, but it was hard to gauge how high it actually was. Was it inside Caroline's house? Jack's? Surely, it couldn't be inside Mom's house, as high as it sat. If it was, the entire town was destroyed.

"We're expecting the eye to blow over in the next few minutes, but we have hours more of this monster storm here on Georgia's coast." A tree limb sailed by the camera.

"Who in their right mind would stand out in storms for a living?" Sloane asked.

I shook my head. Caroline looked pale. "I just wish we would hear from them," she said.

"The second unique factor of this storm is the tornadoes it has brought," Cantore continued, yelling over the wind and rain. "Waterspouts forming over the ocean are making landfall all over the area."

I hit the power button on the remote. Caroline hit it again as a voice off camera said, "We'll keep you posted, but if this storm doesn't start to move out, I can't even imagine the damage it's going to do. God bless those brave souls that stayed on that island."

"Great. That's just great," Caroline said, hitting the power button again. She sighed.

"I tried to turn it off," I said.

"I know, but I needed to see it. It makes me feel weirdly in control."

I nodded.

"That makes sense," Sloane said. "Information is power, even if it's bad information."

"It's only a Category 2," I said. "Think of how many Cat 2s we've ridden out over the years."

"That's exactly right," Sloane said. "They're going to be fine, Car."

Caroline took a deep breath, sitting up straighter. "Right. You're absolutely right. Those houses have been through hundreds of hurricanes, many of them much worse than this one."

I was about to respond when a bang on the front door made me jump. I looked at my sisters, puzzled, and then got up and put my eye to the peephole. Definitely not a stranger. I opened the door and James barged into the living room, still in his ski coat. "Car!" he said, practically falling into her on the couch. "What do we do? How can we get to her?"

I felt like saying, *Well, if you hadn't been such an idiot and had an affair with Edie Fitzgerald and made my sister have to leave you, which turned my niece into this demon who had to be banished to her grandparents', then none of this would have happened.* But James looked so upset I didn't say it. Plus, he had gotten plenty of similar earfuls from me already. Actually, the fact that he'd taken them like a man made me respect him slightly more—ever so slightly.

"They won't let us fly there," James said.

Caroline wordlessly hit the power button on the remote, and James's eyes widened at the total destruction happening on the Weather Channel. "That would be why they won't let us fly," Caroline said.

"Then let's get in the car," he said frantically.

"James." Sloane was very soothing and sweet. I was glad someone could manage that tone right now. "You can't drive there. For one, there's a huge storm that you'd be encountering all up and down the East Coast. For two, even if you could get there, the bridge is up. There's no way on or off that island now."

He shook his head, and Caroline jumped up off the couch. "Oh my God! The boat!"

"What about the boat?" he asked.

I felt my butterflies rising. "Caroline, no," I said. "That's really crazy."

"Why?" she asked. "Why is it crazy? The boat has a water maker, which we know everyone is going to need, and we can fill it up with food and supplies."

James jumped up now too and hugged her. "Yes! You are a genius. Yes!" Then he paused. "Wait, no wait. The boat is in Palm Beach. Remember?"

Caroline put her hand on her forehead.

They were having kind of a weird divorce. Mostly weird in that he still loved her so much and she still tolerated him so fully. But I got it: tolerating someone wasn't love. Tolerance did not a happy and fulfilling marriage make. In fact, it did, quite often, make for a lot of resentment.

"Google if the storm is in Palm Beach!" Caroline instructed me.

She was really scary right now, so I typed as quickly as I could. I shook my head. "No, it's farther north and projected to head inland as it dies down, not back out to sea."

"Perfect!" James said. "It's perfect. We can fly to Palm Beach, and it should only take us two or three days to get to Peachtree Bluff on the boat. If we had to leave from here, it would take at least five or six."

Caroline stepped back. "Who said you were going? Someone has to stay here with Preston."

"She is my daughter too," he said, raising his voice.

"Shhhh," we all said simultaneously. There were a lot of sleeping children crammed in Vivi's bedroom.

"Well, I'm sure as hell going," I said. I didn't even have to ask Kyle. I knew that if we could figure out a way to get to Peachtree, we'd go. All of us.

"Me too," Sloane chimed in.

"Do you think Adam will want to come?" I asked.

Sloane faked a puzzled expression. "Will Adam want to conduct a rescue mission? Hmmm . . ."

In spite of everything, Caroline smiled.

"I don't even know how many staterooms the new palace at sea has," I said. "I've never had the privilege of an invitation."

Caroline rolled her eyes.

"Four," James said. "And two V-berths."

"We can make that work easy," I said.

"I call master!" James and Caroline said simultaneously.

Caroline crossed her arms. Then she said, "Actually, Adam and Sloane get master because AJ and Taylor are going to have to share a room with them and AJ can sleep in their V-berth."

"You get Preston because our captain needs her beauty sleep," I said, smiling at James.

Caroline nodded seriously. "Truth."

Sloane pointed at the TV. "Um, Cap, we can't exactly ride into that."

She rolled her eyes. "I know that, Sloane. Thank you. But it will be at least two or three days until we get to that, and the storm will have passed over by then." She smiled sweetly at her almost-ex-husband. "Can you help me chart the course?"

"We'll just use the GPS," he said. She glared at him, and he acquiesced. "Fine. Fine." Caroline was big on her charts. She didn't trust her GPS when she was out in open water. I, for one, always felt much safer because of that.

She looked back at me. "Take James's credit card. I need you to book us all tickets to Palm Beach."

"So I guess I'm paying for this . . ." James said. Caroline glared at him, and he dug his wallet out. Sloane grimaced. Poor Sloane. She was still afraid to fly, and these past two days had been a real trial by fire.

"Are you sure you want to go?" Caroline asked. "You can stay put and fly in as soon as the bridges open."

"This is the fastest way, right?" James said.

"It's the only way," Sloane chimed in. "Best case, that bridge opens next week. I'm not waiting that long. Even then, probably only power and construction crews will be allowed in and out."

James's eyes widened. "No. That can't be true. They can't just leave people like that."

"That's why it's called mandatory evacuation," I chimed in. "Because if they can't keep people safe, they want them gone." I looked back at the TV. There was no keeping them safe right now.

"Oh God, Vivi," James said. "And poor Ansley. I just hope they're all okay."

We all nodded quietly, in unison, the very scary reality sinking back in.

I held my phone up. "There's an eleven fifteen flight that would get us to Palm Beach before two." Okay, so, honestly, there was also a seven a.m. flight, but it was already four thirty. I didn't think we could get packed and to the airport in time to make it, but I knew Caroline would want to try if I told her.

Caroline nodded. I could see the light had returned to my sister's eyes. We still didn't know if our mother was safe. We didn't know if Vivi was okay. But we weren't sitting around helpless. We weren't waiting. We were going to get them.

Caroline's boat, *Starlite Sisters*, was essentially a self-contained universe, with all the systems needed to not only survive but thrive, to withstand any trouble that befell it. As I looked at Caroline and Sloane, the other two members of the *real* Starlite Sisters, I couldn't help but think that maybe we were the exact same way.

# Vivi: The Trenches

BETWEEN THE CRIPPLING BOUTS OF panic about what my parents were going to do to me if I lived through this storm, I had to wonder: Was the storm of the century a bad time to try to get a boy to kiss you? I mean, was it inappropriate to be thinking about how adorable he was while you were supposed to be looking for binoculars?

We were standing in Sloane and Adam's walk-in closet, which did feel a little wrong since it was such a personal space. But it was practically the apocalypse. Privacy rules went out the window, right?

I was on a stepladder, rustling through some stuff on the top shelf, trying to search for Adam's binoculars as best I could with my flashlight. "Man, this dude has a lot of guns," Tyler said, peering into the locked gun case that was built into Adam's side of the closet, his light reflecting on the glass.

"He's ex-military," I said proudly. "A real-life, serious war hero. He was captured and held captive and everything."

"Wait, I remember my sister talking about that," Tyler said, as if putting the pieces together. "That was your uncle?"

"Yup."

"My dad's ex-military too. Just retired after thirty-five years."

"Wow," I said, feeling around the shelves. "So your parents are pretty old." As soon as the words were out of my mouth, I wished I hadn't said them.

But Tyler laughed. "Not that old. Fifty-three or something? I can never remember exactly."

Okay, so not *old* old. But way older than my parents . . . I felt a small, square box, and I pulled it down. "Bingo!" I said, handing the binoculars to Tyler.

"Awesome," he said. "And, hey, not to be greedy, but I'm soaking wet here from saving *someone*. Do you think it would be weird if I borrowed a T-shirt?"

I shook my head. "Of course not. Adam doesn't care about anything like that." I paused. "I mean, don't even think about touching his guns. But, otherwise, help yourself."

He pulled his T-shirt over his head, and I finally understood what the word "swoon" actually meant. I was a little light-headed. I looked away so as not to be tacky. I stepped forward to look at Adam's neat stack of folded T-shirts right as Tyler did and bumped into him and his bare chest. And I realized that he smelled very good, which was really saying something for someone who had just rescued me from a hurricane.

"Sorry," he said, looking down and laughing.

I laughed too. "No, I bumped into you."

He pulled on a T-shirt, and I looked up at him, and he looked down at me. It was a real-life Hallmark-movie moment where everything went silent, and our eyes locked, and I knew he was going to kiss me. But right as he leaned in, "Kids! Fish sticks and tater tots!" rang out from the third floor. We were eating up there since the unboarded window gave a little light.

It was probably for the best. I mean, I'd just met the kid. But, then again, *he thought I was someone worth saving.*

I turned and walked out of the closet. "It is so, so dark," I whispered, jumping as something crashed outside the window. Tyler grabbed my hand. I kept holding his as we made our way upstairs, presumably because I was leading him. That was legit, right? My heart was pounding, a little because of him and a little because of how scary this storm was.

Up here on the third floor, you could actually feel the house swaying in the wind, which couldn't be a good sign, right? But I felt better when I saw Gransley and Grandjack sitting at the game table, which they had covered with candles to make it almost light. I went to the table, but Tyler beelined for the window seat, binoculars already on his eyes. "Oh man, you guys," he said. "The water is already at the seawall." Gransley and Grandjack shared a look.

"That's bad, right?" I asked.

I could tell Gransley was trying to formulate a response when Tyler said, "Well, it sure isn't good."

I took a bite of fish stick. I was pretty sure I'd never had a fish stick. It wasn't something that my mother would have served in the gluten-free, sugar-free, organic Beaumont household. But, dang, it was good. The tater tots were even better. I was savoring my second one when Tyler exclaimed, "Oh my God! Oh my God!"

Grandjack jumped up, and Tyler practically threw the binoculars at him. "Off to the east," Tyler said. "Blow out the candles! A waterspout is headed straight for us!"

"Downstairs bedroom! Now!" Grandjack yelled.

Tyler grabbed my arm and Jack shooed us all down the stairs. "Behind the mattress!" he yelled.

We all made our way behind the one king-sized mattress that was leaned up against the wall, and Grandjack and Tyler, like they had practiced it—well, maybe they had—each held on to one end of the rope for dear life. We were all panting, partly from exertion and partly from fear. Off in the distance, but getting closer and closer, was a crazy-loud noise.

"Is that a . . . train?" I whispered to Tyler.

He pulled me close with his free arm.

"No," Grandjack said soberly. "It's a tornado."

My heart was thudding in my ears now.

"It's okay," Grandjack said. "The houses are close enough together and we're low enough to the ground that we're fine. We're going to be fine."

I flipped my flashlight on. I could tell by his face he was lying.

The sound was getting louder and louder, and now, even down here, I could feel the house shaking. A shattering sound came from the kitchen.

"Plates," Gransley said. I could barely hear her over the noise, but she was practically yelling.

"Or windows," Grandjack said back. That would be infinitely worse.

I squeezed my eyes shut and leaned into Tyler—not because I was flirting now, but because I was terrified. My breath was coming in short gasps. The sound got louder, and the shaking got worse. I was vaguely aware of how tightly Tyler was squeezing my shoulder.

And then, just like that, it was over. I looked up at Tyler and then over to Gransley and Grandjack. Grandjack let go of the rope and leaned back against the wall, hands on his chest. For a second I panicked that he was having a heart attack. But then he said, "Wow. Haven't done that in a while."

Gransley laughed with relief, and I felt Tyler take a deep breath. "You okay?" he asked, looking down at me, releasing his side of the rope. I was happy to notice he didn't release *me*.

I nodded, brushing the hair back from my face, realizing that I was a little sweaty.

"Oh my gosh," I said. "Can you imagine being outside in that right now?" Which led me to, "Oh my gosh! Tyler! What happened to the kitten?"

"Kimmy has the kitten," Tyler said. "She's fine."

"I hope Biscuit is okay," Gransley said.

"She's fine, Ans," Grandjack said. "She's much safer with the vet than she would be with us right now."

That didn't inspire a lot of confidence. Outside, the rain still pelted and the wind still raged. But, in comparison to the cyclone, it felt slightly less scary.

"What do we do now, weather expert?" I asked Tyler.

"Well, if anyone had a weather radio, I'd be a little better equipped to tell you."

"Well, someone is supposed to be in Australia right now," Jack interjected.

I cringed at the thought. I had made them miss the trip of a lifetime. It was all my fault.

"I'm going to go back up," Jack said, flipping his flashlight on. We all followed suit. The darkness was one of the scariest parts of all of this. "I need to make sure everything is intact upstairs."

"You know what?" Gransley said, suddenly sounding upbeat. "I don't think anyone is getting a lot of sleep tonight. I say we set up a game of Monopoly and a bunch of candles in the dining room, so we'll be close to the mattress just in case." In spite of everything, that actually sounded kind of fun.

"I will warn you," Tyler said. "I'm pretty good. I don't want to hurt anyone's feelings."

I scoffed. "You've never seen Monopoly played until you've seen me play."

He put his flashlight up under his chin. "Oh yeah? We'll just see about that."

Thunder crashed, making me jump a little. "Do you think we're safe to come out from behind the mattress now?" I asked.

"I think so," Tyler said.

"I think so too," Gransley added.

Tyler slid out from his side of the mattress and I crawled out behind him. He helped me up and, as he did, squeezed my hand encouragingly.

I still had knots in my stomach, but there was something about him that made me feel like it was going to be okay. I thought about Adam then, about how he had spent so long never knowing what was coming next, living with something absolutely terrifying around every corner. He always told me that men bond in the trenches in a way that defies anything else. Looking at Tyler, this kid who had been a total stranger to me until a few hours ago, I finally understood why.

# Sloane: Consequences

Dear Sloane,

I bet you thought I'd forget to write you today with everything going on, didn't you? But it is times like these that I am most reminded how very grateful I am for our family. Not just you, AJ, and Taylor, but everyone in the Murphy clan. And I hope you know that my wanting to move isn't because I want to escape from your family, to take you away from them, to separate. You know how I told you that I could never leave the military? That I would never have the bond or the relationships with anyone else that I had with my men? Well, I was wrong, I think. Your family has become my family. They are my troops now, and I will protect them at all costs, just as I know they will me. We'll get through this hurricane together, Sloane, no matter what it brings. We all will. We've been through worse. Brighter days are ahead.

All my love,

Adam

I was reading Adam's letter in one of the two UberXs attempting to get this crowd to the airport—in the third row since I was one of the only family members who didn't get carsick. I folded it and looked over at Adam and then out the window at the standstill traffic. "We're never going to make it," I said, gazing up ahead. "There's no way. We're going to miss our flight."

Adam looked down at his phone. "It's nine forty-five. We might make it."

"We take off at eleven fifteen. We're supposed to board in an hour and we're like twenty minutes from the airport in good conditions."

I closed my eyes and took a deep breath. I could hear Caroline instructing the driver from the front seat, though I couldn't be sure what she was saying. She had gotten in this car with AJ, Taylor, Adam, and me, while James had taken Preston with Emerson, Kyle, and Carter. Usually, orchestrating a family trip like this took weeks, if not months. Now we were attempting to pull it off in a couple hours.

"Car!" I called. "Do you need me to reserve us cars from the Palm Beach airport to the marina?"

"No!" she shouted back. "James is dealing with that. And it won't matter if we DON'T GET TO THIS AIRPORT."

Adam laughed behind his hand. As if the poor driver could control the traffic. But maybe he could. Because just a few minutes later, a miracle happened: the traffic cleared.

We made it to the airport at 10:13, right as AJ was saying, "Mommy, my tummy doesn't feel good."

This was not the moment for me to be trapped in the third-row seat. Fortunately, Caroline was on it, and had him to the curbside trash can right in the nick of time.

Emerson, Kyle, James, and Preston had somehow beaten us to the airport and were in front of us in a security line that seemed to hold all the people in the world. I looked at my phone. "We're never going to make it," I said to Adam.

"Hell of a time for James to let his NetJets membership lapse," Caroline said under her breath.

I didn't point out that he could probably no longer afford it since they were getting divorced.

Twenty minutes later, Taylor was crying because he'd tripped over AJ's suitcase, and Carter was having an absolute fit because Kyle was holding her but she wanted Emerson, whose bag had been detained. The only silver lining was that Carter and Kyle had finally made it through security. The same could not be said for the rest of us.

"I told her that they would think that round lotion was a bomb," Caroline said. "I told her, but she didn't listen, and now we're going to miss the plane."

"Nope," Adam said. "We're not missing it. We're not."

Adam was right. After two temper tantrums—one from a now-starving AJ and one from Emerson, which actually made the TSA agent give her back her lotion—we sprinted to the gate and made it aboard just as the doors were closing.

Two hours later, we had arrived in Palm Beach and gone on the world's quickest provision run, filling carts to the brim with food and water so we'd have enough for anyone in town who was stuck like Vivi, Mom, and Jack. Now, five hours later, I leaned back on the comfortable couch inside Caroline's boat as she pulled out of the marina. I put my hands over my face. "I can't believe we made it." I finally felt like I could breathe, which was weird because, in reality, the hard part was just beginning.

The last time I had been on a big boat like this was when Caroline was attempting to shake loose at least a little of my despair from Adam being MIA. Back then, our fate was so very up in the air. Now he was here beside me on the *Starlite Sisters*, holding my hand, making me strong. I leaned into him.

Admittedly, this boat trip wasn't much better than the last one. We hadn't heard from the rest of our family in more than twenty-four hours. We had no idea what was actually happening to them, and no way of finding out. The last time we turned on the Weather Channel was before we left Caroline's apartment, when the eye had been over Peachtree Bluff. There was certainly plenty of flooding, and it had probably made its way into Caroline and Jack's houses, but, from what we could see, not our family's house.

"Surely, they would have stayed at our house, right?" I asked Adam. "They would have thought to move to the highest ground they could find?"

Adam nodded confidently. "Absolutely. This isn't Ansley's first hurricane. And it certainly isn't Jack's."

"I can't ever remember Peachtree flooding like this, though," I said.

"It's because it's the worst possible timing," Adam said. "It's a king tide, so the water was already high."

King tide. I had always thought it was the most beautiful phrase, the tide when the full moon pulled it highest. But now it didn't sound beautiful. It sounded foreboding. I sighed. Caroline was standing several feet away from us, steering confidently as James, Kyle, and Emerson attempted to make the beds while simultaneously wrangling the kids. I'm not sure they had actually noticed Adam and I weren't helping . . . I was hoping they wouldn't for a while.

"And you're sure this is safe?" I asked Caroline for the hundredth time. I didn't think my sister would put all of us in danger on purpose. But I also knew that she would do absolutely anything to get to her daughter. So I was sort of fifty-fifty on the safety front.

"I promise," she said. "The hurricane is moving inland. It will be long gone by the time we get there." She paused. "Don't get me wrong. I'm not promising bright blue sunny skies or anything. But I'm not nosing us into a hurricane."

Well, that was a relief, at least.

Emerson made her way up the few steps into the salon, looking exhausted.

When Caroline saw her, she gasped.

She didn't look *that* bad.

"Emerson! Your audition!" she said.

It was almost as if Caroline had just noticed Emerson was on the trip with us. Hell, maybe she had. I couldn't imagine what she was going through inside. Fear. Anger at Vivi for putting all of us in this situation, frustration with herself for letting Vivi stay, sadness at what might be happening to our home right now. I looked back and forth from Caroline to Emerson, right as a Taylor-sounding, "Daddy!" rang out. Adam got up and smiled. "I believe that's my cue." He headed downstairs.

"What audition?" I asked, looking from Caroline to Emerson and back again. "What's happening?"

Emerson shook her head. "Caroline, I can't believe you even remember that."

"Remember what?" I asked. "I hate when y'all do this." I crossed my arms.

"Someone had an audition for a role on Broadway," Caroline said.

I gasped. "Emerson! You should have stayed! That's huge."

She waved her hand like it was no big deal. But it was a huge deal. "There will be other opportunities," she said lightly.

"I doubt it," Caroline said under her breath.

"Hey!" Emerson plopped down beside me. For a just a second, I could pretend that it was the three of us, on a fun sister trip. I could pretend we were sitting around gossiping about our lives, chatting, making plans. Almost.

"That's a big deal, Em. I'm sorry you're missing that," I said.

She shrugged. "You know, Kyle and I talked about it. We really did. Because who knows what I can actually do to help once we get to Peachtree? But I knew I couldn't stay behind. How could I even audition as distracted as I am right now? I need to know they're okay. That's all that really matters."

It was all that really mattered. I knew that. But it was easy—especially under the sometimes-harsh glow of the spotlight—to lose sight of that. I was proud of her for putting her family first.

"If I can't do anything, fine. But I need to at least try. Knowing we're doing all we can makes me feel better."

"Me too," Caroline said.

I, like my sisters, had felt my tremendous sense of unease dissipate slightly once I knew we were going to Peachtree, once I knew that we were heading there to rescue our family from the storm. But now, out on these unforgiving waters, I was reminded of how very fickle Mother Nature could be. Would we get to Peachtree Bluff safely? The logic in my head said of course we would. We were on a gorgeous, practically brand-new yacht, with an expert captain at the helm, and we were close enough to shore that the Coast Guard could come to us quickly at any moment along this route. But losing my father—and then almost losing Adam—had trained me to prepare for the worst.

I looked over at Caroline, so at ease on the water, and a sadness that she might lose part of what she loved so much flooded me. The boat was in Palm Beach because Caroline was putting it up for sale.

"Do you really have to sell your boat?" I whispered to Caroline. "You love it so much."

She shrugged sadly.

"Oh no," Em said softly.

"I love it," she said. "But it doesn't make sense to keep it. Between my apartment and James's, the Hamptons house, Peachtree Bluff, and the boat, something has to go. So I think the boat makes the most sense. And the Peachtree house." She shrugged. "Besides, there's no way I can afford the boat's maintenance and the storage and all of that."

"I'm sorry, Car," Emerson said.

She smiled. "The divorce is still worth it."

We all laughed.

She rubbed the steering wheel fondly. "And I'll get a little sailboat or something, keep it at Mom's. It might be more fun, really. We can teach all the kids to sail."

She was lying. It could not be more fun than her gorgeous yacht. But it would be nice to teach the kids to sail. I stretched and, deciding I'd put off my parenting duties for long enough, walked back toward the staterooms.

I was following the small voices, but I stopped when I saw James sitting by himself on the end of his bed. His hands were clamped into fists and he was looking down at them. For a minute, I thought he had been hurt. "Are you okay?" I asked quietly, not wanting to startle him.

When he looked up, he had tears in his eyes. "I'm just realizing that I didn't only lose Caroline in this divorce," he said. "I lost all of you too. I lost you, and I put my daughter's life in danger. If it weren't for my mistakes, we wouldn't be in this mess right now. Vivi would be home and safe. Caroline would still love me."

I wanted to scream at him, unload on him, tell him that, yes, this was all his fault. Yes, he had put his daughter's life in danger, broken my sister's heart, and shattered a piece of our family that we would never get back. We would never be whole again in the way we once were. "I wish things had been different for you and my sister. I wish they had been different for all of us."

I smiled through my sadness as little feet ran by the door and up the stairs and Emerson called from the galley, "Who wants snacks?" A chorus of "Me!" erupted. We had bought like fifteen boxes of Teddy Grahams, and the kids could never say no to those.

James looked up. "I know it's over. I know she'll never forgive me. But she wins, Sloane. In the end, she wins. Because I will regret destroying my family—your family—for the rest of my life."

I smiled sadly. It was nice to hear that he was remorseful. Although I had to think that maybe he was saying all this to the wrong sister. "You're wrong, though," I said. "She has forgiven you. If she hadn't, you wouldn't be on this boat right now." I shrugged. "And you didn't destroy our family, James. No offense, but no one can do that."

He nodded, still looking so downtrodden that I felt sad for him. "Maybe," he said. "Maybe you're right. I just wish I could erase the past." He looked up. "You're so lucky," he said. "You're so lucky to have Adam and your family. You're so lucky that you know how much you love each other."

He was right. Adam and I might not have agreed one hundred percent of the time on things like where we should live and precisely what our future should hold. But it didn't matter. I knew now that that didn't mean I should just roll over and give in to anything he wanted, and that was growth for me. But I did know that something like a house didn't matter at the end of the day. Not really.

I squeezed James's knee and got up. "We are lucky. Let's just hope our luck holds out."

I left James and stood in the doorway of the stateroom I was sharing with my family, watching as my husband fluffed the comforter and spread it out over the top of the bed. I walked into the room and locked the door shut behind me. "Hey," he said, smiling.

I put my finger to his mouth and then kissed him. He pulled back and smiled at me. I kissed him again and lifted his shirt over his head, drawing him close enough that I could feel his heartbeat. My heart swelled with love for this man who was always there for me, who I knew was always on my team. As I lay back on the comforter, everything we'd been going through faded into the background. It was just Adam and I and a bright, shining future, stretched out into the distance like the eternal tide before us. And I knew James was right: we were, without a doubt, the lucky ones.

# Ansley: Pretending

*The Day after the Hurricane*

THE PEACHTREE HISTORICAL ASSOCIATION SELLS luminarias each year to raise money for my very favorite annual tradition: the Starlite, Star Bright Festival, which takes place every Christmas Eve. All season long, neighbors and friends line their front walks with the little bags filled with sand and candles. When I look out my window at night, the glow of those candles lining the streets fills me with the most intense sense of peace, togetherness, and community.

Tonight, now, we needed light. It probably hadn't been the safest choice to sleep in sleeping bags on the third floor, but it was what we had chosen. I couldn't bear the thought of sleeping downstairs and waking up to utter and complete pitch blackness. Plus, the water was rising quickly and furiously, and while I prayed it didn't come into the house, I didn't know what was going to happen. We needed high ground. While cyclones were still possible, they were generally less of a threat. And we needed to keep an eye on Vivi and Tyler. The hormones of teenagers were as dangerous as any hurricane. It was my job to make sure it didn't turn into more than that. Honestly, it was sort of a nice distraction.

By nightfall, the wind and rain had finally stopped, but, as I could see from the windows, the water was high. It had reached my front porch, which meant that, in all likelihood, every shop, home, and restaurant in Peachtree Bluff had flooded.

Jack was champing at the bit to get outside, to check on everything. But the first rule of storm safety was that you never, ever went out in floodwaters. Not only could they rush unexpectedly, taking you with them, but they were also bacteria-filled—and live power lines and even sharks had been known to lurk. Plus, the water was *cold*. Really cold.

There was a sense of relief as Vivi, Jack, Tyler, and I, now downstairs, sat around the fire in the living room, welcoming the morning. We were all trying to preserve our phone batteries and had turned them off. Well, not Vivi, of course, whose dead battery had gotten us into this mess in the first place. I turned my phone on quickly. Still no bars. My heart sank. We were fine. We were safe. But I knew Caroline was absolutely panicking.

I wasn't panicking, but I wasn't calm. Yes, we could live off of the Cheerios and granola bars in Sloane's pantry for a few more days. But we were going to be out of water soon. We could drink what we'd put in the bathtubs for flushing the toilets if we had to. But I really, really didn't want to. The thought made my stomach turn.

We all glanced down at our plates of soggy, once-frozen fruit, string cheese, and cold cuts that were definitely going to need to be tossed tomorrow. "As soon as the floodwaters recede," said Jack, "I promise I will go down to the store and load up."

The store, thank goodness, had backup generators, so, as long as they had turned on, the food would be fine.

"When do we think the water will recede?" Vivi asked.

I noticed that Tyler was looking down at his soggy fruit very intently to keep from meeting her eye.

"We're going to be fine," I said, smiling widely at her.

"Grandjack?" she asked.

Jack looked at me, as if deciding whether to tell her the truth. But then Tyler interjected. "It's going to get worse before it gets better, Vivi."

"But it isn't raining anymore," she protested.

He nodded. "I know. But water from neighboring towns will rush in where the rivers meet the sea. Honestly, though, we're better off here than anywhere inland. Here, the water has a place to go, so it will recede quickly. A few days, tops."

"A few days!" she protested. "No power for *days!*"

Tyler laughed. "Probably days until they can even open the bridges to let the power trucks in."

"Okay," I interrupted. "Maybe that's enough truth-telling for one day. What do you think?"

I heard a really loud banging sound on the front door, followed by, "It's just me! Don't worry!"

"Hal?" I asked, standing up. "What are you doing? You're going to get yourself killed!"

With another ripping sound, the front door was free, and I could see that the water had risen to my front porch—where Hal had a kayak tied to the railing—but not over it. The porch itself was dry.

"Are you insane?" I asked, opening the door and motioning for him to come in.

He shivered in the doorway. "Man! It's cold out there!"

"Can I get you something?" I asked. "Sad cold cuts? Depressing fruit?"

He reached into the back zipper pocket of his waxed Barbour jacket. It was meant for ducks, so it had plenty of space for the bottle of wine and the bottle of bourbon he pulled out. "I just wanted to check on y'all," he said.

Jack laughed, standing up now too. "Good man," he said. "How is it out there?"

Before he could answer, I continued my scolding. "You are never supposed to go out in a boat like that in flooding like this!"

He shrugged. "Well, I know, but I had to make sure that no one was clinging to the roof of a car or tree or anything." He grinned. "And y'all didn't provision. I knew you had to be short on booze."

I shook my head, but inside, I was grateful.

"How is it?" Jack repeated.

Hal clapped him on the back, and Jack and I followed him out the front door.

"The water's definitely in your house, man," he said to Jack. "And, I don't know how to say this, but Caroline's house . . ." He shook his head.

"What?" I asked, alarmed.

"The whole side is gone. The windows are shattered; the roof is blown off."

I gasped, putting my hand to my mouth. "The cyclone," I whispered.

"Thank God it didn't come here," Jack said.

That was true, but I still felt sorry for my daughter. She had had so many losses this year.

"We heard it," I said. I shook my head. Jack's house flooded. Caroline's destroyed.

"I'm really sorry to be the bearer of bad news," Hal said, "but if I had to guess, it's a total loss. I know they don't usually let houses be torn down in the Historic District, but I don't really see much choice in this case." He squeezed my arm. "On the bright side, there's only a little bit of water in Sloane Emerson." He paused. "I, um, sort of found the spare key and let myself in. There was a little water at the front door, but I wiped it up with some towels I found. All your inventory is totally fine."

The towels. The beautiful new Leontine towels I'd just had monogrammed for a customer. *Oh well . . .* I exhaled deeply. "Oh, that's amazing," I said. "Just amazing."

"And the deli looks good too, Jack. The door blew out, but there isn't too much water in there, and the roof looks good." He shrugged. "With the concrete floors, you might be looking at replacing a couple baseboards, but nothing serious."

I shook my head. "Hal, seriously? You've been at this all morning?"

He nodded. "Nothing else to do now. The storm has passed. We must rebuild. That's all there is to it."

"What about everything else?"

"The farther you get back from the water, the better it is. Some minor flooding, but the major damage is mostly contained to this block or two, where the cyclones hit."

I shivered with the realization that we were at ground zero.

"Most of the town is in decent shape," Hal continued. "It's a big mess. Lots of debris. But we'll clean it up quickly. We always do."

I looked out beyond the porch railing at how the water seemed to go on forever now. The walkways were completely submerged, and the floating docks had risen almost above the pilings. And yet, strangely, there was such a peace about the town when it was like this, quiet, calm, covered in water. It was almost the feeling of the one or two times I had seen it blanketed in snow. The calm was a ruse, of course. But sometimes pretending got us through the toughest times.

Jack nodded his head toward the kayak. "Can I get in there with you? Paddle down to the store to get some water?"

"And food?" Vivi asked hopefully, which is when I realized she and Tyler were standing—too close together for my liking—in the doorway.

"Sorry, Viv," Jack said. "There's no room in the kayak for food. We won't starve, but we need water."

I exhaled deeply. "Jack . . ."

"We'll be fine, Ansley," Hal said. "Don't you trust us by now?"

I burst out laughing. "Do I trust the man doing the most dangerous thing a person can do in a flood? No, forgive me, but I do not. Jack, as your wife, I am asking you to please not do this."

He rolled his eyes at Hal. "When she asks 'as my wife,' what she means is that if I don't listen to her, she's not going to be my wife much longer. I guess I'd better stay put."

"Hey, how are Kimmy and my parents?" Tyler asked.

"They're good," Hal said. "Sent me out here to make sure you were okay." He paused. "Hey, I can take you back there if you want."

Tyler and Vivi shared a smile. "I just don't think it's safe," Vivi said.

"Better safe than sorry," Tyler said, shrugging. I could tell from the looks of him that he was the kind of boy who took plenty of chances. I wasn't sure how thrilled I was about my granddaughter quite clearly being one of them. But, well, he had been sort of nice to have around. He'd taken our minds off of things quite a bit. And he certainly was adorable. I could see why she liked him. And he did have nice manners. I guessed I couldn't complain too much.

Jack smiled at me. Tyler was my responsibility now. I couldn't let him go. And judging from the way my granddaughter was looking at him, I was pretty sure I wasn't the only one.

# Caroline: Game Plan

WHEN I LOOK BACK ON my life, I know already that these days will feel like the longest part of it. James and I had taken shifts driving the boat for the first twenty-four hours, but we docked in Fernandina Beach to get a few hours of actual sleep. When he had brought up my taking a break, I said, "I will never be able to sleep. There's no point in even trying."

I was wrong. The minute my head hit the pillow in my stateroom, I was out cold. I woke up in the exact position in which I fell asleep, so I'm pretty sure I didn't move for nine hours straight. But the good thing about boat travel was that everything you needed was right there. Life went on all around you. So, the minute I woke up, we could get back to sea despite the fact that Sloane was making breakfast and AJ was playing games on Adam's iPad and Preston and Carter were singing at the top of their lungs with Taylor leading the charge.

I let James take the helm while I ate, but as Starlite Island finally came into view in the distance, I pushed him aside. "I'm sorry," I said. "I have to do something. I'm losing my mind."

James pulled out the radio. "*Starlite Sisters* to Dockmaster Dan," he said. He paused to listen. Nothing but static.

I eyed him, and he shrugged. "I don't know. I thought I'd try just in case." He paused. "Car, it has to be said: we have to be prepared that the town dock might be destroyed."

I looked at him and said, dead seriously: "Then I'll swim to shore." I meant it wholeheartedly. After almost four days of not hearing one word about the well-being of my child, there was nothing that could stop me.

We could see, as we approached from the water, that there was debris everywhere, and the boardwalk was heavily damaged. I squinted, trying to make out a long enough stretch of undamaged planks where I could dock.

James pointed. "Over there. The whole right side looks fine."

He was right. I knew I had to dock because, well, James wasn't that good at it, and it was a big, tricky boat. But all I wanted to do was jump off the bow and run. I could see that the floodwaters had receded, but the dirty water lines on the buildings on the waterfront showed us that they had been high. Really high. Beyond the partially crushed dock, I could see large puddles and that everything was damp. But it was fine. I knew enough to know that the water would be highest at the sound and lower as you went inland. I could get to my mom's house, no problem. I slid the massive boat side-to on the dock and called, "Get the lines!" I wasn't sure anyone knew how, but I didn't care.

James called, "Caroline, don't run! You have to watch your step."

But I couldn't stop. I still held the sprint record at Peachtree Bluff High. And, as I jumped off the boat and took off toward Mom's house, I was pretty sure I beat my time.

My senses had become hyperactive, and as I ran, I realized that total destruction is something TV can never get right. You can see the big, mangled piles of debris on the screen, the houses gutted, burnt, and discarded as easily as a forgotten toy. Occasionally, you might hear the wails of someone who has lost everything, maybe even a person they love.

But you cannot smell the damp, musty scent of demolition, the burnt, crackling wood ablaze from electrical fires and mis-installed generators. We are born, raised, trained to like pleasant, soft, light, floral smells. Fresh breezes, blooming buds. Peachtree Bluff, a place whose scent generally resembled springtime freedom, now smelled positively decaying. And it had only been a few days since the hurricane hit.

The air was so thick, damp, and heavy that it actually lay over me, making the semicold weather feel practically arctic. I pulled my coat closer to me and sprinted with all my might toward the place I had spent my childhood summers, where I had curled up on the porch swing and read books with my grandmother, where, years later, I had painted walls with my mother, where I had sulked and whined, where I had known real, true devastation—but never panic deep in my bones, lodged in my soul, quite like this.

I dodged downed power lines and avoided loose boards, shutters, roof shingles, entire trees, and a small boat sitting demurely in the middle of Main Street as though that were where it belonged. I noticed them. But I never *saw* them, never saw any of it. All I could think about, all I knew, was that I had to get to my daughter. When I reached the house, the gate I normally would have opened was gone, and the bricks that used to form walkways and flower beds were uprooted and strewn about. Pieces of furniture were still tied to the front porch, where we had left them. The downstairs door and windows were unboarded—a good sign, I thought. I flung the front door open and screamed, "Vivi!" It was an unnatural, guttural sound, something that resembled my voice only vaguely.

Footsteps flew, but they weren't Vivi's. I knew that, in the way a mother does, in the way she recognizes every imprint of her child, in the way that each movement, cough, sound, and smile is a symbol, a signal of something deeper. "Mom," I whispered, as I saw her on the landing of the stairs.

It was then and only then that I burst into tears. For days, I had stayed strong, kept it together. But when I saw Mom, I knew everything was going to be okay. She was dressed in what looked to be a relatively clean pair of black yoga leggings and a white cotton sweater that hit her midthigh, her hair pulled back in a ponytail. A fire roared in the fireplace, making the front room, at least, feel cozy. I knew then that Vivi was okay. If she wasn't, this fire wouldn't be here; Mom wouldn't be clean and calm.

She ran to me and engulfed me in a hug. Then she pulled back and put her hands on my cheeks. "What are you doing here? How did you even get here?"

I knew her well enough to know that she was having visions of me bribing guards at the bridge checkpoint to get in here. But before I could answer, I heard, "Mom!" And there they were, those footsteps I recognized, the ones I knew so well. My formerly distant and withdrawn daughter practically flew to me, going limp in my arms.

I pulled her back after the longest hug of my life and put my hands on each of her cheeks like my own mother had just done to me, studying her. "Are you okay?"

She nodded. "I'm fine. I really am. Everything is okay."

I pulled her to me again, realizing then that I was crying. My baby was okay. My baby was alive. Everything that had happened these past few months faded into the background. All that mattered was that she was safe.

Only then did James appear, panting in the doorway. "How are you so fast?" he asked as Vivi ran to him.

Mom squeezed me to her. "Again, I have to ask: How are you here?"

"The boat," James said, out of breath.

I wiped my eyes and looked at him dully. I'd been telling him for years he was getting out of shape. Maybe now he believed me.

"Brilliant," Vivi said.

"Is everyone okay?" I asked breathlessly.

"We don't know," Mom said sadly. "We are. Our family is. But we just don't know. Is it low tide? How's the flooding?"

I nodded. "It's low tide, but it looks good. Even at high tide, I don't think the water will get back up to the houses." My daughter snuck back underneath my arm. I had so much to say, so much to impart. But, for now, all I could feel was thankful that she was here safe.

"James," I said, "take them down to the boat."

"We need to start helping," Mom said.

I shook my head. "You need a shower, a meal, and sleep." I paused. "Plus, really, Mom, from what I could see, our street is the worst one."

"But . . ."

I put my hand up. "You cannot help this town until you've helped yourself. You know that."

I clapped my hands together, just as Jack straggled down the stairs with a boy I'd never seen behind him. I looked at my daughter warily. "Jack," I said, hugging him. "Thank you for keeping them safe."

"Thank Tyler, Kimmy's brother," he said. "He's the one who rescued your daughter."

I turned to him. "Thank you. Truly. There is a shower and a hot meal waiting for you."

He half grinned with a dimple that made me know that my daughter was done for. "Thank you so much, ma'am."

*Ma'am . . . Ugh. How did I get to be a ma'am?*

I looked around. As much as I wanted to be with my daughter, there was a small part of me that felt a little bit afraid to be. She could have died, and it had been her fault. She had put herself, my mother, and my stepfather—and, evidently, this adorable Tyler person—in extreme danger. I had never faced a parenting challenge quite like this one, one where I was torn between utter and all-encompassing relief that she was okay and pure rage that she had put herself and everyone else in such a horrible position. I had to talk to James before I talked to her. We had to agree on her punishment together. None of this I'm-in-trouble-with-Mom-so-I'll-run-to-Dad stuff.

I stepped back out on the front porch and looked around. The docks all the way down the street were battered, busted, and broken, but I had a feeling that those were the least of our worries. The debris in front of me was so thick it barely looked as if there was a street at all, and I marveled that I had just avoided it as I ran to the house. I finally focused on what was around me and realized that part of the putrid smell was coming from decaying fish, which I presumed had been washed up in the floodwaters and gotten caught here. Poor fish. Poor Mom.

"I haven't been out yet," Mom said. "There were still a few inches of water when we went to sleep last night, and I didn't want to risk it. But Hal said your house is really bad."

I nodded. I knew I should feel . . . something. But all I could muster was pure euphoria that my family was okay. "James, please take Mom, Vivi, Jack, and Tyler to the boat. I'll go check on everything and I'll meet you soon."

"Not by yourself," Mom said.

I rolled my eyes. "Mom, I'm fine."

She put her hands up, acquiescing.

Okay. Game plan. Start at my end of the street. Assess my house, then Jack's, then Mom's. I was grateful I had thought to wear my knee-high rain boots, because every few feet I stepped into water up to my midcalf. Once I got to my house, I pulled my key out of my back pocket and used it to help loosen the screws in the board that we'd covered the front door with. Then I put the key in the lock and pushed the swollen wood hard until the door finally opened. I stepped over the threshold, surprised that it wasn't as dark inside as I had expected. I looked to the right and gasped, my heart thudding up in my throat. It looked like a dollhouse, like someone had cut out the entire side next to the chimney. I put my hand over my mouth, looking out at what used to be a window into the totally open side of the street. Nothing Mom could have said could possibly have prepared me for this.

Shattered glass covered everything. The furniture was drenched, rugs ruined, pillows and accessories in random places around the house—I assumed from where wind and rain had strewn them. It was much too much to take in all at once. I looked straight ahead again. Then back to the right. I tried to picture the beautifully appointed beach house this had once been, but somehow, I couldn't.

I was in shock. I couldn't panic or cry as I walked, gingerly, back through the dining room, where china and wineglasses were shattered all over the floor, into the kitchen. The kitchen was long and narrow and had, at one time, run the length of the back of the house. The window was blown out, and the right side was essentially gone, only a few jagged, busted boards sticking out haphazardly. But to the left, it looked as if it was an ordinary day. Looking from one side to the other made me feel like I was in two totally different worlds.

And how did I not feel more upset by this? Was it because I had just faced a real problem—not knowing whether my daughter and mother were safe? This felt trivial in the face of that. Even still, shouldn't a person have some reaction to her house being destroyed?

I turned and started walking up the staircase, which wove up the right side of the house. I was on the second step when I heard a voice I vaguely recognized yelling, "Caroline! No! Stop!"

I stood, stock-still, my hand on the banister, looking down to see Hippie Hal running toward me. I stepped back down.

"It's okay," I said. "I'm okay."

He shook his head. "You're about to not be okay. The power lines split and are hanging through the roof. I'm pretty sure they're still live. A few more steps and you—and likely this entire house—would be up in flames."

I looked up and put my hand to my mouth. "Oh my God." Thick black wires frayed on the ends looped precariously around what was once a ceiling beam but was now split in half, their gold-and-copper innards looking like fangs. I hoped I would have noticed those wires, but in my shell-shocked state, I'm not sure. The thought that I had come so close to danger made me shiver. Mom was right. I shouldn't have been so cavalier; I shouldn't have come alone.

I felt a sudden need to get out of here, to get my family off this island, my people out of harm's way. If they had evacuated, we wouldn't be here now. There was nothing we could do with no power, internet, or cell service. We needed to get back on the boat. We could go back to Palm Beach. Fly home to New York. Anything. I had to get out of here.

"I've already assessed the damage and taken the photos," Hal said, breaking me out of my tailspin.

I shook my head. "I'm sorry. What?"

Hal shrugged. "What else was I supposed to do?"

"Um, I don't know. Try not to die in the rushing floodwaters maybe?"

He grinned. "Mission accomplished. I'll send the photos to

you so you can get them to the insurance company." He pointed at the space in my house where a wall used to be. "I think you might have a claim there."

It was the exact wrong reaction, the total opposite of the one I should have had, but I burst out laughing. Hal joined me. We were interrupted by James's "Oh my God. Oh my *God.*"

He walked from room to room, continuing this refrain.

"Should I let him go up the steps?" Hal whispered, setting us both off again.

James returned to the entryway, where water the rug had been holding was now seeping into what were supposed to be my waterproof shoes. He looked totally shell-shocked. "That!" I said, pointing to James. "That's the reaction a person *should* have when they realize that their house is totally and completely destroyed. What is wrong with me?"

"How much time you got?" Hal winked at me. "It is my opinion that it's not salvageable at this point," he said. "I tracked down Mrs. McClasky, and she said that—in this rare case only—she will support you if you want to tear it down and start from scratch."

I loved how he said it, like I didn't know he and the President of the Historical Association were secret lovers. *Please, Hal. I wasn't born yesterday.*

"Oh, good. Glad you tracked her down." I winked at him. "But why on earth is she riding out a hurricane? What is wrong with you people?"

"She needs to be boots on the ground to make decisions quickly," Hal said. "We have no idea when we'll get power back, and we can start putting things in motion way ahead of everyone getting back. We have time to get calm and centered before every-one flies in here freaking out."

"So we have to tear it down?" James asked. I had almost for-gotten he was standing there. He tried to put his arm around me, to comfort me, I think. I took a step to the side. I had no interest in being comforted by him.

"No, you don't have to," Hal said. "But it's an option, I think, which shocks me as much as anyone."

"I don't want to tear it down!" James declared.

Again, why was he so worked up while I was so damn calm? We usually went the other way.

"Well, it's my house," I retorted. "I was going to sell it anyway."

"What?" James looked shocked and devastated all at once. "You were going to sell this house? I thought you wanted to keep it."

Most people would have pretended to walk away or distract themselves with something else. But not Hal. He just stood there, as if supervising the fight.

"No. I don't have a single positive memory in this house. You bought this, if you'll remember, to convince me you still loved me after the Edie Fitzgerald scandal. I don't need to remember that." I put my finger to my temple. "It's burnt in my brain."

"But that's why I want you to keep it," he said. "So you can re-member that even though you can't forgive me, we're still a family."

My blood was boiling now. "Right," I said, still calm. "It's all my fault that I can't forgive you. Forget your part."

He sighed. "I can't do this with you today, Caroline. You're right, I'm wrong. You're perfect, I'm a monster. I get it."

I crossed my arms. I wasn't going to argue with him.

"I'm sorry if it shocks me that you want to sell the house. I like thinking of you here, in this place you love, with our children, that's all."

I wanted to roll my eyes, but I refrained. "That's fine. I will be here, at Mom's house, with our children. So don't worry."

"Whatever you decide," Hal chimed in, "you might want to contact your insurance company right away. Or, if you can get me the information, I can do it for you." He snorted. "Once we have any way to contact people in the outside world, that is."

"Who did you insure it with?" James asked.

I racked my brain, unsure what he meant. "I'm sorry. What? What do you mean who did I insure it with? I would assume it's still insured with the same person it has always been."

James got very still, and I could feel my heart starting to race. "Caroline, I've already transferred the deed to you. You signed the papers. Remember?"

"Yes," I practically spat. "I remember. But what does that have to do with the insurance?"

"When I gave it to you, I canceled the insurance, obviously."

"Obviously?" I shouted. "Obviously? How is that obvious, James? How could you do that?"

"Everyone knows you need insurance on a property!" he shouted back at me. "How could you own a house and not have insurance?"

I looked at Hal. He put his hands up. "I can't help you on this one, hon."

That was when it hit me. I didn't feel sad about this house because I never wanted it. It was a symbol, a great metaphor for my marriage, which was a flooded, shattered pile of garbage that needed to be taken out. It *was* being taken out, thank God. I wanted it to be gone. At least this house had probably protected my daughter and had saved my family from a deadly tornado—the exact opposite of what my marriage had done.

"How much do you think it would cost to fix it to put it on the market?" I asked Hal.

He shrugged. "I don't know, Caroline . . ."

"Ballpark," I said more harshly than I'd meant to.

"Two, three hundred thousand dollars?"

My stomach gripped. I felt sick. "And to tear it down?"

He squeezed my forearm as he said, "Twenty-five or thirty."

I probably could have gotten enough for it in the sale to justify fixing it back up. But not only did I not have that kind of cash, I couldn't bear the thought of spending the next year or two of my life going through the process. "Tear it down," I said to Hal as I turned to walk out the door. "Send me the bill."

In retrospect, if I had been this decisive about ending my marriage, we all would have been better off.

# Vivi: The Right Girl

THE WORST PART WAS THE waiting. The waiting for the hurricane to be over, the waiting for the flooding to recede. The waiting for the power trucks—which were now all over town!—to come. And, worst of all, the waiting for my mom to punish me. Yeah, I knew she was happy that I was safe and everything. But this was my mom, Caroline Beaumont, who took no prisoners. Prisoner. Maybe that was the right word, because I figured that's what I was going to be pretty soon.

I was sucking up as hard as I could. I took the last shower on the boat so if we were out of hot water, I was the one who had to deal with it. I played annoying games with the kids for hours on end to keep them safe and entertained. I went with Mom, Gransley, Sloane, and Emerson to Gransley's store. We mopped and opened all the doors and windows and moved everything back where it went.

"It looks beautiful, Gransley!" I said, rehanging the Christmas garland over one of the display cases. "Maybe even better than before." I was trying to be super, overkill positive, hoping that would make my punishment less severe. I wasn't sure if it was working. Mom was in a weird mood. She wasn't mad, but she wasn't happy. I didn't know how to read her when she was like this. It was scary. Really scary.

"It still smells a little musty," Gransley said.

"Yeah, but I don't see any mold," Sloane said. "So that's good."

Mold was something we all knew about now. Because it was already springing up everywhere downstairs at Jack's house. He said we were really lucky that it wasn't hot because the heat would have made the mold come in faster and worse. Adam, Hal, Jack, and Tyler had started cutting out the wet, moldy parts of the plaster. Hal said it was like cancer. You had to keep it from spreading.

But there was no power, so they were cutting it with hand saws and banging it out with hammers since they couldn't use power tools. Gransley was freaking out because they didn't have the right safety equipment and were just wearing masks that Hal had for varnishing boats. She kept saying words like "asbestos" and "mesothelioma," and Jack would say stuff back like, "Ansley, this house was built seventy-five years before asbestos was used. We'll be fine."

Now, in Gransley's store, trying to be the sunshine, I said, "Once the power comes back on, I bet the smell will go away really quickly. Oh! I know!" I exclaimed, ever the helpful, happy granddaughter who was hoping her mother wouldn't kill her. "Let's light some candles and put some dryer sheets around to make it smell nicer." It was still really hard to get used to not having power. I'd walk into a room and flip the light switch, or realize I was cold and go to turn up the heat. But I was sleeping on the boat now. With hot water! And electricity! And TV! I wasn't really watching TV because I was hanging out with my family. But knowing it existed was comforting.

And, second miracle, Mr. Warner, who owned the boatyard, had ridden out the hurricane too. And he had gotten Jack's boat out. The boat was fine, and Mr. Warner said he could put the *Miss Ansley* back in the water today. Jack was making me learn how to turn on the generator and use all the power and battery switches. I was never going to run away again, but it was still a good idea. So now, between Jack's boat and ours, there would be water and power all around. It was kind of funny, because in New York I felt like people got stuff done by being important and powerful. In Peachtree Bluff, it was just neighbors helping neighbors. It didn't matter if you came in on your yacht or a rowboat. Everybody was friends.

I was busying myself with the candles and dryer sheets—realizing that it's putting them on the blowing air vents that makes the room smell good, which obviously wasn't going to work right now—when Tyler walked in. He smiled at me, and I smiled back. It was kind of cold out, but he was still a little sweaty. "I think we got all the mold. At least, we got what we could see. And we hauled all the rugs and the ruined things out to the street," he said.

"I can't thank you enough," Gransley said. She smiled at him. He was playing this just right. If he wanted my family to like him, it was working.

"Hey," he said casually. "I'm going to help Kimmy and Adam get some tables set up. She's bringing down produce, and Adam and Jack are going to donate whatever's in the store in case people are running out of supplies."

"That's a really great idea," Sloane said.

"Do you think, um, you could spare Vivi to help?" he asked.

I smiled at him, and my stomach turned. He was so cute. Did that mean he liked me? Or did he really need help? And was Mom going to let me go?

"Fine by me," Mom said nonchalantly, not even looking up from the box of ornaments she was hanging on the Christmas tree in the corner. There it was again, that very un-Mom-like attitude. Did she even care that I had lived? Did she wish I had been swept away in the floodwaters?

"Okay," I said. "I'll be back soon to check on y'all. Gransley, do you need anything while I'm out?"

"Actually," she said, "if you can bring me some meat, vegetables, and rice, I'll make a thick, chunky soup, and we can serve anyone who stops by Peachtree Provisions tomorrow."

"Will do," Tyler said as we walked out.

I felt butterflies at being alone with him.

"My mom is acting weird, right?" I asked.

"Well, I don't know your mom, so I don't know. But, yeah, if I'd run away and made my family get stuck on an island in a hurricane, then my mom would probably be punishing me pretty hard right now."

"And instead she's just letting me run around town with you."

He grinned at me. "Oh, is that a reward?"

*Well, it certainly isn't a punishment.*

"Ugh," I said. "Maybe that's why she's doing it. Having to be around you is just awful."

He laughed. "Maybe this situation is bigger than your punishment. You know? Like there's so much damage and people are hurting, so it doesn't matter."

A thought crossed my mind for the first time. "What about Christmas?" I almost whispered. "What about the Claus Crawl and the Christmas Market and the downtown open houses?" I gasped again. "And Starlite, Star Bright and the candlelight tour!"

"Well, the candlelight tour should go over without a hitch."

I hit his arm slowly, lingering. I really just wanted to touch him. The feel of my skin on his skin was electrifying.

"You know what? I think if everyone starts coming back in the next couple days and we all work really hard to get the town cleaned up, it might be fine," Tyler said. "The streets behind the waterfront all seem basically okay besides minor stuff."

I looked around at the debris littering the streets. At least the Christmas cottage, which was across from Jack and Adam's store, had been saved.

"Hey," I asked Tyler. "I'm just realizing that I literally know nothing about you. Where are you from?"

He laughed. "We've covered nearly dying together. Time to back it up?"

I smiled.

"We lived all over with my dad being in the military. But, if I had to say I was 'from' anywhere, it would be New York. We moved here a few months ago."

My mouth dropped.

"You are? *I'm* from New York."

"Yes, I know. But I don't think we're from the same New York."

"What does that mean?"

"Well, I didn't live in a fancy apartment or go to a fancy school. I don't know any celebrities."

"I don't know celebrities," I shot back. That wasn't strictly true. I did go to school with a few celebrities' kids, and I did technically know their parents from different parties and school events. But we weren't like friends or anything. I mean, they were friends with my parents . . . And my aunt was a celebrity, and I knew a lot of her friends . . . Okay. Fine. I knew celebrities.

He shook his head. "If we had met in New York, you wouldn't have even talked to me."

*But I would have looked at you*, I thought.

He stopped in front of Jack's store and pulled up one of the tables from the sidewalk and opened it, his muscles rippling through his shirt. I didn't have a defense, and, to be honest, I didn't know if I would have talked to him if we'd met in New York. But we hadn't met in New York. We'd met in Peachtree. And I had to think that Lake, with his trust fund and his designer shoes, probably wouldn't have weathered a hurricane quite like Tyler. He wouldn't have spent his day knocking out plaster and cleaning up debris. He wouldn't be helping his community like this. He might have asked his dad to write a check. But he wouldn't be out here, floodwater squishing in his shoes and mud under his fingernails.

Everything I thought I wanted had changed in the last few days. Everything. My house was destroyed, and that was fine. Because we had made it through the storm. My parents were getting divorced, but they were still here together, both loving me. I did the worst thing I could think of—ran off and made my grandparents miss their trip—and they risked their lives while the rest of my family spent days at sea to come find me, to make sure I was okay. You couldn't buy that stuff. And I knew for sure that Tyler didn't care one bit whether my outfit came from Bergdorf or Walmart. He was the only person I'd met in a long time who I knew, for sure, liked me just because I was me. Well, I mean, if he liked me, that is. No. I knew he liked me. I just didn't know if he wanted to make out with me inside the Christmas cottage like I was currently dreaming of doing with him.

"Look," I said. "I don't know what would have happened if we'd met in New York. But I know for sure that I'm glad we did meet. You saved me, and what's even more amazing is that you kept me calm during this really crazy time. I wouldn't have gotten through any of this without you."

He looked up at me and smiled, still holding the table leg, his hair falling over one eye. I bit my lip. He wasn't mad.

I wanted to step closer to him, but before I could, "Hey there, granddaughter," rang out behind me.

I turned to smile. Grandjack. We had sort of skipped over the huge heart-to-heart we probably should have had about his being my real grandfather. And, really, I kind of wanted to. He'd saved me. He hadn't yelled at me. He hadn't once told me that I'd ruined his trip or cost him more money than I could even think about. And now he'd called me "granddaughter." It was . . . well, it was cool of him, was what it was. I could sort of picture him as a teenager now, and I knew why Gransley must have liked him. "Hi, Grandjack," I said quietly, not wanting to take my eyes off of Tyler.

"You are just the girl I need. I'm trying to decorate this Christmas tree in Peachtree Provisions, and I know it looks bad, but I don't know how to fix it. And I don't need Gransley in here making fun of me."

"You've come to the right place," I said, turning to follow him. Mom had made me help her decorate all of Sloane Emerson New York before we left for Thanksgiving. I mean, that was a little different, obviously. It was more like decorating giant flocked white trees with gold and silver matching ornaments. But still . . . I knew how to decorate stuff.

I followed Grandjack to the door. When I turned to look back at Tyler, he was still looking at me. He winked, and my heart about burst into a million pieces. And I realized that I couldn't think of anywhere I'd rather be right now than in Peachtree Bluff with Tyler—even a luxury cruise to Australia.

# Emerson: Peachtree Bluff Magic

## *Eight Days Post-Hurricane*

I HAD ALWAYS BELIEVED THAT I would love Peachtree Bluff no matter what, but I was starting to doubt that. I knew I shouldn't complain. We were on a beautiful boat with power and water, but there were so many of us under one roof in such a tiny space that things were starting to feel claustrophobic. At least our cell service had come back. The bridge had opened the morning before, and we had all sat on what was left of the boardwalk in utter awe, with fifty or so other Peachtree Bluffians, clapping and cheering as dozens of power and cleanup trucks from places as far away as Ohio roared through downtown. Now, everywhere you looked, men and women on power poles, excavators, and trash trucks were ridding the streets of debris. And, in the most adorable and Peachtree Bluff–ish move, the town trucks were full of men and women rehanging the dozens of Christmas wreaths on the vintage-looking light posts and resetting the giant Christmas tree in its place of glory once all the debris had been scraped away.

As we were sitting on the sidewalk earlier in the day watching the transformation take place, Hippie Hal clapped Mayor Bob—who was standing in front of me—on the shoulder. "Really, bud? The wreaths and the tree take priority?"

He smiled. "People need to come home to Christmas." I couldn't have said it better myself.

Carter, as could be expected, hadn't been sleeping well. Which meant, in turn, I hadn't been sleeping well. And, tonight, with the noise of the power trucks and water crews and street sweepers—all of whom were working on a twenty-four-hour schedule to get the town back into shape—I couldn't imagine how anyone could sleep. Not that I was complaining. I was so grateful. In fact, as I stared up at the ceiling in the boat, Kyle breathing rhythmically beside me, I was focusing on all those blessings, hoping it would help me sleep. Just as I felt myself drifting off, Carter cried out, "Mama!"

I groaned.

Truthfully, in our regular lives, Kyle did more than his fair share of getting up with Carter at night. So, while I wasn't working and had nowhere to be, I thought this would be a good time to return the favor. Plus, I'd never been able to sleep well on a boat. Kyle, on the other hand, slept like a . . . well, I thought, looking at Carter as I scooped her up onto on my hip, not a baby. A sloth, maybe. No, that wasn't flattering. I glanced back down at him. That gorgeous man could never be compared to a sloth.

"What's the matter, baby girl?" I whispered as I walked up the few steps to the salon. But I knew what was wrong. We were all so keyed up, so anxious. And Kyle and I had been debating: What was the right thing to do? Did we try to go home to LA? Could

Peachtree Perk LA run successfully without him for that long? Did we stay until Christmas? Carter rested her head on my shoulder and yawned as I paced the beautiful salon.

I spied Caroline's dark head coming out of her room. "I'm so sorry," I said. "Did I wake you?"

She shook her head. "No. I just couldn't sleep." She pointed. "All those poor people working around the clock."

I nodded. "It's amazing. I know there's no power, but by the time people get back here, it's going to look like nothing ever happened."

I sat down on the sofa, and Caroline followed suit. She sighed. "What?"

"I still haven't punished Vivi. I don't know if we should go home to New York. I don't know if I'm going to blow the sale on this boat by keeping it here for longer . . ." She paused. "And why the *hell* did my idiot husband think that I would know I was supposed to replace the insurance on the house? I had no idea!"

I could feel my eyes widen. Caroline did have a lot of balls in the air right now. She—in her silk gown and matching robe— curled up with a throw on the sofa and reached her hands out to my daughter. Carter went to her instantly, with no complaints. She was the easiest child. She was calm and relaxed. And, while she wouldn't go to just anyone (which I was glad of, really), it was like she knew who her family was.

Caroline sighed. "It still brings me joy," she whispered.

"Your marriage?"

She rolled her eyes. "No. The boat. You keep it if it still brings you joy, right?"

We were both laughing when I turned to see Sloane, bleary-eyed in an oversized T-shirt and boxers, walking into the salon. "I sensed y'all were talking without me, and I got FOMO."

"Oh, good!" Caroline said. "I'm glad you're up because, since I couldn't sleep, I've been doing some thinking. I have the best, best idea."

Sloane and I groaned simultaneously. Caroline's "good ideas" were always huge, terrifying, and impractical at best. Although, truth be told, they mostly ended up being genius and life-changing. Kyle always said I should be more open-minded about them, so I figured I'd try to practice now.

"My house was valuable, but the lot, not so much," Caroline continued, nonplussed by our protests as usual. "You and Adam should buy it. Then you can build whatever you want there."

"Caroline . . ." Sloane started. Then she stopped and raised her eyebrow. We were so practiced at shooting Caroline down before we eventually acquiesced. But this, I had to admit, was a really good idea.

"Right?" Caroline said, smiling. "It's a good idea. It's not even a crazy idea. Y'all can't even argue with me."

"But what about you?" Sloane asked. "Where does that leave you?"

She shrugged. "It leaves me in the same damn place. I'm screwed either way. Seriously, totally screwed. If you at least got something you wanted out of it, it would make me feel better."

I smiled at my sister. This was a really, really nice idea. She had them sometimes. "I mean, I don't know what Adam will think," Sloane said thoughtfully. "But I will definitely run it by him." I felt butterflies welling up in my stomach—that would be the perfect solution to both of their problems. I would do more than run it by him. I would do my best to talk him into it.

I saw a figure then pacing outside on the boardwalk, illuminated by the moonlight. The town was still mostly boarded up, besides Sloane Emerson and Peachtree Provisions. It was eerie out there, so dark and desolate. It looked like a movie set of a postapocalyptic town. I peered out at the boardwalk and then pointed.

"Mom's out there," I said. "Should we go check on her?"

"Should we, Carty?" Caroline looked down at my daughter, who nodded and popped her thumb in her mouth.

I walked out first, my eyes adjusting to the dark night. Although it could only be so dark in Peachtree Bluff. The way the stars and moon reflected off the water created the most peaceful glow, even when the world around us was, as it felt, totally falling apart. Mom smiled when she saw me. Her hair was in a ponytail, and she was wearing the cutest pink patterned pajamas.

"Whatcha doing?" I asked, putting my arm around her as Sloane and Caroline came up behind me.

"Just worrying."

"The town is going to be fine, Mom. The cleanup crews are nearly finished, and it almost looks normal—"

"I'm worried about y'all," she interrupted.

"Us?" Caroline asked. "Why are you worried about us?"

"You have lives to attend to, places to be, towns and homes and businesses. I don't want you to feel stuck here."

"I don't think we feel stuck, Mom," I said. Although I had just been contemplating the right thing to do.

"Definitely not, Mom," Caroline said. "Don't worry about us. We'll go when we need to go."

"Promise?"

I nodded.

Mom reached out to take Carter from Caroline. There really was nothing that could soothe a worried soul quite like a small, contemplative child. I sat down on one of the few boardwalk benches that were still intact. They were all bolted to the dock, but even still, most hadn't been a match for the gale-force winds.

"Don't you think Sloane and Adam should build a house on my ruined lot?" Caroline asked.

Mom's eyes went wide with excitement. I wasn't sure if it was over the idea of getting to build and decorate a new house or because Caroline had found a solution to a big problem.

She nodded. "I think that's a great idea. But, Caroline . . . what about you?"

Caroline smiled and looked slowly from one of us to the other. "The house is going to be torn down, and I don't want to rebuild." She shrugged. "Without insurance, I don't think I have the money to rebuild even if I wanted to. So I just want to stay at our house when I come visit Peachtree. Our old house."

I took my sister's hand.

"You know, I depended on James for everything for a long time," she continued. "I worked and worried to have a husband who would take care of me. But now Sloane Emerson is going well, and I truly believe we can make the stores even better." She paused and locked eyes with me. "I think it's time that I start depending on myself for a change."

I put my hand up, and she gave me a high five. "Right on, sister," I said. I was proud of her. Even after the affair, I assumed that Caroline would always stay with James. She might not be as happy as she deserved to be, but she would stay because her lifestyle was so glamorous. I had felt so badly for her because, once I found Kyle, I knew for certain that I would give up anything—*anything*—to feel that kind of all-consuming, can't-live-without-you love. It was better than any private plane, any once-in-a-lifetime vacation.

It made me proud that my sister was giving herself a second chance. It made me happy that she was opening herself up to find the kind of happiness that I had.

Mom smiled. If anyone knew about suddenly, fiercely having to learn what it meant to rely on yourself, it was Mom. She had rebuilt her life step by step. "So how am I going to tell Jack that I want to move back into our house?" Mom asked. Sloane gasped. I laughed.

Of course she wanted to move back to her house. It was our house, *the* house, the place where everything in our lives had happened. None of us answered, just letting her question float out into the night. Caroline finally broke the silence. "Mom, Jack knows you better than anyone. Maybe even us. I have to think that he already knows."

I nodded in agreement, feeling my heart swell. I knew what it was to feel like that, to love someone in a way that felt like you had known them forever, maybe even longer than time, to be able to read their thoughts even if sometimes they couldn't read yours. Looking out across the dark water at the island that had practically raised my sisters and me, I realized something all at once. Yes, I had been considering marriage. But I knew now that, just like Jack had done for Mom, Kyle had definitively broken down every wall that I had ever built around my heart. I was ready.

"I think I'm going to ask Kyle to marry me," I said out into the night, to no one in particular.

Mom and Caroline shared a glance before Caroline said, "Ew, Emerson. That is so tacky. Please don't do that."

"Yeah," Mom chimed in. "Plus, he's been wanting to marry you for years. Why would you steal his moment from him?"

I crossed my arms. "Geez. I didn't expect you two to be so provincial." I looked at Sloane, hoping someone would be on my side. "Don't come over here," she said. "I think that would be the most selfish thing you've ever done. You don't get to swoop in and be the hero because you suddenly decide something that Kyle has known for years."

I was a little incensed—and surprised they didn't think this was a great idea—but stomping away wasn't really an option. Where would I go? It was boat one or boat two, and they were very close together. "Let's just put a pin in this," I said. "I think you're all in a mood."

Caroline laughed. "Nope. Not in a mood. Literally not ever going to change my mind about this."

I rolled my eyes. Well, we'd see about that. Was it right for Kyle and me to get married? So much of the future was un-known—I didn't even know when we'd go back to LA. It was less than two weeks until Christmas, and I wasn't filming. I didn't have any auditions. I couldn't think of a great reason why I should go back to California. But still. Was it ridiculous to stay here for that long when we had nothing to do and nowhere to go?

Mom took a deep breath. "This has been awful," she said. "It has been terrifying and scary and, in some ways, a lot of my worst nightmares come true. But with all of you here, I know I will look back on this time as one of the very best parts of my life. Everything has gone wrong on the surface. But in some ways, the simplicity of it all has made it feel right. You know what I mean?"

"There's no stopping Peachtree Bluff magic, Mom," I said.

Right then, as the words came out of my mouth, it was as if the town erupted into light. All at once, the twinkle lights on the town square's Christmas tree and all the strands winding the buildings downtown burst into a blazing, glorious, gleaming celebration.

"Talk about Peachtree Bluff magic!" Sloane said.

Caroline and Mom laughed as Carter gasped in all her toddler innocence.

I looked at the smiling faces around me, felt that intoxicating dose of Peachtree Bluff spirit enveloping me. And, in that moment, all was right with the world. Without even thinking about it, I knew for sure that I wasn't going to go back to LA. Christmas season had returned to Peachtree Bluff at last. And I didn't want to miss a minute of it.

# Caroline: All Mariah Wants

*Nine Days Post-Hurricane*

THE DAY VIVI WAS BORN was the best day of my life. Not that the day Preston was born wasn't equally amazing in its own way, but when Vivi was born it was like she was the bow tied on top of the gift of the life the universe had given me. I had wanted to marry one of New York's most eligible bachelors and start a family with him. And it had happened. I had married James, moved into his diamond-studded world, and having Vivi completed the picture, the life plan. I was unspeakably happy. I remember holding her for the first time and thinking that I would never let anything happen to her, that I would protect her with my life, at all costs.

While that sentiment still held true, it had become harder. How could I protect her from the hurt this divorce was causing? How could I keep her safe when she was constantly putting herself in harm's way? I wanted to cover her in bubble wrap and stuff her in a closet for a few years, pulling her out once she had matured a little and the storm had broken.

She was still asleep when the sun rose, and Emerson, Mom,

Sloane, and I decided to try to get a few hours of sleep on the boat before we went back to Mom's and braved whatever was waiting for us there. Now that the downed power lines had been fixed and all the major debris removed, the bridge would reopen to residents in a matter of hours. Peachtree Bluff would rebuild, and we would all be okay. It was a new day. It was shocking how good the town looked, the contrast between now and a few days ago steep, I realized as I looked out the tiny window of the *Miss Ansley*.

And my daughter had been here through all of it. She had narrowly escaped being a part of the destruction. I sat on the side of Vivi's small bed, cross-legged, facing her, and watched her placid, dreaming face.

I remembered being that same rebellious teenager. I remembered feeling so angry and having no place to put all those emotions. After my dad died, I clung desperately to any sprig of control I had over my life, and I'd lost all faith in those who were supposed to protect me. I knew how Vivi was feeling because I had been there too. And that's why this was so incredibly hard for me.

Her eyelids fluttered, and she looked up at me. "Mom?"

I could tell she was groggy, maybe even wondering if she was dreaming.

"You've done a good job," I said. "Cleaning up and helping out around here. I'm proud of you and how you've stepped up."

She smiled. "Thanks."

"But you put yourself and your family in a lot of danger, Vivi," I continued. "I am grateful that you're okay, but you put all of us in a position we never should have been in. This easily could have gone the other way. You could have been hurt." It was almost impossible to get the next words out of my mouth: "You could have died."

"Mom . . ." she protested, but I put my hand up to stop her.

"I know that you are upset about your dad and me. I know that you blame me. I know that you feel like your life is falling apart. I've lived that. I've walked in your shoes, and I can assure you I made some bad decisions in the wake of that." I cleared my throat, thinking about getting suspended from high school for smoking in the bathroom and being so horrid to my mother when all she was trying to do was fix things. In my defense, she hadn't told us that our dad had lost all our money. I might have understood her a little better if she had.

"But I am finished being patient with your tantrums, and I am done tiptoeing around your moods. Your dad and I are getting divorced, and I hate it, and I'm sorry. But we still love you, we're still a family, and we are all going to have to adjust to a new reality." Even as I said it, I wanted to roll my eyes. James and I were still living in the same building, for God's sake. It wasn't ideal for our children that we wouldn't be together. But I had to think that being unhappy together was potentially even worse than being happy apart. Not that I felt happy. But that was neither here nor there.

"Your dad and I have talked about what your punishment should be." I was suddenly regretting telling James that I thought this should be a mother/daughter thing. Weirdly, I wished he were here with me, handing down this punishment. "Our instinct was to ground you, but we know you need your friends right now. So we've decided that you will do one hundred hours of community service, starting now. I know you've already done a lot to help around here, but doing a lot more will make you feel better. I want you to see and feel and remember how blessed you are to have a home and a family who loves you. I want you to understand that there is no time or space for this petty misbehavior in a world where you are full of gifts and talents that you need to let shine."

I felt like I could keep rambling, but maybe it was better to stop now. I had practiced this speech in my head more than once, but, even still, I wasn't sure that I had said everything I needed to say. I wasn't sure if this was the right punishment, but I did know that it would put Vivi's life in perspective. And that was the point, really. I didn't want her to be miserable to atone for her sins. I wanted her to find a way to be happy. And I really thought this would help. I knew I hadn't fully addressed what was perhaps the most important part of the issue, the part about not telling her Jack was her biological grandfather. But we would get there.

"Mom," she said. "I'm sorry. I swear. I really am. I promise you that I didn't mean for this to happen. I went off to think, but I didn't know I'd get stuck on the boat—I'd been planning to be back in plenty of time. I wanted to go on that cruise with Gransley and Grandjack. I didn't want to mess up anyone's plans or anything like that. It's just that my phone died when I got out there, and I didn't know how to get back home."

"Viv, I know teenagers aren't rational thinkers. I get it. I've read the books, and, believe it or not, I was a teenager once too." She rolled her eyes. Right on cue. "But I know that smart, capable, kind little girl I raised is in there somewhere. And I'd really like to have her back if at all possible."

"I know I've blamed you for a lot of things that weren't your fault." She paused and looked down at her hands. "And, if I really, really think about it, part of the reason I ran off before the hurricane was to make you worry." She looked back up at me. "I think that's why I kept sneaking out in New York too. But, Mom, I swear I only wanted you to worry for a little bit. I never meant to put anyone in danger."

I nodded. "But that's what I mean, Viv. You have to think through these things. When you sneak out or run away, you aren't just making me worried. You're putting yourself in danger."

She wrapped her arms around herself, as if realizing that was true. "I get that now. When I was on that boat, when I was all alone, I realized that I could get really hurt. And I'm not going to do that anymore. I promise."

I nodded. I wanted to believe her. But I knew we had a long way to go.

Then she looked back at me, and I saw a conviction in her eyes that hadn't been there before. "But, Mom, you did lie to me. I shouldn't have had to find out that Grandjack was my real grandfather like that. You should have told me."

Damn. I was hoping we could gloss right over the whole my-being-wrong thing and just stick with all the ways that she was wrong instead. No such luck. I nodded. "Baby, trust me, I didn't want you to find out like that. But you aren't too out of the loop. Sloane and I didn't even know Jack was our sperm donor until three years ago."

She shook her head. "Wait. Seriously? So, like, Gransley was dating Grandjack and you didn't know?"

I nodded. Yup. It was just as crazy as it sounded.

Her eyes went wide. "Whoa. Were you mad at Gransley?"

This was my fork in the road. I could tell her the truth: yes, I felt angry and hurt and betrayed. Or I could lie, save face, and make the case that she shouldn't be mad at me either. But I guessed the issue here was her being mad that I hadn't been honest with her. So maybe I should try.

So I nodded. "Yeah. I was very upset. But now I see Gransley's side. Sloane and I always knew we had a sperm donor. For most of our lives it didn't matter who it was because we didn't know him anyway. And then when Mom and Jack got together, she had a hard time finding the right moment to tell us. Just like I had a hard time finding the right moment to tell you."

She nodded. "Mom?"

"Yeah."

"I know that Grandjack will never feel like your dad. But he really does feel like my grandad. Does that hurt your feelings?"

I willed the tears not to spring to my eyes. Inside that brash and bold fifteen-year-old there was still a little vulnerability, that sweet softness that I had missed so much. In that moment, I felt so overwhelmingly grateful for the synchronicity of the universe. I knew now, three years later, that Jack would never feel like my father, biologically or no. Carter would always be my dad. But, as a stepdad, as a grandfather, Jack was pretty fantastic.

"I'm glad, honey. I really, truly am. I want that for you." I paused. "Now, enough of this serious talk. Tell me about the boy."

She shrugged, her messy hair falling over her face. But her grin totally gave her away. "Do you know how it feels when a guy gets you, like who you really are? And you just know it?" she said softly.

I raised one eyebrow. "So you're in trouble, in other words," I replied. I missed the simplicity of those days, when the promise of a future meeting could be such an absolute thrill. I wondered if I would ever get that feeling again.

She laughed. "I don't know. I think he has a girlfriend."

"You think?"

"He's not a big poster, but there are a few pics of him with some girl on Insta."

I pushed the hair behind her ear. "Never, ever be the other woman," I said. "But if you want my advice"—she probably did not—"being friends first is always good."

She flopped back on her bed dramatically. "Friends . . ."

"Get dressed and come on up to the galley," I said. "I'll make you some eggs."

The boys were huddled around an iPad even though they'd had too much screen time lately. I pretended I didn't notice. Sloane was leaning over the small counter with a cup of coffee, talking to Mom and Emerson. "Adam doesn't think Peachtree Perk will need that much work, and fortunately he can do most of the repairs himself."

Adam was very handy. We were lucky to have him in the family.

"How'd it go?" Mom asked.

"She'll be up in a second," I whispered. "But it went well. I feel like I got in there somehow. Maybe." It was hard to know. A notification from my Timehop popped up on my phone, and I gasped when I opened it. On this day last year, I'd posted one of my Christmas card photos. I had almost forgotten to tell my family about my plans . . .

"Everyone," I said, just as Vivi appeared, "I know it's a little late in the season, but due to the unforeseen circumstances of this year, I have scheduled our family Christmas photos with Peachtree Photography for tomorrow."

"Mom!" Vivi practically shrieked. "Do you see this hair? I can't have pictures. I need highlights."

"What?" Mom protested, aghast. "Caroline, don't you think we have enough going on without adding that to our plates?"

I crossed my arms. "We have enough going on that we don't need to commemorate this year of our family's life, that we don't need to take the time to send Christmas cards to the people we love and who love us back?"

Sloane rolled her eyes, and Mom groaned. Emerson was the last holdout. I would convince Mom and Sloane either way, but if Emerson was on my side, it would make things that much easier.

"She's right," Emerson said. "I hate it, but she's right."

"Yes!" I said, knowing I had won. "And, look, the company I use mails them for you. You never even have look at them. If everyone can just send me their holiday card list, I'll take care of the rest." I grabbed my lightweight down parka, which was lying over a kitchen stool, and put it on. "I'm going out for a run. Please be prepared to discuss outfits when I get back."

"I used to think that you were like this because you didn't have a job," Sloane said. "Now I know that you are generally just better at life than everyone else."

I smiled. Lately, I felt pretty positive that I sucked at life. I couldn't keep my marriage together; my daughter was a total train wreck. But I had made magic at Sloane Emerson, and I was still capable of getting a Christmas card together despite a hurricane. So I guessed that was something. I'd take it.

A few minutes later, I was jogging through town, admiring the waterfront and thinking about the randomness of nature. One street back from the waterfront and on many of the side streets, it was as if the hurricane never happened. My house—which was slated to be torn down in three days—was totally destroyed, Jack's had some damage, and Mom's was fine. We had neighbors whose houses and shops were completely untouched, some that had minor flooding or lost a few shingles, and some who, like me, had lost everything. Against all odds, I smiled as I ran by my house, which was surrounded by a huge chain-link fence in preparation for the demo. I had lost tons of money. This had been a major financial setback. But, somehow, that house being gone was a symbol. I was poorer, sure. But, damn it, I was free.

Now more than ever. I loved the way my body felt when it was running, the sun on my face, the wind cooling me, my ponytail swishing. The cold felt nice and Christmasy, adding to the allure of the decorated houses and shops I ran past.

I almost didn't stop when I saw a man waving at me, just assuming he was being friendly. But then I saw that smile, and I slowed down just in time. I tapped my earbuds to stop Mariah's Christmas album—I mean, it isn't Christmas if you aren't all Mariah wants—and said, "What on earth are you doing here already?"

Wes laughed. "I could ask you the same thing." He paused. "I came back to check on my house and my parents."

"And?"

"And all is well." He grimaced. "But not your house."

"And guess who doesn't have insurance?"

He put his hand to his mouth. "How is that even possible?"

I smiled. "It is such a long story."

He raised his eyebrow. "Want to tell me over dinner?"

It gave me butterflies. Besides one date with a guy named Peter from college—where he had essentially proposed and scarred me for life—I hadn't been on a date since I'd left James. Butterflies weren't a feeling I was terribly accustomed to. But they still felt good.

I nodded.

He exhaled deeply. "That took every ounce of courage I had."

"Really? You seemed so nonchalant."

He looked at me very seriously. "I practiced in the mirror. A lot."

We both laughed. "I already said yes," I said. "Seems pretty low stakes at this point."

"Yes. But that was a theoretical yes. This has an actual plan and time attached. It's a bigger deal."

He was so charming. "I'm the one who should be nervous. I haven't been on a date since George Bush was president."

He furrowed his brow. "Oh, wait. You thought this was a date?"

For a split second I was about to be horrifically embarrassed. But then he laughed. *Oh, thank God.*

"I'm going to go back to Atlanta for a few days for some of Brad's Christmas stuff at school, but I'll be back on the nineteenth. Does that work? A couple of the restaurants off the waterfront are already opening back up, I think. But if not, we'll figure it out."

"Wine," I said. "That's all I really need. It doesn't matter where."

As he squeezed my hand in his, my heart raced—and I realized how cold my fingers were. "I'll be counting down the days," he said.

I gave him my winningest smile, tapped my earbuds, and took off again, grinning ear to ear. *Baby, all I want for Christmas is you . . .*

# Ansley: Undeserved Kindness

*Six Days before Christmas*

EVERY YEAR WHEN CHRISTMAS COMES around, I still feel the pang of the loss of my first husband. And I still—whether I want to or not—remember that first Christmas without Carter. On December 19, 2001, ninety-nine days after September 11, ninety-nine days after my world had changed harshly, shockingly, and forever, I couldn't take it anymore. I couldn't spend one more moment in the New York apartment that our family had shared together, couldn't spend one more sleepless night feeling as if I was putting not only myself but also my children in grave danger by staying in a city that was under siege. I cried uncle.

There was this part of me that had, for three months, expected Carter to show up. Maybe he would turn up in a hospital or be discovered amidst the rubble, having survived somehow. But after ninety-nine days, the fires at ground zero were finally extinguished. And so was my hope.

My terror didn't only extend to losing Carter. It also extended to our finances. In the wake of my husband's death, I had discovered that our future, which had seemed so secure, was anything but. My darling husband was in a world of debt and had borrowed from his life insurance policies to keep us afloat. Yes, I had marketable interior design skills, but I hadn't worked in more than fifteen years. I couldn't afford to keep our apartment.

And so, on December 19, I gathered a few friends and loaded the largest size of U-Haul truck. Caroline was furious. Sloane was silent. Emerson was sobbing. But I was out of options. Out of money. Out of time. Out of faith.

And so I drove for ten straight hours, only stopping for bathroom breaks and to eat. I drove away from all my dreams, from my marriage, from my family, from my husband. I arrived in the dark of night to a house that had been closed up for years. We were exhausted, grumpy, starving, and terrified, and I was dreading what was awaiting me inside: a musty, empty house.

Ordinarily, I was the queen of Christmas. I always got a huge tree and too many presents, and hung millions of twinkle lights. A nativity that my dad had carved when I was little would sit atop the mantel, and stockings my mom had knit for each of the girls when they were born waited patiently to be filled. Every decoration, every ornament had a meaning behind it. I always got a warm and glowing feeling inside whenever I thought about Christmas.

But that year, I didn't know what to do. How could I celebrate when my husband was gone? How could I rejoice when the world was being torn apart? How could I praise the birth of a Christ child that—at that moment—I no longer believed in? I had a ten-year-old and two teenagers who didn't deserve to have their holiday stolen from them. But they had been left with an empty shell of a mother who couldn't imagine finding anything to smile about, much less the joy of Christmas. I dreaded having to pick out a tree or find last-minute presents in a strange place that didn't feel like home. I couldn't stomach the idea of putting out cookies and milk without my husband, of greeting Santa's offerings alone.

But when I finally pulled into the driveway of my grandmother's house, I was surprised to see it was all lit up. It seemed warm, cozy even, from the street. A wreath adorned the front door, while fir garlands and lights swooped over the double front porches. When I opened the door, I wasn't greeted by the smell of must and grime. Instead, I was met by the undeniably wonderful fragrance of chocolate chip cookies. Soft music was playing and, as I opened the door, my brother Scott, a globe-trotting travel writer, walked into the kitchen to hug me. I absolutely fell apart.

"You did all of this? For us?"

He shook his head and led me into the living room, where two strangers and two friends were hanging bright, shining Christmas balls on a beautiful tree that filled the front of the house with the scent of pine. Sandra and Emily, two of my best summer friends from growing up, stopped their decorating to embrace my children and me. And that was the day I met Hippie Hal and Kimmy for the very first time.

Christmas came for my family that year. The sky was falling, the world had ended, and yet it came just the same. It came because of my brother and my friends, because of dozens of kind strangers in a town that only vaguely knew us but who, despite that, wrapped gifts for my children and filled up our fridge, cleaned our dusty old windowsills and put fresh sheets from their own houses on our beds. If I live to be one hundred years old, I can't imagine that there will ever be a moment in my life where I will feel so overwhelmingly grateful for that sort of undeserved kindness. Try as I might, it is kindness I know I will never be able to repay.

And now, eighteen years later, eighteen years after the people of this town turned my darkest hour into a bright and shining moment that resembled something like hope, this hurricane, this devastation, was my opportunity to even the score.

"Mom!" I heard from downstairs, followed by the sound of the family house's front door slamming.

"Car!" I shouted. "I'll be down in a second!"

"Oh my God, Mom," she said. "The noise. This is unbeliev-able."

I laughed. I was so used to it I had almost forgotten. The sounds of chain saws, hammers, power tools, and music from boom boxes all over town—not to mention constant limb, tree, and dump trucks driving down the street—were the new soundtrack of Peachtree Bluff. Yes, it could be annoying. But for me, it had become the sound of progress. For the most part, life was back to normal. The residents had returned, the stores were open, and the damage was being repaired. These few weeks had felt like a marathon. We had all rolled up our sleeves, helping where we could. And to see the way that work crews and adjusters were coming in from all over the country to help was truly hum-bling.

As official town decorator, I was busier than I had ever been assessing the situation of the furnishings and textiles in damaged buildings. The library and town hall were both on the waterfront, and both had had a little flooding. Fortunately, the librarians had gathered before the storm to move the books from the lower metal shelves up to the higher ones, so they hadn't been damaged. But two sets of office furniture were soggy and moldy, and the entire building needed new flooring. As for the town hall, only the foyer had flooded, and, with its beautiful old limestone floors, it hadn't needed much more than a good mopping and some new baseboards. But we still took the opportunity to repaint the entire thing. It had been seven years, and it was starting to look dingy despite the housekeeping crew's meticulous work with Magic Erasers.

Kyle and Emerson had decided to stay until Christmas to help, which, at the time, I was very glad of. And, since Caroline had already planned for Vivi to do school virtually, they stayed too, which was wonderful. But, to be honest, quarters were getting tight. We had—very gallantly, I might add—agreed to wait awhile to get the work done on Jack's house so that others who didn't have a place to go could get in their houses first and businesses could reopen quickly. It had helped. Only a few homes were still undergoing repairs, and, by and large, the town was back in action.

But it meant that Jack and I were back in the guest room at what had once been my house, with Sloane, Adam, their two boys, and Preston. Emerson, Kyle, and Carter were staying in the guesthouse, with Vivi and Caroline joining them. In true Christmas fashion, there was no room at the inn.

At least James had hired a captain to help him get the boat back to Palm Beach as soon as Vivi and Preston were settled and was now back to work in New York. So we were down one.

I ran down the steps at top speed.

"Mom?" Caroline called impatiently, sweaty from her run.

"Have they started?" I asked.

"The excavators are here," she said, wide-eyed.

I nodded. Much to my surprise, the Historical Association had agreed that Caroline's house couldn't be repaired. So Sloane and Adam were happily buying her lot. Jack, Adam, Kyle, and Hal had spent the past couple weeks salvaging every beautiful floorboard, piece of molding, and original door or casing that they could. Adam and Sloane had also inherited Ellie Mae the goat, who was getting along swimmingly with the pigs, chickens, and new kitten on Kimmy's farm for the time being. Adam and Sloane said once their house was completed, they would bring Ellie Mae back, but I had my doubts about that.

"Oh, honey," I said. "Are you sad about the house getting torn down?" Right then, Viv and Preston, his arms so full with Biscuit he could hardly see over the top of her fluffy head, came running in the door, the buzzer on the oven going off simultaneously. I kissed them quickly and strode to the kitchen to pull out the day's fifth batch of cookies. Adam and Jack were holding a huge Christmas drive at Peachtree Provisions where people could come get clothes, food, presents—anything they needed, really, to make this Christmas a merry one. And you had to have Christmas cookies, right? Insurance companies hadn't all been quick to pay on claims, so, for some Peachtree residents, this Christmas would be a strain. Hopefully a little holiday sweetness would ease some of that. My specialty was peanut butter drops with Hershey's Kisses right on top.

"Oh, cookies!" Preston said as he followed me into the kitchen.

He took two, and, as if AJ and Taylor sensed what was happening, they flew through the back door too. "Cookies!" they said at the same time.

"Wash your hands!" I shouted over the noise as three excited little boys crowded around my cooling racks.

"They're going to start tearing the house down in a minute, guys!" Caroline said. "Want to watch?"

"Yeah!" the little chorus erupted.

Caroline shot me a smile.

"The house? Your feelings?" I repeated.

"I'm sad a piece of history is leaving our town and mad I made such a stupid mistake. Otherwise, you know, I'm kind of okay." She crossed her arms. "So . . . how's it going?" she asked breezily.

Okay. That portion of the conversation was clearly over. "I'm just thrilled that the whole family is home for Christmas. All is right with the world." I didn't mention that I was a tiny bit excited for December 26, when Jack and I could move into the guesthouse. Jack's house was still a good month away from being finished.

"How are the Peachtree Sloane Emerson numbers looking?" Caroline asked.

She spent a good portion of her days on Zoom with the LA and New York stores, ordering inventory and keeping up with the books. And thank goodness. "Our walk-in revenue hasn't been great with winter tourism down from the storm, but online sales are through the roof." I paused and smiled at her slyly. "Mostly because a few girls I know have made such a huge deal on social media about saving Peachtree and its local businesses."

Caroline smiled back. "People talk about the negative side of social media, but I think we've really been able to do some good for our town."

I nodded, feeling so blessed. Our family hadn't been totally spared, but we had been lucky that our businesses were able to carry on and that we had a place to go home to at night.

"I still can't believe those fully submersible dry bags sold out first in a store that specializes in handmade antique linens and chic designer finds," Caroline said. "Your gut was right as usual, Mom." Fishing backpacks weren't the norm for us, perhaps, but if there was one thing I knew, it was that the men were always the hardest recipients on my Christmas list. I had actually sourced the backpacks for Jack, Kyle, Adam, my brothers, Scott and John—who, unfortunately wouldn't be around for the holidays this year—and yes, even James. I hated him, but he was still family. Isn't that the way sometimes? And, with the absurdly odd type of divorce he and Caroline were having, I had no idea whether he would be here for Christmas.

I took a deep breath, watching my grandchildren inhale my homemade cookies. A peace washed over me as I realized it finally felt like Christmas. Despite the challenges this year had presented, cookies could still be enjoyed. The Christmas cottage downtown was filled with reindeer and, on the weekends, Santa. Storefronts were decorated to the nines with Christmas trains and elves who climbed ladders to chimneys, beautiful murals, and fake snow. Despite the freezing weather and blue tarps on more than a few roofs, the Christmas bazaar at the farmers' market would take place as usual tomorrow night.

But tonight . . . Tonight was a night we'd all been waiting for. At least, I had. Caroline was going on a date!

I looked down at the boys and, figuring they were too young to really get what was going on, asked, "What are you going to wear?"

She rolled her eyes. "Mo-om." She sounded so much like a teenager I couldn't help but laugh. I was just so thrilled. I worried that James had broken Caroline's heart so thoroughly that she could never trust in that same way again.

"Oh!" she said, putting her finger up and turning to rummage in the giant bag she called her purse but that really looked more like a suitcase. She handed me a stack of Christmas cards, which I soon realized were *our* Christmas cards. I gasped at the soft feel of the deckle-edge paper and at the delicate fonts. "Oh, Caroline. They are stunning."

She smiled triumphantly. I put my hand over my heart. In those moments when the photos were snapped, there was devastation all around us. But in the simple smiles of my family members and the beauty of the water behind us, you never would have guessed it. I had to say that my favorite card of all was mine. I had chosen the photo of just my five grands. Vivi was in the middle, smiling at the camera, holding Carter on her lap, who was also smiling at the camera, and the three little boys were all laughing up at Vivi like she was the queen of the world. It was too darling for words. And while, yes, I did like to show off my beautiful daughters, this was a different year. I didn't want to leave Kyle and Adam out of the picture, but I didn't want Caroline to feel badly that there was no James. So five grands it was.

"Is it weird that I am so nervous?" Caroline asked. "I mean, I know it's stupid. He lives in Peachtree. I live in New York. Even if we fall madly in love over dinner there's no future here, which is comforting. But, like, do I even remember how to do this?"

I laughed. "Honey, you're talking to a woman who hadn't gone on a first date in thirty-seven years and then married the man she had met when she was fifteen and had two children with."

She laughed too, much to my relief. I had come awfully close to saying something that resembled the truth. Fortunately, Caroline didn't seem to catch on. My mind wandered back to that rainy night in Georgia, the night I'd never forget, when I pulled up to Jack's house, totally unannounced, my heart beating so loudly it was all I could hear. I hadn't been able to tell him I was coming. I needed to see his face. When he agreed to this preposterous thing I was asking, to father my children, it terrified me how comforting it felt to be in his arms, how the feel of his lips on mine still melted my heart. I had nearly forgotten, in the joy of being with him again, the desperation I had felt for years, the longing for him in the deepest parts of me, the confusion of the push and pull of being in love with two men. But he was here now; it was real. We were together in that way I had always imagined. And while, yes, there was a part of me that wished we had gotten to spend those days of our young lives together, raise a family together, I had to admit that perhaps the here and now was even better. And I would never have traded my life with Carter, even knowing what I know now.

I walked to the stove and filled a saucepan with milk. The kids would be cold while we watched the teardown. Plus, it was nearly Christmas, and we needed hot chocolate desperately. Those snowflake-shaped marshmallows weren't going to eat themselves.

"I think it's good for you," I said. "Dip your toe in the water. Practice how it feels to enjoy the company of a man who isn't James." I looked around. "Hey, where's Vivi?"

"Speaking of enjoying the company of a man . . ." Caroline said, rolling her eyes. "I'll give you three guesses as to where Vivi is. But I'm going to bet you only need one."

I thought of sweet Tyler, of how he'd saved my granddaughter, of how he had helped tirelessly after the hurricane to put this town back together. He was a good boy. I felt it in my bones. Probably quite a bit different from that Pond or Ocean or whomever she was interested in back in New York. She was growing up, I realized then. She was making her own way in the world, spreading her wings, separating herself from us.

The milk began to boil, and I moved it off the burner, looking back at my daughter. Jack walked through the back door, and I remembered that I had been fifteen like Vivi the summer I had met him in Peachtree Bluff. And it made me realize that you have to be careful who you date. Because, like it or not, you might just fall in love. And, if you're anything like Jack and me, that love might last a lifetime.

He kissed my head, and then pulled the to-go cups out of the cabinet, handing them to me one by one so I could fill them and pass them out.

"All right, kiddos!" I said. "Let's go!"

Sloane and Adam were working and Emerson and Kyle had taken Carter kayaking. So Caroline, Jack, and I each held the hand of one of my grandsons as we walked down the block. I could already hear the excavator.

A tall chain-link fence had secured the perimeter for the past couple weeks, but the mesh inset was plenty see-through for us to get a good view. As those massive jaws engulfed what was left of the roof of Caroline and James's house, I gasped, and the boys cheered. I looked over at Caroline, whose arms were crossed. Neighbors and passersby were lined up on the street, watching the action. But I was only watching my daughter. I couldn't quite read her face.

I took her hand in mine and squeezed.

"It's over," she whispered. Then she smiled. I knew then that she was actually happy to see this house go. And, maybe even more, the husband that went with it.

# Vivi: Dazzled

*Six Days before Christmas*

MY FEET WERE MOVING QUICKLY down the Peachtree Bluff side-walk, trying to keep up with Tyler's long-legged, easy stride. I had had exams—virtual exams—the past week, and Mom had practi-cally kept me chained to the house for like ten days, so I hadn't had the chance to casually run into him until now. But they were over! I was free for almost three whole weeks!

"How were your exams?" I asked.

"Pretty easy," he said.

I was super jealous. Mine were not even a little easy. "So, what do you want to do?" I asked.

"Can we go check on your grandparents' house?" he asked.

I sighed. "I get it," I said. "You're a super-selfless do-gooder. But couldn't we just, like, hang out? I'm really tired from all the studying."

As I said it, I realized that, now that I was with Tyler, I some-how felt thoroughly energized. *Tyler.* Who, I might add, still hadn't tried to kiss me. Were we going to be just friends forever? Nope.

Nope. Wasn't going down this path. I could do this. I could salvage this.

"Did you miss me?" I asked, trying to be coy.

"You obviously didn't miss me," he said. He picked up his phone. "Not a word. Not one."

I could feel my heart racing. So he had missed me.

"If you wanted to talk to me, you could have texted me," I countered, wishing he would slow down.

"Well," he said, "as it happens, my *parents* decided that I needed to focus on my exams, so they took my phone."

He could have DMed me or something from his computer, but I let that thought pass. He had to have missed me a little, right? All I knew was that, in between biology and geometry, Honors English II, and AP World History, Tyler was all. I. Could. Think. About. So I had finally given in. I eyed him warily.

"No phone?" I asked. "I would have died!"

He shrugged. "I didn't even have your name saved. It's a good thing you texted me."

I caught his eye, and he winked, finally slowing down a little. "Are you hiding me? Am I your dirty little secret?" That was my sneaky way of asking if he had a girlfriend. No new photos of Tyler and that girl had surfaced, and the more I studied them, the more I realized they looked like pictures taken in New York. But then again, he hadn't posted anything new at all, so that didn't mean much.

He smiled. "If you want to be, you are."

This was what I didn't get. He flirted with me mercilessly. But then . . . nothing. So he had to have a girlfriend, right? We were outside Gransley and Grandjack's house now, and he said, "I just want to check the dehumidifiers. Then I told Kimmy we'd have dinner at her house. Is that okay with you?" he added, looking down.

I smiled up at him. "We'd have dinner, like you and me?"

He stopped and looked around. "Um, yes. Who else would I mean?" He started walking again. True. Who else would he mean? My heart felt like it was flying. But, then again, dinner with Kimmy . . . could be a friend thing.

"Wait." I stopped, something just occurring to me. "What about your parents?"

He shook his head. "They're going out to dinner with some friends. Plus, Kimmy and I have dinner together by ourselves like once a week."

"Aw. So y'all are close?" I was kind of surprised since Kimmy was so much older—and, um, not, like, the motherly type.

He nodded. "Growing up, my parents worked a lot, and Kimmy's like eleven years older than I am, so she took care of me all the time."

Huh. That absolutely shocked me. A side to Kimmy I never would have imagined. But it made me really happy. I worried sometimes that Preston and I wouldn't be close like Mom and my aunts. But maybe that wouldn't be true after all. Maybe I would be Preston's Kimmy.

We opened the front door to Gransley and Grandjack's house. It still startled me to see all that busted plaster. The dehumidifiers were running full blast, but it was kind of smelly anyway. I scrunched up my nose. "Okay. Dehumidifiers are going. Let's go."

Tyler laughed. "Hold your horses. Let me just check a few more things."

*Hold your horses.* He was so cute. He crouched down and slid his hand behind the moldings, which were still standing a few inches up in the air, attached to the floor but not to any walls.

"They're drying out," he said.

I smiled like I was delighted. I mean, I was, I guess. But also, I just wanted to get out of there. All empty and jagged, the house was super creepy.

"Will you check that side of the molding to see if it's drying?" he asked.

Yuck. That's exactly what I wanted to do: stick my hand inside some gross, wet, falling-apart molding. But I wanted to get out of there, so I took the plunge. Oh. It wasn't that bad. It just felt like wood.

"Be careful," Tyler said. "You don't want to get a splinter. And these moldings are old and really delicate, so we don't want to break them."

Not one second later, I had barely touched a section and it fell right to the ground. I looked at Tyler guiltily. But as I studied the baseboard, I realized that the piece hadn't broken. It was cut in two perfectly straight lines. I peered behind it and saw *something.* I put my hand down inside and it felt kind of soft. I screamed and pulled my hand back up.

"What?" Tyler asked.

"I think it's a dead rat or something!" I was full-on panicking, wiping my hand furiously on my pants.

"How's it looking?" Grandjack asked from behind me, making me scream again.

He looked at me, wide-eyed. "Sorry."

I shook my head. "No! No! It's just that I found a mouse or something."

Tyler rolled his eyes, plunged his hand behind the baseboard and pulled up a little black bag. Not a rat.

"What is that?" Jack asked.

The bag was super worn, but it still had velvet in some places. You could tell that someone had sewn it together and it looked really, really old. A rusted safety pin held a piece of paper in place. Tyler handed me the bundle, and I touched the big red piece of wax on the outside of the paper. I blew on it, dust flying, making me cough. I looked up at Jack. Suddenly, the gravity of this moment felt really big. I didn't know what this was, but it seemed like it could be cool.

"'ARS,'" I said, reading the initials on the wax, looking up at him.

He smiled and looked down at it. "No way."

"Who's ARS?"

"Anne Riley Sloane. Ansley's great-grandmother. Your great-great-grandmother."

I pointed to the floor. "She lived here?"

He nodded. "Gransley's house and this house were owned by sisters. That's why she wanted this house back so badly. It was a part of her family too."

I laid the small bag out in my hand and looked at him sadly. "Do you think this is your treasure?" Poor guy. If it was, it sure was tiny.

He laughed. "Well, only one way to find out."

I felt frozen. I just sat there looking at the bag and the paper like they contained something potentially poisonous or explosive. Jack undid the rusted safety pin and handed me the letter. "I can't read without my glasses."

I slid my finger under the wax seal. Now I really wanted a wax seal. I was going to tell Mom. It made me want to start writing letters. It popped open super easily. On the outside, the paper was a little dusty, but inside, it was perfectly legible. It had a couple of small water spots, but that was it. I started reading out loud:

*My dearest, darling children:*

*October 11, 1925*

*The people of Peachtree Bluff have never been particularly fond of hurricanes—and for good reason. The threat of total destruction is always terrifying. But I daresay, if you asked my sister Mary and me, we've become quite fond of them.*

*It seems impossible that someone could not know the troubles that befell us that fall of 1916, but so much is lost to history. Your daddy and uncle were off at war, supplies and food were scarce, and we were getting by the best way we knew how. Mary and I had become quite expert at fishing and rowing, and we had always been more than proficient at sewing and gardening, so there were small mercies. We were also, at that point, without extra mouths* to feed. So it seemed fitting that we would be the ones to take the risk . . .

Pirates were little more than legends to us. But with the men away, and us unprotected as we were, we'd heard stories of modern-day ships coming into towns to pillage what little they had left. Recently, nearby seaside towns had fallen prey to a band of men in a ship with a mast carved into a snake, of plans for them to make their way to Peachtree Bluff.

From the widow's walk, where we were watching to see if a storm offshore would make landfall, Mary and I saw a ship we didn't recognize entering the harbor. It moored out in the distance, something unusual enough to raise an eyebrow. Why moor so far out from town, so near the rocky cliffs, instead of inside the protection of Starlite Island? And then . . . we saw the ship's mast. We watched as a group of men we didn't know rowed into town. We shared a look. And that was enough. Mary was always the brave one, always the one to take a risk. I wasn't. But someone had to save Peachtree.

We watched as the men rowed to the waterfront, studied as they entered the pub. By then, the wind was picking up, the rain falling. We rowed out into the weather, the waves filling our boat. I was terrified. Mary was stick straight and resolved as ever.

I tried to keep her from boarding the ship. Begged and pleaded with her. There could have been other men aboard. She could have been caught. But when she came back a few *minutes later, she appeared to have taken nothing. I was relieved. They wouldn't come looking for retribution for what my sister—sometimes too spirited for her own good—had taken if she had taken nothing.*

*We used the small hand saw we had extracted from the toolshed to release the front line of the giant ship, and, as the weather raged, sawed the thick and sturdy back anchor line as well. It was easier said than done, especially considering the elements. I would attempt to hold the line taut as Mary sawed as best she could. Then we would switch. When the job was finished, we rowed away from the boat as fast as our thin arms would carry us. We watched from the dock, the rain pelting us, the wind terrifying, as the ship began to bounce and turn. We smiled with glee as the men inside the pub rowed with all their might back out to their boat.*

*Once we were inside by the fire, warm and dry, sipping coffee as a rare celebratory treat, our palms raw and bleeding from the ropes and the oars, Mary reached into her skirt pocket and opened her battered palm. I will never forget what I saw. I can't say whether it was wrong or right, but it dazzled me—and I believe the memory will dazzle me forever.*

*By then, the elements had become punishing. With no visibility, we had no way of seeing what happened to the pirates, but, since, we have heard tell of ship remains, crushed on the rocky bluff. I take no joy in thinking of the fates of those men, but I take less joy in the idea of what could have happened to dear Mary and me, to our friends and neighbors, if we hadn't taken matters into our own hands.*

*The moral of the story—if there is one at all—is that the wind and rain can be scary. Storms can inspire great fear. But, if we let them, even our largest challenges can be our greatest allies. As they were for dear Mary and me. I still miss her every day. Now that she is gone, her great treasure belongs to me, to us. Our promise of sunshine on a rainy day. In that way, Mary is still here, keeping us safe.*

*My darling children, storms will befall you; hurricanes will come. There will be, undoubtedly, moments in your life that you need a little help to get by. On that day, you can come here, to our special, secret hiding place, to find this bit of treasure that your brave aunt found for you. I hope it will see you through the way that just the thought of it has seen me through.*

*With all my love,*
*Mama*

When I finished reading, I didn't know how or what to feel except for weirdly proud and excited, as if I had been the one to defeat the pirates who wanted to take my town away. The story Grandjack had told me was real, only the people who had saved Peachtree had been two sisters—sisters related to *me.*

When I looked up, Grandjack, seeming like he was holding his breath, held the bag out to me. "You open it," I said, unable to look away.

Tyler's eyes were rapt on Jack too. He pulled open the drawstring bag gingerly and dumped the contents into his hand. I gasped. And, all at once, I knew exactly what Anne Sloane had been so dazzled by.

# Caroline: Business and Pleasure

EVERY SINGLE TIME WES PICKED me up for a date during those few months we spent together in Peachtree Bluff as teenagers, Sloane, Emerson, and Mom would watch from the top of the stairs. I pretended to be really annoyed by it, but in reality, I think I kind of liked being the center of attention.

Now, I loved that Wes wanted to come pick me up again like he did all those years ago. But I also didn't want Vivi to know that I was going on a date. She was out with—you guessed it—Tyler, so it didn't matter at this point. But I hadn't known that when Wes asked me out, so I had stipulated that I would meet him at the boardwalk. *My date.* And as a bonus, Mom, Emerson, and Sloane couldn't watch from the top of the stairs.

I stood back from the mirror and gave myself a once-over yet again. I wore a white blouse with big gold buttons and a tie at the neck and my skinniest jeans, which were tucked into new boots that had what I liked to call a walking heel. I thought it was a look that was casual but put together, which was key since I didn't know where we were going. I slid my arms into my blue coat, knotted the tie at my waist, and slipped on my cute faux-fur hat. No James, no marriage, meant that my wardrobe budget was about to decrease significantly. I was making the most out of this last really great season of clothes.

Emerson flung the door open and plopped down on the bed.

"I could have been naked," I said.

"So?"

Emerson and I had always had very opposite feelings about whether nudity was a private situation. "You look fab," she said. Then she sighed deeply.

I turned to look at her. "What is the matter with you, and do you have to dump it on me before my big date?" I winked.

She grinned. "No, I guess I don't have to, it's just . . ."

I crossed my arms. "I am leaving in six minutes. So spit it out."

"I just still think I want to get married."

Oh my God. She was so dramatic. And she always put me in these awful positions. I was willing to the bend the truth when necessary, though, and this was one of those times I thought it was worth it. Mom had let Kyle's plans slip, and he deserved his surprise proposal. At least now we knew Emerson would say yes. I also, conveniently, knew how to work my little sister.

"Why on earth would you want to propose?" I asked. "You have been dreaming of being a bride since you were, like, born. Do you remember making me pretend to be the groom and get down on one knee and propose to you?"

She laughed, but then cocked her head to the side thoughtfully. "That would be kind of a nice moment."

There. I had at least made her think about it. "Why have you changed your mind about getting married, anyway?"

Emerson scrunched her nose. "Is it too simplistic to say that I was super influenced by Hollywood, and lately I just want something more traditional?"

I smiled. She was adorable. "Nope. Just sounds like growing up to me. Happens to the best of us, unfortunately."

"Are you going to get married again?"

I looked down at my watch. "Emerson, I haven't been on a date in eighteen years. Maybe let me worry about whether I'm going to get married again after I've survived the night."

She nodded, looking downtrodden. "So, to confirm, you don't think I should propose to Kyle?"

I rolled my eyes. She was so darn stubborn. It would break Kyle's heart if she beat him to the punch. "How many times have you asked me this?"

She looked up at the ceiling. "Um. A few?"

"And how many times have I said yes?"

"Zero. Zero times."

I stepped out of the room and Mom and Sloane were waiting—very obnoxiously—with cameras that began flashing in my face.

"My little girl's first date!" Sloane crooned.

"You two are hilarious. *Hilarious.* And this is not helping my nerves." I kissed them both quickly even though they were annoying.

"Don't do anything I wouldn't do!" Mom called out the door after me. I used to think that was the most vanilla statement in the world because our mother had never done anything shocking in her life. Now, after knowing a little more about her past, I wasn't so sure. Which was good, because depending on how this date went, who knew what I would want to do?

As I crossed the street to the boardwalk, I mused that it was really funny to be going out with someone I had dated in high school. I knew a lot about Wes. I knew his family and his favorite food and his prime, secluded fishing spot. Deep, dark, secret stuff.

And he was one of the only people who knew that I used to sneak out of the house to go clubbing in New York. Come to think of it, with Vivi, maybe the apple didn't fall too far from the tree.

I saw him then, leaning against his forearms on the boardwalk railing, right beside one of the many wreaths that was hanging from it. I pressed up close beside him, leaning over the railing too. I turned my head and smiled.

"Hi," he whispered.

"Hi."

It was a crisp, clear, beautiful night, and the stars shone brightly in the darkness. The docks had all been repaired now—priorities, right?—and this little part of Peachtree looked like nothing had ever happened to it.

"Starlite Island looks like heaven tonight," he said. Then he turned to me. "I take that back. *You* look like heaven tonight."

I laughed. "That's just because you usually only see me in workout clothes."

He raised his eyebrow. "And, don't forget, your bikini."

I swatted him. "That was a very, very long time ago."

He held his arm out to me, and I looped mine through it. It was the right gesture. More intimate than just walking side by side but not as intimate as holding hands. "So, post-hurricane, wintertime Peachtree Bluff presents a few dating hurdles," he began.

I didn't say that this was plenty for me. We could walk arm in arm and look at the stars.

"Azure is closed for the season. Full Moon is closed for repairs. Peachtree Grocery is technically open, but the artfully arranged tarps inside and running dehumidifiers aren't exactly the ambience I was going for."

"Flood chic isn't your thing. Noted."

We turned left on the boardwalk in the direction of Peachtree Grocery, my favorite restaurant, which used to be a grocery store decades earlier. "So, if it's okay with you, I thought I'd show off my mad culinary skills at my house."

My nose unwittingly crinkled at the idea of a newly divorced bachelor pad and the mismatched silverware and blank walls that almost inevitably went with that. But I didn't say anything except, "That sounds absolutely lovely."

In truth, going to his house felt a little too close, a little too serious. But the man was right. The only open restaurants came with bar stools, bowling pins, or pool cues, and the annual Peachtree Christmas concert tonight would no doubt be fun, but it would make for very poor conversation—except for everyone in town, who would have a grand time talking about what Wes and I were doing there together.

I couldn't tell if it was the bachelor-pad aspect or the intimacy that bothered me more as we approached one of my favorite houses in town, located on a side street. It was the palest blue with a big front porch. It was quaint, cozy, and historic: in short, everything wonderful about Peachtree Bluff.

He opened the front door, and I stepped over the threshold, trying to prepare myself for the worst. But I was dead wrong. A fire was burning in the living room, which had low ceilings with exposed beams and an adorable Christmas tree standing in the corner. A mix of white upholstered furniture, a black leather Chesterfield sofa, and English antiques lent a rustic, masculine-yet-modern vibe to the space. Through the doorway, the dining room opened to the kitchen, which had the coolest blue-and-white backsplash and huge, white dome pendant lights painted gold inside hanging over it. Rattan basket chandeliers hung every couple of feet over the antique dining table, which was surrounded by bamboo chairs. A huge coral bowl sat in the middle of the table. The entire thing was done but unfussy.

"This is your bachelor pad?" I gasped.

"You like it?"

"Like it? I *love* it. It's perfection."

He smiled. "Someone you like very much decorated it."

I laughed. "Mom?"

He nodded.

Now that I looked around, yes, that made perfect sense. This had Ansley Murphy written all over it.

I picked up a picture frame that appeared to hold a big black square. "What's this?"

"Hurricane Pearl memorabilia. It's the one shingle that blew off."

I laughed. "And yet you made it."

"We will rebuild," he said wistfully.

We both laughed.

"Come on," he said. "Wait until you see what your mom did to the courtyard." Now I was intrigued, because Mom rarely if ever weighed in on landscape decisions—and Peachtree yards weren't usually large enough to be really "done" anyway.

An oyster-shell path wove around a huge oyster-shell birdbath and a grill, which flanked either side of a beautiful old pecan tree. In the grassy area sat a built-in firepit—already roaring—with a grate on top and Adirondack chairs. Four strings of bubble lights intersected at the pergola in the middle.

"This is really darling."

"I have a confession," he said, opening a cooler next to one of the chairs, pulling out a bottle of champagne and popping the cork. "I wasn't sad the restaurants were closed because I really wanted to show off my new house to you." He paused. "I know that sounds dumb because you live in a big, fancy house, but . . ."

I stopped him and shook my head. "This is hands down my favorite house I've been in in ages," I said, meaning it. It felt like home. It felt like memories. It felt like a place where Santa came down the chimney and "Silent Night" played.

He smiled, pouring the champagne into a glass. I looked at the bottle label and gasped. "How did you know this was my favorite?"

"I have my ways," he said sneakily.

I figured he had asked my mom. But then he said, "I finally joined Instagram so that I could follow you and do a little digging on what you liked. My kid is horrified."

I laughed. We clinked our glasses, and he motioned for me to sit down in one of the Adirondacks, which I did. The fire felt warm and cozy and smelled like every wonderful thing about a Peachtree Bluff Christmas. He pulled a tinfoil packet out of the cooler and opened it to reveal a dozen beautiful oysters. I was already thinking that I would take the shells home so Sloane could paint the insides of them. She had painted one hundred for Black Friday, and we'd sold out of them in the New York store—where we didn't expect to sell a single one—in four hours.

He set each oyster, one by one, on the fire and then covered them with a rough piece of fabric.

"What's that?" I asked.

"Burlap. Helps steam them."

I nodded. "I'm impressed. You've really got this whole thing going on."

"Oh yeah," he said. "Chef extraordinaire. Am I cooking our entire dinner on this fire because I'm a master chef or because I can't figure out how to turn on the fancy stove your mom got me? Guess you'll never know."

"I'm glad you got oysters," I said. "Good source of zinc. Helps stave off mono." I raised my eyebrow, and Wes laughed.

A week after our talk-of-the-town, post-bingo make-out session as teenagers, Wes had come down with mono. Guess who else had gotten it?

"Are you planning on kissing me again tonight?" he asked.

I shrugged. "I guess it really all depends on how good those oysters are."

He laughed and, looking around, said, "Gosh. I never thought I'd be back here. I can't count the number of times as a kid I said I couldn't wait to leave this place."

I smiled. "Yeah, but you didn't know how sucky the rest of the world was yet."

"I spent eighteen years trying to get out of here and the next eighteen figuring out how to get back."

I smiled. "I think it's great you're back. And I'm sure your parents are thrilled." Wes was an only child, and super close with his parents.

"How are things back in New York? Are they managing without you?"

"Yeah. I think being away from Sloane Emerson New York has actually been a good thing. I have a really capable staff, and I need to trust them more."

"Hey," he said, leaning back in his chair. "Have you ever thought about franchising the store?"

This seemed like a weird date question.

"I mean, yeah. All the time. But Mom started it, and my sisters and I are all part owners of the LA and New York stores with her, so it's kind of messy."

He nodded. "I know I don't have to tell you, but anything design-related is really hot right now. If you want to look into franchising, I can help."

I squinted at him. "Are you actually pitching me a business idea on a date?"

He put his hand over his mouth. "I'm sorry. I think I am. You aren't supposed to mix business and pleasure, are you?"

I smiled. "Actually, mixing business and pleasure is my most favorite thing. I like you twenty-five percent more."

"Twenty-five percent? That's a lot."

I nodded. "I know. And I already liked you to begin with, so that's pretty big."

He leaned in close and said, in what I think was supposed to be a seductive tone: "Capital infusion. Investors. New York Stock Exchange."

"Hot," I said dryly, and we both laughed.

"Do you eat red meat?" he asked.

I nodded.

"Thank goodness. Filet and asparagus are the only other two things I can cook over a fire."

He was right: after the oysters, he cooked us some of the best steak and asparagus I'd ever had. He even had untwisted coat hangers at the ready so we could roast marshmallows and make s'mores for dessert. After all the good food, I was feeling much more relaxed. But not *that* relaxed. I was trying to be looser with my gluten-free, sugar-free, dairy-free existence, but a s'more was taking things a little too far.

"Are you too cold for a boat ride?" he asked.

I was so warm from the fire and laughing with Wes that I didn't think I was too cold, but I paused, wondering if that was safe given the recent storm. Then I realized, shockingly, it had been almost three weeks since the hurricane. The beautiful thing about living on the coast was that the sea swallowed up any debris in a matter of days. Inland flooding was a million times worse. The water was probably as clean as ever right now, like nothing had ever happened.

Inside, Wes pulled out two of the adorable Happy Holidays cups we had stocked at Sloane Emerson for this exact purpose and mixed us each a drink. Bourbon for him. Tequila for me.

It was only once we got on the boat that I realized how cold it actually was. I snuggled up beside Wes on the bench of the same Boston Whaler he had had since we were kids. "Wow," I said. "She still looks brand-new."

"Well, her teak and her engine are brand-new," he said. "She's a classic."

I smiled, feeling so nostalgic and so happy that some things never really changed, that some things *did* stand the test of time. Were Wes and I one of them?

Wes cranked the engine and put his arm around me. We pulled up to a spot a few minutes later where several other boats were already congregating.

"What's this?" I asked.

"You'll see," he said back, grinning.

A small skiff pulled up beside us and took one of the boat's lines from Wes, attaching it to a nearby mooring ball. Wes handed me a container of popcorn, a huge box of M&M's, and something that looked like a small radio. Then he brought up a pair of bean-bag chairs and several huge, cozy blankets that had been piled in the stern and arranged them in the bow of the boat. It was only then that I realized there was a gigantic screen set up on the shore. "No!" I gasped. "Is this a drive-in movie?"

"Boat-in," Wes said. "You didn't know?"

I shook my head. "I had no idea. Wonder why Mom hasn't brought us here before?"

"She might not know it exists," Wes said. "It has only been here about a week."

I cozied up under one of the blankets, looking at the stars, almost not wanting the movie to come on. But when the lights began bouncing on the screen and the sound started coming through the speaker, I changed my mind.

"Is *Love, Actually* still your favorite movie?" he asked.

I put my hand on my heart. "You remembered."

"I could never forget, Caroline. Not ever."

For just a moment, I was seventeen again. I was seventeen and *Love, Actually* was a brand-new movie, and I was seeing it at the drive-in with a boy I really, really liked.

Wes put his cold hand on my warm cheek, and, as our faces got closer, I could see our warm breath against the frigid night air. As his lips met mine, Hugh Grant said, "Love actually *is* all around."

And so it was.

# Vivi: Deep-Stalked

*Six Days before Christmas*

SITTING ON THE FLOOR OF Grandjack's living room, holding that delicate, ancient paper in my hands, I blinked up at Grandjack, reaching my finger out, gingerly, to touch what was in his palm. "Is that what I think it is?" I whispered.

"Diamonds," Tyler said, in awe.

"Grandjack!" I stood up to take a closer look, the letter still in my hand. "It's your treasure! It's real. It exists!"

He smiled at me, wide-eyed, touching the dozen or so stones with the index finger of his other hand. I had so many questions. "How are these even here still? Wouldn't her kids have found them?"

"I don't know." Grandjack shrugged. "Mary died of Spanish flu." He looked up at the ceiling. "That pandemic was around 1918, and Anne died in childbirth, I would assume shortly after this letter was written. I don't know exactly when, but she was young and her children were small. Their grandparents ended up raising them."

"How do you know more about my family than I do?" I asked.

"Well, I've known your mother forever. But also, I live in their house. When you live in a historic house, everyone in town wants to tell you all about the original owners."

I shivered. I took one of the stones out of his hand. "So do you think no one knew about the diamonds?"

He shrugged. "They must not have, not really. Her family must have just believed it to be another silly town story."

"Wow!" I said. "This is really cool."

Grandjack looked from Tyler to me. "Can you two keep these a secret?"

The idea of keeping the diamonds a secret made my stomach flutter uneasily at first. Was he going to sell them and never even tell Gransley? They were her great-grandmother's. But, then again, it was his house. So I guessed it was his treasure. "I have an idea," Jack said, "and I'm going to need your help."

As he told me his idea, his face filled with excitement, and my stress melted away. I realized that I was just as excited as he was. Whether it was about the diamonds or about having something special, a secret all my own, to share with Grandjack, I couldn't really be sure.

*Five Days before Christmas*

Lake is so sad you won't be here for Christmas, **the text from Carson read the next morning.** So I think he's still interested despite the fact that you totally blew him off.

I yawned and rolled over sleepily. I had been so excited the night before about the treasure and the secret that I could hardly sleep.

Lake was pretty bummed that I hadn't come back to New York after all the Australia drama—or lack-of-Australia drama. He had called me—like, actually called me on the phone. And he did the thing I'd been waiting for. After months of hanging out, he'd asked me to be his girlfriend. But it was then that I realized it: Lake was handsome and funny and cool. He was fun to hang out with, and he was a great dancer. He was pretty good at lacrosse. But now that I knew Tyler existed, everything was different. Tyler knew how to *build* stuff.

Even still, it wasn't like I totally expected anything to actually happen with Tyler. I mean, we'd hung out plenty, and, for me at least, there had been these *moments.* But he still hadn't tried to kiss me.

I wouldn't tell most of my friends about it, but I had told Carson. When I brought it up yesterday on our every-other-day FaceTime session, she'd said, "Yeah, Viv. If he didn't even try to kiss you when you were in a dark closet together during a hurricane, maybe he just isn't into you." She shrugged. "Maybe he's gay."

I rolled my eyes. "He isn't gay. I know when someone is gay. Half our best friends are gay."

"Well, why else wouldn't he be into you?" She tossed her blonde hair over her shoulder. Carson was probably the most confident person I knew, and, when I was with her, I was confident too.

We both laughed. That's why she was my best friend.

"So maybe I'm right. Maybe he does have a girlfriend."

She rolled her eyes. "We've been through this. There's no way he has a girlfriend." She paused. "So what did you say to Lake when you turned him down, like actually? Was it awful?"

"No! I mean, I just told him, 'Look, Lake, I really like you. A lot. I love hanging out with you, and it has been great. But I'm in a ton of trouble and I'm getting ready to have to do a hundred hours of community service and I'm hardly even going to have time to hang out. Can we just, like, keep talking?'"

"And what did he say?" Carson asked.

"I don't know. He said something like, 'Yeah, I mean. I guess.'"

It was a cop-out. Carson knew it, and I knew it. Lake, who had been my leading man for the last couple months, my obvious homecoming date or person I would to sit next to if a bunch of us went out, was now becoming my safety. I liked him second best, and I *did* want a boyfriend right now. So if the whole Tyler thing didn't pan out—although I hoped it would—then yeah. I'd go out with him.

And so I guessed now was really do or die. I wanted to text Tyler first this morning, but I texted Carson instead because, you know, best friends before boys. Always.

I really like Lake. I just . . . idk

She texted back. Want to hook up with Tyler over Christmas break before you decide?

It's weird when you read my mind.

Then I texted Tyler: Heading to Peachtree Perk. Want to come with?

I didn't know whether he liked me or not, but he sure did text me back quickly. OTW

Maybe he didn't like me. Because if he did like me, he would wait a little bit longer before responding, right? Play it cool? But since I was just a friend, he didn't have to do any of that? Ugh. This was so frustrating. I texted Mom.

Heading to PP. Want anything?

She responded. Ew. From the bathroom?

Mature, Mom. Really mature. Although . . . I'd have to remember to use that one on Preston later. He'd think it was hilarious. I sent her the eye-roll emoji, then put my phone in my pocket and headed down the stairs and out the front door.

A few minutes—and a few dozen waves to everyone passing by later—I walked into Peachtree Perk and sat down behind the shiny stainless-steel counter on one of the bar stools. It still smelled a little musty, but with its concrete floors and walls, Peachtree Perk had weathered the storm just fine, thank goodness. Keith leaned over in front of me and put his fist out for me to pound. "What up, Vivster?" He smiled. "Want your usual?"

Keith was pretty, but, well, he wasn't very smart. I'd told him like ten times that when you ask someone for their usual, it means that you actually know and remember what they like—which Keith definitely did not. But I just couldn't deal. So I just said, "Yeah, Keith. That would be great."

Then the door opened. The sun was streaming all around Tyler, and it was like time stopped. He smiled with those straight, gorgeous teeth, so tall and broad and manly. Oh my gosh. I'd forgotten how hot he was since yesterday.

"Hey, hey," he said, leaning over and hugging me.

Before I could respond, Keith set a cup in front of me. It was actually something iced, which was an improvement over when he made it hot, which I hated. I took a sip. It was an iced pumpkin spice latte, and, judging from the lack of nasty milk aftertaste, it had almond milk in it. My favorite. "Keith!" I said in astonishment. "This is what I drink!"

He nodded, like that was obvious. "You want your regular, T-man?"

Tyler gave me a look like he was in the Twilight Zone. "Okay?"

"He got mine right," I whispered.

"It's a miracle," Tyler whispered back.

Keith handed him a cup. "Happy drinking, bud."

Tyler took a sip.

"This is your drink . . ." he said. "But, hey, one for two isn't bad."

Well, it wasn't good.

"So, last night," he said. "That was pretty crazy, huh?"

It had been so weird at Kimmy's. We'd kept meeting each other's eyes, like we shared this big secret that no one else knew about. Well, I mean, I guess we did.

I nodded. "So crazy." I looked around and whispered, "How many people get to find real-life pirate treasure?"

He laughed and held his hand up to high-five me. And then I was annoyed again. I didn't want to be high-fiving with him. Way too friendly.

"Is everything back to normal at most of your friends' houses?" I asked, changing the subject.

He nodded. "Yeah. It's crazy how bad that hurricane felt when we were in it. But when you think about it, it didn't do as much damage as it could have."

I laughed, thinking about my house.

Tyler joined me. "Okay, so maybe you aren't the best person to say that to. But off the waterfront, it wasn't too bad."

I nodded. "I know what you mean."

"A lot of my friends don't live downtown, so they weren't hit that hard."

I smiled at him for a moment too long, lost in his eyes. I looked down into my drink. "Was it hard moving here?" I couldn't imagine leaving my friends and my school.

He shrugged. "Not really. I made friends with most of the football players pretty quickly. And, you know, I'm used to moving around. I miss my friends back home, but a lot of us got split up into different high schools anyway. And, I mean, I get to go fish every day and take the skiff out and help Kimmy on the farm. I didn't want to move at first, but it has been pretty awesome." He paused. "Hey, what are we doing?" he asked.

I looked around, thinking that that was exactly, precisely the same thing I wanted to know. "Um, this?"

"Yeah. But after?"

I had told the fam to expect me home by curfew, which was midnight in the city but eleven in Peachtree, which I found super unfair especially since, let's face it, there was way less trouble I could get into here. But Mom said she didn't feel like getting into it with Gransley about how midnight was too late at fifteen, and I was still on very, very thin ice, so I didn't say a word. Not one.

"I have a fun idea," he said. "I'll go back to Kimmy's and get the boat." Kimmy had an old flat-bottom skiff that was perfect for pulling up on Starlite Island. "Why don't I pick you up on your dock in like an hour?"

I looked down at my cup. "I'm only halfway done with my coffee."

"Viv, we live on the Intracoastal, and you want to sit inside a coffee shop?"

He had a point. "Are you going to text me when you get close?" I asked.

He scoffed and threw some money on the bar. "City girls," he said, shaking his head as he stood up to leave. Then he winked at me. "Later, Keith!"

"So, then, I guess that's a no," I said to myself as the front door swung shut behind him.

"What's up with that?" Keith asked. "Friend? Boyfriend?"

"Neither," I said, hearing the confusion in my voice as it came out. But that was the truest answer because we weren't really friends, but he also wasn't my boyfriend.

"Been there, sister," he said. "Don't wait too long to make your move. Otherwise he'll be a friend forever."

Wise words from Keith. I got up and rolled my eyes. I didn't want to make a move. I wanted *Tyler* to make a move. How could I be sure he really liked me if he didn't? I guessed maybe he wasn't sure if I really liked him. But how could he not be sure? Unless he had a girlfriend?

Two hours later, the sun had set, and, after picking me up in Kimmy's little boat, Tyler had very handily built a tiny fire on Starlite Island. I had made us some sandwiches, just in case. I was hoping we'd need them because I couldn't think of anything I'd rather do than sit out here on this island with Tyler, all by ourselves, until curfew.

"So how'd you learn to build a fire like this, Boy Scout?" I teased.

He grinned. "In Boy Scouts. You should see me wield a pocketknife and catch a fish."

A real Boy Scout. I loved that about him.

"What did you ask Santa for this year?" I asked.

He rubbed the stubble forming on his chin. "I think it was something kind of like this."

Butterflies filled my stomach. Did he mean time on this beautiful island? Or time on this beautiful island alone? Or with me? As his friend? Or as maybe something more? As I was tossing the options around in my mind, overanalyzing each one of them, he said, "So, look, not to be all up in your business, but who's that guy in your Instagram pictures?"

I smiled coyly. "So you're stalking me, huh?"

"Obviously. And you haven't stalked me?"

I had literally memorized his entire Instagram page, which wasn't saying too much. He only had fourteen pictures on there— including the ones with that girl, which I didn't totally love.

"That's a guy from New York. He asked me out last week," I started casually.

"Oh," he said. "Well, good for you."

I looked over at him across the fire. "I said no." I paused. "But, I mean, you know all about it. I've seen you with your girlfriend . . ."

He held my stare. "We were trying the long-distance thing, but it wasn't really working. I ended it with her a few weeks ago." He shrugged. "But it always seems kind of mean when people take the pictures down."

"Why?" I asked. "Why wasn't it working, I mean?" I wanted him to say it. I needed him to.

"Why did you turn down *Lake*?"

Wow. He had deep-stalked. He even knew Lake's name. But I couldn't be the one to put myself out there first. I just couldn't.

I shrugged. "I mean, I like him a lot. I just have all this community service to do for my punishment and stuff."

Tyler looked over at me again. "I would do one hundred hours of community service with you just so we never had to be apart."

I could feel the smile spreading across my face. He didn't have to tell me now. He didn't have to say it. He had broken up with his girlfriend for me.

# Sloane: Mixed Emotions

*Four Days Until Christmas*

CAROLINE AND EMERSON WERE WAITING with bated breath as I unrolled the swath of papers in my arms.

Vivi ran through the dining room practically singing, "Thirty minutes until the Christmas Market! Aunt Em, I'm borrowing your sweater!" Seconds later, her feet pounded up the stairs.

"I haven't seen her this excited about the Christmas Market since she was like six," I said.

Caroline laughed. "I think it's less excitement over the Christmas Market and more over who will *be* at the Christmas Market."

"Kind of like her mother?" Emerson asked, bumping her hip with Caroline's.

Caroline didn't even try to hide her smile. "I'm not going to lie. It was a fantastic first date. No doubt about it."

"So is he better in bed now, or when he was eighteen?" Emerson asked very seriously.

"Em!" I scolded.

"What?" she asked innocently. "It's a valid question."

"I have no idea," Caroline said demurely. "Because I did not sleep with him either time."

"Really?" I asked, shocked. Granted, I had no real concept of what grown-up people's dating lives look like since I'd been with Adam since college and never really had a grown-up dating life. But I couldn't imagine my sister sleeping with someone on a first date if, for no other reason, then because she was a germaphobe.

"Stop," Emerson said. "For real?"

Caroline pulled her red pencil out from behind her ear and said, "Can we go over Sloane's house plans, please? I don't see how any of this is relevant."

Now I was intrigued too, but, as Vivi had said, the Christmas Market was drawing nigh, and I needed everyone's thoughts on the house plans. We were slated to present them to the Historical Association at their January meeting, and everything needed to be perfect. Even with Mom's major connections, I couldn't believe how fast the architect had gotten the drawings done. Fortunately, Caroline was fine to hang on to the lot until we got approval.

"Speaking of old flames . . ." Emerson said. "You guys are never going to believe this."

I tempered my response because Emerson's *never going to believe this* was often different from mine, and I would get super excited for nothing.

"Guess who called me last night."

"Mark!" Caroline said.

I guffawed. The mere idea of Emerson's ex-fiancé calling her was ridiculous.

"How did you know?" she asked.

"Seriously?" I said. "I thought you were kidding."

"I totally was!" Caroline protested. "What in the hell did he want?"

Emerson scrunched up her nose. "Well, he wants to talk."

"Talk?" Caroline spat. "Talk? What could he possibly want to *talk* about?"

I wasn't sure what she was so outraged about. I mean, yeah, Mark had technically called off his wedding to Emerson, but it wasn't like she hadn't been having major second thoughts. It wasn't like she wasn't majorly in love with Kyle also, which was kind of a problem.

"What did you say?" I asked.

She shrugged. "I mean, I have to go talk to him. But do I tell Kyle?"

As if he'd heard, Kyle opened the front door and sauntered into the room, Keith on his heels. He planted a big, wet, slobbery kiss on Emerson and said, "God, I'd forgotten how beautiful you are."

Keith and I rolled our eyes at each other, but, really, it was kind of sweet.

"Guys," Keith said, "big apologies, man."

"For what?" I asked.

"The drink order situation." He pulled out a cup with my name on it and handed it to me. "That little fire messed up my list, but I thought it would be cool for everybody to try something new every day." He was the definition of a California surfer dude. How he'd made it this long on the East Coast was a total mystery to me. "When nobody said anything, I thought you guys liked it."

I squinted at him. Could that possibly be true?

Caroline looked embarrassed for him, and Kyle seemed a little annoyed. But you couldn't be full-on *mad* at Keith. He meant well. Kyle slapped Keith on the back. "It's all right, man. There's a learning curve."

Well, yes. That was true.

"I got it now, man," he said. "I'm even putting names on your cups." He snapped his fingers like he had invented algebra, not recycled a very, very ordinary solution to a problem.

"That is just great, Keith," I said, not wanting him to feel badly.

Mom walked in, saying, "Oh! Yes! This is so exciting!"

"The coffee or the house plans?" Caroline asked.

"Both."

Keith handed her a cup, and, because he was standing there, she went ahead and took a sip. A few drinks were casualties of this nicety every day. She looked very surprised. "This is a skinny vanilla latte. This is my drink."

Keith snapped at her, "Yup. I'm delivering the right drinks to the right people now. It's my new thing."

I could tell Mom was really having to control herself to keep from laughing. "That is great news, Keith. Really big."

I handed her a red pencil and pointed at the plans.

"We'll get out of your way, ladies," Kyle said.

"I want you to look at the plans later!" I called after him as he and Keith walked out the door.

"Will do!" he called back.

Caroline picked up the top sheet, having to spread her arms wide to do so. She shifted it this way and that and then said,

"Twenty-six hundred square feet. Double front porches. Black shutters. It looks like the exact same house. Literally the exact same."

I nodded and looked at her incredulously. "Well, yeah. Of course it is. We gave the original blueprints to the architect. He didn't even charge us for a full set of plans, because they are basically the same." I put my hands on my hips. "You know the Historical Association will only let us build something that looks identical on the outside."

She dramatically tossed the sheet to the side and said, "Well, then, not much to look at there." She looked up. "So, is Mr. I Have to Have My Very Own House okay with this?"

I rolled my eyes and Emerson rolled hers back. Sometimes it amazed me that Emerson was the actress. Caroline was every bit as dramatic.

I nodded. "He doesn't care what the house is. He just wants to own it."

Caroline gave me a thumbs-up. We had already been preapproved for a loan that would more than cover the house. And when we eventually bought the lot, we would make payments to Caroline each month, as she had asked us to. That way, it was less of a tax hit for her, and we didn't have to come up with a down payment.

"Oh, I love the downstairs floor plan," Emerson was saying as Caroline dissected it with her red pencil. "It's totally perfect."

I nodded. "Yeah. We can do anything we want inside, so we really opened it up."

"You're going to want at least a large door casing there in

between the dining room and kitchen," Mom was saying as she drew in the doorway in red. "This is way too open."

"Oh! With antique pocket doors!" Caroline chimed in.

"Okay," I said, pushing the paper toward them. "Y'all get that all straightened out."

Emerson and I studied the second floor. "Do you really need three bedrooms upstairs and one downstairs?" she asked. "That's a lot of bedrooms."

I held her gaze for a moment and said, "Well, Em, I don't know if you've noticed, but we have quite a lot of family," just as AJ flew by us with Preston and Taylor on his heels, a squealing Carter bringing up the rear.

Emerson laughed. "All this joy these families create, and my evil big sister doesn't think I should get married."

"Caroline!" I scolded. She was such a busybody, always trying to impose her opinions on everyone else. "If I'm not mistaken, you were the poster child for marriage. All you ever wanted was to get married."

A look passed between Mom and Caroline that I didn't quite understand. But it made me know that I should change the subject, so I said, "Do you think a Jack and Jill bath is okay for the boys to share, or do you think I should steal a little from these two rooms to get two en suites?"

Emerson bit the end of her pencil and studied, saying, "Well, a Jack and Jill is fine for families, but I think I'd rather have en suites, personally. Better for resale."

"I think this will get approved, Sloane," Mom said. "I really do."

I looked up at Caroline, who winked at me nearly imperceptibly. Secrets, secrets, secrets.

And, speaking of secrets, I was about to get another one. Once I had wrangled the two boys into their coats, hats, and mittens—or, as Taylor called them, "glubs"—the whole family was off to the market, including Vivi, who was triumphantly sporting Emerson's sweater. "I thought this was the good part about living in Peachtree," Adam was saying to Mom. "You never need winter gear."

Mom laughed. "The weather this year has been crazy. But you never know about the winter. Every decade or so we might even get a little snow."

I was listening to them and keeping an eye on my two boys when Jack touched my arm and signaled for me to stop walking, like he had.

"Em!" I called. She looked back. I pointed at AJ and Taylor and she gave me a thumbs-up. When enough distance was between us and the others, Jack and I started walking again. "Your mom said the house plans look great," Jack said.

I smiled. "They really do. I'm so excited. I hate it for Caroline, but this was our perfect Christmas miracle in some ways. I get to stay downtown, and Adam gets the land he wanted. And we get out of Mom's house, which I have mixed emotions about, but I know it's really the best thing for everyone."

We entered the market. All the booths were filled with goodies, and there were twinkle lights absolutely everywhere. A bluegrass band played Christmas music in the middle of the square, and a teenage girl with a tray handed Jack and me small cups of apple cider. People were selling homemade jewelry and soap, stuffed animals and cards, vegetables and eggs, cookies and bread—anything that could be made or grown here was being sold, and I couldn't wait to make baskets of Peachtree Bluff's finest goodies for my friends—especially my best friend Mary Ann.

I missed the other military wives. No one else understood the lives we led. Being apart from our husbands, learning to rely on each other—and ourselves—for everything we needed, being strong in a way that civilians rarely had to be. I missed it. I missed them. I smiled over at Adam just as he picked Taylor up and put him on his hip, handing him a piece of cookie from a tray. But I wouldn't trade this life we had right now for anything in the world.

I spotted Kimmy leaning down to hand AJ a candy cane—and Tyler, our seemingly ever-present Tyler. I don't know what he said to Vivi, but she burst out laughing. And then they were walking off together. He was adorable. Too adorable. Caroline needed to keep her eye on that one.

Jack smiled at me. "I don't want the others to know . . ." he started.

My heart stopped for a moment. Of everyone in the family, I was the worst at keeping secrets. Or I maybe I just hated them the most. And yet . . . I always seemed to be the bearer of them.

"I want to do something for your mom," Jack said. "It's a special Christmas surprise, and only you can help me with it."

I eyed him warily, but when he told me his plan, I laughed.

There were some secrets I couldn't live with, some I couldn't bear. But this one? This one was pretty great. And, besides, with only four more days until Christmas, this was a secret even I could keep.

# Emerson: Mad About You

IN THE END, I DECIDED not to tell Kyle that I was meeting up with Mark. I could have. I probably should have. And I had ample opportunity while we were walking from store to store putting the finishing touches on Carter's presents the next afternoon. "Hey," I'd said while we were walking. "What are you getting me for Christmas?"

"You will never, ever drag that information out of me."

"Is it pretty?" I smiled.

"Not as pretty as you," he said, leaning over to kiss me.

That was when I was going to tell him, casually, that I was going to have a drink with Mark. But before I could, he said, "Babe, I have a bunch of work to do with Keith at the shop this afternoon. Do you mind?"

He was going to be working . . . so, really, what was the point of telling him? It would only worry him. And I was already worried enough for the both of us. "Of course not," I said. "I'll miss you." I gasped. "But you'll be back in time for the Claus Crawl, right?"

"Wouldn't miss it."

The Claus Crawl was our favorite sister tradition. Five bars. Five signature cocktails. And all the ugly Christmas sweaters you could handle. It was super fun. Although the next day was decidedly less fun.

And now, I realized as I sat on the outdoor porch at Full Moon with Mark, I was getting an early start on things, which wasn't good. I was just going to have a sparkling water, but, before he had even said anything, I was all worked up. I needed a drink to calm myself, so I went ahead and ordered a rum punch to take the edge off. Besides, I usually only had a sip or two at each stop of the Claus Crawl, so I'd be fine.

Mark looked good. Well, I mean, the same. Happy. Had he looked that happy with me? And I shouldn't care either way, right?

"How are you?" he asked. I hated this already. *Don't be cryptic. Just tell me why we're here.*

I smiled. "Oh, I'm good. Weird few weeks, but everyone is okay, and that's what matters."

He nodded. "Yeah. Carter's really cute. I saw her with Ansley the other day."

How could I respond to that? *Yes, my kid with the man I basically left you for is really cute? The kid I found out I was pregnant with that wasn't yours just a few weeks after what was supposed to be our wedding is the most amazing thing that ever happened to me?* I settled on, "Aw, thanks. She's a sweetie."

"Look, I don't want to be awkward or drag this out," he said, "but as you know, the building that housed my family's company was totally leveled in the hurricane."

I was trying to concentrate on what he was saying, but, over his shoulder, I saw a guy on a stand-up paddleboard. And he looked a whole lot like Kyle. And it looked quite a bit like there was some beautiful woman with him. Who wasn't me. It was also cold out, so whoever they were, they were pretty brave. *Focus, Emerson.* "I'm sorry, Mark. I know what that company means to you. That must be so hard. Are you going to be able to rebuild?"

"Well, actually," he said, "that's what I wanted to tell you." I took a sip of my drink and looked out over his shoulder again. It was pretty far away, so I couldn't be sure the man was Kyle, but the guy who looked an awful lot like him was now taking this anonymous woman's hand and helping her to shore.

"I've sold the company."

I almost spit my drink out. But I wiped my mouth and recovered. "I'm sorry. What? It sounded like you just said you were selling the company."

He nodded and smiled. "I did. I sold the company." He paused. "I met someone, and we're getting married. Her career just wouldn't allow us to make a life here."

I could feel myself blinking really quickly.

He was still talking. "I knew you would hear it eventually, and I just thought it might be better if it came from me."

This was one of those moments when I wished I didn't wear my heart so fully on my sleeve. This was one of those moments that I wished I could filter slightly more so I wouldn't say things like, "Let me get this straight. When we were engaged, when I wanted you to live very part-time in LA, that was a total nonstarter. But now you've met someone new, and she is evidently worth changing your life for? Is that what I'm supposed to take away from this conversation?"

I could see in his face that he was getting defensive, and no two people could have a major blow-up quite like Mark and I. I distracted myself by looking over his shoulder again. Kyle or his look-alike had disappeared into the woods now. Still, I barely cared because I was so shocked.

"Oh yeah, our breakup was allll my fault. Sure. Blame it on stubborn, crazy Mark."

I hated when he talked about himself in third person.

"I might remind you," he continued, "that I'm not the one who jumped into bed with the town barista the minute we called the wedding off—or maybe even before. Who knows, really?"

If I had been calm and reasonable, I really could have seen his point. But this version of myself gasped and said, "How dare you?! Do you have any idea what you put me through? I was willing to sacrifice everything for you. I was willing to change my life for you. And you couldn't do the same for me. Not even a little. But, now, *now* all that has changed?"

I stood up. "I get it. You wanted to rub it in my face, have the last laugh. Well, good for you, Mark. If you wanted to be a gigantic asshole and pay me back in the worst way, you've done it. Have a nice life."

The shock on his face registered as he said, "Emerson, I'm sorry. I thought you'd want to know."

Right. Sure he did. I scooted my chair back and turned around. "And I'll let you get my drink with all the money you made selling your company."

I wished I hadn't said that. My previous ending line had been much stronger. But I stomped out of the restaurant. Surprise, surprise, he didn't follow me. He never had.

Caroline was sitting in the living room when I got back to Mom's. "Get dressed," I said. "We're leaving right now."

She looked around. "Okay, well, let me get Vivi all squared away. She's babysitting and—"

I glared at her. "Does this look like a face that cares?"

She raised her eyebrows. "No, it does not. Duly noted."

"Sloane!" I called.

"Yeah!"

"We're leaving right now!"

"The Crawl doesn't start for another hour," she called down.

"It starts when I say it starts," I said.

She peered down the stairs at me. "Yup. I'll be ready in five. I presume we'll cover what all this is about?"

I nodded sullenly.

Three bars and three very strong Christmas drinks later, the whole story had come flooding out. And it was only like eight o'clock. Not a good start for trying not to drink too much.

I had moved on from the furious part of the night, where my sisters had to soothe and coddle me, to the *Girls Just Wanna Have Fun*, maybe-we-should-dance-on-the-bar portion of the evening. "Where in the world is Kyle?" I shouted over the noise as we were dancing. Alone. Just the three of us.

"I think the guys are probably putting the kids to bed before they come," Sloane shouted. "Mom and Jack were going out to dinner."

"Aw, that's sweet," I yelled.

They were so cute. I was really starting to miss Kyle, and I was starting to forget that he was maybe paddleboarding with another woman today.

"Ah!" Sloane squealed, pointing at the door. "There's your guy!"

I got really excited, but then I saw it was Wes she was pointing to. Caroline threw her arms around his neck. He must have gotten an early start too, because he had no qualms about dancing on the nearly empty dance floor with my sister. Although, as I glanced back, that made sense. She was hot. And, what's more, she was Caroline Murphy. Now, then, forever and always.

Finally, Kyle and Adam walked in.

"Let's hit our next stop!" I yelled to them, motioning to Caroline and Wes too.

We all ran outside into the freezing night, giggling, the guys following behind us.

"Wes," Caroline said, "I promise you that I'm not usually like this."

"I hate to hear that."

"You're cute," I said. Then I turned to Caroline. "He's cute."

"Yeah," Sloane added. "But he lives here. Not New York."

"Sad."

"Hey!" he said. "I'm right here. I can hear you."

Caroline took his hand, which was a big deal because Caroline wasn't a hand-holder. "Forgive my sisters. They have forgotten their manners."

"I've forgotten everything!" I said gleefully. But, as I said it, it all came flooding back: Mark's announcement, my horrid over-reaction, my suspicions that *my* Kyle was out paddleboarding with another woman. I could feel my buzz melting away. But by bar number five, the grand finale, Paradise Pub, it was back—and the boys had well caught up with us. We were now dancing our hearts out with a bunch of strangers. Sloane and I dashed off to the bar to get a refill. "Where's Caroline?" I asked.

Sloane looked around and then laughed, pointing. Caroline was in the corner making out with Wes. I mean, it didn't matter because by this point it was really late and everyone left was making a total scene, which, let's face it, was the point of the Claus Crawl.

"Good Lord," I said. "Well, we might never know how he was at eighteen, but I think by tomorrow we're going to know how he is in his thirties."

Sloane laughed.

Kyle came up behind me then, kissing my neck, and I don't know what came over me at that moment, but I was suddenly intensely angry at him. "Is that what you were doing with that woman today?" I asked, pointing at Caroline and Wes.

He was totally taken aback. "What are you even talking about, Emerson?"

"I saw you!" I shouted, pointing at him. "I saw you paddleboarding across to Starlite Island with that woman!"

He pulled me into the corner, which was slightly quieter and less crowded than the bar area and crossed his arms. "And when precisely did this alleged paddleboarding—nude paddleboarding, I'm assuming from your reaction—happen?"

I rolled my eyes. "It wasn't *nude* paddleboarding. I'm sure that didn't happen until later, when you were off somewhere in the woods or something."

He nodded. "Uh-huh. Yes. That sounds plausible. An entire town of empty houses and buildings, but I paddled over to Starlite with a woman who wasn't you to have sex with her amidst the briars and sandspurs in the freezing cold."

"Well, I don't know," I said, hiccupping. "But I was having drinks with Mark and there you were."

I could see Kyle's face getting hot as I felt mine warming. I had just told on myself. And see, this is why you shouldn't keep secrets. Because instead of this being a nothing conversation where Kyle would have said something amazing like, *Babe, I trust you. If Mark has something to say to you, he must need to get it out there. You should respect that,* now it looked like I'd been hiding something, which I totally wasn't. And now, I could see very clearly, the shoe was on the other foot.

"The shoe is on the other foot," I said out loud. "I don't get that. What does that even mean?"

"It means," Kyle said, "that you were accusing me of something and now you've realized that it's because you had something to feel guilty about yourself."

I shook my head and put my finger up. "No, no. You have it all wrong. I don't have anything in the world to feel guilty about."

Kyle crossed his arms. Mark was a tiny bit of a sore spot for Kyle, even still, which made sense. I'd been engaged to him, after all. "So if you don't have anything to feel guilty about, why didn't you tell me?"

I smiled sweetly, hoping to defuse the situation. "Well, I'm telling you now."

Kyle shook his head. "Emerson, just when I think I understand you . . ." He turned to walk away, and I started to feel panicky. I followed him, grabbing his arm.

"Mark just wanted to tell me that he was getting married and moving away," I shouted over the noise.

Kyle stopped and turned. "What?"

I nodded. "We weren't, like, reminiscing about our tragic relationship."

"Oh," Kyle said softly, putting his thumb on my chin. "That must be hard."

I studied his face. I had never, not ever, met a man with so little ego. Or a woman, for that matter. Roles reversed, if he had been the one so upset about an ex, I would have been moody and defensive. And here he was comforting me.

"Does it make you love me less if I tell you that, yes, it's a little hard? I don't know why. I am mad about you. I can't breathe without you. I only feel right when I am literally touching you. But he sold his company and he's moving. And I'm happy for him, but it just sort of stings."

"Of course it does," he said. "That he would do that for someone when he wasn't willing to do it for you."

I snapped my fingers. That is why I was so upset. "Yes! That!"

He kissed me softly and stroked my cheek with his thumb. "And, no, Emerson. That does not, could not make me love you less. Nothing could make me love you less."

Well, that was untrue. But it sounded good.

"You're so mature. I would be so jealous right now if the roles were reversed."

He put both his hands on my cheeks and kissed me again. "The past is beautiful like the darkness between the fireflies," he said into my ear.

I kissed him again. "That is so poetic," I whispered.

"It's Mason Jennings," he whispered back. "So don't be too impressed."

I kissed him again and could feel myself righting, like the storm had passed. I knew Kyle would never make me feel the way Mark had tonight, the way he used to quite often, in fact. Kyle always considered my feelings. "Kyle," I said softly.

"Em," he said back.

"I love you."

"I love you more," he said.

And as I kissed him again, I couldn't imagine—not in my wildest dreams—how that could even be possible.

# Vivi: The More, the Merrier

*Christmas Eve*

DURING OUR MAYBE-SORT-OF DATE ON Starlite Island, I had been practically flying over the idea that the only reason Tyler hadn't kissed me was because he had a girlfriend—who he had now broken up with. We had flirted and laughed and shared secrets all night long. And then we got in the boat and went home. No kiss. I had braved the freezing elements all while trying to be cute for nothing.

I had vowed that I would put him behind me. I'd go home, tell Lake I was ready to be his girlfriend, and forget Tyler had ever existed. As if that were even possible . . .

But now, my phone buzzed. Want to come hang out at the farm today? It was Tyler, of course, and all my resolve to stay away from him melted away.

I had to hold myself back from texting him immediately. Because, I mean, yes. I'd hang out with him at the farm. The street corner. A roadside rest stop. Wherever Tyler was, that's where I wanted to be. Did I feel that same way about Lake? I didn't think so. Had I ever?

I walked downstairs into the kitchen to distract myself. "Oh, good!" Gransley said. "You're up. Can you help me set the table for Christmas Eve dinner?"

Oh God, oh God. That was a way longer task than I could possibly handle before texting Tyler back. But as I was still trying to get back in Gransley's good graces because I ruined her trip, I would have said yes to anything she asked.

She handed me a stack of linen place mats. "Hey, Gransley," I said, testing the waters. "Can Tyler come to Christmas Eve dinner?"

"Well, of course," she said. "If it's okay with Kimmy and his parents, the more, the merrier." Then, pausing her silverware counting, she said, "You two are quite the little item, aren't you?"

I shrugged. "I don't know. Maybe? I think we might just be friends."

I could tell she was about to respond when Mom ran into the dining room. "Mom!" she said. "Leah just called, and there's an emergency at the store!"

"What kind of emergency?" Gransley said.

Mom took the silverware from her hands and said, "I have no idea. But you need to go now!"

Gransley scampered out of the dining room, and as soon as the front door closed, Sloane, Adam, and Jack filed in from the back, loaded down with clothes. I studied the sweater draped over Sloane's arm. They were definitely Gransley's clothes.

"What is going on?" I asked.

"We're finally putting the surprise for Gransley into motion!" Sloane said, her voice muffled by the towering stack of clothes she was carrying.

"What's wrong at the store?" I asked Mom.

Mom shrugged. "Nothing. I just needed to get her out of here for a few hours. I asked AJ to trap a squirrel and set it free in there. I figured that would keep them occupied for a while."

"Mom!" I protested.

"What?" She looked at me innocently. "It's for the good of the cause."

"Couldn't you have just said there was a problem with a client or something?"

She appeared to think that over. "Yes. Maybe that would have been a better idea." She waved her hand. "But I'm sure AJ didn't actually trap a squirrel. Leah probably came up with a better plan."

If I knew AJ, I was positive he had.

The clatter of footsteps down the stairs made me turn to see Grandjack. "Hey, Viv, do you want to talk real quick?"

"No, no, no," Sloane said. "If you think you're getting out of this, you are wrong, my friend. This was *your* idea."

Jack laughed. "It will only take a minute. I promise."

Good. Because I only had about a minute left of self-control to not text Tyler back. I looked back at Mom, and she shrugged. I followed Grandjack back into Gransley's kitchen. He leaned on the counter, looking casual, so I hoisted myself up to sit on it.

"The Christmas surprises are ready," he whispered.

Excitement rippled through me. Had I ever been this excited about a present that wasn't for me? I couldn't imagine that I had been. "Yay!" I whispered back.

"But, really," he said, "I just wanted to apologize. I had no right to drop the big news that I was your biological grandfather."

I shook my head, realizing that this was the window I'd been looking for, the one I'd been too, like, embarrassed or scared or something to find. "No, I want to apologize, Grandjack. I ruined your trip and put us all in danger. If it helps, I definitely learned my lesson."

He smiled in that way that made me know I was forgiven and that, maybe even more important, he could never really be mad at me in the first place. "I really am glad you're my grandfather," I said quietly, meaning it. "I hope you know that."

He crossed his arms and said, "Well, I'm really glad you're my granddaughter, and I'm sorry I'm not better at all this stuff. I shouldn't have told you like I did. It was wrong of me. We were just having a good time and I got excited and . . ."

He was so cute. "I promise it's okay. I'm glad I know."

I hopped down from the counter and hugged him tight. I looked up at him. "And I'll be here to train you, so you don't screw up with all your other grandkids."

He laughed so hard as I pulled away.

"There's only one of you, Vivian Beaumont."

I smiled, pulling my phone out of my pocket, as he said, "I'm going to go get the rest of Gransley's things."

I nodded as I reread Tyler's text: Want to come hang out at the farm today?

I finally texted him. I don't know. What did you have in mind? Want me to help you clean the stables? I was joking, obviously.

I'm going to teach you how to drive.

Oh my gosh. That sounded even worse than the stable thing!

I walked back into the dining room, where Mom was still setting the table. "No!" I said out loud. "No, no, no."

The front door opened, and a very familiar voice, one I really liked, rang out: "Viv!"

I crossed my arms. "I have no interest in learning how to drive."

"Tyler's taking you driving? That's great—you should learn how to drive!" Mom said. "It will be good for you."

Sloane came back into the dining room, holding a toy box. "If I remember correctly," she said to Mom, "getting you to learn to drive at thirty-four basically took an act of God."

Mom smiled. "And now I'm glad I know how. You were right. Is that what you wanted to hear? Are you happy?"

Sloane perked up. "Wow! That was more satisfying than I thought it was going to be. Yes. I am very, very happy, in fact."

Tyler reached out and took the toy box from Sloane.

"Where do you want this?" he asked.

"In the smallest bedroom in the guesthouse." She paused. "The blue one."

"Hey," Sloane said, looking at both of us, "if you guys could help for just a few minutes before you leave, it would be amazing. We're trying to work fast over here."

Old Vivi would have begged off, saying that between setting the table and learning to drive, she had enough on her plate. But new Vivi said, "Sure, Aunt Sloane!"

Old Vivi mouthed to mom, *Community service.*

*You wish*, she mouthed back.

Tyler walked out the back door with the toy box as Emerson emerged from upstairs, a duffel bag on each shoulder.

"You're letting a sixteen-year-old boy teach your fifteen-year-old daughter to drive?" Emerson asked.

"I forget he's only sixteen," Mom said. "He just seems so . . ."

"Capable," Sloane filled in.

"Strong," I added.

"Mature," Mom finished.

Emerson looked at each of us warily. "Okay. Well, if Tyler ever needs an official fan club, he's all set."

Tyler and I helped Sloane for a little bit and then got in Kimmy's truck to head to the farm. "Oh, um, I asked Gransley if you could come to dinner tonight. I mean, if you don't have plans with your family and you want to," I rambled.

Tyler looked over at me and smiled. "Really?"

His question made me think it was too much, too soon. But then he said, "Yeah. That'd be really great."

Then I was happy I'd asked.

As we reached the gate of Kimmy's farm, Tyler put her old truck in park and jumped out. He tried to open my door, but I pushed down the lock really quickly. We both laughed.

"You're being a brat!" he said, smiling. "It's a life skill. You should thank me!"

"Thank you!" I said through the window.

Then I laughed and unlocked the door. Tyler opened it and took my hand to help me down. When he did it was like electricity zapped through our fingertips.

He kept holding my hand as we walked around to the driver's side—and I loved every second, I might add. He finally let it go when he started showing me around the inside of the car. "This is the clutch and this is the gas. And that's the brake, of course." He stopped and looked at me. "Well, go on," he said. "Get in." I did, and, much to my surprise, he scooted up beside me, so close that I could smell the cookie he had just eaten at Gransley's.

"This," he said, taking my hand again, "is the gearshift." With his hand over mine, he moved the clutch from neutral to first, second, third, and reverse. I doubted I would ever drive anyway, but I was totally positive I would never drive stick shift. But Tyler was so warm, and he smelled so good, that I didn't want the lesson to end.

After I had stalled out about a hundred times in one of Kimmy's huge, grassy fields and hit the fence twice, Tyler said, "You know what, Viv, you're right. You don't need to know how to drive. You'll probably always have a driver. In fact, why don't we go walk around downtown instead? Let's practice our walking, since I think you're going to be doing a lot of it."

I was laughing so hard, I leaned over the steering wheel to catch my breath. And when I did, the most miraculous thing happened. I felt it. I *felt* it. The way the clutch lets out just right and you ease onto the gas really slowly. Not wanting to jinx myself, I sped up just a little, heading toward the barn, and held down the clutch again, letting it out to shift into second gear.

"It didn't make that horrible noise!" I shouted.

I didn't dare look at Tyler, and I could tell he was sitting really, really still. I made it from the outside fence all the way to the barn, where I pushed the clutch in again and put it in park.

I looked at Tyler, my mouth hanging open.

"It's a Christmas miracle," he whispered. "She drove. The city girl drove a farm truck four hundred yards."

He opened the door and ran around to the side where he lifted me out of the truck and spun me around. This was it. The moment. *The perfect moment.* It was worth all the waiting, all the missed opportunities, because this was something I would always remember. He was still holding me in the air, and our eyes were locked, my heart was pounding . . . and I heard Kimmy's voice—a voice I usually liked, I might add—yelling, "You did it, Vivi!"

I could have killed her. Tyler set me down, and I smiled disdainfully. He bit his lip and shook his head. "She's a natural," he said, never taking his eyes off me.

I was absolutely not a natural. I was not even in the same zip code as a natural. Kimmy walked over to us and handed me a basket of eggs. "Take these to your grandmother," she said. "They'll be good for that breakfast casserole she makes Christmas morning."

"Sounds great," I said.

"See you at Starlite, Star Bright!" she called as she walked away.

I gasped. I was so excited I'd learned to drive I'd almost forgotten all about my favorite part of Peachtree Bluff Christmas.

I looked down at my phone to check the time. "We need to line up for Starlite by five," I said. I was going to add, *I mean, if you want to go.* But I didn't. Because we were going. No way around it. I wasn't missing it for anything.

"Right," Tyler said. He pointed to the house. "Hey, mind if I shower and change really quickly and we'll go now? We can be one of the first boats out."

I grinned and nodded. I couldn't think of anything I'd like

quite so much. I texted Mom, Okay if I do Starlite with Tyler and we meet you at the house after?

I only assumed you were . . .

She loved picking on me about Tyler.

But thank you for telling me where you are.

Love you, I said back.

I did love her.

I also loved Peachtree Bluff at Christmas, but I had to say, Christmas had never felt this cold here. It wasn't like I wasn't used to the cold. But I wasn't used to cold *here*. I shivered just a little as Tyler and I got out of the car at the town kayak storage. For Starlite, Star Bright, everyone brought his or her kayak, canoe, rowboat, dinghy, and engineless vessel of any kind and dropped it off here, at this tiny stretch of sandy beach on the waterfront, the morning of Christmas Eve. It was maybe one hundred paddle strokes from Starlite Island, so it made it the perfect place for people to stash their boats, and to share them with anyone who didn't have one of their own.

A bevy of volunteers helped any and everyone who wanted to participate get in a vessel and paddle over to the island. There were ferry boats for people who couldn't paddle themselves. But the key to the magic of Starlite, Star Bright was all those vessels in the water all at once and the silence of it all too.

We were only the third people in line, so Mrs. McClasky, bundled up in her parka, clipboard in hand and whistle around her neck, said, "All right, kids. Just the two of you?" She smiled knowingly and I gave her a disparaging *stop it* look as I nodded. I also wondered why exactly she felt like she needed a whistle . . . but I didn't ask.

"Take your pick," she said.

Tyler pointed excitedly. "Canoe?" he asked.

I nodded. I didn't care if we floated over on an iceberg so long as I got to do it with Tyler. The advantage of the canoe over the kayak was that the teak boards that served as seats were situated so we could face each other as we paddled. Tyler helped me in and then, pushing the canoe out into the water, hopped in at the last possible second. He was just so . . . effortless. And he was, as some Murphy woman had said this morning, capable.

Hippie Hal, in his waders, came to the boat and handed us two candles with little cones around the bottom to keep our fingers from getting burnt as the wax dripped and a pack of matches that said, PEACHTREE PROVISIONS. PRESENTING SPONSOR OF STARLITE, STAR BRIGHT. How smart of Adam and Grandjack to advertise during Peachtree's biggest event of the season.

"Don't let 'em get wet, kids," he said.

"Did you want to paddle?" Tyler asked, his face very serious.

I smirked. "Yeah, right."

He laughed.

I sat facing Tyler as he paddled, watching the day merge with the night. He broke the rhythmic sound of his paddle cutting through the water as he said, "Can I tell you something?"

I nodded. We were so close together.

"I'm a little intimidated by you."

"Because I'm such a good driver?"

He laughed. "Yeah."

"I am so not intimidating."

"You're beautiful and smart and you go to this fancy school and live in this fancy house, and there's *Lake . . .*"

"Come on, Tyler. I tried to lock Lake down for like a year. But when he asked me out, I turned him down." When he didn't say anything, I decided to take a chance, to really put myself out there. So I added, "Because of *you.* Not because of my community service."

He smiled. "Really?"

"Really." He seemed happy, I thought. Right? But he didn't say anything else, so I wasn't sure. As the setting sun blazed a hot orange in contrast to the cold day, I looked around. "Here," I said. "I think this is the spot."

"We can pull up on the beach if you want," he said.

I shook my head. "This is better. You'll see."

The sun had almost completely set, and now, as boats were filing in all around us—but not too close—I knew we had to pay attention. We were right in the middle of the waterway, equidistant from downtown Peachtree and Starlite Island.

"Are you sure you don't want to be on the beach?" Tyler asked. "So we can see?"

I shook my head. "I promise this is the spot, Tyler."

A few minutes later, when the sun was all the way down, I struck a match, and, as I did, flames from neighboring boats flickered all around us, the dark sky and the pitch-black water erupting in the soft glow of candlelight. At that moment, someone began singing. There was an order to our caroling. Not too long because it was so cold. But we started with "We Wish You a Merry

Christmas" and then continued with "Joy to the World" and "Jingle Bells." Tyler and I laughed, singing together. I made fun of him when he forgot the words to "It's the Most Wonderful Time of the Year," but I stopped when he squeezed my knee during the line, "There'll be much mistletoeing," which made my heart race out of my chest. I wanted to say, *Promise?* but I kept my cool.

After "O Holy Night," what seemed like much too soon later, the grand finale began. *Silent night, holy night, all is calm, all is bright.* There was a cadence to the caroling, a rhythm, where the bright and tinkling joy trailed off into an almost holy, serious quiet.

"Look around," I whispered to Tyler, pausing my singing. Some people liked to be on Starlite Island to really get a view of these hundreds of vessels out on the water, to see the full effect of all the lights. But me? I liked to be in the dead center, so that everywhere I looked, everywhere I listened, all I could see was candlelight, and all I could hear was the singing voices of people who came together as one for this special night. You could not participate in Starlite, Star Bright and not feel changed afterward, like you were part of something that was bigger than yourself.

"This is the most magical experience of my life," Tyler whispered. I nodded, singing again.

He handed me his lit candle and rubbed his hands up and down my arms to stave off the cold. "Have you ever had something that you wanted to be perfect? That you knew you would want to remember for the rest of your life?"

I nodded. And then he leaned closer to me. I could feel my heart thrumming in my chest. He was so warm. And he smelled so good.

It registered with me that the last line of the last verse of the song was being sung right now. And, despite the fact that I believed something I really wanted was about to happen, I, like everyone else on the water, blew out our candles, the waterway fading instantly into a great, deep, silent black.

I had been waiting for this moment for what felt like forever, and, as Tyler's lips finally met mine, as he pulled me in close to him, I realized that it had been worth the wait. He had been worth the wait. When we finally pulled away, I looked up and gasped.

"No way," Tyler said, looking up too.

"You wanted it to be memorable," I said. "Snow in Peachtree Bluff? I think you accomplished that."

A murmur made its way through the crowd as the people who had begun paddling back to shore started to realize what was happening. Tyler held his hand out, and snowflakes gathered in his bare palm. He touched one on the tip of my nose and kissed me again so sweetly I had to remind myself to breathe.

"A white Christmas," I said. "Can you believe it?"

It was like all the hard stuff this year—my parents, getting in trouble, the hurricane—had just been swept away, that in a few hours they would be covered by a soft, cold blanket of white.

"Hey, Viv," Tyler said, looking at me like I was the only person in Peachtree Bluff, "I know you turned down Lake, but how would you feel about being my girlfriend?"

I peered up at him as if I were considering this matter a great deal. "Was that true what you said? About doing my community service with me? Think seriously about your answer."

He laughed. "For you, Vivian Beaumont, I would spend the

year building Habitat houses and picking up garbage on the side of the highway."

"Ew," I said. "I was thinking about holding babies at the hospital and running bingo at the nursing home." I leaned over and kissed him. "But, yes, Tyler. It would be an honor to be your girlfriend."

As he kissed me again, "Out of the friend zone!" rang out beside us.

"Merry Christmas, Keith," I called, not even turning around. Tyler waved at him.

Then he started paddling. In the snow. In Peachtree Bluff. On Christmas Eve. As the fireworks on the now-cleared-out Starlite Island began erupting, I knew for sure that, like Tyler had said, this was a moment I would remember. My mom, my aunts, and Gransley always said you'd never forget your first Peachtree Bluff summer love, that those days would stay with you for the rest of your life. As Tyler grinned at me, I knew that I would never forget these magical few weeks with him. Summer love was great. But I knew someday I'd look back on this winter love and smile. And I'd remember the warm glow of a white Christmas and, what's more, the perfect hand to hold.

# Caroline: That Girl

*Christmas Eve*

MY SISTER WAS WATCHING MY son, and I had disappeared from the Murphy Christmas Eve chaos to canoodle with a boy I liked. Probably for the last time, since his son would be joining him on Christmas Day after doing Christmas Eve with his mom in Atlanta.

A few days before, I had stopped drinking at my second stop on the Claus Crawl. Which was what made me know that it was probably Wes, not the alcohol, that had made me feel giddy and happy and alive that night. And it was probably the combination of the two that had made me go home with him, a trend that had continued into the next day and the night after that and, well, now.

"Oh my God," I said, lying in his bed. "What if we had stayed married to other people? We would have totally missed out on this."

He turned to me. "Right? I was just thinking that."

I leaned over on my side, propping my head up on my hand. "I'm going to miss this when I go back to New York. I'm going to miss you."

It shocked me that I was saying that. It must have been all the oxytocin. After years of basically no sex at all, my body must have been enraptured to finally have a little of its favorite chemical again. People say that exercise has a similar effect. People are stupid.

"What do you mean you're going to miss me?" Wes asked, turning over to face me.

I was sure I looked confused. "Well, I mean, you know I'm going home, right? I can't just stay in Peachtree forever." For the first time in my entire life, when I said "stay in Peachtree forever," the idea made me feel kind of happy. But, no, I had to go back to New York, back to the store, back to the hustle and bustle of my favorite city in the world and the calm and quiet of my small but perfectly appointed apartment, my friends, my restaurants, my parties. Yeah, I was definitely going back.

"Well, yeah," he said. "I know you're going home, but I guessed I had hoped that we could sort of keep this going long-distance."

The thought of leaving him *did* make me sad. "Oh," I said, not hiding my shock well. "I mean, yeah. That would be great. I guess I just thought that with the logistics being what they are, and our lives being what they are, it might be too . . . complicated." I wanted to find a better word, but that was, unfortunately, the only one that came to mind.

I sat up. "What's our other option at this point? I live in New York. You live here."

"But you're in Peachtree Bluff a lot, right?" he asked.

"I mean, mostly on holidays and in the summer, but yeah, I'm here sometimes," I said, scrunching up my nose and kissing him.

I liked Wes. I wouldn't say I loved him—at least, not yet. I wouldn't even say that I could actually see a true future for us. But I guessed that was more for logistical reasons than anything else. And the thought of getting on a plane and flying away from him in a few days did make me sad. Then I had the most wonderful, golden, glowing thought. I sat up, holding the sheet to my chest. "Do you remember when we were kids, and we'd go away for the summer and have this wonderful, carefree romance?"

"Well, I didn't have to go anywhere. The hot out-of-town girls came to me. But, yes, I remember. It would hit May, and if I had a girlfriend we had to break up because what is summer without a summer fling?"

I pointed. "Exactly!"

"Is that what we are?" he asked. "A summer fling?"

I shrugged now. "Well, I mean, it's Christmas Eve, so no, not a summer fling exactly. But a Christmas fling?"

He looked down and nodded, not meeting my eye. "So what about when you come for weekends or on vacation?" he asked. "What if I just happen to be in New York for a show?"

I smiled at him and looked into his hopeful eyes. "You come to New York for shows?"

He picked up my hand and kissed it. "I do now."

I thought about this briefly. It was hard to really say what I wanted. Well, no, it wasn't. What I wanted was to find an amazing man to share my life with. But I had two children; Wes had one. We lived in different places, led different lives. We had to be realistic about not setting ourselves up for failure. "Did you ever have a girl that came back every summer?"

He nodded.

"How about if I'm that girl?"

He leaned over and kissed me. "You are that girl, Caroline Murphy. You have always been and always will be that girl."

That. That was the kind of stuff that was going to be hard to walk away from.

We bundled up in our coats and walked down to the town boat storage. The candlelit waterway was already full, and the beautiful sound of all those voices merging together brought tears to my eyes. Wes silently helped me aboard a homemade dinghy—one of the only boats left—and, as he rowed by candlelight, I ran the question through my mind briefly before I asked it: "Hey, want to come to dinner?"

"Tonight?"

I nodded.

"Is that too much too soon, or whatever?"

I thought about it. "You know, Wes, I think not introducing people to your kids is great. But my kids know you. And it's fine. You're a nice man they know from Peachtree Bluff. If we never go out again—which I sincerely hope is not the case—you will continue to be a nice man they know from Peachtree Bluff."

He laughed. "All right, then. I'm in."

"Besides, nobody should be alone on Christmas Eve." As I said it, a layer of this equation that I hadn't quite thought of yet hit me. "Um, did I mention that my almost-ex-husband is coming?"

"Great," he said. "Can't think of a better way to forget that I'm not with my son on Christmas Eve."

The mere idea of that made me sad. As he stopped rowing, in the midst of all those boats, I kissed him.

"Speaking of," he said. "I got those franchise documents worked up. Let's go over all the details when it isn't Christmas Eve."

"Business and pleasure. I'm swooning!"

I laughed as Wes, in a very off-key voice, began to bellow, "Silent night, holy night." I joined in, and, as the candles on the waterway went dark, he pulled me into him, kissing me long and slow and sweet. Pulling back, I laughed, pointing toward the sky. "Wes! Look!"

He laughed now too. "Snow in Peachtree Bluff." He looked at me and then up at the snow and said, "I guess sometimes all your dreams really do come true."

Minutes later, as we walked hand in hand down the carless street, the brightly lit wreaths lining the historic streetlamps, candles aglow in the houses and churches, I thought about my mom's house on Murphy Row, the one filled with my children, my sisters, my mother, and, miracle of miracles, my biological father. The day my dad died, it felt like our world had ended, like time stopped. But it hadn't. It went on. We fell down. We got back up. We went on to live brilliant lives full of Christmases and snow angels and handsome men from our pasts to squire us down frost-covered streets.

Marrying James had been my biggest dream come true, but that hadn't worked out like I thought, either. As I smiled at Wes and he smiled at me, feeling all those things I hadn't felt since we were teenagers, I realized that maybe dreams are like people: they change over time, often in the very best ways. The snow fell around me, and Wes kissed my glove-covered hand. It was a surprise, all of it. The snow. The man. And it made me think that we can't plan for happiness, not really. Because, sometimes, the best dreams come true are the ones we don't even know we have.

# Sloane: Finding Christmas

*Christmas Eve*

*Dear Sloane,*

*Merry Christmas Eve! It's here. And so is Starlite, Star Bright.*
*Did I ever tell you about how, every night when I was deployed,*
*I would look up in the sky for the first star that appeared, and*
*I would think of you, wishing to be near you again, wishing for*
*nothing more than to spend the rest of my life with you? Well,*
*I did. I still do. What an adventure this year has been. What*
*an adventure the next year is going to be . . . But as long as the*
*adventure is with you, I'm always up for it.*

*All my love,*
*Adam*

I smiled as I looked out the upstairs window and finished tying
the bow on the very last present. Caroline had already left to go
to Starlite, Star Bright with Wes. Adam and Mom had all the kids,

and Vivi was, as per usual, somewhere with Tyler, who she swore had put her in the friend zone. I had my doubts about that.

I leaned back and admired my gifts. A little box for each person in my family. I piled them up in my arms and carried them downstairs, placing them one by one underneath the already-overflowing Christmas tree.

I wasn't sure how it would feel to leave my childhood home, my safe place. But I had to admit, it felt sort of right. Yes, I was sad about moving, but this way, with my family down the street, it could remain that place of solace and escape, the place where we had visited my grandparents and now would visit my mother. I hadn't wanted to move, not really. But I knew well that life—and marriage—were about compromise. And this was a small one.

"Sloane!" Jack called.

"In here!" I called back.

I got up off the floor, wiping my hands on my jeans, and turned to smile at him. I would probably never get used to truly thinking of him as my father. But sometimes, in moments like this one, it hit me all at once that he was. "Merry Christmas Eve," he said. "Thanks for doing this."

"For doing what?" Mom asked, appearing in the doorway, a case of juice boxes under her arm.

"Sloane and I have a little surprise for you," Jack said.

*More than one, actually*, I thought. Mom winced. She was the self-proclaimed poster child for hating surprises. But, well, in a family like this one, the surprises just kept coming. *Please, only the good ones this year*, I hoped. I mused that, as crazy as the hurricane had made all our lives, the metaphorical storms had mostly been worse.

Mom rolled her eyes. "Please, guys. No surprises."

"You're going to like this one," Jack said.

I started up the stairs, Mom and Jack following behind. I turned to the right, to the beautiful master suite with the stunning view of the water. I was going to miss waking up here every morning. But, well, it was Mom's house.

I turned to look at Mom and she looked around questioningly. "I'm missing it," she said. "It's very clean?"

So, yes, my organizational skills were lacking. Thanks for pointing that out.

"Go open the closet," I said.

She walked into the bathroom and, a few seconds later, walked back out. "Those are all my clothes in there."

I nodded.

She looked at Jack. "Ans, Sloane, Adam, and the boys have very graciously agreed to stay in the guesthouse until their new house is built."

"I don't understand," she said.

He took her hands. "'The Christmas cookies taste better from my oven,'" Jack said. "'I think the bigger tree should go at my house since I have the bigger living room.'"

She laughed, and I recognized those as things Mom had said over the past few weeks.

"Ans, I think I know you better than anyone in all the world, and it has been pretty clear to me since we moved in together that you missed this house, that you wanted to come back."

She looked at me now. "Is this okay with you?"

I laughed. "Mom! It's your house. Of course it's okay."

She looked back at Jack. "But your house. *Our* house."

Jack shrugged. "Maybe this was always meant to be our house. We're the grandparents. We need to have the house where all the kids and grandkids come home to stay. My house will be for overflow."

"You sure? I really don't want to sell it . . ."

He nodded.

She hugged him and then me. "This is the best surprise ever. I have missed this house so much."

I heard a light tap on the door and then saw Mom hugging Adam. "I hope you didn't feel pushed out," she said.

"Never," he responded graciously. "You have been so generous to us. It's time for a fresh start for everyone." He winked at me.

"Okay," I said. "I'll let you two get settled in." Then, to Adam, "Where are the boys?"

"Front yard." He paused. "I told Kyle we'd watch Carter too so he and Emerson could go to Starlite, Star Bright. I hope that's okay."

"Of course," I said, following him down the stairs and out into the front yard. "I actually love watching from Mom's dock anyway. It feels like we're right in the middle of things." He held his arms out and I leaned into them. Despite my biggest fears, he was still that same strong man I had married, still that protector I wanted. He leaned down and kissed me. "Merry Christmas Eve," he said. Then, smiling, "I got you a present."

"You did?" I asked, feigning shock. But then I remembered our deal to only give each other homemade gifts. "No! Wait! Aren't the love letters my present?" I felt a hot panic that he had gone back on our deal and bought me something. I would have been so embarrassed. Although, regardless, I had a feeling my gift to him was going to be hard to beat.

He nodded. "That, and I'm going to get the boys dressed for church."

I laughed. "That is the best present you could give me."

He shrugged. "Well, Caroline also said there was a commission that you had to finish tonight upon pain of death."

I groaned. "Right. I do need to do that." I might have turned Mom's house back over to her, but I was going to have to keep my studio here for the time being. I loved the idea that things would eventually go back to the way they once were. The chaos and clutter contained to the guesthouse, the calm, clean, and creative hitting as soon as I opened Mom's door. It wasn't a bad arrangement, really.

"I'm sorry we aren't doing Starlite, Star Bright," he said. "It's just too hard to wrangle the kids in canoes and kayaks. It's too cold to fall in, even with life jackets. And the candles are dangerous. I thought about taking the skiff, but I don't want to be the jerk that ruins the silence."

I nodded. "I like watching it from here almost as much," I said. "I love seeing all those candles light up the darkness." I felt nervous butterflies welling up just thinking about the gift exchange that would happen later tonight. I couldn't help but say, "I have a Christmas present for you too."

"You made it, right?" he asked. "Like we promised?" I could tell he was feeling the same panic I'd had only a few minutes earlier.

I nodded. "Adam, I don't want to oversell, but it's the best thing I've ever made. And you're the only person in the world I'd want to give it to."

He smiled and kissed my forehead. "It's unfair for homemade

gifts to be mandated when my wife is the most talented artist in the world."

The sweetest part is that I think he really, truly believed that.

As the sun began to set and the boats started to gather all along the waterway, I felt the most tremendous sense of peace wash over me.

The dark descended, and what looked like a thousand blinking fireflies burst out over the water all at once, making Carter say, "Wowwwww." The voices of hundreds of Peachtree residents singing in harmony was one of the most beautiful, ethereal sounds I had ever heard.

The boys had stopped their playing and were standing beside me while Adam held Carter, all of them in awe of the light in the darkness. And, for the briefest of moments, I imagined what it must have been like to be one of those shepherds who saw that star shining bright in the sky, who knew they had to follow where it led. Because this was something I wanted to be a part of too. Right here, right now. I never wanted to miss a moment like this.

Adam leaned down to kiss me and, as my head pointed up at the sky, I gasped.

"No way," Adam whispered.

"Snow!" Taylor and AJ screamed almost simultaneously.

I laughed, taking in the smiling faces of the family members around me, memorizing each one, so I could remember this moment forever. Amidst the chaos and the destruction, maybe it had been a little harder for us to find Christmas this year. But Christmas, it seemed, had most certainly found us.

# Emerson: Grand Combinations

*Christmas Eve*

I ZIPPED MY COAT UP tighter to my chin, still shivering. The year-round warmth of LA had ruined me. But, also, it was just really, really cold. Maybe you never got used to something like this. "Kyle, honey," I said to my boyfriend, who was digging in the sand. "I think it's super sweet that you want to find a piece of staurolite for Carter, but she's two. Maybe we can find one this summer and give it to her next year." Why I even agreed to come on this inane errand with him, I wasn't sure. I mean, yes, staurolite was important in our family. And it also got me out of the fever-pitch cooking, cleaning, and prepping that were going on over at Mom's house. So I guessed I couldn't complain too much.

But I had also been avoiding Kyle a little because, in the spirit of total honesty, I knew I had something to tell him.

"Babe," I said. "Don't get upset."

He stood up, alarmed.

"I went to apologize to Mark today. I was only there for a second and—"

"That's fine," he said.

I opened my mouth, but then stopped. If he was fine, I should just roll with it, right? I had felt like a fool knocking on Mark's door. But I knew I couldn't run away from my mistakes. Letting how I had acted linger made it worse.

When he had opened the door, he just said, "Oh. It's you."

What a warm welcome. He had stepped aside so I could walk in.

I didn't sit or anything. I just said, "I'm sorry, Mark. I totally overreacted, and I wanted to apologize."

He raised an eyebrow. "Wow."

I smirked. "This was hard, okay. Accept my apology and let's move on."

He shook his head. "Fine. I accept. And, you know, I'm sort of used to Emerson Murphy flying off the handle. I wasn't that bothered."

"Ha. Ha." I tried to smile sweetly, but it didn't quite take.

He looked a little sheepish as he said, "You know, Emerson, if I'm being honest, I wanted to hurt you just a little. You deserved to fly off the handle. And I'm sorry. I should have been better than that."

I knew it! I felt very vindicated.

"Well, I'm happy you're happy. I'm happy you're moving on."

He smiled at me. "We're all grown-up, huh?"

I smiled for real this time. "I guess we are." I stepped forward and hugged him, less awkwardly than before. "I wish you nothing but happiness. I mean it."

"I want you to be happy too, Emerson. I really do." He paused. "I always have."

And that was it. Mark was leaving. I would always have those sweet, untainted memories of the kids we'd been in high school when we we'd fallen in love—or something like it—in Peachtree Bluff. But that chapter was closed and finished. Forever.

Now, on the beach, Kyle stood up and turned around to face me. He had a toboggan on, and he looked so darn cute I couldn't help but kiss him. "Also in the spirit of honesty . . . I was here the other day," he said. "I did paddleboard over with another woman."

I gasped. He was becoming less cute by the moment. He took my hand, and I guessed I wasn't that mad because I let him. "So did you bring me over here to tell me so I wouldn't yell at you in front of the entire family?"

Caroline had been right. This was why you didn't get married. When everything fell apart, there would be no messy paperwork.

"The woman I was with was your sister," he said.

He didn't let go of my hand and started walking down a path in the sand, one that I had only traveled once, but one that I remembered very well all the same. Kyle and his friends—with a little help from his grandfather—had built the most adorable ramshackle tree house on Starlite Island when he was younger and used to spend the summers here. I couldn't believe it was still standing. I don't know if none of the powers that be realized it was here or if it had simply become a part of this island's history and lore like every other crazy thing.

"But I want you to know," he continued, "that you would never have to worry about me being with another woman. Because you are a choice I made, Emerson. I know we didn't have the most ordinary dating life, but I knew even before you got pregnant with

Carter that you were the one for me." He stopped walking and grinned. "And I'm grateful for her every day, not only because she is incredible, but also because I know that she is the reason you finally let your guard down and decided to be with me."

As we reached the tree house, Kyle pointed to the ladder, and I started making my way up. "That's not true, you know," I said, the wind cutting through me and taking my breath away. "I was totally miserable without you."

The last time I had been in this tree house was the day of Mom and Jack's wedding, right here on Starlite Island, the day I was supposed to be marrying Mark. Kyle and I had snuck away, and I had finally made love to him in this tree house for the very first time. And gotten Carter. So it was a pretty special spot.

"I thought we could watch Starlite, Star Bright from up here," he said.

I felt a tiny bit sad that Carter wouldn't be here to watch with us, but it was too dangerous to bring a wriggling two-year-old up here in the dark and cold. It was truly, honestly, my favorite event in all of Peachtree Bluff every year. "But don't we want to be in the boat?" I asked, pointing. "We don't have our candles."

"It's okay," he said. "We don't need them."

I was about to protest as I stepped into the tree house. I gasped again, this time forgetting how cold it was—and realizing that I didn't need any candles. Kyle's rudimentary childhood tree house had been transformed. The entire perimeter was lined with huge vases full of flowers and lit by sparkling candles, their flames dancing in the breeze. "If this is your way of saying you want another baby," I said as Kyle stepped inside too, "it is entirely too cold out here for all that."

He laughed, pulling me close to him and kissing me. "This is magical," I said. "Truly, spectacularly beautiful."

Maybe I'm slow, but that was the moment that it all started to add up. Caroline being here with Kyle, my sisters and Mom not wanting me to ask Kyle to marry me. Kyle had been planning this beautiful Christmas Eve proposal, and I had almost ruined it. He stepped back and pulled me over to the tiny balcony on the outside of the tree house where I had kissed him three years earlier. The sun was setting in the most beautiful pink and blue sky, fiery and wild, passionate and free. Hundreds of small vessels were beginning to fill the waterway in these last moments before the world fell dark and quiet.

"Em, this night up here with you was the best night of my life," Kyle said. "It was a confirmation that you felt what I felt, that maybe you could love me the way that I loved you one day."

I smiled, suddenly feeling warm. "I think it's safe to say that that has happened."

"I know that marriage is scary to you. It was scary to me too for a long, long time. But now I see the appeal. Because I *want* to be legally bound to you, Emerson. I want to share a family with you, to make your people my people. I don't ever want to be apart from you for a single moment. I love living with you and our little girl. I love our life together. But I want more, Emerson. I want it all."

I leaned up and kissed him. He was so sweet. And—it really couldn't be said enough—so hot.

He got down on one knee and opened the small box that women wait their entire lives for. "Emmy, will you marry me?"

I could tell that he was holding his breath. We had been down this road before. Maybe not quite this elaborately. But every single time he had brought up the idea of our getting married, I had shot him down.

As the sun finished setting, the waterway sparkled and shone, and it was as if the heavens had opened and the angels began singing.

"Kyle, I did not know that men like you existed, that anyone so generous, so patient, so kind, and so damn good-looking could ever come into my life. I absolutely want to marry you."

I took my glove off and reached my left hand out to him. He slid the most beautiful three-stone diamond ring on my hand, which I could still see a little because of all the candlelight. Past, present, and future. Isn't that what those cheesy commercials said? But wasn't it true too? Because right here and right now, my past, present, and future were all swirling into one, combining into my life. With Kyle. And Carter. And, with any luck, more babies in our future.

He stood up and pulled me up with him, wrapping me in his arms. Just as I said, "I will love you forever," it was as if the sky opened up.

As he leaned down to kiss me, snow—practically Halley's Comet in Peachtree Bluff—poured down from the sky. As we pulled back, we both started laughing.

"Snow!" Kyle said. "Can you believe it?"

"Did you and Caroline make this happen?" I joked.

Kyle nodded very seriously. Then he thought for a second. "Come to think of it, knowing Caroline, she did make it snow."

We stepped back inside the tree house, which was only vaguely warmer. I could finally really take in the beauty of the huge arrangements of greenery, pine, and magnolia juxtaposed by the most delicate ranunculus, peonies, and hydrangeas, all draped around the tree house. Kyle began blowing out the candles, which was going to take a while. There were hundreds of them. "We should have just gotten married right here," I said. "The flowers, the sunset on the water, the snow. What could be better?"

Back on the beach, a light layer of white was already blanketing everything. Snow on sand was one of Mother Nature's grandest combinations, if you asked me. I stood there, awestruck, for just a moment, taking it all in. "You know what?"

"What?" Kyle asked.

"I was going to propose to you."

He laughed. "You were?"

I nodded. "Caroline talked me out of it." I pointed up to the tree house. "Which makes a whole lot of sense now." I paused. "Mom said I'd be stealing your thunder. Would you have been upset?"

Kyle put his arm around me. "Babe, I don't care who does the asking, just as long as I get to marry you."

He always said the perfect thing. I kissed Kyle again as we stepped into the little canoe we had brought over to the island. He began paddling across the sound, back to Mom's, a little to the left of the hundreds of kayaks and canoes that were making their way back to the town dock. "I can't wait to spend the rest of my life with you," I said.

And, really, in true Murphy fashion, I couldn't wait to tell my family.

I smiled at Kyle, thinking about all the perfect moments we had spent in this very town—and the many, many more to come. I was, more than I would like, known for not being able to make decisions, for waffling, for choosing too late, for regretting. Now, as the knowledge washed over me that I was getting married, I felt like maybe I was right on time. As Kyle's paddles sliced through the water, as he grinned at me, making me feel the golden glow that only he could, I realized it: of all the times I'd changed my mind, this might be my very favorite.

# Ansley: The Bell Still Rings

*Christmas Eve*

I LOOKED DOWN THE PEW in our dark, candlelit church, the flames flickering and music filling the space, which had existed since the mid-1700s. For years after Carter's death, being in this space felt insincere, as I believed wholeheartedly that God had forgotten us. There is a point, I learned, at which your fear can overtake your faith. Now, at long last, it felt right again.

Dinner had been a wild and hectic affair as usual, made practically electric by Emerson and Kyle's engagement announcement and the champagne that followed. I smiled down the pew at my youngest daughter, her daughter on her lap. She smiled back at me. I couldn't wait to celebrate this new chapter of her life with her.

My favorite part of this service was the very end. At 7:57, the church went silent and our most talented soprano sang a capella, "O Come, O Come, Emmanuel." It was haunting and beautiful, the kind of music that echoes in your very bones, that reverberates in your soul. As her "Rejoice! Rejoice!" filled the whole of the church, I could feel tears spring to my eyes.

At eight o'clock on the dot, the church bells pealed in triumph. This very same thing would take place at midnight, at my favorite service, where those bells meant that it was Christmas Day, that the Christ child had been born. But, since all these little children born to the Murphy family would be up by six—if we were lucky— even the early service was pushing it.

As we walked outside, I put my arm around Vivi. For all the hurricane had cost us, it had given us something too: perspective. I think my granddaughter needed it the very most of all. She had matured so much in these past few weeks. I could only hope that these hard-earned lessons were ones that stuck.

It was still pouring snow from a deep, velvet sky. I turned to take a mental photograph of my beautiful white church—which had stood in this spot behind my own house for hundreds of years—covered in powder.

"You realize you live in a Christmas movie, right?" Caroline asked, Wes beside her.

"Or maybe a snow globe," Vivi countered.

I laughed. "I wouldn't have it any other way."

In front of me, Caroline, Sloane, Emerson, and Vivi linked arms, leading the way down the middle of the street, their foot-prints patterning the freshly fallen snow. Kyle and Adam loaded the kids into the sleds they'd pulled them to church in and ran down the street, little squeals and giggles filling the air.

It was just Jack and I left, alone. We finally had a quiet moment with the snow pouring down.

He kissed me. "I feel like I dreamed this once," he said.

I just smiled. "The reality," I said, "so rarely compares to the dream." I knew that, for Jack, this life had taken some serious getting used to. He had imagined the two of us together, a simple life where we read the paper in the mornings and took walks and visited each other at our stores. The reality was busy and complicated, filled with children and grandchildren and, well, hurricanes. It was far from the perfection that I too had fallen asleep many a night dreaming of. But it was real, and it was here, and perhaps that was even better.

"The reality doesn't compare," he said. "It is so, so much better."

I laughed. I looked at him curiously as "Santa! Santa!" rang out from the front porch followed by a hearty "Ho! Ho! Ho!"

I raised my eyebrow at Jack.

"I have no idea," he said.

In the dark and the snow, I could make out the figure of a man in a red suit and a smaller man in a green elf costume. As I got closer, I doubled over with laughter. Jack slapped Keith the elf on the back and said, "Man, you drew the short straw, didn't you?"

I couldn't control my laughter as I hugged him.

He shrugged. "Depends on how you think about it. Hal got Santa because he fit the suit, so . . ."

"Santa!" I exclaimed, hugging Hal. "This is the most marvelous, wonderful surprise."

"It's not a surprise, Gransley," Taylor said seriously. "We've been very good this year."

"Santa, Elf, let's get you inside to warm up."

The fire roared and the twinkle lights shone, and the mantels were a wonderland of evergreen garlands and magnolias. And, while I knew Christmas Day was the main event, Christmas Eve was still my favorite holiday. As with so many things in life, the anticipation was the most joyous gift.

Hal started pulling packages out of his sack, handing one to each of the kids and then, curiously, to Caroline, Emerson, Adam, and me. I looked down at the small, wrapped package. "Well, open it!" Sloane said, which made me know it was from her. As I pulled the paper off and admired the small canvas, it took me just a second to realize what I was looking at.

I put my hand to my mouth. "Is this?" I pointed down at the little painting, which, at first glance, I thought was some sort of bean.

She smiled. "We thought you needed another grandchild," she shouted over the noise of the children laughing and chasing each other.

Adam's jaw was hanging open as he pointed to the canvas and then to Sloane. Oh my gosh. He was just hearing this news for the first time too. "This," he said, laughing. He picked her up in the air and kissed her before setting her down. "This is what you got me for Christmas?"

"Pretty good, right?"

He shook his head. "You're right. Hands down, the best thing you've ever made."

I hugged my middle girl and her husband. "We better get a move on that house, huh?"

"Well, thanks, Sloane," Caroline said sarcastically, kissing her sister on the cheek. "You've totally ruined my present now." Emerson and Caroline each hugged Sloane from one side. It took my breath away, seeing the three of them, all grown and happy. But they were still my little girls. They always would be.

Caroline handed gold bags filled with brightly colored tissue paper to Sloane, Emerson, and me. I really hoped she wasn't pregnant too.

I pulled the tissue paper out and felt a stack of papers in my hand. The title read, *Sloane Emerson Incorporated Franchise Agreement*. I shook my head. "I don't understand."

"We're franchising?" Sloane asked.

Caroline shrugged. "Only if we want to. Wes has a private equity group that would like to help us expand."

I studied my beautiful daughter's face, the glimmer that was finally back in her eyes. I never would have imagined that I would wish a divorce on her. But finally freeing herself from James had allowed her to come into her own in a way that I had always hoped for her. She was amazing. The daughter who had pinned all her life hopes on never working had, against all odds, become a brilliant entrepreneur.

"Wait," Emerson said, pointing from Wes to Caroline. "Is that what this is between you two? A business relationship?"

Wes looked at Caroline and said, "Oh God, I hope not."

She laughed and leaned her head on his shoulder.

The kids were running around playing with their toys and Jack said, "Ladies, take a seat. Vivi and I have a special surprise for you."

I put my head in my hands. Oh, the surprises. So, so many surprises. I wasn't sure my heart could take any more. But then again, I guessed that was what Christmas was all about.

As Vivi began handing us each a package, Jack said, "Don't open them yet."

"Do you remember the legend of how Peachtree citizens saved the town from a pirate invasion during the hurricane of 1916?" Vivi asked.

We all nodded.

"Well, it wasn't quite true," Jack said. "The citizens didn't save the town. Ansley's great-grandmother and great-aunt did."

"But do you know what *was* true?" asked Vivi.

"What?" I asked, rapt with attention now.

"There was treasure in the walls of Grandjack's house."

"What?" I gasped. "How?"

Jack filled us in on the story of what they'd found hidden behind the molding. Once he'd finished, he gestured to our packages. "You can open now," he said.

We ripped the paper off our boxes, and there were gasps all around as we pulled out the most delicate, beautiful necklaces. They were identical to one another, featuring four small diamonds linked on an elegant, simple gold chain.

"The women of this family," Jack said, "have obviously always been forces of nature." He paused and smiled at me. "I know one who bewitched me the moment I met her." He winked.

Vivi picked up, "And so each of you gets a necklace made from the diamonds we found, to remind you that the four of you are the real secret treasure of our family."

Jack reached into his pocket and pulled out another necklace, turning toward Vivi. "You get one too," he said.

"Oh my gosh!" Vivi gasped.

"Oh Lord. Don't lose it," Caroline said.

Vivi looked positively thrilled. "I'm never, ever taking it off."

"I have three more," Jack said. "One for Carter and a couple spares, you know, just in case."

"That's a whole lot of diamonds," I said.

Jack smiled. "Your great-grandmother and great-aunt had good taste."

"Oh!" Vivi said. "We had a copy of Anne Sloane's letter framed for each of you too. You're really going to want to read it."

I touched the four diamonds at my throat. One for me. One for each of my daughters. It struck me hard and fast, all at once, that I was the matriarch now. It had been Anne Sloane, my great-grandmother. Then my grandmother. Then my mother. Now that duty fell to me. I was the head of all these brilliant and beautiful people in this room. It was the best job I'd ever had. And how blessed I was to get to share it with the man I had dreamed about since I was the same age as my own granddaughter.

Later that night, when the children and the men were asleep, when the presents had been put out and the cookies for Santa eaten, I found myself standing outside, wrapped in my coat and hat, admiring the newly fallen snow. It had blanketed all of Peachtree Bluff, giving us the gift of a white Christmas. We were going to have a wedding this year, a new baby, a new business—I never knew how many incredible things could still be happening to me at this point in my life. So much to plan. So much to celebrate. But, for now, the world was silent, soft, and new.

I heard the front door close and the crunch of snow underfoot as my three daughters came down the porch steps to stand beside me, all huddled up.

"Merry Christmas, Mom," Emerson said.

"I understand the fuss about a white Christmas now," I said.

Sloane smiled. "Me too."

"I understand the fuss over a truly rock-star Christmas gift," Caroline said, making us all laugh.

Tomorrow evening, we would take down our Christmas wreaths. Inside, we would write down all our hopes and dreams for the year to come and send them out onto the following tide with the assurance that our wishes would come back to us in the same way that the sea returned to the shore. But, for now, I only wanted to revel in the perfect, precious goodness of right now.

As we stood, arms around each other, admiring the golden moon, the diamond stars that shone brighter than our necklaces, the silence was broken by the glad pealing of church bells, loud and vibrant, singing the coming of a new beginning. These women around me knew as well as I that life could be hard. The struggles could seem insurmountable. But the words of my great-grandmother, who had a secret so big and a legacy so lasting, reverberated in my head: *If we let them, even our largest challenges can be our greatest allies.*

She was right. Because no matter what happened, the stars still shone, the snow still fell. The angel still got her wings. The bells still rang as they had for more than 270 years, exclaiming the happiest glad tidings that no matter the storm, no matter the damage, no matter the pain, there was always the chance to begin anew. I inhaled the crisp, clean scent of pine and snow, and smiled. What we had been waiting for had come.

Christmas Day was here.

# Acknowledgments

I said for years that I wasn't going to write any more Peachtree Bluff books. Not because I didn't love them. (I truly do. I might never write women or a town I adore as much.) But because I loved the way the series ended.

Enter: 2020. I'm not sure if it was being stuck at home during a terrifying pandemic and wanting to go back somewhere safe and familiar or if it was because the entire trilogy had been out more than a year and no new Peachtree Bluff books had been announced, but my inbox was flooded, my DMs were full, and every Facebook post had a common theme: When are you writing more Peachtree Bluff?

The holiday season was approaching, and, well, I was a little bummed. Yes, we were blessed and grateful, but staring into the tunnel of a holiday season with no parades, no big family gatherings, and no traditions as we knew them seemed impossible. If I couldn't spend the holiday season like I usually would, where would I go to feel safe and connected, cheery and full of the Christmas spirit? Why, Peachtree Bluff, of course!

A story about a huge hurricane had been nagging at me for years, and I knew in my heart it was a Peachtree Bluff book. I started furiously writing this novel before my publisher had even said yes, which is when I realized that I had known this story for ages. It was just waiting for the right time. (Thank you for saying yes, Gallery!) And the Facebook Live I did to announce this new venture remains far and away the most popular post of my entire career.

So, it seems fitting that the first thank-you would be to you, my readers. This book is for you and because of you. Thank you for loving this quirky town and these flawed yet formidable women as much as I do. Thanks for persuading me with such passion to bring this series back. Thank you for welcoming us into your libraries, your TBR piles, and your hearts. If you're new here, we are so excited to greet you! Because that's the kind of place Peachtree Bluff is. Everyone belongs.

Speaking of belonging, the other place I have found to belong these past couple years? Friends & Fiction. So many thank-yous to the 40,000+ members who join us on Wednesday nights to chat live and who share their book recs and themselves all week long. Thank you especially to Lisa Harrison and Brenda Gardner whose tireless work on the Friends & Fiction book club has made it one of the loveliest corners of the internet. And, F&F Superstars Annissa Armstrong, Sharon Person, Francene Katzen, Barbara Wojcik, Marsha Garwood, Susan Seligman, and Michelle Marcus, thank you for being such an integral part of making this first eighteen months or so spectacular! Dallas Strawn, I just adore you, not only because you think to hand-deliver book plates to stores but also because you always make everyone around you smile—most of all me. And Meghen Kear, let it be immortalized here that you didn't miss a single *Under the Southern Sky* virtual event! Wow! Thank you so much.

Ron Block has long been a favorite human and librarian of mine and now I am so thankful he is heading up the incredible Friends & Fiction *Writer's Block* podcast. You rock, Ron! Meg Walker, how would we survive without you? Thanks for being the greatest. Shaun Hettinger and Rachel Jensen, thank you also for being an integral part of the F&F team.

But very most of all, thanks to my heroes and friends Mary Kay Andrews, Kristin Harmel, Patti Callahan Henry, and Mary Alice Monroe. I love you all dearly and am so grateful we stumbled into this fantastic thing together. And if it weren't for writing sprints, I know for sure there would be no *Christmas in Peachtree Bluff*!

I am so lucky to have the greatest team at Gallery Books. Thanks to everyone who helped make *Christmas in Peachtree* happen! Molly Gregory, thank you for coming alongside me in this book and being there every step of the way to make it the best it could be. Michelle Podberezniak and Bianca Salvant, you are so great at what you do, and I am always amazed. Jennifer Bergstrom, Aimee Bell, Jennifer Long, and Abby Zidle—endless gratitude for all you do. Gabrielle Audet and Sarah Lieberman from Simon & Schuster audio: Thank you for always going so above and beyond!

Elisabeth Weed, I couldn't have a better agent in my corner, and I'm so lucky you came into my life. Olivia Blaustein, thanks for your tireless work on all my books but most especially on this series. Good things come to those who wait, right?

Kathie Bennett, what a year! You certainly rolled with the punches and, as usual, none of the amazing things that happened this year would have happened without you—and the amazing Susan Zurenda.

Tamara Welch, I usually don't put inside jokes in acknowledgments, but, well, just for you: You have *way* more than one job, my friend. And, as your Instagram handle implies, you are truly a rock star!

A million thank-yous to my mom for all the slack she picks up on our blog, *Design Chic,* and all she does to help my writing career. And a huge thank-you to both my parents, Beth and Paul Woodson, for being the best parents and grandparents in the whole world. Love you both! My grandmother, Ola Rutledge, began quite a few of the amazing Christmas traditions inside this book. Thanks for being the ultimate matriarch and *trying* to teach us to make all your amazing Christmas dishes. (And, I hope you know . . . I always hear your voice in my head when I'm tempted to eat raw cookie dough.)

To my husband, Will Harvey, thank you for answering my incessant boating and hurricane questions. And thanks for rolling with my holiday insanity, the hordes of decorations, the giant trees and even the year of the Griswolds. To my son, I hope that, one day, you'll look back on flotillas and tree lightings, candlelight tours and Christmas markets as some of the best times of your life. I love you both and am so grateful for you.

I would not be here eight books later were it not for the tireless word-spreading and good cheer of the Bookstagram, blogging, library, and independent bookstore communities. I have so many people to thank that I will be doing it more in-depth on my blog, but I had to give a special shout-out here to Kristy Barrett, Stephanie Gray, Andrea Katz, Susan Roberts, Susan Peterson, Ashley Bellman, Zibby Owens, Judy Collins, Hanna Shields, Courtney Marzilli, Taylor Lintz, and Jennifer Clayton. And Meagan Briggs and Ashley Hayes of Uplit Reads, thank you so much for introducing me to even more of this fabulous, book-loving community!

Thank you to all the incredible book clubs out there who choose my books for their monthly reads—most especially mine: Booth Parker, Shelley Smith, Leeanne Walker, and Millie Warren. You're always my very first book club, and your enthusiasm and glowing reviews get me ready to take on book tour with confidence! Plus, you are quite simply the greatest, most supportive friends in all the world.

Last but not least, thank you to my town of Beaufort, NC, which inspired Peachtree Bluff. And, specifically, thank you to Patricia Suggs and everyone at the Beaufort Historic Site for throwing the most memorable book launch parties—especially where Peachtree Bluff is concerned. It means more than words can say.

Don't miss the next novel from *New York Times*
bestselling author Kristy Woodson Harvey

# *The Wedding Veil*

Coming soon from Gallery Books!
Keep reading for a sneak peek . . .

# Magic

*June 5, 1879*

SIX-YEAR-OLD EDITH DRESSER'S SKATES MOVED heavily, as if she were rolling through sand, across the patterned wool rug in her mother, Susan's, bedroom. She lived for moments like this one, when she had her vivacious, beautiful mother all to herself while her three sisters continued their skating downstairs in the dining room. Usually, her mother's lady's maid would have helped Susan get ready for the party she was attending this evening, but she wasn't feeling well. So instead, Edith stood—her skates making her taller—admiring the rows of frocks for every occasion in her mother's closet.

"Do you think the pink for tonight, darling?" Susan asked. Edith tried to focus on her mother, but her child's eyes wandered to the back corner of the narrow closet. "I love pink, Mama," Edith said as she clomped ungracefully to a garment she knew well. With a tentative finger, she traced the lace on the edge of her favorite piece, the one she and her sisters loved to try on most: her mother's wedding veil.

Susan turned and smiled, watching her daughter study one of her most prized possessions. In a burst of energy, she moved behind Edith, swept the long veil off its hanger, and motioned for Edith to follow her. Back in the light and opulence of her bedroom, Susan placed the cherished Juliet cap on her small daughter's head, gently touching the rows of pearls at the bottom. She smiled.

"Just look at you, my girl," Susan said as she arranged the lace-edged tulle around her daughter's shoulders, the contrast great against her gray wool dress. Edith stood as still as one of the statues in the yard, holding her breath so she couldn't possibly damage the veil.

Looking in the mirror, Edith felt transformed. It was still her reflection looking back at her, in her usual outfit, with her favorite roller skates. But, somehow, she was completely different.

Susan bent down until her eyes locked with her daughter's in the mirror. "One day," she said, "when you are quite grown-up and find a man you love very much, you will wear this veil just like I did when I married Daddy, and just like Grandmother did when she married Grandfather."

Edith watched her own eyes go wide, imagining. Then she scrunched her nose. "But I want to stay with you, Mama." Edith knew that, in other houses like hers, little girls were supposed to be seen and not heard. They weren't allowed to roller skate inside and certainly weren't permitted to play dress-up in their mother's elegant clothes. Why would Edith ever want to leave a mother who let her keep a dozen pet turtles in the yard?

Susan laughed, moving in front of her daughter to adjust the veil again. She wrapped her in a hug and said, "No, darling. You are going to find a wonderful man and be the most beautiful bride. Daddy will be there to walk you down the aisle, your sisters will stand beside you as your bridesmaids, and I will sniffle into my handkerchief and wipe my eyes because I will be so proud and happy."

Edith was confused again. "If you're happy, why would you cry?"

"Because that's what mothers do at their daughters' weddings."

Edith studied her mother, trying to think if she had ever seen her cry of happiness. She couldn't remember a time, but, then again, Mama had a whole life that didn't involve Edith, many hours that she would never see. And she figured that Mama liked living with Daddy, along with Edith and her sisters Susan, Pauline, and Natalie. So perhaps Edith would come to like it as well. But she had conditions. Thinking of her favorite storybook, *Cinderella*, she said, "If I'm going to get married, I think I'd like to be a princess."

Susan laughed delightedly. "Yes, darling. You, most certainly, will be a princess. You will live in a castle with many acres to roam to stretch your legs and plenty of fresh air to fill your lungs. You will have your own lady's maid and a nursery full of lovely children. You will find a husband who will love you more than the stars, who will give you the earth and everything in it."

This gave Edith a wonderful idea. "Can I marry Daddy, Mama?"

Susan smiled indulgently. "Well, I'm married to Daddy. But you will find a man just like Daddy, who is kind and handsome and loves you very much. And he will take care of you like Daddy takes care of me."

Edith nodded. Becoming a bride suddenly seemed very, very important. She looked back at herself in the mirror, at how beautiful the veil was and, when she was wearing it, how beautiful she became. "Is this a magic wedding veil, Mama?" Edith asked.

Susan nodded enthusiastically. "Why, yes, darling," she whispered. "You have discovered the secret. Once you wear it on your own wedding day, you will be happy forever."

Edith, looking at herself one last time, wondered if she should share this life-changing news with her sisters. But no. That would ruin it somehow. She had a secret with her beloved mother, one to call her very own: The wedding veil was magic. And once she wore it, the fairy tale life her mother had promised would be hers.

# Julia: Follow the Rules

MY MOTHER HAD BEEN TELLING me for months that an April wedding in Asheville was risky. *Snow isn't out of the question, Julia,* she'd reminded me over and over again.

But as I stood awestruck at the brick pathway that led to the conservatory at Biltmore Estate, where tens of thousands of orange and yellow tulips turned their faces toward the sun, it felt like snow was definitively out of the question. One long table sprawled in front of the brick-and-glass space, with a massive garland of roses, hydrangeas, and, of course, tulips running its entire length.

"It's perfect," Sarah, my best friend and maid of honor, whispered in this holy quiet. I nodded, not wanting to break the silence, not wanting to disrupt the overwhelming peace.

Sarah linked her arm through mine. "Are you ready?"

I nodded automatically, but what did that even mean? Could anyone ever be ready? My wedding wasn't until tomorrow, but this bridesmaid's luncheon was the start of the wedding weekend. While my fiancé, Hayes, and his friends shot skeet and drank bourbon and did whatever else grooms and groomsmen did before a wedding, I would be here sipping champagne and eating tea sandwiches with my mother, my bridesmaids, my aunt, and the women in Hayes's family—including his mother. Their difficult relationship made things complicated. What made them simpler was the woman responsible for the splendor of this day: my grandmother Babs.

Maybe a person couldn't be responsible for the *day*—after all, no one could control the weather. But Babs was the kind of woman who seemed like she could. She—along with my aunt Alice, who was my wedding planner—hadn't just picked the brown Chiavari chairs that went around the table and had umpteen meetings with the florist and agonized over every detail of the menu for this luncheon. She had actually, somehow, made this day a perfect seventy-two degrees filled with beaming sunshine and fields of impeccable tulips because it was *my* day. Even if she didn't quite approve of the groom.

Babs never came out and *said* she didn't approve. But I felt it. I knew.

My mother, on the other hand . . .

"It's here! It's here!" she practically sang from behind me. I turned to see Mom and her twin sister coming up the path.

"So getting here an hour early to have a glass of champagne by ourselves didn't really pan out, did it?" Sarah said under her breath.

"On the bright side, Mom *looks* like a glass of champagne," I said.

She was wearing the most perfect champagne-colored sheath with a tiny belt at the waist and chic tan pumps. Aunt Alice was clad in an eerily similar dress in pale blue, but with a wrap. I hadn't actually seen either of these outfits on my mom or aunt, but I had heard about them for months.

"They look gorgeous," Sarah said. "And very well coordinated."

They had perfect matching blowouts, although Mom's hair was much lighter, verging on blonde, while Alice still made the valiant attempt to keep hers dark, even though it meant that covering her grays was a constant battle.

"Did I tell you about the PowerPoint?" I asked.

Sarah furrowed her brow, which I took as a no.

"Babs took an iPad class at the senior center so she could better assist with all of the wedding details. She made everyone in the family send photos of their outfits—complete with shoes, accessories, and purses—for each event. Then she made a presentation and distributed it to the entire family to serve as a packing list. Let's just say," I added, as Mom made her way to us, "some of the first outfits we sent to Babs didn't make the cut."

Sarah burst out laughing. When it came to important family events, Babs didn't leave anything to chance. And, well, Mom and Alice *did* look great.

Mom smiled and leaned over to hug and kiss Sarah and me. "No, no," she said, picking up on what I'd just said and imitating Babs. "Don't think of them as cuts. Think of them as *edits*."

Alice wrapped her arm around me. "Well, girls, we made it. It's here. We're all wearing the appropriate outfits. It isn't snowing."

"What is so wrong with snow?" I asked.

"It's a logistical nightmare," Sarah, who was supposed to be on my side, said.

"Where is Babs?" I asked, finally realizing she wasn't here. We had all gotten ready at the Asheville mountain house that had been in her family for generations, and I had assumed she would ride with Mom and Aunt Alice since Sarah and I had left early.

At that same moment, I heard, "Girls, come quickly! You have to see this!" from behind me. One of the conservatory doors flung open and I saw Babs, all five foot two of her, in a navy knit suit, pillbox hat, and kitten heels, looking as though this estate belonged to her. She waved us over and we hurried in.

I'd been told that we were having this event outside the conservatory in the gardens, another point of panic for my poor mother and her snow. But as I stepped through the door, I realized that wasn't wholly true. Amidst the palms and hydrangeas, orchids, and birds of paradise, and—best of all—what must have been hundreds of butterflies, a small table held a chiller bucket with an open bottle of champagne and five flutes. Quick as a wink, Babs began filling the glasses and handed one to each of us. "I thought we'd toast our girl before we went outside for lunch," she said.

I smiled, looking around at my four favorite women. Sometimes my mom drove me batty, but I loved her dearly. She and my aunt Alice seemed to be in a world-ending spat as often as they were getting along, but they were always there for me. Sarah was my ride or die. She had been since we were five years old, when she had stood up for me after I was wrongly accused of talking in class. Her job as a public defender was no surprise to anyone. And then there was Babs, who inspired me every day with her tenacity, her spunk, and, like any wonderful grandmother, her wisdom.

Now she raised her glass and said, "To my bright, beautiful Julia, who has always been poised to take on the world. May you find your eternal happiness, my darling girl."

Everyone raised their glasses gleefully, but as we all clinked, I felt a familiar panic welling up in my throat. Could I do this? Could I marry Hayes tomorrow? And, maybe more important, *should* I?

*Follow the rules*, I thought. *Follow the rules.* The other women might have been toasting to my wedding, but Babs was testing me. She was asking me why I had changed course so suddenly, why I hadn't stepped into the life I'd always thought I wanted. I stood taller, straighter, convincing myself that I *was* doing that. Hayes and our family were my future. The rest would work itself out.

My friends began filing into the butterfly garden then, a man in a black-and-white uniform appearing to serve them champagne. Seeing all these women gathering to support me, to support my marriage to the man I loved, reminded me that my uneasy feelings were silly. Every woman felt nervous before her wedding. Right?

I looked up at the ceiling of the conservatory, the dozens of panes of glass—handmade, no doubt—that formed the roof of this historic building catching my eye. I wondered what it would have been like to draw the plans for this ceiling and the massive arched windows inset in this beautiful brick. Realizing I was jealous of the architects who lived more than a century ago, I wondered if perhaps I had done the wrong thing, walking away from my dream career. I looked down to see that a butterfly had landed on the rim of my flute. Sarah snapped a picture with her phone, startling me out of my thoughts, as Babs clinked her glass with a fork. "Ladies, we have a quick surprise before lunch is served."

I moved over to Babs as the guests started murmuring excitedly. "Being inside the conservatory isn't enough of a surprise, Babs?" I whispered so as not to scare off the butterfly.

"In life, and especially at a party, there can never be enough surprises, Jules." She raised her eyebrows. "It's the surprises that direct our path."

As if she'd heard, the monarch on my glass spread her orange-and-black wings and flew off into the orchids, back where she belonged.

A woman who looked to be in her midfifties, dressed in a black-and-white Biltmore guide uniform, appeared in the doorway with a stack of books. "I am delighted to introduce one of Biltmore's finest guides," Babs said to the group, "who is here to take anyone who would like one on a tour of the conservatory and gardens. And, in honor of Julia's wedding, we have a very special treat. With the help of the Biltmore staff, we have compiled a book of photos from Cornelia Vanderbilt's wedding day for each of you."

I put my hand to my heart. "Babs! You didn't!" I had visited Biltmore Estate with Babs many times while growing up, and over the years, I had developed quite a fascination with the house and maybe even more so with Cornelia Vanderbilt, the little girl—and later, woman— who grew up and lived here. I knew she had been the first bride of Biltmore, but I couldn't recall ever having seen any photographs from that day. As the guide handed me a book, my heart swelled. Babs was so thoughtful.

"Do you remember the first time I brought you here?" Babs asked. "You were the only six-year-old in the world who was as thrilled about the architectural details of Biltmore as you were about the candy shop."

I laughed. "And you were the best grandmother for getting me an annual pass every year for my birthday."

"Some kids like Disney World."

"I guess this was my Disney World." I smiled.

Babs put her arm around my waist and squeezed me to her side. "I love that we get to have yet another memory here at Biltmore, that this place we've always loved so much gets to be a part of the most special weekend of your life."

I opened my photo book to the first page, and Babs clapped her hands with excitement at the photo of Cornelia Vanderbilt, standing by the grand staircase at Biltmore, exquisitely dressed in a satin gown and holding a streaming bouquet of orchids and lilies of the valley. The guide, smiling at the group, said, "If you look at the first photo in your book, you can see that Cornelia's original veil included Brussels rose point lace." I really zeroed in on it. Babs and I leaned closer, gasping in unison.

"It is a sight to behold, isn't it, ladies?" the guide asked.

I could feel my heart racing, but that was silly, wasn't it? I was just so keyed up about this wedding, the excitement of this day. But then again . . .

Sarah glanced over my shoulder. "Whoa. That's crazy."

"Isn't it?" I replied. "Is Cornelia's wedding outfit on display somewhere?" I asked the guide.

She shook her head ruefully. "The gown has been lost to history, as has the heirloom veil worn by Cornelia Vanderbilt; her mother, Edith; and Edith's sisters, mother, and grandmother. Their whereabouts are a mystery. But a team from London re-created Cornelia's wedding outfit from photographs in painstaking detail and with some difficulty. It is a part of the Fashionable Romance Exhibit, which will be opening here at Biltmore soon."

"Jules! We should go!" Sarah trilled.

I locked eyes with my grandmother. She had seen it too, hadn't she? "Babs?"

"What, darling?" Her face was a blank canvas.

Turning away from the guide, I said in a low voice, "It's just that . . . don't you think this looks like *our* veil?"

"I think so," Sarah chimed in.

Babs smiled. "Oh, Jules, I think your love of Biltmore has gotten the best of you." She looked down at the picture. "I can see how you would think that. Won't it be great that you get to wear something that looks kind of like the Vanderbilt veil on your special day?"

I peered at her, but she just smiled.

"All right, ladies!" Aunt Alice said. "It's time to celebrate our lovely bride!"

I laughed as my bridesmaids gathered around, champagne flutes in hand, to corral me to the table.

I looked down at the photo again. That veil just looked so similar. Then again, I was at Biltmore—the place where I had spent so many hours dreaming of finding my own happily ever after—the day before my wedding . . . Babs was probably right. Maybe my Vanderbilt obsession had finally gotten the best of me.